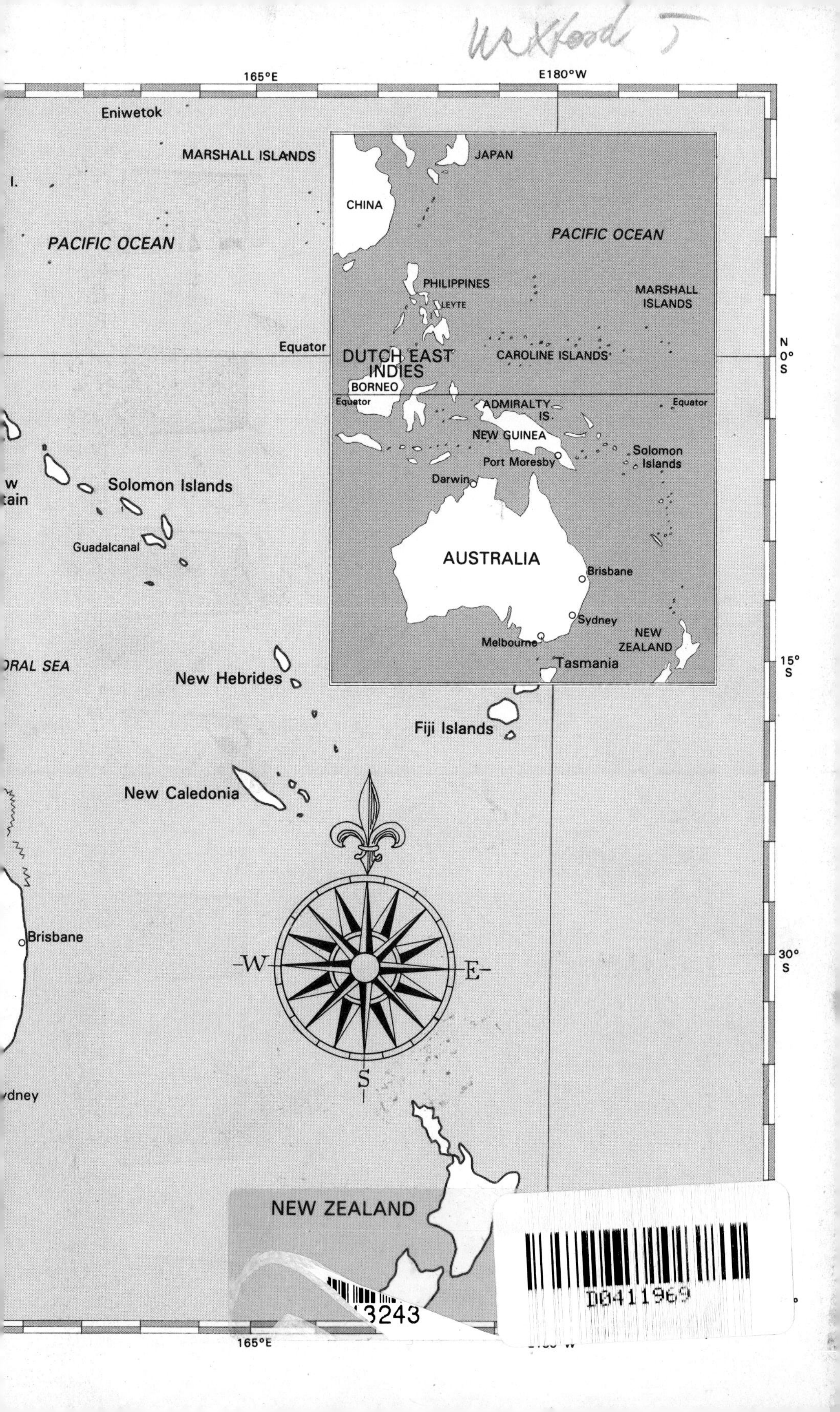

165°E
E180°W
Eniwetok
MARSHALL ISLANDS
PACIFIC OCEAN
Equator
Solomon Islands
Guadalcanal
New Hebrides
Fiji Islands
New Caledonia
Brisbane
NEW ZEALAND
N
0°
S
15°
S
30°
S
W
E
S
CHINA
JAPAN
PACIFIC OCEAN
PHILIPPINES
LEYTE
MARSHALL
ISLANDS
DUTCH EAST
INDIES
CAROLINE ISLANDS
BORNEO
Equator
ADMIRALTY
IS.
NEW GUINEA
Port Moresby
Solomon
Islands
Darwin
AUSTRALIA
Brisbane
Sydney
NEW
ZEALAND
Melbourne
Tasmania
165°E

COYLE, W.

CHIEF OF STAFF

BOOKS BY WILLIAM COYLE

Act of Grace

CHIEF OF STAFF

a novel

WILLIAM COYLE

Chatto & Windus
LONDON

Published in 1991 by
Chatto & Windus Ltd
20 Vauxhall Bridge Road
London SW1V 2SA

A CIP catalogue record for this book is
available from the British Library.

ISBN 0 7011 3258 2

Phototypeset by Intype, London
Printed in Great Britain by
Mackays of Chatham plc, Chatham, Kent

PART ONE

Temperate

Chapter 1

Well-Tailored Men

THEY BOTH LOOKED very pleased with themselves as they got down, out of the first-class carriage. Their uniforms seemed lighter, cooler, better cut than those of the young militiamen hurrying up and down the platform in heavy wool tunics. The militiamen all at once saw these two lean, ageless, well-tailored men and – oh shit! – remembered to throw them a salute. The autumn humidity seemed to have stewed every other face on the platform, but the faces of the two officers were tanned and calm and dry.

Dim, feeling a little stewed herself in her own woollen private's uniform, was waiting at the ticket barrier. In American films, people were allowed on to railway platforms without tickets. There was never a ticket barrier when Veronica Lake waited for Robert Taylor. Dim had sometimes wished it was like that at Spencer Street Station.

When for instance her mother used to come down from Maneering to visit her at boarding school, Dim had stood by the ticket barrier in a different sort of uniform from the one she was wearing now, the uniform of the Presbyterian Ladies' College, and wished that like girls in American films she could have run beside the train, laughing up white-teethed at her mother in the arriving carriage.

Tonight however she was pleased not to have the option of being out there. Because the two men, her husband in his lightweight, barely beige, tailored Australian army uniform, and the British naval officer walking even taller than *he* was beside him, looked as if the work they'd recently performed together had made friends of them. Nothing sinister, nothing like *that*; just honest male stuff. She would have felt uneasy to have intruded.

The apparent *closeness* of the two men, as they came down the platform, made her decide at last to turn towards the tall pale young woman near her, the only other figure at the barrier. This woman was slightly beak-nosed but strangely handsome and very well dressed, in the mode they called casual in these brave precarious days – a floral dress and a scarf around her neck. She was holding a baby easily on her hip as if she enjoyed being a mother.

Dim said, 'You're not Commander Runcie's wife, are you?'

The woman turned towards her. Front on, the beakiness was gone. Lean bones like these are the ones I want, Dim thought. And the voice that came out now! It had all the vowels the elocution teachers at the Presbyterian Ladies' College had tried to beat into the voice-boxes of Australian girls.

'Yes, I'm Honor Runcie. Of course.' Her long fingers scooped the light bonnet back from her baby's forehead. 'And this is little Katherine.'

'Yes, well I'm Dim. I mean, that's my name. Dimity, for God's sake. It was my Scottish grandmother's name.' Once more she cursed the long-deceased Scots who had named her grandmother. For her grandmother had probably been able to survive a Scottish childhood without being called Dim, able to survive, too, life as the spouse of a Scottish grandee in the Australian bush. But there was no way you could take such a name to the Presbyterian Ladies' College in Melbourne and not come away labelled *Dim* forever.

The Englishwoman said, in that peculiar, British, unabashed way, 'You don't look so dim, I must say.'

'Neither do the men,' said Dim. 'They look so well.'

'Oh, yes,' said Honor Runcie, almost aiming her baby's head down the platform towards its father in his naval uniform. 'I believe it's very beautiful where they've been.'

Dim reconsidered the men and felt a sort of pulse in her womb. She wanted to be a young mother, unaged by giving birth, in a floral dress. Just like Honor Runcie.

A porter was following the two men, wheeling a large trunk up the platform on which was written in white paint, 'Gordon

Runcie, Tangin via Mandalay,' and then in big letters, BURMA. Tangin, wherever in God's name it was, like Mandalay and Burma, was now in the hands of the Japanese. But the white paint said that Gordon Runcie seemed to have few doubts that he would go back there one day, and take Honor and Katherine with him.

Also on the trolleys were Captain Allan Lewis's, her husband's, more modest ports, suitcases, survivors from his days at university.

They were only thirty or forty yards away now, the angular, rakish Englishman and the six-foot slim Australian, sandy-haired beneath his cap. All at once she felt very old, because she saw Allan as so painfully young. She saw him as a ninety-year-old might see him, and she felt a ninety-year-old's amazement as she thought, *that's my husband!*

She turned to Honor Runcie and the baby.

'I'll queue for the cab,' she said in a panic.

She could see that Honor looked a little startled, but it was a reasonable idea just the same, and as soon as Dim got to the cab rank outside it seemed a really good idea. The queue was full of girls and American soldiers, officers interspersed amongst them. At least the US Army was a democratic army. The officers didn't jump the queue. Amongst this military mass was an occasional Australian officer, or an old farmer, probably wealthier than he looked, down from the bush to see his lawyer.

The Americans were early arrivals from the 41st Division. Everyone seemed to know that a few months ago they had been on their way to the Philippines to relieve the embattled American garrison there. Then the United States had despaired of saving the Philippines and diverted them here, to Melbourne. They could have been up to their shoulders in muck and death in Bataan or Corregidor, but a shift of destiny had brought them, in their well-pressed uniforms, to a cab queue in Melbourne.

She joined the queue. An American sergeant with his forage cap slung tenuously on his springy, brilliantined hair, said to her, 'Why, miss, you can share my cab.'

'I'm waiting for my husband,' she said.

The cabs kept coming. Sometimes the drivers refused to pick up Australians, pretending they were at the end of their shift.

They knew the Americans paid recklessly. The Americans had the idea of tipping, which was totally alien to the Australians. We believe, she thought with some pride, that wages should be adequate to relieve a man or a woman from the need for tips.

The sergeant said to her, 'I can't believe a little thing like you is married, ma'am.'

'You'll believe it when he turns up,' she said. She was aware then of her hard laugh. I'm a tough little tart, she thought. That's no good for Allan.

For Allan had what he called a great uncertainty. She knew she was useless for people who had uncertainties. If they had doubts, she increased their level. She didn't see how it could be helped. If she tried to be artificially kind, things ended up even worse. As they did with Allan.

They all turned up in the end, with the porter and the bags, and Dim found herself embracing Allan yet feeling far away. He kissed her full on the lips, as if he couldn't wait to get her home, and she couldn't help hoping that was the truth. Their military training was so demanding that it might have changed him, made him hungrier.

Honor Runcie introduced Dim to her lanky husband. The man was leathered from the sun. It was hard to guess his age. He could have been thirty or fifty. She knew Allan thought he was wonderful and had lived a *proper* life. This meant that he'd served as a young man in the Royal Navy, gone to Burma teak farming, then escaped with a boatload of British wives and children and sailed to India, where he had been immediately recommissioned as a full lieutenant in the Royal Navy and now, just a few months later, promoted to Lieutenant-Commander.

She could tell Allan was flattered that a man of such broad experience should have become his friend. That's the terrible thing about growing up in country towns, Dim thought, and being something like local gentry. It made you think you were leading a richer life than you were. Her own father was a landowner, a *squatter* she supposed he'd be called, in the town of Maneering north-east of Melbourne, and Allan's father was the solicitor in town. Their futures were right there. Dim was meant to marry another sheep farmer, Allan was meant to succeed his father in the family office. The years away at boarding schools in Melbourne were a preparation for these two high destinies. You could be really big people in a country town; country towns even seemed to be built for that sort of thing. Ordinary people, tradesmen and their wives, even seemed willingly to defer – in a nation as democratic as Australia – to the local landowners and doctors and lawyers. So that even a bank clerk was considered a branch of the aristocracy in a country town.

Somehow, Dim had always known it was a trick, that there was no *real* bigness or stature involved in small worlds like Maneering. And now it seemed that, through his contact with this strange-looking, gangling Englishman, Allan was just finding out the same thing.

The cab driver could not refuse to pick up these two officers – Runcie had an air of important friends about him, even if Allan didn't. If I were on my own, Dim thought, in my private's uniform, I'd have to wait out here as long as that rich, close-fisted old cow-cocky farmer.

The cab was a big Buick with a jump seat, so that they could all sit in the back. Honor Runcie said to her husband, 'I hope no trouble with the malaria, Gordon?'

'Of course not.' Commander Runcie frowned and nodded towards the cab driver's back, meaning that she shouldn't ask such careless questions.

'Come on, Gordon. I'm all for security and not giving secrets away, but what harm can it do for me to know that you two have been to New Guinea?'

Allan looked momentarily astounded and then smiled wanly at Dim. Dim found herself looking at her husband though with a new interest. Had he been to New Guinea? There was no one up there, really, except a few commandos and native militia awaiting the Japanese hammer-blow.

'Wherever we've been, my dear,' said Gordon, 'my malaria gave me no trouble.'

The cab dropped the Runcies at their fairly scatty-looking South Melbourne flat. They climbed out like two angular cranes, honking away. Honor, child on hip, called out an invitation to dinner the following night. Dim was sad to see them go. She thought that she and Allan were not quite ready to be alone together yet, but had no choice in the matter. At least there lay this fresh idea of New Guinea between them.

Ten minutes later, they reached at last their pleasant flat in South Yarra, which they rented from Dim's father. The dinner she had left in the oven also came ultimately from the 'old home in the bush', as Dim's father liked to call it. It was duck, shot in Maneering billabong and brought down to Melbourne wrapped in a bag of ice by Mr Herbert, a friend of her father's, who delivered it to her as a present.

When the duck had been served, Allan eating it without much appetite, and the wine poured, Dim said, 'That's true, is it? New Guinea? Really?'

Allan moved his shoulders evasively, but he wanted to tell her. 'You know I'm not allowed to say, Dim.'

'Tell me. Allan. Tell me. I'm your wife. Don't treat me like some spy for the Axis out of some awful picture.'

'Not beyond this kitchen then,' he said, settling himself to tell his story.

'I won't talk if the duck won't.'

He leaned over his plate, smiling shyly. 'It was astounding, Dim. One day I'll write a bloody book. But don't ask me for details now.' He lowered his voice. 'It's wonderful to be going forward when everyone else is going back.'

It was fair enough: in the newspapers the Allies only retreated. Allan and the Commander had – it seemed – gone forward.

'Cripes!' said Dim, putting on a face of mock awe, and Allan looked solemnly at her before they both collapsed laughing. She was sure that everything would be all right now.

But in the bedroom he could do nothing. He was such a tender man – he kissed the nape of the neck and the hollows of the shoulders. He mouthed her breasts so delicately. But then either fear of failure, or genuine failure, overcame them both, and she was no use to him, neither her body nor what she thought was her forthright attitude. The dreaminess and grace with which they had moved was now replaced by a sweaty, mechanical endeavour to make his genitals work. It was so sad, so demeaning. The one time they had slept together before they married it had seemed all right, not absolutely magnificent, but something that would work perfectly once Allan was over his normal and endearing shyness. He had certainly achieved an erection, and now she wondered if he hadn't pretended the rest. It was an awful suspicion, because after all, however lovable he might be, if her doubts were correct he had wilfully condemned her to a barren marriage. Or perhaps he'd thought too as she did, 'This is the low-water mark of love. I'll naturally do better.'

The idea that anyone should have this sort of trouble hadn't occurred to her before. Even in primary school, two-thirds of the boys sat behind their desks lewdly pointing to their erections. Boys she'd waltzed with at boarding school dances pressed themselves against her, going as far as they could beneath the combined supervision of the Reverend Doctor Speechley, Headmaster of Scotch College, and of Miss McTavish, MA (Edinburgh), Principal of the Presbyterian Ladies' College. And her father's rams at Maneering were astounding – achieving in seconds what even the most boastful boy took minutes to do.

Tonight, as happened at the worst times, Allan had begun to weep.

'In New Guinea I thought of you one night, and I was able to do it all for myself. You understand what I mean.'

She couldn't help herself saying, 'It must have been the excitement of the surroundings.' She was pleased he didn't seem to detect the edge of bitterness. 'Don't cry,' she told him.

'We went up the Sepik River with native bearers,' he said through his tears. 'Then over a mountain track. We had young fellows from the New Guinea administration with us. We dropped them off here and there so that they could go on arranging supply dumps and bearers to carry the stuff up the trail. We had a few native militiamen with us too, and two NCOs from Special Reconnaissance.' Special Reconnaissance was the organization Allan worked with. Its headquarters were in a terraced house near the Botanic Gardens in Melbourne.

He was telling his tale as if he were complaining to the gods: how can a silly thing like this happen to a Special Reconnaissance man who has been up the Sepik River with native bearers?

He went on with his account: 'At last we came down into a

great grassy plain. It's lovely there, on the north coast of New Guinea. We delivered the ammunition and supplies to our commandos over there, at Salamaua. They're wonderful boys, really tough, really determined.' His voice broke up into sobs. Even behind her disappointment, Dim was astounded by what he was telling her. He must have looked at those suntanned commandos and thought, 'Yes, we're all men together. Brave men. Our manhood can't come into question ever again.'

'Then we looked around the plain over there for an airfield, a place where transport planes could land – Gordon Runcie had done that sort of work in Borneo, and Special Reconnaissance have trained me for it, too. And for other things!' Again he sounded as if he were choking. 'But not for the most important thing of all!'

She couldn't think what to say.

He muttered, 'I shouldn't have said any of that. I could be shot for saying any of that.'

'Do you think I'm unreliable with secrets?'

She'd been to talk to a surgeon in Collins Street – again an old friend of her father's. The surgeon had said that something could be done these days. Depended on the cause. She couldn't tell Allan that she'd sought that advice – he was insanely sensitive about telling anyone. She said however what she safely could. 'I read there are operations now . . . '

'Where did you read that?'

'The papers are printing all sorts of astounding stuff these days. People want to enjoy life's simple joys while they can, old mate. Perhaps if you had a talk with your medical officer . . . '

'They'd throw me out,' he said. He began to sob again. 'They don't tolerate imperfection!'

'Jesus!' she shouted, suddenly angry. 'But I'm supposed to, eh? I don't give a damn about all your journeys. I just want you to survive them. I want to be able to sleep with my husband!'

'I can't tell another *man*, Dim! Don't you understand that? I can't do it.'

She just stopped herself from saying, 'Then you can go up the Sepik and over the mountains a dozen times, and I still won't believe in you.'

Chapter 2

Landing with Big Drum

GALTON SANDFORTH RAISED himself on the harsh metal and ribbing by the bomb-bay doors and looked across at Ernie Sasser, who had somehow fallen asleep, his face as grey as that of a man sleeping off an anaesthetic.

'Good luck to you,' Galt said, though he couldn't be heard for the engines. He looked aft, to where a mattress was spread beneath the waist gunner's position. Mrs Wraith was asleep on it. She was a beautiful woman even asleep, with a faint froth of air sickness still in the corner of her mouth. Mrs Wraith was what was called 'ethereal'. She was the sort of woman Galt could admire in pure aesthetic terms, a little too angelic perhaps, a little undernourished, her relationship to her husband more that of a brave votary towards a high priest than of a woman towards a lover.

The little boy, Little Drum, was sitting up in the arms of the Chinese nurse, Ling, and was retching weakly, with scarcely a string of bile left in him. He had been seasick all the way from Corregidor to Mindanao in the motor torpedo boat. And now, for the whole miserable flight across a dangerous quarter of the world, he had been continuously airsick. Amongst everything else the Japanese had captured, they had captured also the world supply of quinine, but Galt hoped there would be enough in Australia for the doctors to give the child once the plane touched down, *if* the plane touched down. Otherwise the kid, Little Drum – Corporal Drum, the GIs used to call him outside the tunnel at Malinta – could die, simply perish for lack of body moisture.

A little forward the General, Big Drum, sat in the radio operator's seat. Galt couldn't tell whether he was asleep or awake – Big Drum had the power to sleep quite soundly yet with his back still straight.

Dangling forward of Big Drum were the legs of the pilot and the co-pilot. What a cool kid that pilot had been! Taking off from Del Monte field on the island of Mindanao in the dark, with nothing but a flare at the end of the field to guide him, and the superchargers in his engines misfiring. Implementing the order of the President of the United States. Getting Big Drum out of the Philippines before the Japanese captured and humiliated him, and through him the American spirit. And yet likely to land them all in the Del Monte pineapple plantations at the end of the runway if the superchargers didn't work. Yet calm as hell, like someone delivering the mail, like any old pilot on a milk run. History – Galt was sure of this, as was everyone around Big Drum – history, of which Big Drum was a vast part, depended on whether a magneto did its stuff or not.

So what a good American kid, that pilot! Flying up half a day from Australia in the first place to collect them, landing amongst the plantations by flare light, guzzling a pot of coffee, taking off again with Big Drum and his staff, persuading the superchargers, intimidating the magnetos, and getting the whole of history, incarnate in Big Drum, into the air.

Galton Sandforth hated the feel of a uniform which had been sweated into profusely for some days, which had absorbed a certain amount of fear as the Japanese stalked the torpedo boat off Tagauayan. It had also soaked up tropical rain, the fever he had suffered while waiting at Del Monte for the planes to come for them, and now the high altitude chill of a B-17. It was inhuman to be stuck in such clothing, and degrading. He had known men who liked it – the simplicity of the field, the sweats of manoeuvres and of the camp, the jokes you could make of all that, the jokes about underwear, the shared, pungent stink of men thrown together companionably around a map or a compass or a campfire.

He himself had never liked it. It was not what he had joined the army for. He had joined the army for tradition; for the sake of his ancestors dead on various Virginian Civil War battlefields; and for the instinctive inherited sense that women were excited by men in mess uniforms.

He had been drawn to soldiering by the theory of it, too. The

Clausewitz aspects. He wanted the godlike overview a well-accoutred general enjoys; not the grime and stink of GIs.

These terrible clothes he was trapped in, the clothes of defeat he wore in the belly of the B-17 – he hadn't finished adding his sweats and odours and terrors to them yet. Because the B-17 was still over enemy country, enemy sea. He might actually die with Big Drum in these stinking fabrics. His great grandfather, the Confederate Major-General, who'd died perfectly at Chancellorsville, would not recognize his ghost when it turned up in Hades in these foul, undignified fatigues.

Beyond the pilot's and co-pilot's legs, the Navy man Hogan slept unapologetically, slumped forward in the bombardier's nose turret. Face down to islands which three months before had safely been someone's colony – Britain's, Holland's – and which were now the enemy's.

In a gust of turbulence, Galton Sandforth fell against the ribbing of the fuselage hard enough to break a rib.

'Fuck you, lieutenant, and damn you to hell!' he screamed in the direction of the legs of the pilot who had altered history. But no one could hear.

The plane banked again, and then again, over islands. Anxious lest the Japanese were waiting for them, high up in the sun.

Somewhere in all this air, with any luck, were two other B-17s bearing the residue of Big Drum's staff. Unless they had been pounced on from above by Japanese fighters.

Thoughts of these fighters, despised by the Allies until a few months ago, thoughts of Mitsubishi Zeros, of Nakajimas and Kawasakis, were enough to make General Sandforth flinch when he saw the navigator pass a note to Big Drum. There had to be bad news in that note! Big Drum read it, looked around, raised his eyebrows, and passed the slip of paper down to Galt himself.

It said, 'Darwin under attack from Japanese bombers. We'll need to divert.'

Galton Sandforth raised his eyebrows in return. Divert to where? he wondered. Darwin was the only town of any size in all that empty northern sector of Australia. Big Drum smiled momentarily at him. Big Drum was able to convey the idea, no matter what he thought secretly, that small inconveniences were not necessarily dangerous. They would point up his final triumph all the more. When you saw the large placid face, the empty cigarette-holder clenched in its teeth, you nearly believed it yourself.

The plane veered again and Sandforth gave up trying to kneel or stand or take any other dignified posture. He subsided crookedly to the floor again. Grey-faced Ernie Sasser was still in an exhausted sleep. Harry Strudwick, the chief of intelligence, was staring wanly forward over Mrs Wraith's prone body. Little Drum was being ill again in the arms of the nurse. If anything happened to him, how would Mrs Wraith take it? She was one of those strong Southern women, genuine Daughter of the Confederacy material, but she was so fragile, and the tropics didn't suit her, and Big Drum was probably too old to give her another son.

The B-17 went into a terrible corkscrew which wrenched the stomach and made the brain buzz. During it, fighting nausea, Sandforth saw crookedly – through the observation window beside Big Drum – a mangroved coastline. He hoped it was Australia and not just another of the innumerable islands of the Celebes or Timor or Arafura Seas.

Big Drum turned around in his seat and held his cigarette holder stem upwards, as if it was the head of a riding crop, and jiggled it in the air. This was for the sake of Mrs Wraith, who came not only from a Southern family but from a horse riding one. The gesture said, 'All's well, we've beaten the course.'

Galt hoped it meant that they were approaching a serviceable landing strip, and the deceleration and changes in engine noise seemed to indicate that too. The air grew warmer and warmer in the fuselage of the plane. Could the blessed heat of an *Australian* day be reaching up for them?

Galt saw Big Drum mouth the words, 'Hold on tight!' The engineer, Ernie Sasser, had woken now – the increasing pressure of descent must have done things to his ears. Galt could see the long face of Harry Strudwick, chief of intelligence, staring forward, tight with hope, from the depths of the plane beyond the mattress where Ling and Little Drum and Mrs Wraith had huddled and puked for hours.

At least I am surviving with all my enemies, Galt thought. Amongst them, Major-General Harry Strudwick, born Hans Strudewicz, a Pole or German from the borders of Silesia and Saxony.

The bumpiness of the landing was so prosaic that it was hard to believe they had arrived.

This arrival on Australian soil had none of the drama of the take-off from Mindanao. When at last the staff, having followed lithe Big Drum in a very athletic vault from the forward hatch, all stood on the ground, everyone looked without comprehension at the gravel runway in the bush where the B-17 had deposited them. Nothing about the place looked very special. Nothing about it matched the idea of deliverance. Sure, they were safe, but they seemed to have landed in a vacuum.

Two young officers were hurrying towards them from some combination ops room/foxhole on the edge of the bush. Galt noticed now that there were drums of aviation fuel covered with camouflage canvas and a few US Army Air Force ground-crew staggering disconsolately amongst tents set in the shade of gum trees.

'Well, Galton,' said Big Drum, his empty cigarette-holder in his mouth, 'it seems we came through. Though it doesn't yet feel like it.'

'I was thinking the same thing, General,' said Galt.

Some of the crew of the B-17 had opened the large door towards the stern of the plane and were helping Mrs Wraith and the Chinese nanny and her charge, Little Drum, down to earth. A freckled boy still wearing his flying helmet carried Little Drum across to where his father stood. Big Drum and Mrs Wraith exchanged chaste but strangely affectionate kisses.

'We are all saved, my dear,' said Big Drum with a smile. He looked ready for business, and Sandforth noticed how everyone, himself included and Mrs Wraith as well, adjusted their features so that they showed energy, a will to work.

Yet the idea of work also seemed so unreal here, in this desert-like scrub bush, like Africa, not like the Philippines. Despite the long escape, Galt couldn't believe in the place. He felt they had all merely travelled to some botanic gardens down the road from the Hotel Manila.

The two young USAAF officers arrived, a captain and a lieutenant. Their eyes were wide. They knew Big Drum from the press and newsreels. By the way their faces worked, it was obvious they had belief problems of their own. Had the greatest American hero dropped from the sky to their despicable little gravelled strip in the Australian bush? Had the front cover of *Life* materialized in their midst?

They saluted and reported who they were, and Big Drum reported who he was, very genially.

'We have a flight of Kittyhawks here, sir,' said the young captain, 'but they've gone off to Darwin on patrol.'

'Excellent,' said Big Drum, chewing ferociously on his cigarette-holder, back in business. 'Captain, I must put myself in contact with the American forces on this continent. I believe there has been a great build-up here. I presume most of the troops are still in the south-east of the country, however, in training.'

The captain flushed, as if personally responsible. 'Sir, I have to say I'm not aware of any big build-up.'

Big Drum fixed him with that eye, placid as the eye of a bird of prey.

'There's the forward echelons of a few divisions arrived, sir,' the young man explained. 'The 41st in Melbourne and the 34th Infantry in Brisbane. But that's all I've heard of.'

Big Drum absorbed this. 'And you?' he asked.

'We're forward elements of the Fifth Air Force. But that exists mainly on paper, sir.'

'Very well, my boy. Do you think we could have some breakfast?'

Soon everyone was seated round an ammunition table in a shack amongst the trees. And again it was so strange to be here, so anti-climactic, as if they hadn't escaped the Philippines by torpedo boat at all, or come all that way in a B-17.

Mrs Wraith fed Little Drum some of the juice from a can of peaches. Big Drum and everyone else ate baked beans. They were terrible, Galt thought – typical Department of Defense contract baked beans, bought at best for the sake of cheapness, at worst because some bureaucrat took a bribe from the cannery.

He was sitting on Big Drum's right side. He could tell Big Drum was bewildered but doing his normal good job of hiding the fact.

'It's that Democrat scapegrace in the White House,' Big Drum murmured to Galt. He liked old-fashioned words such as *scapegrace* or *rapscallion*. But he was not using the term lightly. The whiteness of his hands showed that he was furious. 'Firstly, he cheats me in the Philippines, tells me all the time that he was sending troops. And when they didn't arrive, he says it's because they've been sent here! The great build-up! And what does that amount to? Forward echelons of two divisions, that boy said.' Big Drum called across the room to his wife, who now sat wanly on an army cot as her son drowsed. 'Eat up, dear. Keep your strength up.'

He wanted her there when he himself got to the White House. He wanted her around for the punishing of all the Democrat scapegraces.

Mrs Wraith smiled weakly and waved. Big Drum returned his attention to Galt. 'I despise myself,' he murmured, 'for believing them in the first place. If we fail here, Galt, and the Japanese put my head on a pole, the Democrats in Washington will hold a ball to celebrate it!'

Even for such an extraordinary day, Galt felt that his chief must be buoyed. He felt no exaltation himself. He kept actually forgetting that they had escaped, that *this* was not *there*.

He said, 'We won't be able to be sure about anything, General, until we get south. An air force captain wouldn't know what was happening.'

The same young captain appeared with a radio flimsy in his hand. 'General Pendle in Melbourne has arranged for two commercial DC-3s to land here and take you south, sir,' he announced. He seemed ecstatic at the arrangement.

In the subsequent silence, everyone could hear Mrs Wraith say to Hogan, the Navy man in charge of the General's personal and travel arrangements, 'Please, Mark, I don't want to take

Little Drum south by plane. I want to go by train and build him up.'

Sandforth knew then that that was the way it would be. Mrs Wraith had uttered her quiet ultimatum.

It was night in the saloon car. The lights were down. Under a robust moon, the Australian paddocks swam past the windows. There was something about their monotonous expanse that made General Galton Sandforth, chief of staff, aware that he was tired. A very fine sleeping car lay beyond the saloon, and most of the party – Mark Hogan and Colonel Winton the surgeon, Ernie Sasser and Harry Strudwick – had already retired there, as had Mrs Wraith and Ling and pallid Little Drum.

Big Drum, however, had already got some nine hours' sleep on the far more primitive train which had brought everyone south from Alice Springs. He needed only one good sleep every three weeks or so. And in any case nothing made him wakeful as much as bad news.

'Perhaps you can work this out for me, Galt,' Big Drum was saying. 'I am on the cover of *Life* magazine and the President praises me on the radio waves. The American Ambassador to Australia tells me the columnists in the United States are saying I'm a successor to Pershing and Lindbergh. Well, that's OK, though I was never a respecter of Pershing. All this is a matter of indifference to me, Galt . . . '

Galton nodded. It was not a matter of indifference; no one liked destiny nor toyed with old-fashioned concepts of immortality as energetically as Big Drum.

For example, at some desolate water bore south of Alice Springs, some Australian cowboys – *stockmen* they call them – stopped the train, and Big Drum thought they had come to see him. Even for such a small audience, you could see, he was preparing a memorable speech, something to etch on to the ranchers' imaginations. He had even been a little disappointed when he found out they were meeting the train because they'd heard there was an American surgeon on board. One of them had been hit in the eye with a steel spike, that was all, and he needed treatment.

And if Big Drum wasn't indifferent to the opinion of Australian ranchers, he certainly wasn't indifferent to seeing his aquiline face, surmounted by its campaign cap, on the cover of *Life*.

The Big Drum party had boarded that first train in Alice Springs, right in the geographic middle of Australia. Alice Springs had struck Galt as being like Arizona about 1912, and then some. The enormous flies which harried them were, Ernie said, the Australian national bird. The train sent to meet the General's party had also been something out of the set of a Western movie, an absolute contraption. It had been at least fifty years older than this new, smooth train they had joined in Adelaide and which was now sweeping down a wide-gauge rail towards Melbourne.

Arriving in Adelaide from Alice Springs on that first, awful, vintage train, they had been met by the US Ambassador who had come eight hundred miles from Canberra to greet them. The distances in this country were horrifying, yet maybe they could be of use in a campaign against the Japanese, the way the Russian steppes had been against Napoleon. The ambassador was a lawyer, a self-made man, a friend of the President's. He affected a rustic sage's manner. Being a Democrat – and therefore, as Big Drum would say later, a liar – he had been effusive about the build-up the President had promised. Nonetheless Galt could see Big Drum wanted to believe the man. He himself wanted to believe him!

Big Drum had actually turned to Galt right there on Adelaide railway station and murmured, 'This man is more likely to know. Rather than that young captain up north there, where we landed.'

But a few telephone conversations with American officers in Melbourne and with the USAAF commander in Australia, a man called Pendle whom Big Drum didn't like anyhow but now liked less as a bearer of bad news, had given the lie to what the ambassador had said. This great continent, which the Joint Chiefs of Staff had chosen as the ultimate American fallback, was naked.

It had been Galton Sandforth's task to introduce the General gently to the figures. There were maybe thirty-four thousand

American and Australian troops available to rebut the Japanese. Very few of them had jungle training. The best Australian troops were still being shipped home from Egypt and Libya, against the wishes of Churchill. In any case, though an army of some hundred thousand men or more, the Australians were veterans of the desert, not of the jungle. There was one brigade of the Australian 6th Division training in Queensland, a tropical state of the enormous Australian continent. They were the best troops available just now. The young conscripts of the 34th and 41st Infantry Divisions of the US Army, former National Guardsmen and farmboys, had no jungle training at all.

At the moment a few battalions of Australian militia held New Guinea, together with a couple of companies of Australian commandos. This was the extent of the land-based screen against Japanese invasion. A cursory look at a map indicated that New Guinea, directly north of Australia, was the key. Galt already knew that. But no one he'd talked to by telephone expected it to hold. It had been exhausting just listening to them explain how hopeless everything was.

Item by item it was appalling. The Japanese had gobbled up the Dutch East Indies in a week in early March, and only a token number of Dutch soldiers had got out to Australia. So nothing of substance could be looked for from them either.

When it came to aircraft, there were a hundred or so, including the slow Australian fighters called Wirraways and even some Tiger Moths of 1920s provenance.

The naval resources: the Americans and Australians had lost an entire destroyer flotilla in the Java sea. The elderly seaplane-tender USS *Langley*, laden with aircraft, had been sunk on the way to Java and the heavy cruiser USS *Houston* had been lost in the Sunda Strait.

Such was some of the comfort and advice Galt had for his chief on the Adelaide-Melbourne special that night.

While Galt was gathering this information, Big Drum had stood on the railway station in Adelaide facing reporters, American and Australian. He made a little speech: 'At my President's order, the enemy saw me retreat. But they shall soon see me return.' The press had loved that. Harry Strudwick said he'd seen the tips of their pencils pick up for a second as they absorbed a sentence which had the sniff of history about it, and then return in furious movement to the pages of their notebooks.

But at that stage the General hadn't been acquainted with the full story, the dismal news Galt was acquiring by telephone: that Australia looked untenable.

So, night in the saloon of Big Drum's Adelaide–Melbourne special and, even at this hour, not all the sad news uttered!

'Back to the question of there being two Australian armies,' Galt told the General. 'In the Great War, the Australians suffered massive losses, but they were all volunteer troops. The present Prime Minister of the country himself campaigned in his youth against attempts to conscript soldiers. The cry is that Australians shouldn't die in some foreign place unless they choose to. As a result, they have a volunteer army, well-trained – according to what they tell me – and then this militia, conscript army which can serve only inside Australian territory. Thank God, that includes New Guinea. The Prime Minister is a socialist, and won't hear of sending conscripts *outside* Australian territory.'

'A socialist!' said Big Drum dolefully. A muscle at the right corner of the General's face dragged down. Galt couldn't stop himself feeling responsible for the ideological quirks of Australian politicians.

But he had to press on with the last of the dismal assessment: 'The Australian headquarters staff have devised a plan for dealing with Japanese invasion. It hasn't been accepted by the government – it would be political suicide for them to do so. But the generals believe that the country can't be held as a whole. Only the south-east has a chance of being held. And so, if the Japanese arrive, the Australian generals' plan is to make a line from Brisbane in the north to Melbourne in the south. The rest of the country they'll just have to give up. Of course, this line and its feasibility is the first thing we have to look at.'

'Tell me, Galt,' Big Drum pleaded. 'Will we really have to fall back on such a stratagem?'

He was mortally sick of retreats.

'Not if we can hold them in New Guinea,' said Galt, trying to make it sound as if that could be easily done.

The General covered that side of his face which was dragging down. 'So what we have is that the President of the United States asked the Prime Minister of Australia if he will kindly ratify my appointment as Allied Commander-in-Chief in the Southwest Pacific. The Australian Prime Minister happily agrees. But all the two of them between them can give me is this tatterdemalion collection of barely trained, barely floating, barely airborne forces.' His voice was by now nearly inaudible. Galt had to resist the tendency to lean forward, which would have implied a certain criticism of the General's delivery. 'I am sixty-two years old,' murmured the General. 'It seems to be my destiny to be given lost causes to play with. Have my wife and child escaped, Galton, from a trap in the Philippines to a trap in Australia?'

Even behind Big Drum's nineteenth-century style and melodramatic delivery there was real pathos.

Galt, in fresh clothes provided by the American mission in Adelaide, with his Lieutenant-General's stars glistening as they had never done on Corregidor – they'd been buffed up by a US Army private attached to the mission – picked up the sudden stench of his own stale fear; of what he had been living with since before Christmas. Yet he believed primitively in the General's ultimate success. That's what kept all the staff going, against all the evidence. That's what had sustained them even in the bitter days in the Malinta tunnel, when it became clear no reinforcements were coming; even in the days before the Joint Chiefs in Washington and the President ordered their escape. If Galt perished, he would perish believing viscerally in Big Drum. The trouble was he could not convey this certainty to Big Drum himself. He wondered what it was that kept Big Drum going.

The General rose from his chair in the saloon.

'I might just go and speak to Mrs Wraith,' he said. It was the greatest confession of weakness which he would ever make. He would go and wake his wife – she would be instantly alert – and together they would discuss events, and she would say the sort of thing he listened to only when it came from her. 'Dear,

we can't do anything about it until we get to Melbourne anyhow. So why don't you rest?'

But he probably wouldn't rest, and they would sit together until dawn; while Little Drum, whom Colonel Winton had had to put on intravenous fluids for a few days but who was now recovering, got his sleep, which was all that mattered. For he was the coming Drum. The Wraith of the future!

Galt was left alone. He rang the bell and a somnolent Australian corporal entered, still putting on his white steward's jacket.

'I wonder could I have some coffee?' Sandforth feared a little what he might get, since they didn't seem to make coffee in the accepted way down here.

'No problems, sir,' said the Australian in the broad, loopy vowels which characterized the Australian tongue.

'That's what you think, young man,' said Galt, but with a grin that let the corporal off the hook. 'And do you have any such thing as brandy?'

'Not French stuff, sir. We've got some South Australian brandy. What we call *plonk*, sir.'

'Plonk?'

'You chuck the grapes up in the air and they come down *plonk*,' explained the corporal.

'I'll try it anyhow.'

He was sad to see the corporal go. I'm actually lonely, he thought with astonishment.

In a numb sort of way he missed his Chinese-Filipino mistress, Teresa Chung. He was grateful he had done the provident thing and got her out of Manila in time – otherwise his moral and personal misery this night on the Adelaide-Melbourne train would have been more acute. While three divisions of brave young Americans held off the Japanese to the north-east of the city, while American equipment and men crossed the Calumpit Bridge into the Bataan Peninsula – a manoeuvre ordered by Big Drum and executed by Galton Sandforth – Galt had made sure that a small detachment of headquarters staff got Teresa to Clark Field. On New Year's Eve, on the last evening of a year the Japanese had made a pretty grievous one, she had boarded one of the few transport planes going out to Hawaii. Galt had sent five hundred dollars in currency with her – his own money. She had signed a receipt for the package at the airfield, and a sergeant had returned the signed receipt to him. It was all he had of her now – he carried it in his wallet, that peculiar spidery signature the Chinese have, which Chinese script imposes on their hands when they come to sign their names in English.

He wondered how she was doing in Hawaii. And though he would have loved to have been with her now, he doubted in his blood whether he would contact her when all this ended, if it did. Perhaps she might go to the mainland and parlay the money into a deposit on a bar, something with a little style. For she did have style, and she was hard-headed. She was only twenty-eight years old – nearly half his own age.

That was one of the benefits of the military situation in Galt's view of the world. Your wife, whom you married in your youth from a narrow circle of acquaintances which you were innocent enough then to believe an immense circle; whom you courted from a circle of girls whose grandfathers had also been senior officers of the Confederacy, from a small sorority who had attended the North's best schools yet had returned faithfully to Virginia – this wife of your youth, a mature woman with her own fish to fry, chose politely not to escort you to tropical postings.

Galton Sandforth's predecessor with Big Drum had been killed in a plane crash outside the Filipino city of Baguio two years before the war began. Galt, then a mere major in the peace-time army, in an era of appeasement and isolationism, had grabbed at the chance to go to Manila as Big Drum's Chief of Staff. It was a strange posting, in that Big Drum had at that stage ceased being an American officer strictly speaking, was in fact the commander of Filipino forces and a Filipino Field Marshal.

Galt's wife, Sandy – Alexandra – Sandforth had grasped the opportunity not to join him. She pleaded that she needed to be on hand at their estate outside Charlottesville to supervise the Sandforth horse stud. She had pleaded, too, a great sensitivity to tropical heat. Her doctor had advised her against it. Good old Sandy. *Her* grandfather had been a young brigadier in the

Corps commanded by *his* grandfather in the Peninsular campaign of 1862. People of such breeding knew the score, didn't need a program, and were gracious at extricating themselves.

In Manila Galt had enjoyed Teresa's sensuality and mental liveliness. Yet he had never felt so close to her as to consider annulling a marriage over her, especially a marriage to the granddaughter of his grandfather's comrade-in-arms. He did wonder, however, in those company he would spend his old age, if he had an old age. Would it be in Sandy's? The prospect didn't delight him.

He hit the buzzer again. He really wanted the company of that Australian corporal.

Chapter 3

Jungle Knives

DIM AND ALLAN went to the Runcies' flat by tram, and in the blacked-out city there was nonetheless an atmosphere of hope. They could see it in the faces which came aboard the tramcar out of the darkness; in the joviality of the woman conductor who took the fares. The legendary Big Drum had come! His train had rolled into Spencer Street station that morning.

His words had been played on the Australian Broadcasting Commission network all day, every half hour. 'In any event, I shall do my best. I shall keep the soldiers' faith.' He had called up his connection with Australians on the battlefields of France in 1918, where, he said diplomatically in the broadcast, he had been honoured to serve with them.

It had all been like the homecoming, perhaps not of a father, but of a favourite uncle arriving by train to deal with a family disaster.

In the Runcies' sparsely furnished flat, Honor served a lamb casserole. She apologized for the plates she served it on – she had escaped from Rangoon with one suitcase, and given the wartime austerity of Melbourne, had nothing that she wanted.

'Even my clothes,' she said, 'came to me from the British Empire Association, some kind women there. Not very stylish.'

She waffled on about how hard it was to build up a wardrobe under the austerity conditions imposed by the government. 'I mean,' she said, faintly accusatory, '*you* have a uniform – your fashion is laid down for you. I wish I had a uniform. They probably do in the Soviet Union, you know. A uniform for mothers. I would wear a Mother of the Masses uniform grade five, I suppose.'

Dim watched how Allan and Gordon Runcie sat together, still

totally happy in each other's company. The worldly Englishman who had let Allan, a boy from protected Maneering, cross New Guinea with him.

'They get on so well, those two,' murmured Honor without jealousy. She seemed secure in her own connection with Gordon, whatever it was, companionship or passion. They never *seemed* ardent, but maybe that was just their Englishness. In any case they were friends. Dim wished that that sort of friendship was enough to satisfy *her*.

The lamb dish was very good and seasoned with spices like cumin, foreign to Dim's palate, which Honor had bought from a grocer in St Kilda.

They drank a burgundy as well. Gordon had bought it 'semi-black market' he called it – from the porter at the Melbourne Club, the premier club of the state of Victoria, a devout imitation of the best British clubs. Jews and Catholics weren't tolerated there. Gordon, with his offhand English style, was probably a favourite drinking companion of the good Melbourne Protestant burghers and Anglophiles.

'And what do you think of our new master?' he asked Dim at the table.

'Master?'

'This Big Drum fellow. What an extraordinary name!'

'Is he our master?' asked Dim. 'Or our saviour?'

'Our saviour, of course,' said Honor, as if she had rehearsed this two-handed argument with Gordon. 'But once they've saved us, we won't be able just to thank them, kiss them goodbye and wave them off.'

'It's the new empire,' said Gordon wistfully. 'America!'

'You talk as if you're sure they'll save us.'

'A good point,' said Gordon. 'The guard of honour who met our friend the Big Drum at Spencer Street this morning was made up entirely of signalmen and engineers, Brigadier Leslie told me at the Melbourne Club. There aren't sufficient American infantrymen in Melbourne to mount an honour guard! So perhaps, Dim, as you so correctly point out, the matter of the Yanks and what they'll do for and to us is academic.'

Dim noticed now that Gordon was not using his knife and

fork conventionally. He was spearing chunks of lamb onto the point of a very long, very sharp, very dangerous-looking jungle knife which he had produced from somewhere. He used it elegantly, so that even if he had produced it in similar circumstances in the Melbourne Club – as he probably had – no one could complain. She noticed simultaneously a slight tremor in Honor's right hand as she raised her fork. It was talk of the coming enemy which might have done that. Honor had already escaped from Burma and then, carrying her baby in her arms, made a further dangerous sea voyage from India. There was nowhere further to go – Tasmania perhaps, where she could raise her daughter wild in the mountains. But that was a fantasy. All that lay to the south was Antarctica, unreachable and uninhabitable in any case.

'As long as they let us return to Burma, eh, old girl?' Gordon asked his wife.

The baby, Katherine, suddenly wailed from the bedroom. Honor excused herself and went to attend to it. As she went she was frowning, Dim noticed. Perhaps she didn't look forward to a lifetime on a teak plantation. It was peculiar how people worried about all the potentialities of their life at the one time, especially if they were tired, as Honor seemed to be. For example, Honor was worried about becoming a serf of the Japanese or – more likely – at being driven to rebel against them; and at the same time, about a future of endless teak. The prospect of victory might disturb her as much as the idea of defeat. Maybe more so tonight, now that the good uncle – Big Drum – had arrived to take the situation in hand.

Though he *had* issued a warning outside Spencer Street station, to the crowd of childlike Australian faces, turned to him like daisies towards the sun, 'I cannot do the impossible. I *will* need men adequate to the enemy's strength, and in the same measure, I *will* need material.'

According to Allan (who had been with Gordon to the Melbourne Club and had drunk with generals there), people expressed some fear that the Democrat President of the United States might not properly supply Big Drum, whom the Republicans wanted to use at some stage – in a future not too distant

– as their Presidential candidate. The question was this: could the President be willing to write off Australia as a means of discrediting and eradicating Big Drum? For the Japanese would hang him high if they came here.

That was the humiliating aspect of belonging to a small nation, Dim thought. On the one hand, it was God's gift to the immigrant. Her Scottish crofter grandparents had become in Maneering the closest thing to aristocracy Australia had. On the other hand, you were a pawn. In Washington they had no regard for the special subtleties of Australian life. They had no regard for the special subtleties of *her* life.

The baby had quietened down. Dim saw the door open from the bedroom. Gordon was still talking to Allan, was in mid-sentence, his jungle knife held loosely between index finger and thumb. Quicker than she could see, he changed his grip. The knife became a blur, travelling towards the doorway in which Honor stood looking paler than when she'd gone in to attend to her daughter. The point embedded itself with a *thunk* in the door jamb by her elbow.

Gordon sat smiling at her subtly.

'Oh, really, Gordon,' said Honor. 'I've asked you *not* to do that!'

She pulled the knife by its handle out of the wood, walked the length of the table and laid it down with a slight emphasis of annoyance by her husband's hand.

'You love it, old girl,' murmured Gordon, grinning like a schoolboy. 'Keeps you interested . . . '

Dim was appalled to see the gleam of admiration in her husband's face. Allan envied Gordon those nights of knife practice in the lonely plantation houses of Burma.

Later, when they managed to get a cab, Allan said to her in the back seat, 'What do you think of Gordon, eh? What a character with that knife!'

'One day he'll miss,' said Dim. She wished she could laugh too and feel enthusiastic. It would be good for Allan if she could. Some women would be more generous when their husbands were being clearly enthusiastic about a mad friend. 'He'll end up explaining himself to a jury.'

'He's too good at it for that,' said Allan.

'He's not God, you know. Or do you think he is?'

Allan turned his head away. She knew she shouldn't have said that, shouldn't have brought up the question of magnetism between men. *That* wasn't Allan's problem.

It was as if some of the tiredness and pallor she had seen in Honor's face had entered her now. But why not challenge him? she thought then. If he was brave enough to walk up the Sepik and sit still while his friend threw knives at a woman, missing by a hair's breadth, shouldn't he be brave enough to go to a urologist and see if something could be done?

'I'm sorry, Allan,' she murmured, putting her hand on his sleeve. 'I don't know where I am with you. I don't know whether to be sympathetic or a real bitch.'

'You're succeeding better with the latter than the former,' Allan told her.

'All right. I'll try. But you must try too.'

'You won't have to try after next Tuesday,' he said.

For on Tuesday he would leave again for a Special Reconnaissance training camp somewhere in the bush north of Sydney.

Private Dim Lewis worked as a purchasing clerk in the office of the Allied Officers' Club near the Botanic Gardens. She knew she was competent at that – at ordering in the sides of beef, the claret, the towels, the toiletries for the club's rather ornate men's lavatories and less well-provided ladies'. She had done the same sort of work on her father's property. He was sad to see her go, though she could not have happily opted out of the broader opportunities and possible excitements of the war.

Before she had left Maneering six months ago to enlist in the newly formed women's services, her mother had taken her aside for a talk. She had wondered what would be imparted to her. Advice on how to deal with adulterous officers? Or perhaps some worthwhile and practical tip about birth control. Her mother had not mentioned any of this however. Instead, she said with a composed seriousness, 'They will try to make you type.'

Dim remembered that her mother had a prejudice against typing. She had not let Dim attend typing classes at the Presbyterian Ladies' College. 'A woman who types locates herself for life in a slavey's job. Typing is an excuse for men to boss women around, lean over them, ogle them, paw them. Honestly, Dim, for a woman to take up a job which involves typing is the female equivalent of Samson letting Delilah cut his hair.'

Dim remembered that her maternal grandmother had had the same obsession. The old lady had always put it less democratically: 'Ladies don't type!'

Maybe there was something genetic in this hatred of the typewriter the women of her family harboured. She felt that way too. She felt that she would be diminished by learning to type and take shorthand. She would be doing away for good with her own chances of ever being in the position to dictate to someone else. Old Captain Cahill, a white-haired veteran of the Great War and manager of the Allied Officers' Club had already tried to get her to go off on a typing course, but she had refused – a hard thing for a private to do – and backed up her refusal with a certificate from a colonel, a friend of the family's serving in the Australian Medical Corps. A slight tendency towards tennis elbow, the medical certificate said. So Captain Cahill was reconciled and Dim remained at the work she most enjoyed – the telephone and the control of all the club's buying.

Captain Cahill, whose wife tended to shame him in public with her drunkenness, didn't want to be too hard on Dim for fear that – with her contacts – she might get herself transferred. Then he would have to take the bulk of the purchasing himself. Out of pure justice and to keep her happy, he had already recommended her promotion to the rank of sergeant. As yet only the most senior women were being commissioned in the Australian Army, but Captain Cahill and Dim took it for granted that in time she would become a second lieutenant.

Dim liked – in an innocent sort of way – the male ambience of the officers' club. Dutchmen, Americans, British and Australians came and went, young men clean-shaven and in tailored uniforms. Some of them showed a little wear from the campaigns they had been blooded in – Libya, India, Java. Largely they were genial and brave men. She did not deal with them face to face, but she liked it when groups of two or three of them strolled past the open door of the management office. She hoped that strong resistance would stop the place ever becoming a Japanese Officers' Club. She could imagine herself happily spending the war working here, building up relationships with the suppliers of wine and beef, fish and fowl.

Amongst her other work, she was responsible for hiring from the distributors recent films to be shown on what Captain Cahill called 'picture nights.' The films came reel by reel in canisters, and a corporal from the Service Corps projected them in the ballroom on Wednesday nights for the entertainment of the Allied officers and whatever women guests they chose to bring. On Dim's part this wasn't difficult business – it involved a telephone call or two to a clerk at the distributor's, and a further telephone call to a local depot so that a truck could pick up the canisters.

Mundane enough, but in this weekly chore lay the seed of Dim's whole extraordinary future.

She got a call from, of all places, Big Drum's headquarters, which as everyone knew, were located in an old insurance building in Collins Street. Melbourne people had taken to Big Drum very warmly, and stood outside his headquarters in the morning and afternoon – sometimes a thousand at a time – to see him arrive and depart from his office. There was no attempt to keep his headquarters secret. Dim wondered sometimes if an enemy agent would shoot him one morning. But then Melbourne wasn't the sort of place for enemy agents. It was very unlikely that any Melburnian was either a Nazi or a supporter of the Japanese Emperor.

The call that came through to Dim was from a Captain Duncan in Big Drum's Chief of Staff's office. He sounded remarkably young and like a supernumerary in some American picture, a press or talent agent say.

'Private,' he said, 'I believe you're the Aussies' number one girl for hustling up movies.'

'It isn't such hard work, sir,' said Dim.

'My chief, General Sandforth, would like you to know that the Great Man himself is very enthusiastic when it comes to the movies. I mean, very enthusiastic. War movies and Westerns are his favourites. Particularly westerns. Randolph Scott is Jesus Christ himself to the Great Man. I believe there's a new one with Errol Flynn as Colonel Custer. The General has apparently already mentioned it, in spite of the overtones of military defeat, overtones the General is not too keen on. Lieutenant-General Sandforth wants you to be the Movie Procurement Officer for us. Would you do that?'

'By all means, sir.'

'*By all means!*' he said, laughing gently, as if she'd said something charmingly British. 'Movies will be shown at least three times a week at the Menzies Hotel, where the General has his quarters. We can't expect you to deal with the distributors unless you have some muscle, so we're arranging for you to be promoted straight to full lieutenant. It will be your task to ensure that the distributors don't palm off any old movie on us. If there's any doubt, General Sandforth will have first choice – he knows the Great Man's taste. By 14.00 hours on Fridays, I'll require on my desk in Collins Street, a list of available motion pictures, including the latest titles that have made it here. From this list General Sandforth will make his choice. You must impress on all the distributors, beginning now, that they need to have at least one print held in reserve for every title on the list, and we want the list to be comprehensive. Understood?'

'Yes, sir,' Dim told him.

'It may be necessary to give you an office here in Collins Street at some stage. For the moment, stay where you are, but in all dealings with the distributors, style yourself Lieutenant Lewis. Understood?'

Again Dim assured the captain that it was understood.

'Take this seriously, lieutenant. There are two or three things the General, Big Drum himself, loves in this world. One is valour, two is his wife, three is movies. Do I make myself clear?'

As she hung up, Captain Cahill came into the office, looking for a file.

'I've just had a call from Big Drum's headquarters. A Captain Duncan.'

'Oh?'

'He says that I'm a lieutenant. An officer and a gentlewoman.'

'Check it wasn't one of your friends,' Captain Cahill advised her. Yet he was anxious.

By mid-afternoon Captain Cahill himself had been notified and a set of lieutenant's pips arrived in a sealed envelope. There also arrived an invitation to Government House, where next Tuesday the Governor, Sir Henry Keeble, was to hold a reception for Lieutenant-General Galton Sandforth, Chief of Staff to the Supreme Commander, Southwest Pacific Area. The invitation was addressed to Lieutenant Dimity Lewis. Though the card was printed, her name and rank had been filled in in copperplate by someone at Government House.

The speed of her elevation and her new status left her breathless. She went to the women's lavatory, attached the new pips to her shoulders, smiled broadly at herself in the mirror and then emerged feeling foolish.

'Dearie me,' said Captain Cahill.

Chapter 4

Pacific Size

IN THE OLD insurance building at 401 Collins Street, Melbourne, the operations room sported an enormous map of the Pacific. Lest newly arriving officers have any doubt about the size of the task which lay ahead of them, Big Drum had ordered a blue-taped outline of the continental United States to be superimposed on it. The outline fitted in quite neatly between New Guinea on the south side, the Philippines on the west, the Marianas on the north and the Marshall Islands on the east. In fact, the General's blue-taped blob representing San Francisco lay just south of Manila on this vast Pacific map, and New York was merely one of the Marshalls. Immensities of North and South Pacific Ocean lay all around and outside this taped outline. New Guinea, the Solomons, the New Hebrides, Fiji, Samoa, New Caledonia, New Zealand, Australia lay far beyond its boundaries. The Hawaiian group, the great half-way archipelago, was as far away from the Marshalls as Russia was from Ireland.

Big Drum wanted his officers to know that they weren't dealing with tiny spaces.

Galt knew quite well that what was making Big Drum pensive these days was not the amazing size of the Pacific. It was that the Japanese dominated now so much of it, and that daily he expected instructions and a promise of new forces from the Joint Chiefs of Staff in Washington, and that still the forces or even the promises refused to arrive.

Throughout late March and early April 1943, Galt personally took into Big Drum each day radio flimsies bearing bad news. For example, the Japanese had landed at Lae and Salamaua on the north coast of New Guinea and were being watched by a thin screen of Australian commandos. Big Drum would suck on his empty cigarette-holder – he had given up smoking at his wife's request five years past – and wince at its sourness, as at the sourness of the news.

'It's the old Chaumont gang,' he'd say at least once a day. 'They would rather see me humiliated than the enemy defeated. My head on a pole would be a beautiful sight to those boys.'

Galton Sandforth had been hearing about the 'Chaumont gang' for four years now. They were all officers he knew or knew of, but he had never heard this name for them or seen them as a political bloc until he'd joined Big Drum's staff in 1938.

During the first Great War, when Big Drum had been the youngest and most decorated brigadier-general in the US Army, with six Silver Stars, two or three wound stripes and the Distinguished Service Cross, the staff at General Pershing's headquarters at Chaumont, men as young as he was but jealous of his combat success, had begun to thwart him and given him trouble.

Big Drum did not consider for a moment that it was because in some lights he might be considered an arrogant sonofabitch. He saw it all purely as the hatred of the mediocre for true talent.

For example, Big Drum had told Galton Sandforth that when his brigade came out of the line at the Côte de Châtillon in 1918, having lost twenty out of every twenty-five officers and men, the inspecting officers had been there, at the crossings of the Aisne River, looking for faults in their march order and deportment. Another time, after terrible hand-to-hand fighting in the forest of Fère, he had given his brigade leave passes, only to see military policemen, on the orders of the Chaumont crowd, send the soldiers back to their positions behind the line.

Once, in the mid-summer of 1918, when Big Drum had been loading his brigade into trains at a depot on the Moselle, moving them north into Champagne at the orders of the Chaumont gang, those staff headquarters gentlemen had pointed out to General Pershing the disorderly way the troops were boarding: every man for himself, their leggings, their uniforms, their rifles muddy. General Pershing had upbraided Brigadier-General Wraith right there in the depot yard, in the midst of a summer shower, while Big Drum's enemies and contemporaries stood about witnessing it.

'These men are a filthy rabble,' Pershing had been instigated – that's how Big Drum saw it – into announcing loudly.

Big Drum liked to say that he had observed aloud, with respect, that some of General Pershing's staff officers would look likewise a filthy rabble if they had been in the line for six weeks and were being rushed to another sector. Pershing had demanded an apology for this outburst, which Big Drum had given. And all around the railway depot, as Big Drum told the story, his rivals – the men who had resented him since West Point – rejoiced.

And in Washington now, elevated to high posts amongst the Joint Chiefs of Staff, they were rejoicing again, Big Drum was sure. Above all, General George Channing, a bright colonel in Chaumont, these days the generalissimo of the Joint Chiefs.

While Washington starved Big Drum of orders and men, there was still enough to make the days constructively busy, both for the General and for his Chief of Staff.

In a DC-3 they flew up to Canberra, Australia's capital in the bush, and Big Drum was allowed on to the floor of the Parliament, where both sides applauded him, including the supposedly socialist Prime Minister.

Over tea in the Prime Minister's office, the soft-spoken, fairly tormented-looking socialist and Big Drum reached a kind of unminuted agreement.

'Prime Minister,' said Big Drum, 'you will forgive me for feeling there's a little inequity here. Our government conscripts young men from Wisconsin and sends them to fight on remote islands in the Pacific. Your government will not send its conscripts outside Australian territory.'

The Prime Minister adopted a pained half-smile. 'General Wraith, I am hopeful that when our regulars return from the Middle East we will have as many fine Australian volunteers as we can train. But if not, I'd be grateful if you spoke to me, person-to-person, and pointed out in a private way any shortcomings.' The Australian even gave a little groan. 'I would have to bring my party around gradually.' The man's eyes flinched. According to Harry Strudwick's intelligence, he was a reformed drunk, but he had a fine whimsy and gentleness.

'As you know,' he went on, 'in the Great War we put an enormous army of volunteers into the field, and that war didn't have the justice of this one. Bear with us for the time being, General Wraith. Australians are very keen on the idea of volunteers and dead against the idea of conscripts.'

Surprisingly Big Drum seemed happy with that sentiment from the Prime Minister. He had really hit it off with the man. Happy for the first time in his life with a radical idea like not conscripting young men! For the time being anyway. The Prime Minister and Big Drum seemed actually to liven each other up and be odd mutual supports.

At the tea party afterwards – the Australians were tea-mad – the Prime Minister's press man told Galt, 'The boss hasn't had more than an hour's sleep at a stretch since the Japs captured Singapore. But he's a new man now that General Wraith's arrived.'

Galt was not to know then how this friendship and chemistry, the Prime Minister bending to Big Drum's position on conscripts, Big Drum bending to the Prime Minister's, would in the end be used by Big Drum in his ambitions regarding the White House. But that was two improbable and chancy years or more off, and for the moment there was the strong smell of heartily brewed tea, and a sweet air of spiritual comfort prevailed.

Together with Galton Sandforth and the General, the Prime Minister went on to a big war loan rally in Sydney, the city with a great natural harbour to defend.

The Australian currency was based on the English pound, and at the rally Big Drum made a donation of five hundred pounds, and the Australians thought that was extraordinary and wrote it up in all their papers.

Galt liked the way Big Drum made his promises to the Australians, and the confidence he gave off like a shimmer of body heat as he stood up there on the rostrum in Martin Place wearing his combat uniform of jungle greens, the same uniform he'd worn in Bataan and Corregidor, his campaign and medal ribbons dating back to the battles of World War I, and his barracks hat on his head, worn jauntily as he had worn it since those early days, with the wire frame taken out. All over the world, according to report, American officers were taking the wire grommets out of their caps so they could imitate Big Drum! And the Australians loved him too, loved this informal cap he wore. After all, they were supposed to make a virtue of informality.

Galt looked at their troops, both the militia and the returning veterans of the Middle East, and thought that maybe they made too much of a virtue of it. They looked like big gangling boys in ill-fitting uniforms; or else ferrety little guys with disrespect always there in the corners of their eyes. They didn't look like an army. But then Galt remembered that when he arrived in France in 1918 as a young captain of infantry only four years out of West Point the British said the same thing about the Americans.

In any case, the adulation of the Australian crowds, the frankness with which they greeted his promises, were good for Big Drum. He was pure public figure, only really alive in public, and he and the Australians breathed vitality into each other. In public then he was able to believe things he had no grounds for believing in private.

I shall reserve judgement on the Australians, Galt told himself, and see how they perform.

One Tuesday morning after Big Drum *had* slept well, he ordered Galt and Harry Strudwick to make a complete listing of all landing places, bays, inlets and beaches on Australia's coast, with tidal charts and moon readings – all of it to be accessible at a moment's notice. 'Since a moment's notice is all we'll get,' Big Drum announced.

'Jesus, Galt!' he heard Harry say when Galt passed on the order.

He and Strudwick studiously used first names, even though they did not like each other. They could not afford to alienate each other too badly, because Big Drum respected both of them. But at this game, Galt knew he had a greater advantage than Harry. Strudwick had not been tacitly promised any cabinet post in Big Drum's future government, and given the fact that he was German, however innocently, till the age of five, was unlikely to be offered any in the present climate. 'That's a big order on short notice. Can I bring in the Australian naval men?'

'Big Drum doesn't want any of the other Allies here at headquarters.'

For Big Drum wanted to be able to say with truth, when it *was* all done, that it had been all done by an American staff.

That made Big Drum uneasy about the senior Australian general, a Falstaffian, genial fellow called General Billings. Billings had been declared Chief of the Allied Land Forces under General Wraith, but it was clear to Galt that Big Drum wanted to deal General Billings out of the game, to let him have his own headquarters, to keep him as far as possible from Collins Street, and to dream up ways – or to have Galt dream them up – of ensuring that American troops weren't commanded by Billings, even though he seemed competent and had successfully led the Australians against the Panzer Corps in North Africa.

'By all means, draw on any Australian records you can get your hands on,' Galt therefore told Harry, 'but we don't want Australian officers hanging round Bataan.'

The building in Collins Street where Big Drum's headquarters was located had been called, at Big Drum's fiat, *Bataan*, after the peninsula in the Philippines where Big Drum's troops had put up such a brave resistance against the Japanese.

'Christ, Galt,' Harry protested further. 'If my staff is to do this in time, we're going to need the Aussies. The last I heard, they weren't actually the enemy.'

In such a circumstance, Galt decided to draw on his natural hauteur. He knew that, controlled by judgement, it was his greatest weapon.

'Listen, Harry. When we win, it must be because of American boys led by Big Drum, and because of a staff which is seen to be totally American. We can hold the line by depending on the Australians, but we can't win with them because there's just not enough of them. We're on a continent the size of the continental USA, and with a population of seven million! You can't raise an army these days from a population base of seven million, not one big enough to face an army from a population base of ninety million. If we win, it will be only because the US President and Congress backs us. And it will back us only if we have American – not Australian or Dutch – but freckled-faced-farmboy American victories to give to them.'

Harry lowered his voice. There was too much of the teacher-with-slow-student about the way he did it, but maybe he was only reacting to Galt's didactic manner.

'Galt, I understand how it's heresy to say these things aloud, but we're not going to get any victories yet out of the Americans we have. Corregidor and Bataan taught us that much. For the next six months, maybe for the next year, the only trained troops we have are the Aussies.'

Galt chose to smile as if there was genuine amiability between them. 'OK, Harry. But if on top of everything else we invite the Australian staff in here, then we'll never be rid of them. Let's send some of your officers to plunder the Aussie files, and ask General Pendle for any reconnaissance back-up you need.'

There was silence. Harry Strudwick could not bring himself actually to *assent* to Galton Sandforth's decrees. He never said, 'By all means, Galt.' 'I'll do what I can, Galt.' 'I'll put my men on it straight away.' Though he did usually get the job done in the end, whereas a lot of men who gave assurances didn't.

Harry said at last, 'Oh, Jesus! Don't misunderstand me, Galt. I've got no objection to providing that sort of minutiae. But I don't have the staff for it. What I do have is taken up with what the Japs are actually doing. Bombing Broome in Western Australia, for instance, and building up on the north coast of New Guinea. We're fully stretched, for God's sake, don't you see, Galt. Just taking care of what might happen today and tomorrow, without worrying about next year.'

Galt hated this – the way Harry complained about a job which he had to do anyhow, and which he was *bright enough* to know had to be done anyhow!

On an impulse, he said, 'I thought you were meant to love this sort of stuff – efficiency, long-range planning. That's what they tell us anyhow.'

That's it, Galt saw. Harry Strudwick will resent that slur for the rest of his life.

'It'll be done, Galt,' said Harry at last. He didn't want to sound offended, for that would be a signal to Galt that the jibe had worked and could be used again.

'I mean,' said Galt, 'I'm just observing, Harry. You must retain some of your ethnic characteristics, I hope. You can't be entirely a good ole boy. None of us need good ole boys. *They* put us in this mess.'

And so, fairly neatly, Galton thought, I've turned my reckless insult on its head.

'It'll be done,' was all that Harry said.

A major on Sandforth's staff reminded him one Tuesday morning that the Governor of Victoria, a retired British army officer of the kind the Australians seemed to like for their vice-regal personages, was that afternoon hosting a reception in his honour. It was a day cold enough for Galt to wear the tailored heavy-weight jacket he had had made by a tailor since his arrival in Melbourne. But underneath it, he wore for symbolic reasons the shirt he had brought with him in the B-17 from Mindanao, and the same cap with its wire removed.

The Aussies seemed to get great comfort out of beholding Big Drum and his staff dressed not-so-elegantly, in the beaten-up manner of the Philippines campaign, in the style of Bataan or Corregidor – even though Bataan and Corregidor had been military disasters.

There was further irony to all this that day. As Galton entered his car for the short journey to Government House, his staff had messages in their hands, as yet unconfirmed, that the American forces in the Philippines had surrendered. This news did not shake Galt, though he had been taken by the poignancy of a hysterical radio transmission up from Corregidor in the small hours of that morning. A flimsy of it had been on his desk in Melbourne when he'd got there at breakfast time:

Corregidor here Corregidor here 02.00 5 May 1942 They are not here yet They are waiting for God knows what

How about a chocolate soda Lots of heavy fighting going on We may have to give up by noon We don't know yet They are throwing men and shells at us and I feel sick in my stomach They bring in the wounded every minute We will be waiting for you guys to help The jig is up Everyone is bawling like a baby They are piling dead and wounded in our tunnel I know now how a mouse feels Caught in a trap waiting for guys to come along and finish it up Got a treat Canned pineapple My name is Irving Strobing Get this to my mother Mrs Minnie Strobing 605 Barbey Street Brooklyn New York

Galt was sensitive to the fact that but for the President's order to Big Drum, he himself would have been in the Malinta tunnel with that radio operator. He hoped he wouldn't have been 'bawling like a baby'. But the Japanese, with their great navy and their big guns positioned along the shoreline of Bataan, had been able to starve and pulverize Corregidor, the island south of Manila, the island from which, a bare month past, Big Drum and his entourage had fled by motor torpedo boat.

So, at the end of such a day as this, Galt felt mute and dazed. But no one could tell.

By comparison with Manila, Melbourne was a shuttered, ordinary, verdant little city. A quiet place. No New York, it got most of its glamour from the fact that Big Drum had come, and that the Japanese might be following him.

In accord with the spirit of this pleasant place, Government House was a slightly excessive nineteenth-century mansion in the style of British country houses. It was set in the midst of wide and impeccably kept grounds. He had heard that the Victorians, the people of the state of Victoria, had had a great nineteenth-century gold rush, and some of that money had gone into this structure. The spacious garden was filled with a fantastic combination of plants and trees, some of them native Australian and therefore odd and of great interest to Galton Sandforth's eye. His family had – like other great Virginian families including the Jeffersons – always taken an urbane interest in exotic plants from far places. All their founding wealth had been based on exotic plants, one growing wild in the American hinterland, the other from Egypt by way of England. The names of the plants in question were tobacco and cotton.

So by the time the small honour guard of *diggers* – as the Australians called their soldiers – had presented arms, Galton Sandforth, led by a young Australian aide, entered the reception hall of Government House with a little more interest than he originally thought he would take in this ritual event, especially one which occurred on such an evil day, a day which might well have done for Mrs Minnie Strobing's signaller son Irving.

'I think your gardens here are exquisite, Your Excellency,' Galt was able to tell the Governor, a genial man in his early seventies who would not fare well in internment camps, if it came to that, if the Japanese arrived.

The old man warmed to Galton's genuine praise for the grounds.

General Sandforth's enthusiasm was about to be turned up by several notches in any case. For in this severe but opulent mansion, he saw all at once a young Australian woman, an army officer, chatting with some naval people on the far side of the vice-regal drawing room. And he wanted to meet her.

It wasn't banal sexuality which awakened his interest. At least that was what he would always afterwards tell himself. He would in fact tell himself that even then, before they had exchanged any words, he had been engaged by the girl's blend of liveliness and intelligence, its survival inside that terrible uniform which seemed designed for lumpier, heftier women. It was – above all – what, watching her, he diagnosed as the girl's seeming frankness of expression and lack of posturing in the way she held her body.

He felt warmly, *This is the sort of woman the Australians are good at*! *This is* the *Australian woman*.

Suddenly he relished being guest of honour. For he did not have to seek the other guests. They would all be brought to him if he stood still.

When it was her turn to be introduced she barely lowered her eyes, as he would have expected a male officer to do even momentarily. It raised his hopes that he had not been deluded.

‘Well, welcome to Melbourne, sir,’ she told him. ‘It may seem a bit small to you, but we’re very proud of our city.’

‘With good reason, lieutenant.’ He found himself remarkably willing to like her antipodean town. ‘Needless to say I’m very pleased to be here.’

‘It must be hard, sir,’ she said, looking him in the eye, ‘to know whether you like it in itself, sir. Or by comparison to the alternative.’

He could see, though, she already regretted having said that. She was telling herself, *You fool*! And, *What a thing to say to someone who fled the Philippines*!

For some reason he found it not only forgivable and endearing, but also amusing. He thought, *You fool, you’re liking this*! This very proper opening move of courtship. He’d always presumed that courtships of young women by men his age could only proceed in an underhand, risqué way. He *heard* himself laugh. He felt he was outside of himself and not quite in charge.

‘That’s quite a challenge to put to me, lieutenant.’ But he’d already forgotten what she had said. In her straightforward, accessible way she was so beautiful. He had watched her mouth uttering the sentence but missed the meaning altogether. ‘Though,’ he said, retrieving ground, ‘chiefs of staff are supposed to lie most of the time, so that they’ll be proved right at least half the time. What did you ask? Oh yes. Well, I’ll still say I like Melbourne in its own right.’

Off the hook, she began enjoying herself too. ‘And so . . . can you guarantee to save us, sir?’

‘Consider it done,’ he told her. Though he wondered what Signaller Strobing would make of such glib chatter as this. ‘It’s my honour to help the Australians save themselves *and* us.’

With the gift for peripheral vision he’d built up in his years as a professional officer, the sort needed at regimental dances and social events in particular, he detected a flicker of amusement not on the face but more in the eyes of the staff aide he had inherited here in Melbourne and who had accompanied him this afternoon. This was a young West Pointer newly arrived in the country, a Captain Duncan. Galt had no reason to mistrust or dislike him. Nonetheless, one more flicker like that, boy, Galton mentally promised the young man, and you'll be back with the infantry.

'And what is your part in this great endeavour of ours, lieutenant?' he asked the young woman.

She winced but got a laugh off as well. 'A not very glamorous job, sir,' she told him. 'Though an officer of your staff told me it was a very important one. I'm to provide the latest motion pictures for General Wraith and his staff. I've been told I'm to give you a list of latest releases every week.'

He had to keep reminding himself of the content of what she was saying. For he simply liked her accent. It had a breadth to it. He liked the blend of carefully schooled vowels and Australian twang.

'Of course,' said Galt, strangely delighted to find that she was virtually under his jurisdiction, 'I told Captain Duncan to locate someone with experience in that area. I hope you'll do a good job, lieutenant. The General is in a movie-going phase and holds me ultimately responsible for the motion pictures he sees. I remember that even in Alice Springs he dragged us to the open air movie house. We saw a really bad Western. I want you to send us only the really good ones. And don't forget a cartoon or two – Mickey Mouse and so on. The General likes watching his son laugh. It's a common parental entertainment.'

'Well, is there any subject matter I should avoid?' she asked solemnly. 'For example, does the General like musicals?'

'Not particularly, lieutenant. But Mrs Wraith does. And that's the General's other main entertainment – watching his wife enjoy herself. In his own terms, though, he likes to see the Indians defeated. His father was an Indian fighter and didn't always quite manage that!'

They laughed together so thoroughly that Sandforth very nearly forgot to keep an eye on Captain Duncan. He cast about for something to say and gratefully found it.

'You have a movie for us tomorrow night?' he asked.

'Sir, I've already provided your office with the list. There are half a dozen possible pictures standing by.'

'Oops, lieutenant. I'll have to attend to that in the morning.'

'Well, I hope it's all suitable, sir.'

But she didn't sound as if his disapproval would make her scurry around to the distributors and find a replacement.

'Sure it will be,' he told her.

This was such ordinary talk and yet it enchanted him and had a weight greater than the individual words justified or bystanders might suspect. And he wanted to keep the conversation going.

'Tell me a little more about this list you make up.'

'Yes. Of course, the distributors give me all the information. I'm not an expert in judging films.'

'I thought everyone was. Surely it's the art of ordinary people.'

'Yes,' she admitted. 'But I lived in the country and the nearest picture theatre was forty miles away.'

He thought, *This is astounding. She's frankly telling me she's no film buff. She's secure enough to do that.* Maybe this was an Australian trait, confessing one's limits because they were nothing to fret about.

'The distributors tell me, sir,' she went on, 'that they've got a special coming next week. A sad tale of Welsh miners. *How Green Was My Valley*. Do you think the General would like that?'

'Sure he will, as long as there aren't unionists in it. But there's tomorrow night. What would you choose for tomorrow night, lieutenant?'

'Well, as I said, the list should be with you, sir.'

'Yes, but what do the distributors say?'

'Well, there's *Road to Morocco*. They say it's been a big success in the United States. Bing Crosby, Bob Hope, Dorothy Lamour. It's supposed to be lively. I haven't seen it myself.'

The frankness had struck again. *I haven't seen it myself.*

'That will be fine, lieutenant. Let's make that tomorrow night's event. Captain Duncan, we must make sure that the lieutenant is invited to tomorrow night's screening. The ballroom at the Menzies Hotel.' Galt got a salute from Duncan and then turned to Lieutenant Lewis. 'I'm afraid it's a little early. Six-thirty. So Little Drum can see the cartoons before he falls asleep. He's a brave boy, Little Drum.'

'I know. I read newspaper articles on how he and his mother lived on Corregidor.'

‘So come and watch him laugh.’

Captain Duncan can’t make anything special of a normal, courteous invitation like that, Galt Sandforth told himself. Even if he wanted to be snide. Even if – and it was paranoid to believe this – he were an agent of Harry Strudwick’s. Which he certainly wasn’t. He’d just been waiting there in Melbourne when Galt turned up.

Later that evening, when Galt reminded Duncan to make sure that Lieutenant Lewis would be admitted to the Menzies, which was after all an American fortress, Duncan gave no sign, however minor, that he was reading General Sandforth’s desires and finding them a little bit comic.

As for Dim, though she thanked the general without gushing – as her mother had taught her – she was excited. Events had brought her in a few days from Captain Cahill’s front office to a reception at Government House, and so by way of General Sandforth into the presence ultimately of Big Drum, the greatest American hero.

Later, leaving the reception, as his car pulled out of the gates of Government House, Galt saw the young woman crossing the wide street in a shower of rain. She had her head tucked in under a large frumpish black umbrella, but her style gave a grace to the whole scene. Galt toyed with the idea of stopping and giving her a lift. But it wasn’t feasible. He could do it only for someone he liked less. He could not risk having Captain Duncan see him warming to the Australian girl. He noticed that Duncan looked at him, as if to suggest the possibility of giving Lieutenant Lewis a ride. Galt, however, looked straight ahead.

(a) She won’t get a cold, not at her age.

(b) I’ll see her tomorrow night.

That night, Honor Runcie phoned to find out if Dim had heard anything from Allan. The call revived in Dim a guilt at having so easily shelved her memory of her own husband. It was obvious from what Allan had said about his journey up the Sepik that Dim and Honor would not know on any given day whether their husbands were in training camp outside Sydney or in New Guinea or – for that matter – Java. The thing which made Dim uneasy was that she did not even try to *imagine* the location he was in and what he was doing. Whereas Honor could not stop her mind running on that.

All afternoon, while Dim was too easily forgetting Allan and glorying in the company at Government House, Honor, tethered by her baby, had been keeping alive the vivid flame of wifely concern.

Suppressing her own futile remorse, Dim told Honor, 'I'll let you know exactly how I feel about all this. I trust your husband. I took one look at him, and I thought there's a traveller, a man with staying power. It's easier for me because I just believe that if Allan sticks with Gordon, then . . . '

She did not finish the sentence. Everyone knew that if you speculated on people's survival, then perverse chance would move in on them. All the same, it was true that Gordon Runcie – despite his habits with jungle knives – took off Dim some of the onus of fretting about Allan. Surely an expression of belief in Gordon was a comfort to Honor.

'Oh,' said Honor. 'It's funny. I tend to think of Allan as a moderating influence on Gordon. He won't do anything foolish because he doesn't want Allan hurt . . . '

Dim had a sharp image of the jungle knife quivering in the door jamb beside Honor. Surely, now that she was off the moral hook, Honor would put down the telephone and go and feed the baby. End of uneasy topic!

'You must be so lonely too,' Honor said then, in a peculiar voice, a voice which, even to her, seemed to give too much away, Dim thought, with a shock and a kind of envy, 'She *loves* him. He's one of the staples of her life. Like bread and water. She believes she can't live if anything happens to him!'

Whereas Dim could live without Allan. She knew it in her blood and couldn't pretend otherwise. She would be bitterly sorry if the worst happened. She would shed tears. But her very proper hysteria would be more for Allan's thwarted manhood and modest dreams than for her own desperation.

'Look,' Dim said firmly, wanting to reassure herself as much as Honor. 'They are both going to live to be old men. They will sit by the fire in the Melbourne Club, and the young members will try to avoid them. I can foresee it, clear as day. Believe me, Honor!'

Before Honor had properly hung up, Dim remembered with a pulse of joy that the next evening she was going to the pictures with the greatest man in the southern hemisphere. She would watch the same screen as Big Drum. A ridiculous and – she didn't doubt – *shallow* excitement, which had nothing to do with Allan, entered her body as a sort of shiver.

You're a shallow woman, she thought. But the idea of shallowness filled her with joy rather than shame.

In the grand ballroom of the Menzies, Little Drum fell asleep in the middle of a Bing Crosby number. Dim, who was only one row behind what the Americans called 'the brass' and could see the back of Big Drum's leonine head, watched the Wraiths' Chinese nurse gather the little boy up and tote him out of the room. The eyes of both Mrs Wraith and Big Drum followed the exit of Ling and Little Drum and thereby missed a Bob Hope joke. What – again to use the American idiom – was called 'a sight gag'.

The husband, tall and straight-backed, and his small-boned wife exchanged satisfied glances, rejoicing together in their son, before returning their eyes to Bing and Bob and Dorothy Lamour.

Throughout this fascinating passage of events, Dim could see in profile the lean but compact features of Galton Sandforth. He had the sort of face which did not particularly age. So, in a different sense, had Big Drum. Some women, she thought academically, would consider them both very glamorous. And sitting near them, she felt glamorous herself. There was an extra glow about her. If Maneering knew about her tonight, they would be astounded. Her radiance in this high company, she was sure, was greater than the combined street lights of Maneering after closing time.

The street lights there were in any case switched off now, Maneering had blacked itself out. The town fathers were quite certain that the Japanese empire and its plan to capture Australia was all a not so subtle ploy just so that it could possess the core of the nation – beautiful Maneering.

But what about her school teachers at the Presbyterian Ladies' College, the ones who had always predicted a bad end for her; the ones who told her in Mathematics classes that she would never get a job? Well, she had her job. She was on the staff of Big Drum.

The picture was going down well. Captain Duncan, who sat beside her, mentioned at the changing of the first reel – there was only one projector – how thoroughly Big Drum liked it. 'You find out if he doesn't like it,' he told her. 'He just walks, just that. He ups and walks.' Duncan adopted a rural drawl which wasn't his normal accent. 'And when that ole boy walks, he *walks*! He don't wait for any actor to finish his sentence.'

When the film ended, with a spatter of applause from the American officers and their women guests, the General stood and the entire room also stood as if in respect for him. Even Mrs Wraith seemed to be doing him honour. Big Drum turned towards the audience. At first Dim thought he intended to address them.

Instead, he said to Dim in a low conversational voice which enabled the rest of the room to get on with their own discussions, 'Thank you, lieutenant, for a very fine movie. When I think of the primitive motion pictures I watched as a boy in army forts in Wyoming, I have to say they now have it to a fine art, a fine art indeed.'

He seemed to be thanking her for the American film industry, and with a sense of the exorbitance of this she began to blush.

'I hope I can satisfy you as well every week, sir.'

Fragile Mrs Wraith, her handsome face on its side, regarded her with a smile.

'Dear,' said Big Drum. 'This is the young woman who acquires the movies for us.'

Mrs Wraith said in a soft, Southern accent, very different from her husband's more patrician one, 'Why, lieutenant, you managed to satisfy the toughest critic you'll ever encounter. I mean my son, Drummond Wraith III. Both the cartoon and the main course were exactly to his taste.'

And she laughed, and the General laughed and then said goodnight. Out of such simple conversations with the great come the often repeated tales of grandmothers, Dim knew. If she ever became a grandmother.

General Galton Sandforth strolled down the aisle of chairs, a half smile on his face. 'You didn't fail me, lieutenant,' he said, looking both at herself and at Captain Duncan too, as if he wanted Duncan to take notice of his words. 'You've managed to divert for a few hours the centre of our world. Believe me, we will profit richly from this small service of yours. Good night.'

Then he turned precisely and went.

Marching alone out of the ballroom, Sandforth felt hollow to be leaving her. If he knew Duncan and could trust him, he would have spoken with her longer. Duncan was a cool contemptuous Yankee and difficult to assess.

Outside the hotel, Duncan opened the door of a large army Buick for Dim. She would travel home alone in its cavernous back seat.

'Lieutenant,' said Captain Duncan, bending over so that the driver could not hear, 'I wondered if you'd do me the honour of letting me take you to dinner one night. I'm a little embarrassed to remember that when I first spoke to you I used a lot of military slang, as if I was talking to an infantry section. I'm capable of better. Likewise, they say the Hotel Australia is better than the Menzies, and I'd like to get away from this zoo in any case.'

Dim said, 'That's very kind of you, captain. But I *am* married, and my husband is on active service.'

'Forgive me, ma'am,' said Duncan, and unlike an Australian, he did not either go on insisting or show any confusion. 'I didn't understand your situation.'

He closed the door, stood back on the steps of the hotel and gave a very companionable, very well-tutored wave.

As for Dim, she had asserted her married status automatically, without thinking about it. She had had no preparation. She had sat beside Duncan all night without thinking of herself as a person a young officer might desire.

A dinner. Duncan had mentioned a dinner. The Americans had the right to order big in a country where all the meat was being shipped to Britain. So maybe if Duncan asked again, she would say yes. After all, he didn't seem to be the sort of officer you would have to fight off. He had already taken *no* the way a man should.

Chapter 5

Bataan, Australia

FRED, THE AGEING Australian corporal who acted as door-guard and concierge at the Allied Officers' Club, appeared in the doorway of the front office Dim shared with Captain Cahill.

'Madam,' he said, 'there's a young Yank officer out there. He's come by car and he says he's got orders to take you to the Menzies.'

She stood up, and did not yet grab her hat, the flat-crowned, wide-brimmed affair they made servicewomen wear. (Only men were allowed to wear the famous slouch hat with its left side turned up and held in place with a badge.) She wanted to check with Captain Cahill.

She found him in the hallway, engaged in conversation with an elegantly uniformed American officer. It wasn't Duncan, as she'd suspected and half hoped it might be.

'I hope this isn't permanent,' Captain Cahill was saying to the American. 'Lieutenant Lewis is absolutely essential to this club.'

Dim was flattered to hear this but nonetheless wondered why it had taken the Americans to promote her above the rank of private?

The American officer saw her. 'Ma'am,' he said, 'could you fetch anything you wish to bring with you to Bataan?'

'Bataan.' Dim knew it was the name of an ill-fated peninsula in the Philippines.

The officer said indulgently, 'United States Army Headquarters in Collins Street.'

At Big Drum's headquarters, Dim entered an American world. From the lobby onwards, there was not another Australian uniform to be seen. Even the corporal who worked the lift – which the Americans called the 'elevator', as if they were imitating people in motion pictures – looked more fashionably dressed than most Australian majors. She didn't doubt the worth of her own countrymen. An Australian major, especially after three years of war, was many times the professional equivalent of an American major, who was still becoming accustomed to the idea of battle. And everyone took that for granted.

It was just that the Americans were – to grab at a term she had heard *them* use – more snappy.

She would have to resist their glamour. For all over Melbourne there were women who didn't. Light-headed girls who thought that if they were with a Yank they were closer to Hollywood.

As Dim emerged on the third floor, the officer escorting her said, 'There's something Big Drum insists we take everyone to see.' He took her into a barn-like room. Once walls had divided this up into dreary offices, but every partition had been knocked out, and now the space was taken up with desks and telephones, teleprinters and radio transmitters, amongst which officers and staff-sergeants hurtled, serious business written all over their faces. At one end, above a raised platform, sat the same immense map of the Pacific which Big Drum had earlier ordered Galt Sandforth to have erected. An outline of the United States was marked in blue tape and occupied only as much space as Australia did. As she was intended to, Dim found the sight of the immense Pacific chastening. She thought, too, that towards one of the small islands set in that immensity Captain Allan Lewis might at the moment be in transit.

After she had considered the map for ten seconds, the officer said, 'General Sandforth will want to know that you've seen it. He says you guys are just about as ignorant of the Pacific as we are.'

'He's right,' Dim admitted. 'Until all this happened, we thought we were moored off the south coast of England.'

The officer took her up two further floors, along a corridor and to a door on which a US private was scraping off paintwork which said Mr C.H. Evans, Rural Division. 'This will have your name on it,' said the officer. It was a pleasant office, medium-sized. It had a view. Through the taped glass of the window she could see the grandstands of the Melbourne Cricket Ground.

The officer said, 'You're a Headquarters Procurement Officer slash Motion Pictures. Your orders have been cut.'

She wondered why the American said that – *orders cut*?

She noticed there that there was a typewriter on a side table. She hesitated but thought she must make her position clear.

'I don't type, you know.'

'Ma'am, you don't have to. You're an officer and a gentleman. You'll have access to the typing pool.'

He showed her where the stationery and procurement forms were, and then he left her. She was uncertain what to do. She sat down in her chair and swung it to face the view of the venerable cricket ground. Her father was a member there. A metal Lady's Pass tied in her lapel, she'd sometimes attended test matches between England and Australia as a girl.

Now here she was, high in Big Drum's fortress. High above the esteemed playing pitch. She knew she should be happy, but she was bewildered too.

And a little fearful. Procuring movies for Big Drum's showings took at most a day a week. How was she to spread that work over six days? She could become lost and forgotten in this room.

She was considering this, and working herself up to make a reconnaissance out into the corridor, when her telephone rang.

'General Sandforth,' said the voice. And it sounded familiar to her. She had kept, without knowing it, a memory of the modulations of Sandforth's voice. 'You're settled in, lieutenant?'

'Yes, sir.'

'You sound doubtful about it.'

'Well, it's simply that organizing picture shows for the General doesn't take so very long. I feel a little unreal here. I don't want to waste my time or yours.'

She didn't doubt a second it was best to let him know, even though he sat on Big Drum's right hand.

Sandforth was laughing. 'My God, you really *are* a civilian, aren't you? I shouldn't confirm your worst suspicions, but armies are great time-wasting exercises. Accept that, and nothing worries you as much. Let me reassure you, lieutenant. You will be working with the Senior Entertainment Officer who is located at 41st Infantry Division's headquarters out in the hills. For practical purposes you'll be doing his work. I will deny I ever said this, but he is not very efficient. You will be providing movies for the various battalions of our 41st Division. I believe that up to now they've been watching re-runs of Hopalong Cassidy, grainy old stuff from the early thirties. Captain Duncan will be giving you the name of a useful contact in the divisional entertainment office. It may become necessary for you to arrange live entertainment as well. Welcome to Bataan, lieutenant! Or – to put it more bureaucratically – Southwest Pacific Area Supreme Command.'

She thanked him. But he rushed on to other matters, with a breathlessness more appropriate to that of a younger man trying to get something difficult uttered. 'And in that regard and to celebrate the day,' he said, 'I would be honoured if you would join me for dinner in my quarters tonight. Twenty hundred hours, sixth floor of the Menzies. Would you do that?'

'Of course, sir.'

For Sandforth had a compelling rank, to which even a civilian soldier had to defer.

Nor was she conventionally concerned. He was not a sexual possibility, as Captain Duncan was. He was old enough if not to be Dim's father at least to be her father's younger brother.

She heard him say that Captain Duncan would meet her at the door of the Menzies at eight and bring her up to his quarters. Her first job in her new office would be to let Captain Duncan know to which address a vehicle should be sent to collect her that evening, and at what time.

'And now,' he said, 'you must be a little disoriented and surprised. You're dismissed for the remainder of the day.'

Having said that, he hung up. Later she would know that he had been hiding behind the military forms, of which the brusque hang-up was a notable example.

She wondered if the rule about being five minutes late for dinner appointments applied to someone of Sandforth's distinction. However she had been brought up, she decided not to test the matter fully, and as soon as her car dropped her at the front of the Menzies, even though it was still seven minutes to

Sandforth's nominated time, she walked up the steps and into the lobby.

Captain Duncan was there as promised. He bowed. 'Good evening, ma'am. I shall take you to General Sandforth's quarters.'

As he led her to the lift, he half-turned towards her. He smiled. 'I understand that you have reasons for dining with General Sandforth which didn't apply to my invitation. The one I made earlier, remember? I'd be grateful, ma'am, if you omitted mentioning to General Sandforth that particular overture of mine.'

He cocked an eyebrow. He certainly had style. For an instant Dim had an insight into the world of the professional soldier, where careers were blighted by one ill-considered invitation directed to the wrong woman. She was nonetheless puzzled why Duncan thought any table talk between herself and Sandforth should include such a random item of information.

Upstairs at that moment, Galt was welcoming what might be called his dinner guest of convenience, an old North Carolinian friend, Brigadier-General Bryant Gibbs.

Gibbs and Galt had graduated from West Point in the same class. Even tonight, under the shadow of the great Japanese military *tsunami*, they wore their class rings. Bryant Gibbs had just been promoted and appointed to command of a brigade of the 41st Infantry Division, and, given that he had a classmate who had the area commander's ear, could expect any merit he showed to be rewarded with further promotion.

He was a tough, intelligent little man and he liked operations in the field as passionately as Sandforth preferred staff work.

'Bryant,' Sandforth confided in his friend after they both had a drink in their hands, 'there's a young Australian officer coming to dinner. She is at the moment the only exception to Big Drum's rule that no Aussies or Dutch or other breeds be admitted to Bataan. Let me tell you frankly, I had her appointed.' He let Bryant absorb this information. He was playing at letting Bryant feel that he had a lever he could use, whereas both men understood that all the main levers were, if not exactly in Sandforth's hands, at least within his reach. Sandforth knew, and the Brigadier-General knew he knew, that Gibbs had kept a mistress in the mid-1930s while he was military liaison officer with the British in New Delhi.

Galt Sandforth continued: 'What I'd like you to do, as a friend, is that you should get an urgent telephone call about nine-thirty. Just as dessert is served. You can arrange that?'

All business, Gibbs nodded as if responding to a fully professional request. There was no smirk or leer in his reaction, and Galt was inexpressibly grateful for that.

'Give me a telephone now, Galt, and I'll arrange it in ten seconds.'

Dim was shown into Sandforth's quarters, a fairly gloomy suite built originally for wealthy miners or sheep barons down from the bush on business – a suite which had that Australian feel about it, not the aura of General Sandforth's enormous power. Gibbs was just putting down the phone and wearing the appearance of someone who has heard faintly bad news.

'The newest member of our headquarters staff,' said Sandforth as she entered, as if it were his duty to announce her.

She inclined her head, throwing doubt on all overdone gestures, particularly the kind Galt had a secret, rarely indulged appetite for. She's perfection, he thought, and she's not even scared of me. Oh Jesus! There was a frank sweetness and a subtleness around the mouth!

He said, 'Lieutenant, may I introduce you to the newest general in the Southwest Pacific Area?'

He did it. He watched her shake hands with Gibbs, who suddenly gave a sort of harmless crooked smile, that rictus of hopeless desire which – since it didn't threaten any crass action – women didn't seem to be offended by.

But something else, he could see, was worrying the girl. It didn't take much of her native intelligence, he had to admit, for her to understand the peculiarity behind tonight. Her elevation to the lieutenancy was being honoured at the same meal that went to honour Gibbs's new general's star! She spotted the disproportion, and it confused her.

Galt Sandforth rushed in to reassure her. 'It's pure good fortune that my friend General Gibbs is here. He was commanding an infantry battalion in Hawaii. And one of the generals of the

41st Division took ill. Bad luck for him, but the opposite for General Gibbs and his friends, amongst whom I count myself.' You're sounding a little flatulent, he warned himself. For Christ's sake, stop trying so hard. 'General Gibbs is drinking bourbon. What would you like, lieutenant?'

Dim asked for a sherry. A young American steward in a white coat put it into her hands within seconds.

'Here's to Australia and its robust health!' said Sandforth, smiling at her and raising his own glass of Scotch.

Galt Sandforth was delighted with Bryant Gibbs. Before the soup was even served, he had the girl laughing about the General he had replaced. The poor fellow had had cruel piles, and in the hope that it would render him ready for combat had undergone a painful operation. But the operation hadn't been much of a success; when Gibbs had last seen him, the man was being loaded on a sort of whoopee cushion or inner tube into the belly of a B-17. Going Stateside, his big chance of combat cruelly snatched from him.

'The poor guy,' said General Gibbs. 'He has to put up with all these jokes about fundamental military principles!'

'And you yourself have no affliction in that direction?' Galt asked, knowing what the answer was.

Gibbs drained his glass. 'None, sir. I am fit to occupy any office chair that presents itself.'

They sat down to soup.

'And your husband?' Gibbs asked Dim at one stage. Galt was angry with himself for not recognizing that, of course, she'd be married. He had not noticed at Government House, but she must have been wearing the same ring she wore tonight.

He wondered whether Bryant was playing with him, asking that question, or alerting him to unexpected hazards. Galt looked at the wedding ring on her hand again. It wasn't a bad design, he thought. Melbourne had good jewellers.

'My husband's an Australian officer,' the woman said without any apparent discomfort, any guilt for his not being here.

'Infantry?' persisted Gibbs.

'Yes, he's an infantry captain. But he's involved in something secret. He can't even tell me much about the details. But it's something to do with reconnaissance operations against the Japanese.'

'I'm damned glad to hear someone's doing that sort of thing,' cried Gibbs.

'Yes,' she said. 'Even he says it's good to be going forward when everyone else is going back.'

Galt thought, with some bewilderment, *This is not Teresa Chung. This is not convenience or cosy arrangements.*

He was so tongue-tied that there was a danger that Bryant would be the man Lieutenant Lewis remembered from this evening.

Gibbs himself was settled in and enjoying himself. He winked at Sandforth. He really approved of this girl. *She's the girl to keep you honest*, the wink said.

'Now perhaps you could advise us on a peculiar Australian matter,' said Gibbs cheerily. 'Your longshoremen – you call them wharfies here – what's the story with those guys? What I mean is, I hear from my friend, he of the whoopee cushion, that when our brigade transport was being unloaded, these guys just walked away all at once. A *stopwork meeting* or something. Trucks and armoured cars were left dangling from the winches. What I'm getting at, Mrs Lewis . . . their country's up to its neck in trouble, and they hold a stopwork meeting! Are these guys a fifth column or what are they?'

Dim Lewis said, 'I can't defend or explain that, sir. The wharfies have always been radical. I don't approve of it, but some people say it's not entirely the pigheadedness of the men concerned. They see it as their struggle for just pay and conditions, but they don't see that if the Japanese come there'll be no such thing as pay and conditions.'

Galt said, 'They're so slow even when they are working.'

'Perhaps, General,' said Dim. 'But they behaved even worse before Russia was involved in the war. It was definitely a capitalist war until then. Since Hitler invaded the Soviet Union last year, it's become more of a people's struggle.'

Both generals laughed as if at her acuteness. There was gratification in the laugh too, since it seemed her political opinions were set round about the same point of the spectrum as theirs.

'Just the same,' she concluded, willing – politely and firmly – to modify Gibbs's opinion, 'I think it's a bit extreme to call them a fifth column.'

Sandforth murmured, 'We should have Lieutenant Lewis down there at the wharf. To speak to them in their own language.'

General Sandforth was not pleased with his performance as a conversationalist tonight. Because the girl was so desirable, he felt that what he said to her creaked with a kind of engorged pomposity. It was chastening to face what he rarely had to face: that no degree of power or promotion could ever make him at his ease in front of a woman like this one. So Brigadier-General Gibbs had exerted all the effortless charm.

Galt was delighted, therefore, when, at 9.31 – a little late, though Sandforth wasn't going to blame anyone, since this was an army of civilians now – the telephone pealed and one of the young stewards went to answer it. The steward returned, Gibbs's ear was whispered into, and he crossed the room to take the receiver. After listening and then muttering into it for a few seconds, he placed it down, came to the table and bowed stoutly.

'Sorry, Galt. One of my battalion commanders wants to talk to me. Ma'am, it has been an honour.'

Dim noticed that the steward who showed General Gibbs out did not return. Before going, he had deftly wheeled a coffee trolley close to Lieutenant-General Sandforth's elbow.

Dim became uneasy now. Sandforth was being too solicitous about pouring her coffee exactly as she wanted it. It didn't make sense, the Chief of Staff to Big Drum fussing over the exact measure of sugar a lieutenant needed in her cup.

'Is anything the matter, lieutenant?' he asked her, passing a plate of after-dinner chocolates.

'No, sir,' she said, but then thought better of it. 'Well, yes. But I don't want to sound ungracious. I'm a little overwhelmed, that's all. I mean, dinner with two generals! It's not a common experience for sheep farmers' daughters from Maneering.'

He sat back, considered the ceiling for a while, and cleared his face of all expression. It gave Dim a chance to examine his features in repose. They were lean though not as aquiline as Big

Drum's. In another life, if he hadn't been a general, you could almost imagine him as a scholar or an Anglican bishop.

Meanwhile Galt hoped to God his pitch would succeed. He was in a state of divine anxiety appropriate to a boy of seventeen, and it both excited and terrified him.

'Do you promise not to interrupt?' he asked her at last, as a kind of safe starter.

'Of course, sir. I don't have any track record for interrupting generals.'

Sandforth laughed at that briefly. She had a good, informal humour, a little like the informal humour of the Australian Army itself. But he could not enjoy that yet. He was too busy being clever. 'Actually,' he said, 'I wouldn't be surprised if you did. But let me get on with what I was going to say.'

Dim's blood itched with fear of what might come out. It *can't* be the normal male speech he's about to make? Surely not? Yet even from her limited experience, she could spot the signs, the gravity, the clenching of the features, the uneasy postures.

'I need a companion, lieutenant,' he told her. 'Inevitably, I would look for someone young, someone I don't have to fear, someone of intelligence but set apart from the sort of power manoeuvres which go on amongst the staff of a great military endeavour. You understand, I'm sure. I need someone to have a meal with, share an outing with, even someone who won't *yessir* me all the time, someone to contradict me, if you like. But not the way I'm normally contradicted. There, that's my speech.'

He sipped his coffee but obviously hadn't finished talking yet. Dim could think of nothing to say.

'Now when I first met you,' Sandforth continued, 'and when I first framed the speech, I didn't know you were a married woman. And so, if what I've said is offensive, I need to beg your pardon.'

Dim closed her eyes. She felt powerless to think of what to say, or she could think of a number of things and couldn't find the words for them.

'Well?' he asked. 'What do you think?'

Dim said, 'The idea of a friendship is all very well. But other people might think it's more than friendship. That might hurt both of us.'

'It will always be a discreet friendship, Lieutenant Lewis. All these other men here have their discreet arrangements too, far less innocent than the one I'm suggesting.'

Oh God, he thought, I've made it sound as if she's to be my good-time girl. He rushed in to shorten the frown she was wearing.

'Just the same, I shouldn't be hypocritical about this. If anything further came of our arrangement, anything more intimate . . . I would treasure that. But I'm not talking about that now. I swear. I'm speaking of friendship, Lieutenant Lewis.'

Though to him her name as uttered by him sounded like a lie, so bloated with his desire, it was at that second that a crucial shift occurred in Dim. She ceased to consider him in the abstract way as a distinguished older man. She noticed in a new way that yes, suddenly he was appealing as a human rather than as a study, that his features were as taut as a young man's, that he was obviously still a player in the sexual game. That he was a potential seducer.

You learn, she told herself. You really learn things suddenly here!

'If we're to be friends,' she heard herself say, 'you'd better call me Dim. The shortened version of my grandmother's name. Australians shorten everything.'

'So you compensate for the name, Dim, by being sharp as a knife.'

She re-achieved a sort of control, and saw herself as she must appear to God or a fly in the corner – a young and easily influenced woman from the bush sitting in a plush chair and listening to a pitch from a lonely American officer. She felt distaste for herself and a little anger for being in this situation through none of her own fault. She smiled bleakly and Galt thought, what a terrible thing – to have to bullshit someone you want to love and take care of.

She said, 'All this makes me uneasy, General Sandforth. I know you don't mean it this way, but I can't help but feel my job depends on . . . well, on my friendship.'

'No! Never, lieutenant!' said Sandforth, laughing edgily. She noticed that his laugh had increased in attractiveness also. She was rendered uneasy by the rate at which he was becoming alluring, right in front of her. Her friend, Galton Sandforth. 'I'm a tough old rooster, I pay debts back, I settle people's hash if they're inefficient or if they lie or if they betray Big Drum. If they betray me I'm hardly any more lenient. But I swear to you, Dim, that your place here at Bataan, as Big Drum insists on calling it, is secure. It doesn't affect your position one jot, lieutenant. Big Drum and his troops are movie-goers. I didn't make that up. In *your* job, you will rarely encounter me, if at all. Unless – and I hope this is what will happen – it's by your choice.'

She thought, *this* is what they mean by deep water. I'm in deep water. There were extraordinary and alluring and improper possibilities here, in the deeps, possibilities which earlier in the evening she hadn't even known to exist.

When she spoke, she heard her own voice as a croak.

'I have to know. I have to know something about you.'

He nodded, doing her the honour of taking her seriously. Because he sensed he didn't stand a chance otherwise. If Teresa Chung had asked questions like that it would have very likely been the end of the liaison.

'Let's have one more drink for the evening. A port for you and a Scotch for me.'

He went across the room and poured them both at the drinks cabinet. He returned to the table, set her port gently beside her, and then sat himself.

'OK,' he said. 'I'm a Virginian. I get the impression you come from a family which is Australia's nearest thing to landed gentry. Well, Virginia has rightly or wrongly possessed a landed gentry since the seventeenth century. My own forebears first began commuting across the Atlantic late in that century, and then in the early years of the eighteenth settled for good near the upper waters of the James River. We also owned an enormous tract of what is now West Virginia. It was a good scheme for those early people – plenty of land in the tidewater, and even more – a kind of echo of what they already owned – up over the Blue Ridge and the Appalachians. Sandforths sat in the Virginian Assembly during colonial days. They helped finance the revolution against the British. You probably don't approve of that, but let me tell you that the revolution was good business. We were slave holders – humane ones according to the family history, though we probably did awful things to coloured folk – and we fought with the South in the Civil War. Half a dozen of us, uncles and great-uncles of mine, along with my grandfather, reached the rank of colonel or higher, and two of us, including my grandfather – were corps commanders in the Confederate army. I'm just filling you in, you see.'

For he wanted the friendship to start as soon as possible.

'My father was a West Point graduate and spent five years in the army. He made a further Sandforth fortune late last century and early in this one, shipping coal and steel along the Ohio. He owned mills on the Allegheny too. I grew up in polite society, in a house near Charlottesville, not so far as the crow flies from Jefferson's great house, Monticello. I was an outdoor child. The family passion is horses, and it was fortunate that I liked them at that stage or at least tolerated them. In those days they were the essence of being a military man, which everyone seemed to think I'd be. I'm glad they dropped out of the scene since then. I graduated from West Point, class of 1908, and I served in the Philippines when Big Drum's father was American commander there. Then I was a young staff officer in the canal zone in Panama.'

'Dear God,' said Dim, 'I don't have any history at all by comparison.'

'That's because you're young. It's better to be young than have a history.'

'Please go on,' she urged him. He was happy to see she was fascinated.

'Well, then 1915. In 1915 my father died of a stroke. My mother had already died of pneumonia when I was at West Point. So I was an orphan. I found myself in Vera Cruz on the coast of Mexico with General Gaines's force and that's where I first met Big Drum. He was a captain, a Lawrence-of-Arabia type of fellow. He went inland, a law unto himself. His job was to discover if the railroad was intact and if there were locomotives to haul our supplies when we advanced towards Mexico City. I was told to accompany him. I was a little uneasy about it, but once I met Big Drum I felt nothing could go wrong.'

That rang true. It was obviously the way Allan felt about Runcie.

'It was cowboy stuff,' said Galt Sandforth with a laugh, looking back ironically at the bravery of his youth. 'Arid plains, big mountains and no lack of hostile territory. On the third day out Big Drum and I and our three Mexican scouts were surrounded by fifteen guerrillas – they were either guerrillas or bandits, there wasn't any time to ask – and somehow we survived. All because of Big Drum. He took out both his Colt revolvers and shot six of them before I'd even cocked my pistol. I thought afterwards, if I keep near this fellow, I'll live forever. I hope it turns out to be the truth.'

He looked at Dim. She was waiting for more. Maybe she was waiting for news of his marriage.

'By then I had married Alexandra Curtis Lodge. She was a wonderful girl, champion point-to-point. She used to go to England every summer to compete.'

'And you're still married to her?'

'Yes. Of course, we lead our separate lives. You'll find that amongst professional soldiers. We haven't really lived together since the summer of '37. She runs the horse breeding side of the Sandforth operation. My older brother, whom I rarely see, runs the iron and steel and the shipping. And I'm the soldier.'

'Do you have children?' she asked, as if this too was an essential consideration to their friendship.

'Three,' he said. 'For the first fifteen years of marriage they went everywhere with me. Army brats. But then Sandy – my wife – got fed up with these army postings. The army sounds adventurous, but the wives see only the most dismal places on earth. Anyhow, my son, Galt, the eldest, is working on Omar Bradley's staff in England – he's a West Point graduate, a good man, a more genuinely gentle fellow than me. I have a daughter Alexandra – she's called Sandy, too – who's let us down by becoming a famous Broadway actress.'

'Let you down?'

He laughed. 'In the circles I grew up in, the stage was an indecent or frivolous profession. But I'm really proud of that girl. My second daughter, Abbey, is learning Japanese at Harvard. She's reflective, an outsider, a slow starter. Yet there's something about her which makes me think she's the one everyone might end up remembering. I'm lucky in my children.'

'But what about in your marriage?' Dim challenged him.

'My God, do all Australian women ask pointed questions? No, the marriage hasn't been as happy. There are certain . . . temperamental problems.' One of them was that Sandy asked such direct questions. And here he was trying to enchant another woman who asked direct questions. What did *that* mean? 'But you see, we army gentry never divorce, not if we want to be promoted. Now Big Drum *is* an exception. He married a flapper in 1926, all in good faith. His mother had just died, and he was demented with grief, and this really Bohemian girl turned his head. She was so immediately unfaithful to him, so openly, so flagrantly, that everyone knew he had either to shoot her or divorce her. That was OK, that was permissible.

'But you can't divorce a woman like Sandy, a woman everyone respects, and rightly so, a woman of character, of what they whimsically call *breeding*, without ruining yourself in our old-fashioned army. Mind you, if we all survive, I look to this war to change a few things that way. The old, tiny, inbred army I come from is what we call *stitched-up*. If you like – and if you'll forgive the impropriety of what I say – it's *tight-assed*. But for the moment, that's the army I'm operating in, until the civilians take over with their more liberal ideas. So, no divorce. Just genteel separation. And a coldness. Which isn't Sandy's fault. Coldness is one of my greatest strengths and failings.'

He had not mentioned the Big Plan, the strategy to get Big Drum to the White House, and his part in it, and how it would be disadvantaged by any scandal. Maybe she would become acquainted with all that if, as he hoped, they became close. For the moment though he was astonished that having made a start he was telling her all he was. And she seemed astonished too. It was a continuation of the bemusement she suffered at dinner.

'You can't be too cold,' she told him, looking for the good points of the experience, 'if you're willing to make a clean breast like this. And also, there's the way you talk about your children . . . '

'Well, I love them. On the other hand, lieutenant, I dearly want to be your friend, so I'm trying hard. I won't rush you, I promise, and you don't even have to think about the prospect of fighting off advances tonight. I respect you too much.'

Lieutenant Dim Lewis frowned deliciously. I am in love, he thought, and I must have her.

But it was too serious a matter for the *having* to be immediate, as he might have wished it to be with someone he felt attraction but little warmth for.

'Will you come to dinner again on Tuesday next week? Tuesday next week is a good evening for me. Big Drum is going out to the 41st Division camp in the Dandenong Ranges. I'll have a quiet afternoon to practise my table manners. Will you come?'

'Of course,' said Dim dubiously.

She knew an honest woman would say something else. She knew what people like her mother would say if they knew: that she'd been sucked in by the idea of dining privately with generals in what they would call in Maneering *flash* surroundings. Therefore that she lacked solid character. And what about her husband, poor Allan? He was a favoured son of Maneering, far more than she'd ever been a favoured daughter. Maneering people less than forty-five years old could foresee a time when they would bring their wills and conveyancing to him, and feel secure about it. Whereas they didn't have many expectations about her, and they would despise her for doing this, agreeing to a second meal with a Yank (as they called all Americans, even Southerners like Galt); with any Yank. Everyone believed they knew what Yanks were like.

She felt in a way lost, therefore. She knew by the reality of her present impulses that the people whose ideas had framed her picture of the world had been working in half-truths. She knew they'd given her only a partial map, and she was now pushing on beyond where it gave out.

But though she was bewildered, she was sure she didn't want

to be cut off, by a Maneering view of what virtue was, from meeting with Galt again. He combined the offer of friendship and the sharing of powerful secrets so succulently in the one being.

And it was an attractive being too, she told herself again. Just short of six foot, smooth-faced, even-featured, and no longer an Anglican bishop or a scholar; more like the presence of an actor, the kind they call *distinguished men of the stage*.

She understood that in the deeps of night, when the question would keep coming up, she would ask herself how it was possible to fight him off? She would have to face up to it that he wouldn't ultimately be happy with shared port and coffee.

But for the moment she told herself – with a confidence she genuinely felt – that *she* would set the bounds of the friendship he'd spoken of. On these terms, it might not last a long time, she knew. So be it.

'It's very confusing,' she almost pleaded then. 'Perhaps one more dinner.' She laughed. 'I sound so ungrateful, don't I? But bear with me for the moment and let me say that. *Just one more.*'

It struck her that beyond her polite pretence the thing might have developed its own sinister velocity. Both of them wanted there to be not only many more shared dinners ahead of them, but also for those dinners to be given an extra piquancy by the possibility of something happening.

In the following days she kept tracing these circular arguments with herself. There was not a second she was alone that she didn't begin running through it all. There was one time where she stood at her office window and looked out at the Melbourne Cricket Ground, and said, 'I'd be happy never to sleep with him.' It was the truth too. Since he was as old as her father, why shouldn't she maintain a niece-uncle relationship with General Sandforth?

But somehow the nature of their new friendship had nothing to do with uncles and nieces. There had been something in its origins, something she wasn't guilty of, which stopped it from being that.

Sometimes she would think of the coming dinner with Galt

Sandforth with the purest exhilaration. These were the most significant moments of all. Their quality ensured she would keep her appointment with him.

The coldness Galton Sandforth had confessed to Dim Lewis was – as he'd also said – something suitable for a Chief of Staff. It was something which Big Drum treasured in Sandforth, and which Sandforth was called on to exercise the next morning, before the 10 a.m. staff meeting.

The daily meeting always took place in what had been the boardroom of the insurance company. Sandforth, however, sent Duncan down to the lobby to wait by the elevator doors and to make sure that Big Drum's air force chief, General Pendle, was brought to Sandforth's office and not permitted to go to the boardroom. Pendle already knew he was in trouble with Big Drum, who had not liked the standard of aircraft which Pendle had sent to the Philippines to extricate his party. There were other bad marks against Pendle, too, so he could be depended on to be early for the meeting.

As it turned out, Duncan was able to lead him into Galt Sandforth's office, panelled in sombre Australian hardwoods, at three minutes to ten. There was an exchange of salutes and Sandforth motioned Pendle towards a chair.

'If you don't mind, Galt, I'll stand. I don't want to be late this morning. I fear I might be under enough of a shadow as it is. Until I can reassure Big Drum . . . well, I don't want to provoke him.'

Pendle was a plump man. In the past year he had probably aged somewhat and become jowly. After today, as Galt knew, he'd have plenty of time to devote to becoming a comfortable-looking middle-aged man.

'You don't need to worry about this morning's meeting,' said Galt, looking him full in the eye and not letting any trace of empathy enter his own face. No flinch, no part of fellow feeling. 'You have been relieved of the command of air forces in the Southwest Pacific Area by order of General Wraith. You are to hold yourself available to confer with your replacement, General

Bernard Clancy, though he may not arrive for some weeks. In the meantime, you will not be needed at these daily meetings.'

Pendle looked ill and even seemed to waver sideways before collecting himself.

'If he blames me for sending defective B-17s to rescue him, he ought to be told they were the only planes I had. It seems poor grounds for ending a man's career.'

Sandforth considered this analytically, without showing compassion. 'I doubt anyone could say that General Wraith would act out of pique, or narrow interest of the kind you specify. Sure, he was angry about the planes you sent, but he's a reasonable man and your problem was reasonably explained to him. And after all it was a successful operation – Big Drum arrived in Australia. No, General Pendle, it's more what's happened since. The Japanese have captured and are reinforcing Rabaul. It will be the base from which they strike in other directions – eastward towards the Solomons, New Caledonia, Fiji, southwest towards Port Moresby and Australia. You have not managed yet to mount a bombing raid on Rabaul, and you are providing us with very little reconnaissance. Our planes are arriving by ship, crated. They are not being assembled fast enough. The General is just not satisfied with the rate of progress. If you want to be told straight, the staff work in your force is below standard. There is a perceived need for someone to tighten it up, to deal with the logistics, to get those planes assembled and airborne and probing out over the Coral Sea.'

'You mean you want someone to go off half-cocked and squander half our planes in a day.'

Galt made a mild soothing motion with his hands. 'Russ, I don't expect you to be thrilled at this news. I wish you well and thank you on behalf of General Wraith for your services to this command. Now, I'll call Captain Duncan to escort you to your command car.'

Pendle flashed a half-crazed, sickened smile. 'Maybe not so fast, Galt,' he said. 'Until my replacement comes, who will organize these bombing and reconnaissance raids that you're so keen to have?'

'The Supreme Commander himself will take over the direction of air operations until Buck Clancy arrives.'

'You mean, *you* will take over direction. *You* will choose the targets and dispatch the planes. Fuck you, Galt! This is damn typical. You and Big Drum want to centralize all decision-making. You don't want to listen to reasonable, professional objections. You want to get all power into the hands of the Bataan crowd. Well, you had all the power you could want on Bataan and in Corregidor, and you still screwed up. The Japanese tanned your ass. Thousands of American men are paying for your arrogance right now in prison camps throughout the Philippines.'

Galt found it supremely easy not to rise to the bait.

'You're not doing yourself much credit, General Pendle,' he said with a ferocious iciness he really enjoyed projecting. 'Take time to compose yourself here, in my office, and leave when you're under control again. If you'll excuse me, I have the staff meeting to attend. When I say I wish you good luck in your future career, Russ, I mean it.'

And no one would need luck more than Pendle. For if it was known you'd been sacked by Big Drum, not even the old Chaumont gang around General Channing in Washington would want much to do with you.

Pendle didn't take Galt's offer of a chair. He raged out. Galt called Duncan in and gave him an order for transmission to the airbases in Northern Queensland. The Japanese in Rabaul would now begin to be accustomed to the sight of Flying Fortresses.

When Big Drum announced that General Pendle had – as he put it – *been recalled*, there arose around the conference room the middle-aged, military equivalent of naughty laughter. Pendle had never belonged. He hadn't been on Corregidor. He hadn't seen the stream of wounded being brought into the Malinta tunnel. The staff were aware too that he had sent those three deficient B-17s to fetch them from Mindanao. Not only did he not belong to the club. He had let the club down.

'The substitute in question, by my own request,' said Big Drum, 'will be General Buck Clancy, arriving any day.'

An ambiguous mutter running like an electric charge from Ernie Sasser to Sam Winton to big Russell Morgan, the dour quartermaster, to Harry Strudwick. Clancy was popular and loud and decisive and had been at West Point with at least two of them. But he was a devout Catholic as well. Including him in the team would demand an effort of tolerance.

Now Big Drum had Galt refer to the minutes of the past meeting, and summarize what everyone had said they would do by now. It could be an uncomfortable time, as section heads heard their rash promises read out. Next, Big Drum launched into agenda items. 'After weeks of delay,' he said, 'my orders from the Joint Chiefs of Staff have arrived.'

There was unspoken disapproval around the table. The Joint Chiefs of Staff were the enemy, committed to Rainbow Five, the plan to defeat Germany first, and only then turn all resources to the Pacific. Rainbow Five was the excuse for disadvantaging Big Drum.

'My orders are sublime, gentlemen,' said Big Drum. 'I am to recapture Rabaul and Bougainville Island. I commend this to you as a superb idea. There is one problem. Logistically, I am to be starved.'

But despite all the evidence, when you were with Big Drum, you felt it was *all* possible. On Corregidor as at Santa Cruz in 1915, Galt had even felt it was possible to die a brave death with Big Drum. And here, somehow, it was possible to recapture Rabaul, the greatest Japanese stronghold in the region. In the end. In the long, long term.

He opened folders and turned pages as he spoke, his eyes flitting between print and the faces of his staff. It was from oceans of print that he was abstracting the first principles he uttered here. That was of course his gift.

If Australia was to be held, he stated, first there must be a build-up of naval and air forces along the north coast, along the coast of the exotically named Coral Sea. His naval staff officer reported on the thin screen of Australian and American ships operating from Townsville, a tropic port a long way up the eastern Australian coast. Everyone here, including Big Drum's naval adviser, subscribed to the idea that far out in the Pacific, the 'big admirals', the deputies of Admiral Kremnitz, were trying to make the war their own and keeping their carriers to themselves. They would surely have to strike, though, if Japanese fleets approached Australia.

Galt himself, now that Pendle was gone, had to report on the slow deployment of squadrons of P-40s and B-17s throughout northern Australia.

'And the striking range of those B-17s, Galt?'Big Drum asked him.

For this war would be one of astounding distances. Walking on the fortified heights of the island of Corregidor, watching the artillery flashes from over on the Bataan Peninsula, Galt and Big Drum had argued their way towards this idea. War was no longer a question of the distance between one trench and another. It was the limit of an aircraft's range. The enemy knew this. That's why they were gobbling up the world.

Galton Sandforth, replying to the General, explained that the range of the B-17s, fuelled and with full bomb load, was nine hundred and twenty-five miles. On that basis, the air forces in Northern Australia had been able to bomb the Japanese-held port of Rabaul twice in the past week. The General had a report on yesterday's seventeen-bomber raid. It was intended, said Galt, that now the raids would be increased.

At this, the memory of General Pendle ran through the room, but attracted no recognition.

Then Harry Strudwick briefed the staff on Japanese build-ups on the north coast of New Guinea. To get to Port Moresby on the south coast, Harry asserted, the Japanese would have to cross an enormous series of mountains called the Owen Stanley Range, across a track which led through Kokoda and took its name from that place. 'The terrain is impossible,' said Harry. The so-called *trail* scarcely exists and runs through jungle rainforest. It isn't possible to move artillery through country like that. However, I think we know by now, gentlemen, that if something doesn't absolutely defy Newton's Laws, the Jap – in this case General Horii – will try it.'

This drew gentle and rueful laughter from around the table.

Next, Ernie Sasser, the engineer, began to report on road-building operations; in tropical northern Australia, across the centre of the continent; south of Sydney to the industrial city of Wollongong.

Captain Duncan entered the room with a large envelope he placed in front of Sandforth. While listening to Sasser, the Chief of Staff opened the envelope and saw what was inside. It was the Special Reconnaissance Department confidential file on Captain Allan Lewis. It had been couriered to him by a senior Australian aide on the staff of General Billings, the Australian commander of Allied Land Forces. Duncan had not known what was in the envelope, had been told only that a specially sealed report was on its way from the Australians and was to be brought to General Sandforth at once, wherever he might be at the time.

Galt was tempted to read the report at once, right there in the midst of the staff meeting, especially since Ernie Sasser was not a riveting speaker. But this would be a betrayal of one of the principles of successful participation in staff meetings: never let them think you're not listening. Once they know you have periods of inattention, they'll slip things by you.

So, after glancing at the first page of the file, which included the significant information of Captain Lewis's marital status, news with which Galton Sandforth was familiar but which had a radiance on the page, Sandforth put the file away again in its envelope.

General business arose. It was time to think grand strategy.

'Galt?' Big Drum asked.

'Thank you, sir,' said Galton Sandforth, looking off through a screen of smoke from Harry Strudwick and Ernie Sasser. He had never been a smoker himself, having been a West Point track star who would have run in the 1912 Olympics but for a sudden hamstring injury. He had always liked liquor but seen no profit in smoking.

'Our men – I include the Australians in that overall title – will have to fight the Japanese in New Guinea or in northern Australia. Though there's nothing to stop the Japanese landing anywhere in eastern Australia, our reconnaissance aircraft would spot a long-range convoy, so that New Guinea, to the north of the Australian mainland, is the most likely arena. The Navy out in the Pacific is not within our control, as we all know and regret, but it may contribute to our success through its operations. We *may* hold the Japanese in New Guinea. General Horii in New Guinea *may* find that he's outstripped his supply line and run out of string. On the other hand, if he captures Port Moresby he'll then move on to the mainland of Australia. Our best hope then is that he'll land in northern Australia and be punished and defeated by distance and desert.

'But even in New Guinea, he might find he's come too far. When he begins straining like a dog at the limit of its leash, we must have solid thinking in place. It will not be enough simply to cheer and welcome the fact that the Anglo-Saxon race has reasserted itself. Now I know the General has devoted much thought to this question and is familiar with Orange Plan Hucker.'

Hucker had in fact been a major on Big Drum's staff in the Philippines in the mid-1930s. He had devised a plan which worked from the premise that the Japanese might capture the entire Central and Southwest Pacific and that the Americans might need to operate from Australia. That idea alone had brought him into universal derision. His young wife had left him for the more feet-on-the-ground commander of an armoured battalion. In 1937, Hucker had been killed in a pig-hunting accident, and some of his friends had indicated that they believed he had deliberately placed himself in the path of a shotgun charge.

Hucker had lived and died before his time. The premise of his plan had now been realized, five years after his death. For in the tunnel on Corregidor, Galton Sandforth found he still retained a copy of the Hucker plan amongst his papers. Barely interrupted by the quiet customary thud of Japanese artillery, he had read it, suspecting its time had come, and had been excited by its scope. He had brought it with him in the one suitcase he'd carried from Corregidor to Mindanao to Australia, and had begun to discuss it with Big Drum as soon as they arrived in Melbourne. He was raising the matter here therefore not to enlighten Big Drum but to enlighten the others.

'Hucker's plan,' said Galt, 'proposes a means of fighting and outflanking an enemy in the Pacific in a situation of logistical attenuation. I mean by that, a situation where you're not being supplied properly, because there's another war being waged in a more popular arena – Europe, say.'

There was laughter again. In-club laughter, them-and-us chortling.

Big Drum took over then. 'As Galt points out,' he began. For Galt was the senior favoured son. When ideas came from him he was verbally credited with them. Whereas when Big Drum announced ideas which came from less beloved sources or outside the Corregidor group, it was as if they had come directly to him from on high. 'As Galt points out, the crucial thing is the capture of airstrips. Major Hucker knew about the B-17, and other bombers still on the drawing board at the time he drew up the plan. The new planes mean that for any mile of airstrip you capture today, you can add a thousand miles, since that is in effect the range of your bombers. Under the bombers' umbrella, you jump, you *leap-frog* by means of amphibious landings. There is no predictable quality to the nature of your amphibious landings, since the enemy cannot guess where they will occur along a given chain of archipelago. You can stretch the enemy's resources. . . .

'And so, these are the mental possibilities I want my staff to adopt. First, the repulse of the enemy, wherever *that* is possible. Second, great bypassing actions, impossible just now but possible in the future and once we have met this present emergency. For that reason, the *entire* Southwest Pacific and the Philippines must be our study. Galt will answer your questions.'

There was an outburst of questions. Harry Strudwick felt bound to ask if this wasn't a matter of whistling in the dark, but he kept his voice low so that Big Drum couldn't hear. Galt referred the gentlemen of the staff again to the copy of Orange Plan Hucker which was included amongst the tabled papers. When they had fully taken its details into account, he would entertain any questions they might have.

Like the others, Sandforth was excited by the great communal zeal which seemed now to fill the room, cobbled together out of simple but revelatory ideas and sanctioned by Big Drum as prophet. If the enemy advance could be stopped, then the victory was possible. All according to the ideas of poor damned Hucker, thought Galt, who had let himself be shot for no particular reason. For love, was it? Or was it a kind of vengeance directed at the mockery of these his brother officers, who knew in 1936–7 that the Japanese could never achieve the conquest of the Pacific.

Big Drum launched into a few concluding remarks. He complained he had heard of recently appointed staff officers, fresh from the United States or the Canal Zone, referring to the enemy as 'little' and 'inefficient'. That was outmoded thinking. It was actually dangerous. American armies fell to pieces when faced with the reality. If the enemy was 'little' and 'inefficient' then it had encountered more success than any little, inefficient army in history. Young officers were to be upbraided for indulging themselves with these irrelevant forms of thought and expression. An observed continuing tendency to write the enemy off was to be considered by all staff chiefs as grounds for dismissal . . .

One of the General's secretaries entered and came to Galt. There was an urgent telephone call for him, from the United States.

Galt excused himself, went outside and down the corridor to his office. He hoped it wasn't Sandy calling him from Charlottesville with some meaningless item of horse business – to tell him that certain contract papers, for example, needed his signature. When he picked up the phone in his office, he found that indeed it was Sandy.

'Galt,' she said. No one said it her way, and he remembered briefly that old passion, and the family it had produced, and even the cosy spikiness of a marriage which had outlasted its time.

'Sandy,' he said. 'Nice to hear from you. But things are a little desperate here . . . '

'Here too, Galt. I don't know how to tell you.' There was silence. One of the girls is pregnant, he supposed. He didn't want Sandy to be coy, anyhow.

'Sandy,' he said for the sake of speed, wanting to end this

awkward call, 'these are wild times and unspeakable things happen. Feel free to tell me things straight.'

There was silence for a while, to the limits of his patience. He wanted to be back amidst the staff's enthusiasm for dead Hucker's ideas. But then it struck him: this *is* your wife, and she's calling all the way from Virginia, across the hours and the latitudes. Be gracious. Also beware.

'It must be very late there,' he said all at once, to help her, certainly, but with a sudden fear that he might hear something he *really* did not want to hear.

'About 11.30 at night, Galt. General Bradley's people wanted to call you – Bradley himself wanted to tell you. But I thought it was better if we kept it family.'

'Kept it?'

'Young Galt. He was flying from London to Cairo for General Bradley. Some meeting with the British. The plane disappeared over the Mediterranean. He's missing, Galt. They're using the term: presumed dead.'

He could hear Sandy begin to weep economically on the other end of the phone. She didn't wail. She was a woman who knew the limits of everything, both of marriage and of the degree of grief a mother should show at a time when so many sons were perishing.

He felt cold invade his arms and legs. 'Galt?' he said.

A good-looking boy who lacked coldness. 'Galt Junior?' he asked again.

'I'm sorry,' said Sandy. 'Our son is missing, Galt.'

Sandforth had not sat down at his desk to take the call, but now he did. There's nothing left, he thought simply. Galt is gone. I hold fast to chief-of-staffdom here so far from where he vanished. There was only one lasting value on earth, and that was his fierce belief that his son was better, braver, cleverer than he was. This was waste. This was outrage.

Sharply and graphically, he remembered Galt Junior as a sleepy-eyed boy of eight, still attached to some stuffed toy or other, leaving in early morning, swaddled in an overcoat, to travel by train with his parents from an army base in North Carolina to an equally dismal one in Nebraska.

'There's no hope?' he pleaded of Sandy.

'The plane went down three days ago, it seems. Nothing's been found. Oh, Galt, I wish I was there so I could hold you.'

'Oh, Jesus, so do I.' And he meant it.

'I persuaded them not to let Big Drum know yet. I know how you hate expressions of sympathy. But now that you've been told, Galt, the news must be released to the press and of course to Big Drum and others.'

'Do the girls know yet?'

'I still have to face that,' said Sandy. She began to weep again. 'I've got this awful suspicion that once they hear, it will blight them – block them from being the women they already are.' It was as if he could hear her thinking, but there was nothing he could contribute. 'Galt, I suppose there's no chance you could fly home?'

'Oh, Sandy,' he groaned. 'Have you looked at a map? I can't leave here anyhow. Things are so tight, dear Sandy. I can't tell you the details. But Australia is wide open . . . '

'It was like this when you were playing peacetime soldiers,' said Sandy without malice. 'So – I suppose – all the more so now. Let's leave it then . . . Except, Galt, do you think you can handle the condolences down there. They're going to have to signal Big Drum. It'll come through on your headquarters press office ticker machines anyhow.'

'Yes,' he said. 'Yes. I'll handle the condolences. But he might be found.'

Sandy said nothing. He thought, *she knows he's dead.*

To his surprise, he wanted the condolences Sandy mentioned to begin rolling in straight away. He wanted people to tell him that Galt Junior was a loss beyond bearing. He wanted Big Drum to tell him that and then drop the subject.

'Sandy,' he said. 'To hell with my fear of having people tell me they feel sorry for me! It's you who's suffering most. I know that.'

He listened to her weep at the other end of the long, long line. If only we weren't strangers, he thought, I could utter simple consolations. I could futilely say, *Don't cry, dear.* By which I would mean, *Weep to the limit. Weep all you want.*

*

The Wraiths invited him to drinks that night. Big Drum greeted him after their butler, Sergeant Hynes, opened the door. 'Oh Galt, I know how you hate this stuff – people approaching you and pretending they can understand an iota of your grief. Please believe me, I *do* understand it dimly.'

'Thank you, sir.' Contrary to what he had expected, he didn't want Big Drum to stop talking.

'Galt Junior would have risen to high command. Everyone said that. Bradley thought the world of the boy.'

'He would have overshadowed me,' Galt risked saying, his voice breaking. But he wanted the General to confirm that much.

'Galt, you're an organizational and logistical genius. But Galt Junior showed every sign of being at least up to your level.'

'He had Sandy's flair as well. He would have achieved overall command.'

Big Drum patted his upper arm. 'Oh Galt, you dear man. Yes, he had Sandy's flair, too. Come and have a drink.'

Mrs Wraith stood up as they entered the living room, and sought his hand and kissed his cheek. 'I can think of what you're going through only if I think of Little Drum, and how I would feel . . . '

Her voice broke and her eyes misted. Yet Galt remembered how on Corregidor, as the wounded appeared overnight from the mainland, she had prepared to die with Big and Little Drum. No one was sure whether Big Drum intended that they should all take poison pills or whether he would finish them with a loving bullet before taking his own life. But that wouldn't have been the same as this. It's living on that hurts. If one of the bombers which came over every night had landed one on Little Drum's bedroom, she would have been crazed with grief.

Big Drum had mixed the cocktails himself – he believed he was good at it, whereas he was only passable. And he was a very poor drinker, too, in the sense that Galt had never seen him finish a drink. Handing Sandforth his, Big Drum said, 'I would keep it out of the newspapers here if I could, Galt. But it's obvious from the wire services that as we speak it will be already appearing in today's London and Washington papers.'

'That's OK, General. Don't concern yourself about that.'

'I do concern myself. Once more, I know how you hate it. You should put on an extra secretary just to deal with the condolences.'

'I might. Of course, I actually want to read some of them. I didn't think I would, but I *do*.'

The General drew near conspiratorially. Mrs Wraith was temporarily cut out of the conversation but did not seem to mind. *She* was the ideal General's wife. She had no existence outside Big and Little Drum. She was no less formal in speaking to Big Drum than any of his staff were. People jokingly wondered if she used the full form of address – frequently she addressed him as 'General' – in moments of intimacy.

'Let's dedicate this campaign to that boy of yours, to his memory,' said Big Drum. 'His fine young voice is stilled, but it lives on in the cries of our young men. The young men you and I shall send ashore in a thousand places.'

Galt felt an urge to ask, 'Which young men?' The most likely near-future amphibious landings would be Japanese. And yet he was touched by Big Drum's intensity. Big Drum was the only human being he knew who could talk like someone in the movies and yet have it make sense, have it reverberate, have it make a difference, have it change things.

'Thank you,' said Galt. 'Thank you, General, thank you.'

He just prevented himself from the effusion of saying it a fourth time.

The next morning, after a night in which he'd slept little, drunk much, and talked briefly with General Bradley by telephone, ascertaining as Sandy had that Bradley and his people held little hope for Galt Junior, Sandforth was at his desk a little before the normal time. He read files and memoranda he had brought from the previous day's staff meeting, giving everything equal attention. For, even in these remarkable days, everything seemed equally not to matter.

Then the visits and the phone calls began. Tall Harry Strudwick, Chief of Intelligence, what they called G2, arrived first. Of course, he had to be asked to sit down. He seemed to tremble with compassion, and Galt was touched by the way he spoke.

'Everyone will tell you to be consoled, but there is no consolation.'

Galt was relieved to hear someone say this. It was as if he wanted to be told that words and time could not mend things or diminish the loss. That Galt Junior's death would hold the same bitter meaning in twenty years' time as it did today.

Harry Strudwick went on, 'George Bernard Shaw tells us that the key to happiness is work. It's obscene to speak of happiness in view of what's overtaken your family, Galt. But I have to tell you that we may be very busy indeed in the next few days. An Australian coast watcher on Woodlark Island, near Rabaul, reports seeing an enormous Japanese fleet heading south for the Coral Sea. I'll be sending you the details, but it looks as if Admiral Takagi is on his way to Port Moresby. Our reconnaissance planes are patrolling out of north Queensland looking for him. So are Admiral Andrews's carrier-based aircraft. As soon as there's contact . . . '

Galt felt suddenly strong in an arid kind of way. If things went well, if the fleet was intercepted, Australia would be saved for the moment. If the other happened, then he could join Galt Junior in nothingness – a Japanese invasion force would ultimately see to that.

In the next twenty-four hours he barely slept. He and Big Drum spent most of the time in the operations room. Reconnaissance planes from US Navy Task Force 44 located the Japanese Port Moresby invasion force north of Woodlark Island, and Galt, after talking it over with Big Drum, ordered the B-17 squadrons in Queensland out into the Coral Sea to bomb the Japanese ships.

Other reports came in. The Japanese invasion force had been joined by three Japanese carriers from Tulagi in the Solomon Islands. There was a vanguard consisting of the carrier *Shoho* and a number of cruisers. Galt ordered the Queensland B-17s up to attack this screen. The size of that act awed him. He was making command decisions. American sons might die of valour over the Coral Sea. If the carrier-borne fighters sprang the Fortresses, Galt's painfully assembled bomber force might be reduced by half, leaving northern Australia wide open.

Numbly, he committed them in any case. He did not wait and bite his thumbs – he was too busy dealing with the radio signal traffic. He received a message; the bombers reported sighting the carrier and the cruisers. It seemed only an hour or so – even though it was probably three or four – before he heard that the Fortresses had returned intact, and jubilant, to Townsville, reporting hits on the carrier and on several of the cruisers.

But the Navy had sighted yet another Japanese force, Admiral Takagi's carriers, rounding the Solomons and steaming in to support the *Shoho* and the Japanese invasion force for Port Moresby. Galt again ordered the B-17s, crewed by other people's sons who had been both brave and lucky today, to be ready to go out and attack *Shoho* and the cruisers again the next morning. This even suited the Pacific's chief, Admiral Kremnitz, who for once was grateful for all the help Big Drum's air force could give him.

Before Big Drum went off to sleep on a couch for a few hours at eleven that night, he grasped Galt by the shoulder. 'Good work today, Galt. Thank God we sacked Pendle. If we hadn't he'd be standing there in front of us now, telling us that perhaps if we gave him a week to service the aircraft he might be able to get them into action. Pendle is the sort of commander who wants superbly maintained squadrons to hand over to the enemy.'

It was obvious as Galt looked down on Big Drum's face in repose that General Wraith was happy now that something crucial was at last happening. He himself went off to his office and wrapped himself in a greatcoat and slept dully for two or three hours, awaking cold at three and thinking, Galt is dead. No matter what we do to the *Shoho*, that's irreversible.

The B-17s took off again. At 10 a.m. they were off Misima Island, east of New Guinea and just south of the Japanese invasion force. A little over an hour later, they reported that *Shoho* and a number of the cruisers had been hit and sunk. The Japanese vanguard was in ruins. Sandforth found himself shaking hands heartily with Captain Duncan.

It was the first Japanese carrier of the war to be sunk. A

precedent had been set. From signals which came in during the afternoon, it was apparent that there would be a small-minded squabble about whether the Navy or the B-17s had sunk the thing. Such were the inter-service battles which followed the real battles: the ones in which for the vanity of older men young men like Galt Junior were snuffed out for good.

On another night, Galt might have planned the strategy to undermine the Navy's arrogance. But he was still weak with grief. He suggested that the General's press officer draft a statement for release to the American press. If he were fast enough, Big Drum could make it seem as if his planning and his B-17s were what had done it. The public, who loved Big Drum, would be gratified. And the Navy would at best learn a lesson and at worst be chagrined. To hell with them!

Late on the second day, when it became clear that Australia and its front door, the New Guinea port called Moresby, had been saved from an enormous Japanese thrust, when reconnaissance reports from excited boy pilots far out in the Solomon Sea told Big Drum's headquarters again and again that the Japanese Invasion Group had turned and was retiring in the direction of Rabaul (the JIG, as one of them joked, was up!), Galt felt his grief, partially postponed by battle, suddenly hollow him out again. And in one far corner of that vacancy the battle of the Coral Sea had done nothing to fill, in that great cold hangar of his waning life and his shrunken hopes, there was still one vivid image, a flame, a radiance.

How had Dim spent this day of extraordinary victory? Talking to the local representatives of MGM? Or to the entertainment officers of the 41st Infantry Division?

He knew mourning demanded certain politenesses of him. He knew how officers like Captain Duncan and other junior men not without influence or contacts would think it improper of him to entertain a young woman in his quarters, to laugh with her and pour the wine himself so soon after his son's loss. Little they knew! It was exactly because the loss was insupportable that he *needed* to laugh and pour wine.

Big Drum left headquarters at 10.45 that night. His press office had prepared the resounding communiqué Galt had suggested.

Already, throughout the United States, throughout the free world for that matter, it was emerging from teletype machines, arresting the gaze of sub-editors, and being taken on the double to editors' officers.

Big Drum was on his way home therefore to Mrs Wraith and Little Drum, after the best day's work he'd had in this war, the only good day so far, the start of many more good days he intended to have.

Galt Sandforth returned to his office. Captain Duncan was still working at the outer desk. Inside, Galt poured himself a drink, put it down on his bookshelf and forgot it. On his desk were his files from that staff meeting an age ago. He wondered whether it had been yesterday morning or the morning before that? Amongst the files were the Special Reconnaissance documents on Captain Allan Lewis, AIF. He opened that file. He did not read it fully. He merely let his eye land on this or that sentence. Because he feared discovering that Allan Lewis was just another young man of talent like Galt Junior, and certainly everything he saw confirmed that fear. A law student. Good family. A year younger than Galt Junior. Marital status: well, the divine Dim Lewis, of course. And an address in the part of town called South Yarra. He and a British Naval officer had been right across Papua-New Guinea to Salamaua with an ammunition and supply column of New Guinea natives and militia. Now Captain Lewis was on his way with the same Naval officer to Buna, again on the north coast of New Guinea, taking a small group of American engineers with them to find a site for an airstrip suitable for heavy bombers. This was an initiative Big Drum and Galton Sandforth had authorized – the finding of a suitable airfield location so far north. He had never suspected that Dim Lewis's husband would be one of the reconnaissance party or that Special Reconnaissance would be the specific commando organization used to take the engineers in. They were all British and Australians, Special Reconnaissance, Sandforth knew. And they were never decorated. That was Special Reconnaissance policy. Yet the boy was a hero. Whereas he himself was an old man with a dead son, and he wanted to take a hero's place in Dim Lewis's arms.

His in-tray was full of letters and messages of condolence. Flinching again, he began to leaf through them. There was one from the Governor of Virginia, Everett Morley, an old boyfriend of Sandy's. There was one from the President, and a separate gracious one from the First Lady. General Bradley had stated his personal grief and said there was no further news.

It occurred to him that if Galt Junior's body came ashore, it would very likely roll up on some German-held beach. Galt hoped they would treat it gently.

Amongst the raft of condolences was one informal-looking one in a blue envelope. Galt opened it. It was from Dim Lewis. It was written in a generous copperplate which spoke well of the school she'd gone to.

Dear General Sandforth,

The news appeared in this morning's Melbourne Age *of the sad disappearance of your son.*

I am very shocked for your sake and I know that there is nothing I can say to lighten the bitterness.

I cannot imagine what service I can offer you in this sad situation. But if there should be anything, please do not hesitate to call on me.

Yours sincerely,
Dimity Lewis
Lt 2nd AIF

Australian Imperial Force. That's what they call themselves, despite the fact that the British and their empire had been willing to write them off, to abandon them to the Japanese, to fight for Europe first and only after that for the Pacific.

I can't imagine what service I can offer you in this sad situation . . .

He reopened the file on Captain Allan Lewis. The address in South Yarra caught his eye. He wrote it down on a sheet of paper. Then he telephoned Captain Duncan.

'I'd like a car,' he told Duncan. 'But no markings of rank on it. And no driver. I'll drive myself.'

He heard a certain hesitation at the other end of the line. 'Yes sir,' said Duncan. 'Sir, may I just say that after the last few days you've had, a driver might be the advisable option.'

Sandforth swallowed the chagrin he felt. 'I appreciate your concern, captain. But my capacity to handle a vehicle hasn't been impaired.'

'Of course not, sir. Unless you hear otherwise from me, the vehicle will be downstairs within five minutes. And sir . . . '

'I know what you're going to say, Duncan. Could you leave it unspoken, and could I just say *thank you*?'

'Tell me if there's anything at all I can do, sir.'

Sandforth began to choke with tears. 'Thank you,' he managed.

He left without saying goodbye to Duncan. Outside the vehicle was waiting, a large Buick. As he had asked, it was not his assigned vehicle, the one with the three stars on the metal plate on its bumper bar. The soldier on duty at the door went to escort him aboard the car, and opened the back door from habit.

'Oh, I'm sorry, sir,' he said, catching up with Sandforth as he entered the front seat and took the wheel. It was, thank God, one of the left-hand drive vehicles. Even driving on the other side of the road from the one Americans drove on, it seemed easier to Sandforth to control a wheel located on the left, non-British, side of the vehicle.

He drove away from headquarters and then parked further down Collins Street, using a torch to discover in a road atlas of Melbourne where South Yarra was, and Lieutenant Dim Lewis's address.

A little after midnight, he parked the vehicle and entered the Lewises' small apartment block. There was no doorman as in American apartments. Just the cold entryway, and unlit steps rising to the upper floor. He stumbled up them, using his torch. He knocked on the door of what was – according to the file on Allan Lewis – her apartment, number three. Everything felt cold, and the knocking resonated. The door felt to Galt like the door of an empty apartment.

But then a beady light flashed on behind the glass panes of the door. Dim Lewis opened it a little way. She was wearing a quilted gown and her hair was tied up with a ribbon. Her face was barely marked by sleep. Only the middle-aged and old were offensive to behold when woken.

'General,' she said. She looked at him with mild concern.

'In your kind letter, you mentioned services you could offer me. Lieutenant Lewis, I would like to go driving. Up into your hills. What are they called? The Dandenongs? Who thought up these names? Will you come with me? My car's downstairs. No driver. I'm driving.'

'General,' she said. 'It will be very cold.'

He liked the unawed way she didn't ask him in at once.

'I'll get some rugs,' she said. 'And I'll fill a thermos with coffee.'

'No,' he said. 'Make it tea.' He laughed. 'You guys are good at tea and rotten at coffee. I'll wait in the car. Please don't worry, it has a heater. Take your time.'

Within ten minutes, she appeared, fully uniformed, out of the apartment block door. He got out to open her door, but she was there before him. She carried two rugs and shook a thermos in her hand. He went back to the driver's side and they both got in the car at the one time.

'You're the senior officer,' she said, disposing of the rugs and thermos on to the back seat. 'So I should be driving. But I've never driven much in Melbourne – only Maneering, where you really have to concentrate to hit someone.'

He laughed but said nothing. He started the engine and released the brake.

He drove through the blacked-out streets of the city for ten minutes. She said nothing in that time, because he didn't seem to want to talk.

Then she took the initiative and began to speak. 'I'm sorry I've got no conversation,' she said. 'It's because I can't imagine what to say. When you were talking to me the other night, about your daughters and then about your son, I could see how much special hope you'd invested in them. I mean, one of the daughters was a Japanese-speaker and the other was an actress, both very honourable achievements, according to my book anyhow. But that son of yours . . . he was the one marked out. Wasn't he?'

He grasped the wheel and kept on driving numbly. Soon they were amongst market gardens and farms. Occasionally he would ask her for directions. The road rose into foothills. It was – as she had promised – cold in the car. He was pleased that he wore his trenchcoat.

'Any water we can watch?' he asked.

'Water?'

'Lakes or dams. Don't worry, Lieutenant Lewis. I'm not suicidal. Too big a conceit for that. Besides I have to be back at my desk at 9 a.m.'

'There's some water at Silvan,' she told him. 'Or else Emerald. No, let's make it Silvan. You turn left at the next crossroads.'

Soon they were amongst gums whose trunks were streaked with moisture. To their left lay a pleasant expanse of misty water. The dawn began to come up behind them, through the back window of the car. He was not pleased to see it. For some reason to do with his own private mourning instincts, he wanted the sun to hit the water before it hit him. But in a foreign country, fighting in a foreign war, he had to take the daybreaks which came his way.

Soon they came to a wet picnic table and the water view he had wanted. He drew the car in and parked.

'Do you know,' he told Dim, 'we've had a great victory. It will be in the morning papers and on the radio. The Navy and our B-17s – or let me put it another way – our B-17s and the Navy stopped the Japanese on their way into the Coral Sea. The Japanese fleet has withdrawn. This country of yours, Lieutenant Lewis, is safe for the moment. What do you think of that?'

'Praise God from whom all blessings flow,' she said, genuinely awed and to her own surprise reverting to the opening line of a boarding school hymn.

'Well said,' he told her. 'These are enormous operations. Astounding operations, Lieutenant Lewis.'

'Why don't you begin calling me Dim as everyone else does?' she asked.

'Because in my opinion the shortened name demeans you, that's why.'

'I don't mind,' she said, smiling richly at him. 'With a name like that, everything I do becomes an achievement. Besides, you can use it ironically. In the Australian manner. The way we call tall people Shorty and redheads Blue. You could call me Dim and imply I'm bright.'

He laughed and then grew quiet.

'Enormous operations,' he said again. 'One boy . . . one boy counts for nothing in all this . . .'

His voice cracked. Her hand rose and covered his gloved left hand. Then it withdrew and began to pour tea into one of the thermos cups.

'It's frightening,' he said. 'This great machine I myself serve. It should frighten everyone. It should frighten me. I mean, its size and its inefficiency. Not that we have nearly enough men and machines . . . '

'Drink up,' she advised him.

'You don't have gloves,' he said.

'We girls from Maneering are very tough. You can believe that. *Very* tough.'

All at once he collapsed on the wheel and began weeping. It seemed that what she had said precipitated this. If so, she was pleased. She held his wrist and put the other hand on his shoulder, not thinking of telling him to cut it out or remember who he was.

When the spasm had passed, he said, 'I want you to understand. I've seen your husband's confidential records. He's involved in something. A reconnaissance. For us. For all of us, I suppose you'd say.'

He saw she was waiting now for the word on her husband, almost like someone wanting an explanation.

'He's very brave,' he told her. 'He's really a very brave young man. I'm ashamed to be wanting to take his place. I *should* be ashamed . . . '

'Yes,' she said. 'I should be ashamed too. He's a young hero, and I sent him off with harsh words.'

'I can't imagine that,' said Sandforth.

'Oh yes. We have enormous problems. Enormous problems. You see, I'm not very generous . . . '

But she had taken his cup and begun to pour more tea into it, and the gesture seemed to belie her claims to callousness.

The light was sharp now. A crisp antipodean autumn day had begun. In their hot berths in the tropics, the victorious pilots of the Coral Sea would still be stunned by victory and exhaustion.

'Are you hungry, General?' Dim Lewis asked him.

'Yes,' he said. He was surprised. 'There's nothing more extraneous or unnecessary than the hunger of the parent of a dead child? What's it there for?'

'It's so that you can be back at your desk by nine o'clock. In *Bataan*, as you call it. That's what it's for.'

She gave him directions to a country bakery. It stood on a bush road beside a closed general store. A storm lantern glowed beyond its window.

They parked amidst the dripping trees. Though the bakery's front door was not open, Dim went to the side and knocked. A middle-aged woman baker wearing a white cap and coat answered. 'Yes, love?'

'The General and I have been travelling all night,' Dim told her. 'I was wondering if we could have some of your fresh-baked bread, and if you had tea that would be marvellous.'

The woman looked at her wryly, as if she presumed *travelling* was a euphemism for something else. 'Bring your General inside, love,' she said at last.

The woman and her husband cut them great slabs of steaming bread and spread them with butter and jam. 'Legal butter, General,' said the woman. 'We have a farm as well.'

'Where have you come from overnight?' the baker asked, eyeing the two of them with genial and irreverent suspicion.

'We left Albury,' Dim lied, 'at eleven o'clock last night. The General has to be at a conference at 9 a.m. in Melbourne.'

'You're a bit off the road, aren't you?'

'My family used to bring me here whenever we came to Melbourne. That was when I was just a child. I remembered it. And thank God you didn't let us down.'

'My son is up in Port Moresby at the moment,' the baker said to Galt, politely challenging him. 'He's a bit hotter than we are.'

Sandforth laughed. It was astounding the way the Australians challenged you, no matter how much braid you wore. Maybe because of it. It disoriented him, but in a way he felt it was good for him.

'Well,' said Galt, temporarily a magician and a harbinger of good, 'you'll hear on the radio this morning . . . we've stopped an invasion fleet on its way to Moresby. It's the first happy news for quite a time, wouldn't you agree?'

As the baker stared, wondering if Galt was pulling his leg, Galt and Dim exchanged glances, and then she smiled confidingly. Jesus, I want to live, thought Galton Sandforth. I want to make love to this woman, even in younger men's place.

They left before full light. She thought Sandforth looked very hollow-eyed, but that he was entitled to do. She said nothing. Part way down the mountainside, he reached out and took her hand.

'How is the film and entertainment business, lieutenant?'

'The fact is, I *am* starting to branch out into entertainment. I'm working with the USO to create an itinerary so that Australian and overseas performers can cover all the army bases. I'm pleased to say, that will keep me relatively busy.'

'And what do the entertainment officers of the various divisions think of this? Are they jealous of your power?'

She laughed. 'I think they're busy enough on base providing pingpong tables and venues and projectors and microphones and loudspeakers and all the rest of it.'

'So, you've expanded your mandate somewhat?'

'Do you rank that as insubordination?'

'Rank insubordination,' said Galt Sandforth, laughing at his own pun.

The sun began to enter her side of the vehicle now, throwing some radiance around her profile.

He said, 'I hope you'll understand, but I don't think I have enough spirit to entertain folk in my quarters in the next few weeks. Also, it wouldn't be appropriate. Can I visit you at your place?' He held up the hand which had been around hers. 'Now

I know you've got ration problems I don't have, so I don't want a meal. But maybe some tea and cookies.'

'We call them biscuits,' she told him. She turned her head away. 'You can come,' she said. She was looking out of the window, at the wet ferns on the mountainside.

In the next few days he kept an eye on Allan Lewis's reconnaissance group. On Sunday they were ready to leave the Buna area. He took special notice of this fact amidst the raft of radio messages which crossed his desk. He authorized a signal both to their transport aircraft, which lay under camouflage at Buna Mission, and to the airfield at Port Moresby, where they would have to land to fuel for the long run to Brisbane: *In view of the strategic importance of Buna airstrip site, Buna party engineers required to remain at Moresby to confer with 14th Battalion US Army Engineers there stationed.*

A week ago it would have been immoral to suggest that anyone stay an unnecessary hour in threatened Port Moresby. Since yesterday, however, Port Moresby was no longer immediately imperilled. And there was something to be said for the men who had been on the spot now going to advise the Port Moresby engineers, who would soon have to be flown across the high peaks of the Owen Stanleys to begin work on the proposed airstrip, something better than the fringe of crushed coral which comprised the present airstrip, something further inland and more defensible.

And it was not so much that he wanted Melbourne and, in fact, Australia clear to himself. It was more that he did not want to be shown up by what he thought of as *that gallant young man*.

The following Tuesday Big Drum called Galton Sandforth to his office. Ernie Sasser and Harry Strudwick were there already. Everyone was standing, and Big Drum had his straight-backed posture on – if he'd been a foot and a half shorter you might have been justified in calling it Napoleonic. It was the posture he used for his memorable harangues, and he had it now in this semi-private gathering. In such surroundings he sometimes admitted to despair, but the events of the past few days had confirmed him in his public air of confidence, and he seemed confident right through now.

'Galt,' said Big Drum. He was playing with his cigarette-holder, really worrying it round in circles, 'What do you say about this Buna airstrip business? How soon do we need it? Oh, I know it's desirable in terms of the B-17s and their range. But Ernie says it's logistically impossible to get his engineers over there. Or to put it another way – since we know Ernie is a man of adventurous disposition – logistically difficult.'

Dark, wiry Ernie said, 'The transport planes aren't made yet, Galt, to carry the earth-moving equipment.'

Big Drum nodded, but everyone knew that didn't necessarily mean agreement. 'Ernie says to get him and his engineers a month to plan, and a month for the right transport planes to arrive, and we can fly everything in in one hit – a week at the most. That way, he argues, there won't be engineers over there, exposed to the enemy and waiting for things to arrive. The question is, has yesterday bought Ernie time enough?'

Galt could tell, almost from the way Big Drum's eyebrows moved, that he wanted support for moving fast. But that it was a thing of small margins – that he was willing to be persuaded to give Ernie's engineers their time.

And Galt's instincts, too, were to get the men over there. There were some Australian positions over there, and if they and the engineers had to fight, they had to fight.

'I have to say, General, that if I was Yamamoto I would now authorize an invasion force to leave Rabaul for the *north* coast of New Guinea. It would be a shorter business for him than coming down through the Coral Sea, the way he tried in the last few days. In the first place, if he went to the Buna side, there'd be much less chance of our reconnaissance planes spotting him, or of our bombers interfering. I have to say my instinct tells me he won't leave it very long. The Japanese don't leave these things long.'

Big Drum began rolling his cigarette-lighter more wildly still through his large but extraordinarily delicate hands. 'But Harry here has decided after all the enemy can't send an army across New Guinea. Land in Buna, yes, spread out a bit . . . '

'But not cross the mountains to Moresby,' said Harry Strudwick, picking up the argument. 'I've had very reliable scouts up in those mountains now. They tell me there's no chance of the Japanese bringing a modern army, with its supporting artillery and baggage train, over those mountains. There's no road, only a track crawling with seepage and mud, nearly vertical in places. We'll all be getting the reports soon, Galt.'

Galt knew it was his job to be dubious about this, but he sincerely felt dubious in any case. For hadn't the Japanese been doing the impossible for the last six months? They'd followed a whirlwind schedule and had, until yesterday, success which made your head swim.

He said, 'If we want to stop them from landing, and if we want to be able to bomb their bases in New Britain and the Admiralties, we ought to press ahead with all speed on that airstrip.'

Ernie closed his eyes. He was believed to have Cherokee blood, and he could do all sorts of telepathic parlour tricks, squinting his eyes up like that. 'My engineers will be very exposed up there at Buna. If I send them now. Without proper support.'

'Of course it's a risk. But it seems to me we have no choice.'

When Harry spoke he sounded a little temperamental, sulky. He got that way when people cast doubt on his advice. Or more exactly, when you cast doubt on information people he trusted sent back from the field. 'I've had some really competent men up into those mountains,' he murmured.

Big Drum put his cigarette-lighter down and clapped his hands.

'Ernie, I want a concrete timetable from you, just in case we decide to do it your way. Harry, I want you to talk to some of the Australians about this.'

'The Australians?'

'Yes. Discreetly. It's their backyard, after all. Speak to some of the Aussies in General Billings's headquarters. What do *they* expect the enemy to do? I want a further assessment on my desk before I go home this afternoon. Thank you, thank you.'

That's how the decisions were made – very often by Big Drum walking about in solitude and gesturing with his empty cigarette-holder, conjuring up an answer. Or else it might be a quiet and not too coherent conversation over coffee with his Chief of Staff.

And if it turned out to be the wrong decision, as some of the decisions in the Philippines had been, they were not mentioned in future conversations. Sandforth liked that principle of consigning mistakes to verbal if not mental oblivion. He followed it slavishly, even forgetting past wrong decisions totally until you needed them as a guide to present behaviour.

For example, there had been Big Drum's decision, which he himself had heavily influenced, to send the B-17s from Clark Field outside Manila to hit Formosa on the morning the news of Pearl Harbor came to Big Drum's headquarters. The air force general at Clark had already ordered them to be bombed and fuelled up for the mission. Galt and the General between them decided to cancel the raid. Why? Well, it was Big Drum's idea – and on December 7th, 1941 it seemed a not unreasonable one – that the Japanese might treat the Philippines as a non-war zone, might even offer terms for excluding the Philippines from their attack on the Pacific. There were good intelligence reports (from Harry Strudwick) to this effect. Of course now, in Melbourne, it seemed a grotesque idea. But on December 7th, there had been reliable information that the Philippines *would* be spared, and Big Drum was keen to spare them.

Because at base he knew they had been starved of resources and that they could not be held. And so the bombers were told to stay on the ground, not to jeopardize the neutrality of the Philippines.

Now, six months later, Galt was – despite himself – embarrassed occasionally by the memory of that day. He knew instinctively that military historians might puzzle over it, might wonder what Big Drum and he were dreaming up between themselves that day. Especially since, later on the afternoon of December 7th, most of the B-17s were caught on the ground by the Japanese air force anyhow and blown to pieces. Galt had ordered their dispersal, but they were still being fuelled and serviced at a pace appropriate to peacetime, a pace for which the Japanese now punished them.

The conference over, Ernie and Harry and he were leaving Big

Drum's office, but the General called him back. He waited until the others had gone before he spoke low to Galt Sandforth.

'Galt, all that Chaumont gang, all those staff officers and chairborne geniuses from World War I who are now on the Joint Chiefs of Staff, are sniping at me because I have my wife here. As if a man of sixty-two isn't entitled to the comforts of family!'

'I wouldn't be worried about that, General.'

'Oh no, well I'm not.' But it rankled with Big Drum. He was at the same time above all such criticism and yet felt it intimately. 'What I was thinking though was: would you like your wife to join us here in Melbourne? I know . . . well, I know she doesn't like base life. But in the sad circumstances . . . '

Even though this was Big Drum's own second marriage, he still believed in the old-fashioned Protestant virtues, and in such things as bereavement reuniting an estranged couple.

'It's very kind of you, sir,' said Galt. 'But Sandy's set in the life she leads now. To be honest with you, we're strangers, sir.'

Big Drum considered him dolefully. Surely, Galt Sandforth thought, he has no inkling of my interest in the girl. Surely some chance joking remark of Brigadier Gibbs, on one of Big Drum's camp inspections, hasn't caused the General to suspect?

No, that was impossible. Big Drum's offer was brotherly and not sinister.

'I don't think it would be fruitful, sir,' he said with more confidence. 'Not for Sandy nor for me.'

'Very well,' said the General, looking away. He almost seemed embarrassed. 'One man never knows how things stand with another . . . I just thought . . . '

'It's very kind of you, sir, as I said.'

But Galt knew that he would have to go to some trouble to keep his *affection* for Dim Lewis a secret from Big Drum. Or if not exactly a secret, something which need not offend Big Drum's sense of virtue. Something which above all did not make him or the headquarters vulnerable to scandal-mongers and to such people as the Chaumont gang.

It was possible, Galt decided then, to love Dim Lewis and not to let the fact intrude into Big Drum's line of vision. Or if it intruded, to write it off as a peccadillo, not a serious attachment.

And as yet, there wasn't a peccadillo anyhow. Given what he knew about Harry Strudwick and Ernie Sasser and all of them, it should be quite easy to protect himself if there were.

That Sunday night, Mrs Wraith had all the senior staff to dine in her and Big Drum's suite at the Menzies Hotel. These Sunday dinners were becoming a ritual. Galt could see in Mrs Wraith the classic Southern hostess who liked nothing better than a full table, plentiful food, and a measure of humane noise. She always had Galt at her right side, and Harry Strudwick sat down the table beside Big Drum. Little Drum and his nurse had a place in the middle stretches of the table, where they fielded the joky inquiries of those staff officers who wanted to flatter Big Drum by amusing Little Drum. The boy and his nurse would studiously debate such things as the value of eating parsnips, and people would join in.

The little boy was still thin, even now, after nearly two months since the escape from Corregidor by way of torpedo boat and the Del Monte airstrip on Mindanao. Galt remembered how Little Drum had been a brave, bewildered small boy in the tunnel at Malinta, in those last days, when the wounded were coming in and the Mitsubishi dive-bombers were overhead all day. But he'd had a fragility which – Galt was sure – Big Drum hadn't had even at the age of four. He had entirely a different sort of sensibility and intelligence from Big Drum's. And yet he spent all his time in the company of Ling and of middle-aged soldiers. It was interesting to speculate how he would grow up. If, that is, Big Drum succeeded with the enemy, and – as now looked more likely than it had – he did grow up.

Galt hoped that there were not too many more extreme adventures ahead for the boy.

The arguments about whether this or that vegetable should be eaten, conducted in the little boy's level, reasoning voice, reminded General Sandforth of his own lost son – both the lost infant and now the lost man. He was pleased that Mrs Drum carried on a lively, prattling conversation at this end of the table.

'I heard just yesterday from my sister-in-law. Did you know my brother has taken over the whole chemical side of the war effort in Britain? She tells me they have it very hard, the British. That they live like cave dwellers. She actually said something a little subversive, Galt. She said, *Makes you wonder why they're fighting the enemy so hard*? I have a letter drafted back to her, in which I make bold to give her the answer. Even the poorest people will fight for their own brand of squalor, I say, over that offered by an alien regime. I mean, didn't we Southern folk see that ourselves during the war of Northern Aggression?'

Galt laughed, because she always called the war between the States the 'war of Northern Aggression'. And Big Drum, who would have considered such a term seditious if it came from the mouth of anyone else, Big Drum whose father had fought for the Union at Gettysburg and in the Peninsular campaign, didn't chastise her.

'You look at our army!' Mrs Wraith invited Galt. 'Half those boys in the 41st and the 34th and the 29th and all the rest – they haven't grown up in bountiful surroundings, General Sandforth. But they are fighting for what they know. For what they perceive to be themselves.'

Galt secretly hoped that the untrained cohorts of the three divisions Mrs Drum had mentioned *would* fight for their image of themselves. And that this would be enough.

The meal was very gravy-ridden and British – roast beef and Yorkshire pudding, and a fine rice pudding. When everyone was finishing the pudding, Big Drum boomed towards Ernie Sasser, who was in the middle of the table opposite Little Drum, 'Give us one of your fancy mental tricks, Ernie.'

The engineer made a gesture which asked that he be let off the hook. But everyone at table began to cheer. Some of them had begun smoking cigars and drinking heavy Australian ales. The mood was definitely after-dinner and trick time.

'I'll need two sheets of paper and two pencils,' Ernie warned, as if this was beyond the logistical resources of the Menzies Hotel to supply.

Ling went and fetched them. She handed both pencils and both sheets of paper to Ernie. Little Drum looked at Ernie fixedly, as if he was about to pick up a trick he himself could try amongst the children of Australian officers and politicians who were brought to the Menzies occasionally to play with him.

'I need a subject, and I believe that in social terms Mrs Wraith would be the suitable one,' announced Ernie. 'It is by no means a case of playing on the supposed feeble-mindedness of women, which – ma'am – is entirely a piece of mythology in my book. If you consent, Mrs Wraith, I shall have this pencil and this piece of paper passed down the table to you, while I retain the other pencil and the other sheet of paper.'

Mrs Wraith said, 'Why General Sasser, I accept your items of stationery in the spirit in which they are offered.'

One of the stewards took the sheet of paper and the pencil down the table and handed it to Mrs Wraith.

'Now what do I do with this, General Sasser, sir?'

'Ma'am, I'll tell you what I shall do. I shall think of a famous person. Not necessarily a military one, although you may have noticed, Mrs Wraith, that we live in a military age.'

There was laughter.

'This personage I think of, and I shall think of him or her very hard, ma'am . . . I shall write his or her name upon this piece of paper with my pencil, and as seems appropriate I shall deposit the sheet of paper with our Chief of Intelligence, General Strudwick. Then I shall concentrate very hard again upon this personage's features, and when I point to you, ma'am, you will also think of a well known personage. The first personage to enter your head – I insist, the very first, Mrs Wraith – you will write his or her name on your piece of paper and hand it to General Sandforth. If the name on your piece of paper coincides with the name on the piece of paper which General Strudwick is holding, then perhaps the company will agree that I have concentrated well.'

There was a spatter of anticipatory applause for Sasser's showmanship. He bent over his page and, shielding the pencil with a hand, wrote a name. He then doubled the page over and passed it down the table to Harry Strudwick. Harry opened the paper, read the name and raised his eyebrows melodramatically.

'I shall now take the liberty, ma'am,' said Ernie, 'of closing my eyes tight at your handsome table and fixing my mental resources upon the features of the personage I have named on the paper. The one I passed down the table to General Strudwick.'

Galt smiled, looked at Mrs Wraith, shook his head. 'What a wizard!' he told Mrs Wraith.

Ernie, however, began to concentrate with a seriousness which had nothing to do with his showmanship up to the moment. So intense did he become that some of the younger officers at table began to titter with nervousness. It was almost beyond the bounds of what should be tolerated in an officer, this degree of spiritualist intent which Ernie seemed to be practising in front of them. It lasted perhaps ninety seconds or two minutes, an uncomfortable time, and then Ernie, without opening his eyes, pointed in a fairly commanding manner at Mrs Wraith, who took one look at her husband and then at Galt and wrote down a name and, awed by the exercise, handed the sheet of paper to Galt.

Ernie Sasser's eyes snapped open. He shook his head as if to clear his vision.

'Ginger Rogers,' he stated. 'The name you wrote on your piece of paper, Mrs Wraith, is *Ginger Rogers*.'

'Yes,' said Mrs Wraith, astounded. 'I did. Ginger Rogers, the cinematographic artiste.'

Galt thought it was pure *Southern* to describe Ginger Rogers, after whom nearly every young man in the 41st, 34th and 29th divisions must have lusted unremittingly, as a 'cinematographic artiste'. Yet he saw that her name *was* the one Mrs Wraith had written on the paper she'd handed to him. He held it up to show people.

Ernie asked, 'And what name do you have written on the piece of paper you hold, General Strudwick?'

An old central European ham like Harry Strudwick milked it for all he could. 'Ginger Rogers,' he announced at last.

There was a burst of automatic, relieved applause. Galt joined in it with the same sort of gratitude as the rest. A few days ago he had lost his son, but here for three or four minutes he had been caught up in the question of whether Ernie Sasser could be depended upon as a mental trickster. And the answer now was – gratefully – *yes*.

'How did you train yourself for a trick like that?' asked one of the officers in the middle of the table.

'It wasn't a trick,' said Ernie Sasser. 'I just learned I could do it, that was all. I found myself doing it, this very trick, in high school. Little else to do to fill in the time in Norman, Oklahoma. Maybe it comes from the Cherokee side of my blood. But I don't have any other gifts of mind reading. I can't tell you, for example, what General Drummond Wraith is thinking.'

Again there was laughter.

'It's just something I do,' Ernie repeated. 'No other gifts, no other tricks. Just this one.'

The following Tuesday night, Galt again drew a car from the headquarters motor pool and drove to South Yarra. When she answered the door, she was still wearing her uniform, including the asexual, matronly breasted heavy jacket the Australian Army favoured. Leading him into her living room, she seemed uneasy. But a bottle of whisky and a soda siphon was waiting there on a tray. There was no ice. He'd noticed before that Australians didn't bother with ice when it came to whisky.

'You'll have to forgive me,' she said, standing by a settee, her hands joined. He could have studied her frown all night, yet he wanted her to be at her ease. 'I'm still finding my way. I didn't know how to dress. And the flat was so cold anyhow, that I just stayed in uniform.' She laughed. 'I suppose you think that's pretty funny, eh?'

He feared it was all going to be this awkward. 'Not at all,' he said. 'I know this isn't exactly a convenient set-up for you – Big Drum's Chief of Staff calling round for a supposedly friendly chat.'

He was aware that they were nowhere near back to the intimacy which had existed the week before in that bakery in the hills. 'May we sit down?'

'Oh, I'm so sorry.' She laughed at her own tension. 'Of course.'

He sat. But the atmosphere in the room seemed so contrived and hopeless.

She began pouring him a drink. 'And this terrible thing with your son . . . Any news, General?'

'No body has been found. I wish it would be.' He could not help his voice breaking on that. 'For Sandy's sake, and so that the girls will feel easier. There's a big family mausoleum on its own land outside Charlottesville. The first Sandforth grave there is dated 1726. It's the resting place of the nineteen-year-old wife of some ancestor of mine, dead in childbirth. I know it's not very important in objective terms, not the way the world's going, and yet it's very important to me for young Galt to be there. That's where he belongs.'

'Of course it's important,' she told him. 'My grandfather and grandmother are buried on our property. In a grove of pepper trees, with just enough elevation above the river to keep them safe from floods. When I think of death, I think of myself being there. Nowhere else. Certainly not in some city cemetery, surrounded by the dust of strangers.'

'You put it exactly, Lieutenant Lewis,' he said, lifting his glass of scotch to her as grief kept nipping off the ends of his sentences. Yet it was suddenly wonderful to be here, talking about this issue. Not the death, but above all the disappearance – more sinister than death, more laden with questions – of his son.

Because even to Big Drum now the disappearance had become a settled matter, something Galt would gradually get used to. Something you didn't need to keep referring back to. With Lieutenant Lewis, though, Galt didn't have to get used to it. Galt could still talk and rail and discuss.

'General Sandforth?' she asked.

'Better start calling me Galt,' he said. 'In a way, it honours my son, who had the same name.'

'Very well, Galt.' Yet she still seemed very hard-edged, as if she were coming to bitter conclusions. 'I wanted to say . . . Let's come clean! I mean, let's sleep together. That's what all this is about.'

His lungs seemed to have expanded inside him, leaving him with only a crumb of breath in a small corner. He doubted he could speak. 'You're right,' he said. 'It is what it's about. It's desire. It's infatuation. But I don't want anything cynical or sad. And for God's sake, I don't want it to have anything to do with relative rank, yours and mine.'

It was a mistake to say that. She flushed. Scottish anger, he thought. It reminded him of the energetic temper of his daughter the actress, Sandy. 'I couldn't give a damn about your rank,' she said. 'I'm a civilian and always will be.'

It was funny the way the Australians flaunted the word civilian like a badge of honour.

'Okay. Forgive me.' He thought. 'What about your husband, Dim?'

'Better stop mentioning Allan,' she said briskly. 'Allan isn't part of the question.'

What a discussion! he thought. He'd never conducted a seduction this way before.

'I'll take your word on that,' he said, and he was grateful.

'Look,' she ordered him. She was close to tears of rage. 'For God's sake don't argue with me about it yet. Think what you like about Allan and me. Or think what you must. That isn't the question. The question is: Do you want to sleep with me?'

'Oh Jesus, yes.'

'Well, that at least is simple, General Sandforth.'

She smiled bitterly then and shook her head. At last her face unclenched and she came across the room, refilled his glass, and kissed his forehead. All of which was unutterably and exactly what he needed. She didn't bother with any justifications. She didn't utter the stupid sentiment about how she didn't normally behave this way. She knew he knew that, and it didn't matter if he didn't.

Within seconds his head was on her breast and he wept, for what would be the last time for a long while.

Chapter 6

Love as a Campaign

ERROL FLYNN AS General Custer was riding to his death at the Little Bighorn that Thursday night, in a movie provided by the MGM distributor through the good services of Lieutenant Dim Lewis, when a signals officer entered the ballroom of the Menzies Hotel and whispered to Big Drum. Galt saw Big Drum rise and leave the room.

The officer then spoke to Harry Strudwick, and Harry rose too. Galt did not wait to be summoned but left by a rear exit and doubled around to wait in the suite which served as Big Drum's office away from the office.

'Thank God you came, Galt. Come in, come in. And close the door.'

Galt obeyed him.

'This is a conversation we've already had,' said the General. 'But we've *got* to settle it now, because it's given extra point by the latest reconnaissance. One of our B-17s has sighted a Japanese convoy leaving Rabaul. The enemy is on his way again. I have no doubt it's aimed one way or another at Moresby. But indirectly. My money is on that place up north – Buna. The place Ernie Sasser doesn't want his engineers sent to yet!'

Harry made his doubtful face. It had the unfortunate quality of just about adding up to a music-hall sneer. 'It's only one sighting,' he said. 'I'm sure the force will move in the other direction, towards the Solomons. That's the assessment of my office anyhow.' Harry was very jealous of his sightings, and the interpretations his officers put upon them.

'General,' said Galt, directly to Big Drum, 'we have only a thousand Australian militiamen in the Buna area. My suggestion is that we throw in as many men by sea as we can, now.'

'We're not ready,' said Harry. 'I'm getting sick of this subject.'

'If they take Buna,' said Galt, 'you'll be sicker, Harry!'

'When they come to Moresby, it will be by sea and by the direct route!' Harry's German accent thickened under siege. 'They won't come by the back door, by Buna. I'm willing to stake my reputation on that, General.'

'What should I do, Galt?' Big Drum pleaded. Galt thought he was extraordinarily patient with Harry's Prussian insistence.

'If they land at Buna, it's going to take us a long time and gallons of blood to win it back.'

Big Drum thought a while and shook his head. 'I want more reconnaissance, Galt. Put up as many planes as we can.'

'With respect, General, we have to get men in place now. Whether we think they're ready or not. For example, we could airlift in General Gibbs's brigade. Then we'd know it was well commanded whatever the shortcomings of the troops.'

Halfway through this sentence, it struck Galt that he might be condemning his friend Bryant Gibbs to death. He became sharply aware that he himself did not want to die. He wished to spend years within the clasp, within the wrapped legs of Mrs Dim Lewis.

Big Drum shook his head. 'I wonder if Errol Flynn is faring better than us,' he murmured.

Harry and Galt said nothing to ease the moment. But they knew that Big Drum was to choose between their views. Rejection and triumph were equally on the cards.

'As I've said, Galt, I want lots of reconnaissance. Meanwhile, I have to take Harry's word. He's chief of intelligence, and that's what chiefs of intelligence are for. To be believed.'

Galt could feel like an electric pulse the *frisson* in Harry. It's going to be a mean and temporary triumph! Galt mentally promised him.

'I'll be as delighted as you, General, if he's right,' said Galt, trying to sound sporting.

Big Drum shivered. 'I hope those Japs are on their way to the Solomons. That's outside our zone.'

In those seconds, before he returned to Hollywood's version of the Little Bighorn, he looked – as he sometimes had on

Corregidor but rarely did these days – like a man of more than sixty years; one whose life has been too hard.

It was cold in Dim's flat, with a moist, seeking cold which reminded Galt not of his postings in Wyoming and Montana but of night in a low, damp city like Richmond. He encountered the cold when he left her bed, left her arms, her neat breasts which seemed so familiar and mothering to him now, her rich, symmetrical thighs in which he'd sunk himself twice in an hour before entering an ecstatic sleep. From it he emerged now with an aching bladder.

He ran to her bathroom where, shivering, he happily relieved himself.

Then he went back to her drowsy warmth. He pushed his face into the smooth indentation between her breast and her shoulder. This is the province of a younger man, he thought – not for the first time. Captain Lewis's Buna reconnaissance party was still, however, in Port Moresby. Galt kept track of that small group. They wouldn't be leaving New Guinea for another week, and the slow flight down the coast of Queensland to Brisbane might take them three or four days, what with waiting between planes. It might then be a month before Captain Lewis got leave.

Men were astounding, the way no sooner had they married themselves to a ripeness like that of Lieutenant Lewis than they found reasons to be absent. He had been the same with Sandy. There must be something young men found threatening in the permanent presence of a beautiful and avid young woman.

He noticed she was awake and reaching for him. 'Did it make you happy?' he asked. 'When we were so close, Dim. Did it make you happy?'

She gave a brisk little shake of her head and he could almost hear in the darkness the small crackle of her smile. 'Well, I knew I was alive, Galt.'

He cherished that directness. She didn't lie and simulate. And again he took unexpected delight in the fact that he had not simply put aside rank when he took to her bed. He was in a world where all that was gone, was not even a lever between them, did not add to or take away from their delight.

But even here, as he held her and she drowsed again, he found himself asking what he would do if Big Drum kept putting his money on Harry Strudwick's intelligence? That is, if he kept ignoring Galt's advice? It's like a testing, Galt told himself. Without being too fancy about it, it's like God testing Abraham, demanding Isaac's blood. Isaac being in this case the composite young man who would have to die getting Buna back if the Japanese landed there.

If Galt were forced to resign through Big Drum's ignoring of his advice, the Joint Chiefs in Washington would probably snap him up, just to milk him for information to serve their long feud against Big Drum. Christ knew, though, he didn't want to serve them. He would lose his soul doing that.

And as regards his career, how far would *they* let him go anyhow? He would probably have to revert to a field posting if he wanted to become in the end one of the Joint Chiefs himself. He would probably have to go back to being a Major-General and take a divisional command in Europe or Africa or somewhere. After having almost direct control of an entire air force, the sacked General Pendle's Fifth Air Force, he would find it pretty small beer working an infantry division of draftees.

His fear was too that he would never follow Big Drum to the White House or become his Secretary of Defense. For with Big Drum, it was a case of either total loyalty or of being the enemy. There were no shades of friendship or dissent with Big Drum. Big Drum was lucky to have found a woman who thought him infallible. And sometimes, in his larger moments, he conveyed a sense of infallibility to absolutely everyone. That's what Galt sometimes thought he himself feared the most: being cut out of Big Drum's literal charm, the enchantment of certainty he was able to impose with equal ease on his staff and his wife despite all the evidence.

That was Big Drum's strength. Even worldly men like Galt Sandforth needed to be near him for succour. He was the swami, he was the prophet, and in his presence the world shone.

But he had now made two wrong as hell decisions about Buna.

And there was also the question of Dim. She was not Teresa Chung, whom he could send off to the airport with $500. She had become a companion he could not contemplate losing. Away from her, he felt the magnetic pull of her flesh, a yearning for her face.

He raised his head to take in that sleeping face and was surprised to see it regarding him with a wide-open gaze.

'There's something you must know,' she said all at once, when he had thought she was asleep. 'Something utterly in confidence which you mustn't mention to anyone, or make use of in arguments between us, or refer to at all ever again.'

He gave the promise at once, blind. He realized that it was a dangerous thing for a soldier to give blanket promises, but he had been seduced into it.

'My husband and I have never had sex with each other,' she told him. 'You could exclude one time perhaps.' She smiled wistfully at the memory. 'We got some result, but it had all the charm of saving a bogged ewe. He doesn't desire me. Or the other thing is, he doesn't desire women. I don't mean for a moment he goes for the other. That's why you mustn't mention any of this. The most precious thing to him is this work he does. He's a success at Special Reconnaissance. I just think he's one of those men who don't need much sex.'

Galt felt strangely embarrassed and found himself muttering dopily. 'I've known men . . . of course, I've known them . . . similar dispositions.'

'I want him to go to a doctor,' Dim explained. 'Or I should more correctly say, I *wanted* him to go to a doctor. I don't care any more. He said no anyhow, at the time. He didn't want anything to appear on his medical record. To hurt his big chances.'

'And he's probably bashful,' muttered Galt. He felt stupidly bashful himself.

'When he said no, I have to tell you . . . I felt something harden inside me.'

It sounded like a pun on Allan Lewis's condition, and Galt in a panic felt a berserk urge to pick the pun up. 'Something hardened in you, but not in him. Is that it?' Even the impulse made him feel like a barbarian.

Thank God the perverse temptation passed.

Dim said, 'I know it sounds as if I'm making excuses. Because here I am. *Adultery*. This is what they call adultery, isn't it, General?'

'Oh Jesus, Dim, it happens all the time. It feels natural as hell when you're involved.'

'It's the first time for me,' she told him. She drew her hand over his brow, gently, as if she wanted to see him as clearly as possible. 'I take it by the way you're talking, it's not the first time for you.'

He knew that answering was full of danger.

'Dim, I've been married thirty years.'

'That's not answering the question,' she told him. 'Your wife wouldn't consider that an answer.'

'Sure, I've had women. For God's sake, believe me, it was never anything like this. This is the biggest thing since . . . '

'Since you got married?' she asked, still forcing the issue, wanting everything out in plain view, in ungarnished language.

'Christ, Dim! It doesn't do to examine some things up too close.'

'I do examine things up too close,' she acknowledged with so much solemnity that he wanted to enter her again, to make himself part of what he saw as her unvarnished and colonial honesty.

'Never anything like this,' he said. 'I swear to you.'

'You'd better get used to the idea,' she announced, utterly in control and nursing his head to her breast. 'That I can't stand lies, Galt.'

'That's the point,' he told her. 'That's the point of what I'm saying. With you, Dim, I strain to be truthful.'

'You'd better keep doing that,' she advised him.

The nights he was away from her, he'd wake trembling after no more than forty-five minutes of sleep and begin to grieve for Galt Junior. The world after midnight seemed not large enough to contain the sorrow for what had happened to Galt. It was the child whom he quivered for, the young Galt, whom he'd occasionally struck out at, on whom he'd exercise some small fatherly petulance or other, he now remembered with a grief that took his breath away.

Yet he hadn't been a bad father, no worse than any other officer. Nothing could have made up to Galt Junior for the fact that he would die young, falling out of the sky, that the Mediterranean would be either the wall of steel he hit or else the medium which smothered him.

But when Galt was with Dim, it all seemed soothed, all that regret, and even Galt Junior's death, though terrible, seemed part of the normal order or disorder of the universe. So he went to her as many nights as he could. And he kept an eye on his aides, particularly Captain Duncan. Just in case the word got round from the motor pool that Big Drum's Chief of Staff was driving *himself* round Melbourne a number of nights a week. Harry Strudwick, in his struggle for control of Big Drum's ear, would love to hear tidings like that.

The news came in by radio and then on teleprinter: the convoy which had been sighted near Rabaul had obviously turned up at Buna, even though Harry Strudwick said it wouldn't. The Catholic priest at Buna Mission, who had bravely stayed on there against all advice, had witnessed the landing and then taken to the jungle. Australian positions on the north coast of New Guinea were also sending frantic warnings by radio, as were Australian coast watchers from their hideaways behind the beaches.

So the Japanese would have an airfield at Buna. Would they try to march across New Guinea to Port Moresby? Harry was still confidently saying no. It was as if he had no consciousness that he'd just made a howling error. Maybe he believed that if Buna had been garrisoned, the garrison would merely have fallen into Japanese hands. But now it was the Japanese who would build that north coast air base for which Allan Lewis and Commander Runcie and the boys had gone reconnoitring.

The gloom in Bataan, Collins Street, was frightful. Big Drum had promised to win back the Philippines. But with his resources, and with the raw and outnumbered Australians, could he even win Buna back?

However, Big Drum did not publicly announce Strudwick's

error, or make any references to it in staff meetings. That was one of his strengths, and one of the reasons he was loved. He never humiliated any one of his staff publicly and the habit bred loyalty in them. Galt, nonetheless, was sure that Big Drum always remembered. That was what was important. Harry's credit was partly blown away.

As the southern winter struck Melbourne with the coldest weather Big Drum and his staff had experienced in years, news came through that the American fleet had inflicted tremendous damage on the enemy navy at Midway. The news did not create much excitement in the insurance building in Collins Street, Dim noticed. She discussed this with Captain Duncan, whom she met on her way out the door to catch a tram home.

'Well,' said Duncan, winking urbanely, 'the truth is that if Big Drum isn't involved, then it can't have been much of a victory!'

Dim had felt defensive for some reason. A need to protect General Wraith. 'Maybe Big Drum's right not to be too excited. It isn't as if this finishes off the Japanese. They'll try again.'

'Oh sure,' said Duncan. 'They'll try again, lieutenant. But next to the Japanese winning the war, the next thing Big Drum most fears is the Navy doing it.'

Outside it was one of those blustery Melbourne days. It never snowed here, but the wind seemed to come all the way from Antarctica. The tram was crowded with Australian militia and Yank enlisted men, and wan young wives whose husbands were probably away. A militiaman gave up his seat to Dim yet called her 'Sir' in a joking sort of way.

Holding on to a strap, there was an Australian major in a well-tailored uniform, polished Sam Browne and all, who seemed to inhibit the boy. The young militiaman made a face and moved further down the tram. The major, who was fairly young and smooth-faced himself, smiled down at Dim.

'Are they working you hard, lieutenant?' he asked with a smile.

'*They*'re not, sir. The hard work is my idea.'

'Goodness,' he said. 'That's against the best traditions of the military life. Making work for oneself.'

Though he was obviously an Australian, he affected the manners of an English gentleman. He might as well save himself the trouble, since the English would never accept him as one of them. Dim knew this. But it was one of the ironies of colonial life. The provinces futilely aping Rome.

'It's probably because I'm a civilian through and through,' smiled Dim, a common cry of hers, in this case called in to serve to explain her work ethic.

'Me too,' said the major. 'A barrister in civvy street.'

'Perhaps I should tell you I'm a married woman, major,' she said, feeling a fake.

'Are you now? I'm a conversationalist myself. Are you a conversationalist, lieutenant?'

'I'm sorry if I misunderstood you, sir.'

At her stop he stood back to let her off, but he followed her.

'Oh my God,' she said stopping on the pavement and facing him as the tram receded clanging. 'You said you were just a conversationalist.'

'I just want to chat with you, lieutenant,' he told her. 'It's business, as a matter of fact. I know you're a married woman. In fact I even know him to whom you're married. I also know him to whom you are not married, if you understand me.'

'Where are you from?'

'You could say from Australian Land Headquarters? But if you called and complained, they'd say they didn't know me. So don't call and complain, because I'm more or less speaking for myself. Although I'm not. Again, if you understand.'

She began to tremble. 'Get to the bloody point, major,' she told him.

'I'm sure you're a loyal Australian, lieutenant. Even though the Yanks have subsumed you, or more or less digested you whole. Do you remember the Australian Army? It's a better army than they have. And even according to the Yanks, General Billings is the commander of all land forces, including theirs. For what theirs are worth. At least, he's the commander in theory.'

She looked at him, sceptically inviting him to continue.

'The Southwest Pacific is our area, lieutenant. It's not *theirs*. We bloody well live here! But they're dealing us out of the game.

Oh, certainly, they'll use us against the Japanese. If any bloody Allied army is going to turn back the little yellow men, it's going to be us. We're the only qualified body in the world to do it. But they don't want us to have any influence. They don't want any of us at their headquarters. They haven't invited any of us to their game! They have plans to exclude General Billings by this stratagem and that. And you know why that's so? I'm *sure* you know why that's so. You've probably picked it up, along with other things, from him to whom you are not married.

'It seems that Big Drum is meant by God to become Republican President of the United States, and General Sandforth his Secretary of Defense or of State under God. But after the débâcle in the Philippines, he can become the Lord's Anointed on earth only by seeming to manage the whole bloody affair of the Nips on his own. He won't share a fragment of the credit with General Billings, or with the Australians. He'll just let them *do* it. Do his work for him. People like your husband, lieutenant. Him to whom you *are* married.'

She stared at him hard. She was angry, and yet knew that in a way she deserved his contempt. 'I don't like you, major.'

'We're not in it for likes and dislikes,' he told her. 'As I said, you're one of the few Australians who's allowed to work at Bataan. You're certainly the only one who's managed any penetration of that place. Or do you think it would be more accurate of me to say that it has managed a certain penetration of you?'

Dim could feel blood prickling her face. 'You shouldn't talk to anyone like that, no matter what they've done!'

The major smiled. It was a savage smile, but it was obvious that the major thought it was disarming. 'Well, at least you would admit that you're rather uniquely placed. That Bataan thinks more warmly of you than it does of poor old General Billings.'

'How does anyone know that?' Dim asked in sudden bewilderment. If secretiveness was a virtue in lovers, then Galt Sandforth and she had been very secretive.

The major wasn't saying how anyone knew, but at least he'd dropped his smart alec smirk. 'I think you should meet me regularly, lieutenant,' he said. 'I think you should ask your friend about Big Drum's intentions for the Australians. Ask above all whether elements of a new US Army Group, the VIth, are beginning to arrive. It is very important for us that it be put under General Billings's direct command, as the arrangement between our two nations allows for. But we fear there may be some other plan. No one is as well situated as you are to get the good information, my dear.'

Dim said, 'I can't do that. I *won't* do it. I can't work that way. And besides, I respect him. We're all on the same side, aren't we?'

'For the time being we are. We would be delighted if the Americans extended us the courtesy of being on the same side. Equal partners instead of servants.'

Dim laughed painfully. 'I won't do it.'

'Then your parents will be told all about you and your liaison.'

Dim remembered what she thought of as her parents' old-fashioned rectitude, though she'd once heard them fighting over the fact that her father had danced too long with some other woman at a tennis club party. But the idea that they should know about her *adultery* was beyond bearing.

'And of course we would need to let your husband know, though it would have a terrible effect on the poor boy's morale. And then we would leak it to certain members of the press, so that you would always be known in Melbourne for this affair of yours. Under censorship, perhaps nothing would be published on the subject, not immediately anyhow. But as soon as Bataan *knew* that the press knew, you would be thrown out of Bataan.'

Dim shook her head in confusion. 'Why don't you take this threat straight to General Sandforth?' For Galt would know how to treat a blackmailer.

'We can't get near him, dear girl. There are only two Australians he speaks to. You and the Prime Minister. Besides, I think we could put more reliance on what he tells you out of – what shall I say? – *gratitude*, than on what he might tell us under coercion.'

'I won't see him any more then.'

'We'll still let everyone know, my dear,' said the major. 'Look, you live life as you usually do, and I shall contact you once a week. I mean, General Sandforth knows you're a good Australian girl, and questions about the future of the army in which you are a lieutenant would naturally occur to you.'

Another tram was rattling down the street, and the major began to signal it, as if he meant to go now. 'I'll contact you next week. Sorry love, but all's fair, etcetera.'

She was in turmoil. She certainly could not face the prospect of Allan or her parents finding out. That made her a classic hypocrite, she supposed, but knowing it was no comfort. She could not live in a Melbourne where rumours circulated about her. She wanted to be known as an honest, straightforward woman. This was an ambition she took seriously. It was one of those essential pictures of herself which she cherished.

For some hours therefore she entertained ideas about suicide, but that was so stupid and such a waste. In any case, mightn't the Japanese turn up and do the job for her whether she wanted it done or not?

Captain Allan Lewis . . . he might not secretly be as hurt as her parents would be. He would after all know she had a sort of reason. But it was a cheap reason. And the public scandal would torment him.

In the end, if this affair lasted and Allan and Galt and she lived, then he'd have to know about it. But it seemed crucial that *she* tell him, that he not find out about it from a stranger, from someone like the major, muttering to him in a tent in New Guinea.

Towards midnight she began to understand that since there was no perfect world left, the one that would cause the least pain was to renounce Galt. She could barely imagine a life without him. But she knew that such a world had existed, that she had recently occupied it, and that she might be able to re-enter it. That it was better to live without him than betray him to this poisonous major.

'I have something to tell you,' he announced. 'May I come in?'

'Of course,' she said. Because he must have already sensed the refusal in her face. She stood back from the door and let him enter.

'Have you heard something, Dim?' he asked her.

'No,' she said. She felt unlovely in her flannel dressing gown.

'It's cold in here,' he said.

'Well, they'll let us have only so much coal,' she said, more aggressively than she wanted to.

'What's happened to you?' he asked.

'Come through into the lounge-room,' she said. 'I want to talk to you.'

'Sure,' he said, 'because I have something to tell you.'

He followed her through and they sat at either end of the floral settee. The marriage settee, as Galt thought of it. The one Dim and Allan Lewis had bought before the wedding. Before they really knew each other.

'Well, who goes first?' asked Galt Sandforth.

Perhaps he had had second thoughts. She hoped and feared the possibility. Perhaps he was going to make the usual speech an older man makes sooner or later to a younger woman. She gave in to an instinct for cowardice and said, 'You go first.'

He looked at her from under a cocked eyebrow. 'OK, lieutenant. Big Drum has decided, at my urging and that of the Australians, to move Bataan twelve hundred miles north, closer to the enemy. To Brisbane. This is absolutely confidential at the moment. But the move will be made soon, some seventeen days from now.'

'Ah,' said Dim Lewis. She began to cry – she couldn't help herself.

He put his arm out as if he were a stranger visiting and touched her wrist lightly. 'What's the matter?'

'No,' she said. 'No. It's good. Nothing's the matter. I understand. I suppose it's a sign that the important battles are close. I suppose that's what it's a sign of.'

'It's certainly that,' Galt conceded.

'It's just as well. I've been thinking of Allan. And of my parents. I couldn't stand it . . . ' But what she couldn't stand now was the thought of Galt going away.

He raised his head again, the inquisitive mouth, the jaw cocked as if for debate.

'But you're coming, Dim. For God's sake, my girl. You're

coming with us! You didn't think I'd leave you when I've just damn well found you?'

'How can you manage that? How can you manage to bring me with you?'

'*Movies*! And their place in the lives of Big Drum and others! You have the clout with the distributors, Dim. I've arranged it. We're travelling by train. Seventeen days' time.'

So since he had not ended it, it was up to her.

'I can't go,' she said.

Galt looked at her narrowly. 'I could tell you you were a soldier, and that you have to go,' he said with a half smile.

'I won't go, Galt.'

'For Christ's sake, why ever not?'

She thought for a while. 'What do you intend to do with the Australians, Galt? What place do you see *them* having in this war?'

He grimaced but then looked levelly at her. 'They're the only trained roops we've got just now, Dim. Why are you asking that?'

She shook her head. She couldn't answer.

'OK, I'll be honest with you. I *do* see them being superseded by our boys once we've got round to training. It's a question of numbers. We've got them, you don't. It's even, some would say, a question of politics.'

She shook her head in an attempt to clear her vision. She said stupidly, 'Thank you for being honest with me about that.' For some reason he had established his good faith by confirming what the major had said.

'I tell you things, Dim, I wouldn't tell the Prime minister of Australia.'

'Well,' she said, 'it's all safe with me. Even though we won't see each other again.'

'For Jesus' sake, don't say that, Dim. Why wouldn't we see each other again? Don't play with me. I'm besotted with you.'

'Well, I think that perhaps I'm just overwhelmed by your status, General Sandforth. I think I've been a very foolish girl from the bush. I think you ought to go. I think you ought to issue orders sending me back to the Allied Officers' Club.'

'I can't believe you're talking like this,' he said. *I can't believe it myself*, she could have told him. She heard him ask her, 'What's happening, Dim?' There was a new, very surprising, very martial toughness in the question. 'What's happening? This isn't you. This is someone outside you. Maybe someone from inside Bataan. That's it. Someone knows. Isn't that the case? Isn't it?'

She would not answer.

'I don't know how it's come out though. We've been very careful. Very careful. You haven't spoken to anybody?'

'I've spoken to no one,' she said angrily. Except, of course, the major from General Billings's headquarters.

'I have enemies inside Bataan, Dim. We're not all a happy brotherhood. Has one of them got to you? Is one of them *blackmailing* you?'

'No. It isn't that.'

'Let me be honest, Dim. I can't afford a scandal any more than you can. But I love you, and that's the most important of all.'

There was already a shift in him. What he was doing, though she did not know it, was gauging perhaps for the first time whether it was worth risking the future status of Secretary of Defense of the United States against the sweetness of her company. He was discovering with some astonishment that her value was supreme with him.

He returned to easier questions. 'If it's one of the people at Bataan, I have the means of frightening them off. Honestly I have. And if it's someone else, I also have means.'

'Please go, Galt. Don't make it hard.' One thing she found she couldn't do was to betray another Australian, even one like the major. For behind him was General Billings and Australian Land Headquarters.

'Tell me!' Galt insisted. 'Who is it?'

She stood up, getting desperate. 'Does it have to be anyone? Can't I make up my mind for myself? I just don't like what's happened! Can't you understand?'

He was standing too, but they were still separate from each

other. Blows and caresses seemed both equally likely. She was thinking of landing blows because he wouldn't go away.

'I know it isn't that, Dim. The passion's too large. I know that sounds like the movies. But it's just too great, Dim. Because, believe me, I've known the *other*. The liaison that's just a liaison. The mere arrangement with a woman. Something that can be ended easily, without either party feeling that they've lost a limb, or had their entrails fall out. But this isn't one of those arrangements, Dim. Neither for me nor for you. So I ask you again. Someone is twisting your arm Dim, aren't they? I know it. I can swear to it. And unless it's Big Drum or God, then I can stop them. I swear that to you.'

'Will you go?' she cried, wanting to tear his face. 'Will you go for dear God's sake! Not everything is wide open to Yank-power, you know, or to your influence! I've got my pride, too! I'm not interested in who you can silence and who you can frighten. That's a side of you I don't like. That's *the* side of you that's not worth loving. I just want you to go, don't you understand? Just to go!'

He stopped arguing. He retrieved his cap and the fawn, well-cut greatcoat he'd had made by a Melbourne tailor. Then he moved out of the room and down the hallway and through the door of her flat with its frosted glass panels, ordinary dimpled glass which until now had always shone with promise. Downstairs, he stood just inside the doorway of the block of flats, looking up the street to the right, and down it. Sadly the view was complicated by trees. Not native gum trees, but English beeches which the Melbourne folk, with their nostalgia for England, seemed to favour. He could see no one though. There were a few parked cars with wartime coal gas bladders in wooden racks on their roofs. Was the spy in one of them? he wondered. Or did whoever it was already know enough, not needing any more to follow him every time he made his pilgrimage? Needing only to check when he took out his driverless car from the motor pool.

In the morning Dim felt aged and entered Bataan tentatively. Like some crone, she avoided the crowds in the ornate elevator cage and took instead to the stairwell. American officers seemed to avoid stairs, and there was hardly anyone on them this morning.

But the ascent to the remote corridor where her office was located seemed hard and long. She didn't have enough oxygen.

She made her normal phone calls to distributors and army camps. She authorized transport for two comics and four dancers from the Tivoli in Sydney to travel to Queensland by train and entertain the Australian 7th Division and the American 34th Infantry, which were both in jungle training in the rainforest. She wrote letters to entertainment officers whose names were becoming familiar to her. For she had been permitted to create a network of distribution of films between camps as far away as the bush north of Adelaide in South Australia or remote airstrips a thousand miles north of Brisbane.

So – this morning – at least she didn't have to fill in time.

She had earlier made an appointment with a gynaecologist, not the one her mother and she had visited on a journey to Melbourne from Maneering, but one recommended to her by Honor Runcie. She had wanted a contraceptive device, because she did not intend to have abortions if she became pregnant by Galt, even though Galt could arrange it all in a trice. But now she would not need the thing. She wondered if she should cancel. But it had been so hard to arrange and she spent an hour fretting over the question.

A little before noon fire alarms began to clang in the corridors of Bataan. She heard military police knocking on doors. She felt ill disposed to rush; very fatalistic, in fact. She took time to extract from her bottom drawer a portrait photograph of Allan, with brilliantined hair and newly authorized second lieutenant's pips on his shoulders.

'We're married again, Allan, love,' she murmured. 'For bloody good and ever.'

She looked at that ingratiating grin in the photo. It was a grin from before the time he knew himself flawed, an impaired man. She shoved the thing in a leather valise she carried these days, stood up, and began to leave the office. Before she got to the door, however, Galt appeared through it, shut it behind him, and locked it.

'There's no fire,' he said gently. 'I set the alarm off. A little bit hard on some of the crowd who were with us in Corregidor and who flinch a lot these days. But desperate situations demand . . . '

There was a knock on the door – some young MP. 'Anyone there?' A hand tried the doorknob and found it locked. The shadow from beyond the glass moved away. The MP must have presumed the office was vacated and that the security-conscious officer to whom it belonged had locked up all papers before fleeing.

The alarms ceased, and in the building there was a great silence. But as if by mutual consent, Dim and Galt spoke in hushed voices.

'I can't stand this, Galt,' she told him. 'I can't stand not having my word taken!'

She could tell, though, that there was a new ferocity in him, a quiet one, very frightening.

'Listen to me. I don't believe you, so you might as well be quiet. I've come to the conclusion that the chief of intelligence, Major-General Strudwick, and perhaps one or two of his allies, such as Brigadier-General Ernie Sasser, are blackmailing you. And rather than betray me, you have very sportingly decided to end the affair. So no one will see me draw a vehicle from the motor pool anymore, no one will see me drive it to your apartment, and you won't be forced to give them anything!'

She felt a panic at being so closely but inaccurately read.

'Dim,' he continued, 'you survive in a place like this, in a command like Big Drum's, amongst people like Harry and Ernie, only by having something you can control them with. Bcause if you think my ego is large, theirs is absolutely imperial. Now, I know something about Harry Strudwick and little Ernie. Something they did in the Philippines, before the war. In the salad days. Nothing criminal, mind you, not in the direct sense. They didn't rape or strangle a Filipino girl. But something extremely improper. Something that could end them.

'I am about to use this precious bit of information, Dim. For your sake. I thought I would use it for some military purpose – I would use it, for example, when Harry Strudwick advised Big Drum one way, and I advised him another, and knew that I was right, and knew that my view would save lives. But I'm going to have to use it now, to keep you. That's the most important issue in my life. I'm amazed to say it. But I'll say it again. *You're* the most important issue. If I don't hear the truth from you, then I'll use what I have straight away. If you'd just tell me the truth though, maybe something less extreme – some weapon not quite so radical – might be available to me.'

Dim was shaking her head. 'I swear to you, Galt, it isn't anything to do with Strudwick and Sasser.'

'I don't believe you,' he said.

It might be a simple statement, but it had utter and final authority.

'It isn't them,' Dim repeated. 'I could swear to that, Galt.'

'Then it's someone else. It's not a decision you came to on your own. It's someone else!' He looked at his watch. 'Quickly, Dim. Everyone will be back upstairs within a minute or so. If I have no clear word from you, then I go outside and use this once only and very precious device of mine. Against two generals, Dim. Think of that! But if they've hurt and confused you, I'll get great pleasure from doing it. Please understand that. I won't let anyone hurt you!'

Dim sat down in her office chair. She hauled the photograph of Allan out of her valise and put it face up on the table. 'For Christ's sake, here's the reason. Believe me. He's the reason!'

'With his dead prick?' asked Galt and his savagery seemed to penetrate her, jolted her.

He turned and was at the door. There wasn't any doubt that he was going and that by dusk that winter's day Strudwick and Sasser would be faced by Galt's sudden accusations, whatever they were.

'It's the Australians,' she called out. 'They feel you're using them. That you won't let them into the spoils. If there are any spoils to be had when the Japanese are finished with us!'

'Billings?'

'No,' cried Dim, not sure that she was telling the truth. 'Not

Billings. A major. He said a new army corps was coming from the United States, and that it should be under General Billings's command, but that you and Big Drum would try to take it away from Billings somehow, that the war was just the way for Big Drum to become President, and that he didn't give a damn what happened to us Australians after the war.'

She covered her eyes with her hand.

'Oh God,' she said, 'now I've ratted on my fellow countrymen.'

'No, Dim, they *ratted* – as you put it – on you,' Galt said. There were noises in the corridor. People were returning. False alarm. Galt was willing now to risk someone seeing him emerge from her office.

But he was not about to leave yet.

'What was this major's name?'

'I don't know.'

'Is that some dumb antipodean sense of honour operating again?' asked Galt with a half smile.

'I don't know. And don't ask me for a description. And don't let anything happen to him.'

'I *will* scare him off, Dim. I *will* frighten him. What do you expect?'

She thought about this. She didn't like the imperial tone. 'You bastard! Give my countrymen their due. At least they've been fighting this bloody war from the start.'

'I acknowledge that.' He looked at her and the smile came again. 'I happen to think they're amongst the best troops in the world. There just aren't enough of them, Dim. You know that. Here you have a continent, Australia, the size of the continental United States. You have a population of six or seven million. I know one Aussie regular is worth a company of Illinois draftees at the moment. But can you look me in the eye and tell me there are enough Aussie regulars to beat this enemy?'

'What about this new army corps?' she asked, unrelenting. 'Will you give it to Billings?'

'That's ultimately Big Drum's decision, Dim.'

'Will you argue and vote for giving it to Billings?'

'I've no objection. He's Allied Land Commander, for Christ's sake.'

She looked him in the face, suddenly searching for treachery in the features.

'Listen,' he said. 'You're not to worry, Dim. From now on I can come and see you, and no one will know. No one, I swear. Please, Dim, trust me on this. Please believe I wouldn't lie.'

Her face was still clenched. 'What if I have a child?' she asked.

She had thought the idea would panic him, but he looked at her with a calm frown. 'Are you pregnant, Dim?'

'That's not what I mean. But what if I were?'

He thought. 'I believe I'd want to keep it, Dim.' That too was a new feeling for him. To be a potentially re-emerged parent.

Dim said, 'I'm seeing a gynaecologist today.'

'You mean you'll take precautions?'

'Yes. What do you think?'

'No. That's good. Jesus, I love you, Dim.'

General Galton Sandforth had in his office a captain whose chief task was intelligence liaison with Harry Strudwick's office. He was fresh from America, this boy – he had not been in the small party which had escaped from Corregidor and travelled to Australia by way of that terrible B-17 flight. But he was discreet and a graduate of the Point, and Galt sometimes set him intelligence tasks in his own right.

Now, on the way to an afternoon conference with Big Drum, Galt asked the young man to produce the records of the senior NCOs and officers of the Bataan motor pool, which was situated around the corner from Collins Street in Little Bourke Street in what had formerly been a commercial garage.

He went into the conference feeling renewed. He would get that Aussie major. He would hammer his hide to the wall.

'You look well, Galt,' remarked Big Drum. 'Mrs Wraith's been saying how chipper you've been looking. I tell her it's the tension between the improved regional situation and the deteriorated local situation that's doing it. She laughs at that.'

The stuff of the conference was the standard quandary over Buna, which the Japanese now held. They would surely not attack Port Moresby on the south coast directly. Harry Strudwick still said – on apparently good evidence – that that was an impossibility. But their navy might make a run around the eastern end of New Guinea, capture Milne Bay right on the tip and thereby acquire an even more convenient bombing strip and depot than Buna was.

So the decision Big Drum and Galt had reached was to put the best of the Australians at Mile Bay. Their convoys had sailed from Queensland, escorted by USAAF bombers, and the Aussies had made it safely to Milne Bay where they were already digging in, waiting for what Harry Strudwick called 'the inevitable amphibious attack'. If the Australians handled it well, Galt saw, it would be good for the war effort and his own reputation.

That afternoon therefore, Galt had a sweet sense of having done everything possible for his own happiness and that of the world, with the exception of the Japanese task forces in the Southwest Pacific Area and one Australian major.

Late that afternoon the motor pool files he had asked for appeared on his desk. The sergeants all had Polish and Italian names. Galt skimmed through the undistinguished military histories of young or youngish civilian mechanics. The dispatcher, Galt saw, was a man in his early thirties called Lieutenant Ticino.

Galt dialled the number of his young intelligence liaison officer in the outer office.

'There's an officer in the motor pool. Aldo Ticino, lieutenant. Find out what you can about him. His habits, I mean. Question some of the others about it. Operate with normal secrecy. I'd like to know something by tomorrow morning.'

If it were not the dispatcher, then he'd move on to the others. One by one. It could take two or three days.

He called Dim at home that night. 'We have something big planned for you Aussies.'

'Exactly,' said Dim. But she didn't sound as aggrieved as this morning. '*You* have it planned.'

'The other . . . I think it's our motor pool that's to blame.'

'Um,' she said.

'You saw the doctor?'

'He said the new devices are fine.' He had recommended a

cap to Dim, but that piece of technological information was secret to herself. 'He said that one day science would make it possible for girls to avoid the wages of sin. "The myth that young women should live like nuns while their boyfriends are away is under siege," he said. He seemed pretty happy about that. True equality for women came from contraception, he said.'

'Fascinating,' said Galt. 'Look after yourself, Dim. More news tomorrow.'

Lieutenant Aldo Ticino, a grizzle-haired man in his early thirties, not unattractive-looking, was shown into Galt Sandforth's office the following noon. There was some sweat on his face, although it was winter in Melbourne. Captain Duncan withdrew. He didn't want to know anything; why a lieutenant-general would want to interview an obscure lieutenant from the motor pool. For that very reason, Galt thought, the boy might go far.

Ticino saluted and Galt told him to sit down.

'Lieutenant, I won't waste time. You've been speaking to the Australians.'

'Don't know what you mean by that, General,' said Ticino.

Sandforth could imagine Ticino in some suburban auto shop explaining to some sucker why the entire gearbox had to be replaced. The brilliant boy in the outer office had found out everything Sandforth needed to know about Ticino. He had a wife back in Philadelphia. He had a girlfriend in the Melbourne suburb of Fitzroy. He was a gambler – he went to the Flemington and Caulfield racetracks most weekends. He lost at poker. The young intelligence officer had found this out from various staff-sergeants who had lately been repaid by him. So there had been a recent bonanza for Lieutenant Ticino. An Australian bonanza.

'I'll tell you what I mean,' said Galt. 'The Australians have been asking you for information about the movement of cars from the motor pool. You were not authorized to give that information, but you did. Now I know about your tart in Fitzroy and your wife at home, and I have the power to transfer you. You speak straight to me, and your reward will be a posting to Townsville in North Queensland.'

'That's a reward?' asked Lieutenant Ticino.

'Comparatively,' said Galton Sandforth. 'When compared with the other possibilities. Reduction to private's rank and transfer to New Guinea. We're not having some sonofabitch in Bataan who passes out information to strangers. Who sells himself just because he's lost a few games at poker and backed the wrong Australian horses.'

Ticino began to look from one wall to the other. 'Shit, General,' he said. 'You play it dirty.'

'I would never have known of your existence, lieutenant. Except that you've been stupid. Did the Australians come singly or in a team?'

'Oh, Jesus,' Ticino was sweating madly now. 'One man. I thought he had authorization. That's why I showed him the dispatch sheets.'

Galt Sandforth stood up. 'You bastard!' he whispered. 'You *thought* he was authorized. That's horseshit, Ticino. You don't give over papers because you *think* someone's authorized. The bastard could have been a journalist in fancy dress.'

Ticino, flinching, conceded this with a mad smile.

'I want to know three things. What did he say his name was? What did he look like? And what did he pay you? And I want the truth on the whole three within the next minute, or else you're on the next train to Queensland and the first DC-3 into Moresby. As a private. I swear, lieutenant. As a fucking private!'

Ticino wiped his face. He still kept his handsomeness and a kind of composure. He did not go utterly to water. But he was a sensible man. 'Oh, Jesus,' he said. 'It'll take more than a minute to describe him, General. But I can tell you one key piece of information. He was a fairy. You know, a faggot.'

'The way you're a fool,' said Galt. He handed Ticino a sheet of paper. 'You can write, I suppose. I want a written description of the man, no shorter than a hundred words. Everything you can remember. If it differs from reality in any way, then again you won't find yourself nicely located in Townsville, lieutenant. You'll spend time in the compound before being sent to New Guinea as a buck private.'

As he watched the head bowed over the paper, Galt felt like

hitting him. Ticino did seem anxious now. Threats of the compound, delivered by a lieutenant-general, would frighten any sane man, and by being perturbed, Ticino showed his sanity.

When he had finished writing – there were two pauses in the middle – he found the General still glowering at him. 'Is that all?' asked Galt.

'I swear it is, General. But if I think of more . . . '

'Don't worry. You won't be in Melbourne long enough for any more face-to-face discussions.'

Dismissing Ticino, he kept his eye on the man, exacting from him every iota of the proper military deference.

Galt called the office of the Brigadier-General who ran the Military Police in the Melbourne area. He was not a member of the Bataan crowd, the select corps who had escaped from the Philippines. Instead he was another late arrival from the States; in peacetime, a captain of police in one of the medium-sized cities in the Midwest. Galt could not think of which one. Maybe Bloomington, Indiana. Throughout his entire military career though, Galt had found it useful to have a good, no-questions-asked friend in the Military Police.

After the pleasantries, Galt said, 'You must have amongst your officers a reliable man who's worked in vice somewhere or other.'

'What area of vice, General?'

'Homosexual soliciting,' said Galt.

As she came up the stairs to her flat, Dim was surprised to see lights shining from inside through the glass of her front door. Perhaps she had left them burning, against all the rules of rationing. She had certainly been sufficiently confused in the past two days to forget simple things like that. She unlocked the door tentatively. Could this be Allan suddenly returned? But surely Galt, who seemed to know about Special Reconnaissance and its movements, would have told her.

Unlocking the door, she saw her parents rising from the sofa in the living room down the corridor. *Not now*, she thought. But she couldn't flee, she was committed: they had sighted her. Advancing towards them, she saw them for the first time as if they were strangers, two quite good-looking members of the grazier species. Her father in the typical grazier's tweed jacket and wool tie, his big hat beside him on the seat. He wore, too, the tight moleskin trousers of a man accustomed to working on horseback, and his brown boots sparkled.

Her mother was dressed in stylish black. They were clearly on their way to some half-formal dinner where they would meet others of their background and celebrate both the easing of tension since the Japanese were defeated in the Coral Sea battle, and the high price of wool generated by the war, by the demand not so much of armies in the Pacific but of all the Allied armies in the northern hemisphere.

'Don't you look handsome in your uniform?' remarked her mother. 'And yet you're so pale . . . '

Her father, who had served with the Australian Light Horse in the Middle East in the Great War, who had once even met Lawrence of Arabia and entered Damascus on his heels, gave her a mock salute.

'My daughter the military man,' he said, laughing. It was strange how parental jokes always fell flat; they were directed at the parent's image of the child as child and therefore missed the mark by some years.

'We got your letter about the posting to Brisbane,' said her mother. 'We're really proud of you. You must be doing wonderfully. And it's such a nice climate up there. I went there by ship once, it was a sort of consolation trip to make up for becoming engaged to your father at Christmas time in – when was it? – my God, 1913.'

Dim had somehow forgotten that they had a key. The flat, after all, belonged to them. It meant that there was a risk that they could have arrived from the country at any time and found General Sandforth there. And that would have taken a lot of fast talking to explain. Not that they'd ever turned up unannounced before.

'I wish I'd known you were coming,' she said, hoping they might take the message. 'I could have got some food in.'

Her mother brushed this aside. 'You know, you may see more of Allan up there. Is there any chance of that?'

'Jingo!' said her father, not waiting for her to answer. 'That would be nice. I hadn't thought of that.'

'You don't hear much from him, do you, dear?'

She felt she had to give them something, some particle of information. 'I've heard a few things since I've been at Bataan.'

Both her parents looked mystified.

'That's what they call Big Drum's headquarters,' she said. 'General Wraith's headquarters. They call it Bataan. They say they're going back there. To the Philippines.'

'Good for them,' said her father.

'And I've heard a little,' Dim pursued. 'He's been out of the country, though you have to keep that a secret. But he's in a safe area at the moment.'

Though she couldn't be sure of that.

She was very pleased to find her parents were staying at the Windsor Hotel. Her father was well known at the Windsor from all his years of coming to Melbourne for wool sales, the Royal Show, the cricket Test matches.

'Watch out for the Americans,' said her mother, winking, as they started to get ready to leave. 'You'll be surrounded by them and they're real skirt-chasers. Even married women aren't safe.'

Dim noticed that a frown of serious anger crossed her father's face. He was the more old-fashioned of the two and didn't like his wife talking about his daughter as if she was an object of possible desire. Dim wanted him never to know that the night before Galt Sandforth, a man *his* age, had been with her. As indeed he had, three-quarters persuading her that the Australian major had been found and frightened off. That the affair could safely continue.

Dim had the strange feeling now that she was in some sort of alliance with Galt Sandforth, against her father the grower of fine wool. Against all the possible judges and dismissers of what she did.

Hearing nothing but reassurances from Galt, Dim began to prepare with some reviving excitement for the Brisbane move. In view of the relocation of Bataan and all the disorienting grief of the past few days, Dim thought there was one social call she should make. It was to old Captain Cahill at the Allied Officers' Club. She took the tram into town early in the evening. She knew Galt would come to South Yarra about ten, and she wanted to be back by then.

Old Cahill was delighted to see her too, admiring her lieutenant's pips, taking her hand in a fatherly way and dragging her into his office, where he propped the door closed with the Melbourne telephone book.

'It's been chaos, Dim,' he said. 'The new girl is hopeless. Barely able to read and write. She gets the reservations mixed up and she doesn't know how to deal with the business houses. Here.' He pulled out a bottle of sherry and grabbed two glasses. 'I'm happy for your success. It means that you are now entitled to dine here, my girl.'

'On my own?' she asked, smiling.

'Why not? Unless you have someone you would like to bring?'

'No. I don't have anyone. My husband is away training somewhere.'

Again there was a momentary pang at being a hypocrite.

'Why don't you dine tonight? You don't want to go home to your flat, do you, and have to cook some miserable little tea?'

'Thank you, captain. But I can't dine here. Not on a lieutenant's pay.'

'My dear, this is on the house.'

He showed her to a table, and all the orderlies she had known during her time here made a fuss of her. Some British naval officers asked her to join them at their table, but though she spoke freely with them, she fobbed them off either with stories about her husband or about it being her duty to dine alone, since she had to write a report on the standard of service and food.

Later in the evening, about the time she was having coffee – it was coffee not brewed but made up of essence and chicory, a concoction the Americans, Galt particularly, really abominated – some Yank officers arrived and began chatting to her. They were never like the outrageous officers of Hollywood films. They were always so courteous. There was an inevitable *frisson* of thinking how they would feel if they knew that she was a general's woman, the girlfriend of such a general too – Big Drum's right hand.

Dim was just about ready to leave when she was astonished to see Honor Runcie appear, escorted by an Australian Naval officer perhaps two or three years younger than she. She was wearing a black suit cut to show off her fine shoulder blades and neck.

She hadn't been seated long when she saw Dim. Dim could tell she was surprised to meet her here, but she did not try to dodge the issue. After a second's quavering, which was very like her normal way of coming to a realization anyhow, she waved and smiled at Dim. A few minutes later she excused herself from her companion and came over. She and Dim held each other and brushed their lips against each other's cheeks.

'Have you heard from Allan?' asked Honor.

'Just the normal letters.'

'I know. You get the normal guarantees of eternal fealty, but because they can't tell you where they are or what they're doing, there's no substance to it all.' She suddenly seemed very serious, defining this core problem of the letters of Special Reconnaissance men. 'Anyhow,' she said, 'I think it's very brave of you to come here on your own. This place is full of lonely men, Dim. I mean . . . ' She looked around in a second's confusion, again the very model of the pretty but fey Englishwoman. 'But then, that might be the very point. And I wouldn't blame you a bit. After all, I'm here with another man, and I'm not going to ask you to believe he's my cousin or my brother. He's certainly not my uncle. Look, I'm going to the ladies' sanctum up the hall in a few minutes. Why don't you join me there?'

And still quavering, but with a smile, she turned away and receded across the dining hall, murmuring to her companion and then steering onwards towards the sepulchral corridor where the lavatory could be found.

Dim made herself wait a minute before rising and following. The women's lavatory had been very dismal when Dim first went to work there. Captain Cahill had been content to have it that way – he was the sort of man who didn't understand why men would want to bring women to an officers' club instead of keeping them stashed away in some other comfortable location. Therefore he had been content to allot them the darker and more ancient convenience room. At Dim's insistence, he had been persuaded to put in a few mirrors, and had had the place painted a standard-issue navy grey which was at least better than the stained distemper colour it had been.

Honor was looking at herself in the mirror, doing nothing, just flatly regarding herself. No devices to keep her busy – no rouge, no lipstick. She didn't seem to go in for that kind of thing.

'I thought I'd be safe here,' said Honor, still looking in the mirror. 'Gordon himself considers this place a little *déclassé* and never comes here. He says it's for solicitors' clerks who've become officers by accident. A genuine snob, my husband.'

She turned to Dim. 'I can't get through all this like a good little wife, taking her little daughter for walks every afternoon and listening to the radio for good news every evening. I have to have the occasional company of a man, and you won't believe me perhaps, but it's because I miss *him*, and I require a distraction from that, of course. Does he miss me? In a sort of way, sentimentally. Men are such sentimental bastards. I'm something he can return to when the adventure's over. I'm the face of home every sailor, especially a sailor like him, has to have. But that's all there is to it.'

'So you're getting even?' Dim asked despite herself. Because there had been something of *getting even* in the start of her affair with Galt.

'Oh, I'm not saying *you* have to feel like this. If you don't, thank your lucky stars. I'm not proud of myself. I just want you to know where I stand. Because we're bound, Dim. Those two, our husbands, are so damned close. If you feel you must tell Gordon at some stage, then do so. I'd just advise against it, that's all. At least till he's back.'

'I'd never tell him,' said Dim. 'And I do understand.'

'Well, that's generous of you. A lot of faithful wives get very angry at the so-called *unfaithful*. I think sometimes there's an element of jealousy in it.'

Dim smiled. 'Well, that young fellow out there *does* look fairly handsome . . . '

Honor spoke unambiguously. 'He's seduceable.' But then she became serious. 'Of course the other thing to understand, just in case you ever have to speak about this to anyone, is that this isn't any grand *amour*. I never go out with them more than a few times. I go for three weeks at a time, dressmaking and cooking and doing all the appointed things. Then I break out.'

'How do you meet them?' asked Dim.

Honor laughed. 'Are you looking for tips, Dim?'

Dim felt a kind of flippancy overtake her. 'A girl never knows . . .'

'Well, it's tawdry, really. I get someone to mind my daughter, and I tart myself up and go to a hotel. From that point on I can leave it to the young heroes.'

They kissed again, with more feeling this time, and began to leave. Honor had become very sombre. 'Those two are not innocent, you know. They're both guilty of a sort of infidelity. I don't mean they're nancy boys. But you know what I mean. It's not that they're involved in the war. It's that they're *too* willingly involved. They want to be more involved than anyone else.'

Dim thought about this. She found it reverberated within her.

'I know what you mean,' she said. 'Look after yourself.'

'I do,' whispered Honor. 'In every way. You know, they have the most remarkable contraceptive devices these days. If you talk to the right doctor.'

Chapter 7

Bataan, Brisbane

ON A COLD Saturday night in July an exceptionally long passenger train, interspersed with freight cars, many of them carrying manned anti-aircraft guns, waited at Melbourne's Spencer Street railway station. Every doorway on every carriage was surrounded by contingents of US Military Police. On a flat car near the rear, military engineers were working on the mountings which held down Big Drum's huge black limousine.

Like all the other junior officers, Dim was required to arrive early. Her mood was a mixture of expectation and melancholy. Part of the melancholy was that she was not used to being in love with someone like Galt Sandforth and not ready to leave her home town for him. She could say she was leaving for duty's sake, but in fact she was travelling further than she ever had before, and she was doing it for her lover's sake. Her life had become unfamiliar to her, less manageable if more marvellous. She had found that even a simple thing like facing her parents had become dangerous.

She occupied her seat by a window in a carriage to the rear of the train for an hour and a half before the main party emerged through the ticket barrier and came tramping up the platform at a pace imposed on everyone by General Wraith. Big Drum was dressed a little more formally than Dim remembered him having been in the past. He wore a uniform jacket, not quite as elegant as Galton Sandforth's, a little more battle-worn. Big Drum managed to give everything he wore an *on-campaign* look, whereas Galt preferred to be natty.

On Big Drum's chest there were eight inches at least of campaign ribbons. He carried a cane and gloves, but the cane did not seem entirely a matter of jauntiness. He looked a little lame tonight. His throat had an old man's scrawniness. Yet even with all that taken into account, he still looked like a strong fellow. Under siege, yes. But resisting with determination.

On Big Drum's right side walked pretty Mrs Wraith in a fashionable hat and a burgundy overcoat. A little behind her, jogging to keep up but seeming happy to be there, was Little Drum, carrying the stuffed toy he had brought with him on his escape from the Philippines, his hand held by his Chinese nanny, Ling.

Two or three inches shorter and at Big Drum's left side strode General Sandforth, his medal ribbons not as expansive as Big Drum's but his jacket better cut, his fawn tie more carefully knotted, and on his right breast an order awarded to him by the Philippines government before the Japanese attacked.

Flanking Big Drum and his wife and Galt were all the others she knew from remote sightings at Bataan, or else from what Galt Sandforth told her. Harry Strudwick, the lanky chief of intelligence. The dour Methodist quartermaster-general, Russell Morgan. The surgeon Winton. Ernie Sasser, the engineering chief of staff who had the power to do telepathic tricks.

The Australian colonies had built their separate railroads without reference to each other, and the result was that the lines in the state of Victoria were some inches wider than the lines in New South Wales and Queensland. It meant, too, that at the border into New South Wales, in the dead of night, everything – including Big Drum's limousine – would have to be unloaded from this train on to another. But in Albury there would be sleeping cars, and everyone would be able to lie down.

Until then Dim shared her compartment with Bataan's chaplain, a sober Episcopalian minister with premature silver-grey hair; with a middle-aged woman whose job it was to distribute nurses around the hospitals of the Southwest Pacific zone; with an education officer who was really a professor of sociology at the University of Southern California (Dim overheard this and did not know what sociology was, only that it was something new and American); and with the officer in charge of catering.

The catering officer was a captain in his early thirties, very handsome, and he smiled frequently at Dim as if sharing with her a private knowledge no one else in the compartment had.

These Americans were pleasant company but they kept on wanting her to explain why the switchover at the border was necessary. Even when she had done so many times, the woman who administered the nurses kept saying, 'Yes, but I can't see why they had to let it happen in the first place!'

'It was a case of regional competition,' said Dim. 'It was because they didn't like the idea of each other. They wanted to stop farmers in one state shipping their goods into another.'

Again the catering officer smiled at her as if she'd been especially clever, and again the nursing administrator failed to see how anyone interested in efficient rail services could have let it happen. Even the aristocratic-looking chaplain got sick of her and said charitably, 'Every country has its own mysteries, major. They make sense in context.'

Dim felt grateful to the man and, as less than a practising Presbyterian, her regard for Episcopalians – or Anglicans as they were called in Australia – increased in bounds.

The train screamed through Maneering, which was blacked out lest the Japanese bomb it. It looked a small, cold town when seen from the window of the carriage whose own lights were hooded and turned down. The town seemed almost alien to Dim, as if she was seeing it for the first time through the eyes of these foreigners. A negligible little hamlet. A place you'd never want to settle in. As the train rounded a bend past Maneering station, she could see straight down the main street. Finnigan's Rural Stores, the stock and station agent, and next door to that the office of Mr Lewis, the country solicitor, Allan's father. After all his adventures, how would Allan settle down to working in that little shopfront legal office when the war was over? If the war was over. If he lived. If any of them lived. If the laws of Australia had any application in the post-war world.

There was a stop at the town of Wangaratta, and everyone got out to walk about the platform just for something to do. Walking and clapping her gloved hands, Dim watched boys too young and men too old for military service hauling stainless-steel canisters, filled with live coals, into each of the carriages. They called these *foot-warmers*. She remembered them from her girlhood travels to and from boarding school in Melbourne.

The Bataan catering officer who'd been in her compartment approached her. He was very mannerly.

'Ma'am, would you be offended if I said that you were a handsome woman?'

'Not at all. But I'm also a married woman.' Though when she said *married*, it was the musk of Galt Sandforth which came into her mind.

'Let me introduce myself. Milt Freeman, former food and wine manager at the St Regis, New York.'

She told him her name, doubting the wisdom of it.

'Perhaps we could take in a movie together once we get to Brisbane,' he suggested.

'No,' she said. 'No, I'm sorry. We can't take in a movie.' She was feeling a litte desperate and far from home. Even though she had just passed through her home-town, it had looked uninhabitable. 'We can't *take in* a movie or dinner or anything. I'm very sorry. I'm married.'

'To an Australian guy, I suppose.'

'Exactly,' said Dim.

'Not to this faggot, I hope,' said Milt Freeman. As his smile had had a cutting edge to it, so now did the way he spoke. She had offended his pride. He pushed an evening newspaper into her hands. 'You read that, honey. It'll make you glow with pride.'

Then it was time to board the train again. She went to her seat, avoiding Freeman's eyes. She shook out the newspaper he had given her. It was an early edition of the scandal sheet, *Truth*. It told how a major in Australian intelligence, Major Summers, had accosted a plain-clothes officer of the US Military Police in a public toilet in Fitzroy Gardens and had as an outcome been charged with homosexual soliciting. It said that the military censor had attempted to suppress this news, but *Truth* had felt every Australian had the right to know. The Australian Army, said *Truth* piously, didn't need men like Major Summers, and it wondered how he had risen to such a relatively high rank.

Dim looked up. Milt Freeman was staring at her, wearing his pretty-boy smirk. She turned her gaze away and pretended to sleep.

When at last at one in the morning the train reached Albury, they were allowed to cross the freezing platform and go to their sleeping berths. Australian Army privates carried their baggage for them. Looking for her sleeping compartment, she saw the administrator of nurses following her. Perhaps, Dim thought, she'll be my bunkmate. As long as she doesn't spend the whole time telling me how *primitive* everything is and asking me *why*.

But she found that she had a sleeping cabin, both the upper and lower bunk, to herself. Galt must have arranged this. Perhaps he intended to visit her.

She was safe from exposure now. But it had been done so savagely. She felt a little sorry for Summers. She felt astounded by the reach and deftness of the things Galt Sandforth did, proud and ashamed of them at the same time.

He woke her just before dawn. He was holding both his gloves in his left hand and carried in his right a cup of tea, which she took. He kissed where her neck joined her shoulder.

'I read about the major,' she said.

'Yes. You see, I told you I could handle it.'

She did not reply to that.

'You don't seem very happy about it.'

'It's very severe, Galt.'

'My dear, *they* try to be severe on me. Listen, Dim, I love you. I would never be ruthless with you. But military affairs are rarely all politeness. Do you think a man can stay where he is without taking tough initiatives?'

'I'd hoped he could,' said Dim. She smiled without any real joy.

'No moping,' said Galt.

She murmured, 'I still have to get used to being in love with someone like you.'

'Maybe if you'd met your great grandfather or some other of those menfolk who started your family here . . . you would have met my type then. Major Summers showed you no mercy, Dim. Yet you seem to want a soft landing for him.'

They lay together as the train scuttled through the outer suburbs of Sydney. She thought with real joy of what the nursing administrator would say if she could see this, she and Galt entwined. 'But *why*?'

Lieutenant Dim Lewis found herself quartered in a medium-sized bedroom on the third floor of Lennon's Hotel in Brisbane. Across the street from her window stood a park with palm trees and memorials to Brisbane boys who had fallen a quarter of a century past, in the Great War. There were swings and a large sandpit as well for children to play in, and one Saturday afternoon, when Dim was standing at the window, she saw Big Drum take Little Drum there and give him a ride on the swings, and build sand fortresses with him in the pit. Citizens of the city of Brisbane stood around laughing and applauding, and press photographers alerted by the General's zealous press officers got pictures for the newspapers of the free world.

Standing at the window, she looked at Big Drum and wondered if he knew about her. Had he asked Galt about her? What had Galt said? She understood and accepted that Galt would not yet be fully frank about her. She hoped nonetheless for the day he could be.

Big Drum and Mrs Wraith, together with Ling and the little boy, lived on the top floor of Lennon's. There, too, Galt had a small suite. Bataan headquarters themselves were located in yet another insurance building, this one two blocks from Lennon's.

By telegram and telephone, Dim ran her business of distributing motion pictures around the Southwest Pacific from a fairly small office in a rear corridor of the insurance building. She found transport – truck, rail, plane – to send comedians, tap-dancers, ventriloquists (Micky Mahon and Porter the Puppet), vocalists (Whispering Billy Day, Sheila MacNeish the Lilydale Nightingale, Phil Fish the Yodeller, Crooning Harry Whitmore, and others) to army camps throughout Queensland, especially to north Queensland, a thousand miles and more from Brisbane, where the climate was tough, the infantry training intense; where Big Drum's squadrons, the ones who bombed Rabaul, were located.

It was a strange life in some ways, for she had never been a show-business enthusiast. Occasionally she had to collect a so-called star from Archerfield airport and take him or her up into the Lamington Plateau in a jeep, where she would watch a performance in some dismal army camp. But most of her work was routine – she moved the entertainers around the map as someone else might move battalions, she assured their accommodation and their rations, and she wondered why she found it all so fulfilling.

And every evening at Lennon's Galt came to her, or else invited her to dinner in his quarters. The first time she dined alone with Galt, the catering officer, Milt Freeman, turned up along with the waiters and the dinner trolley to express the wish that the General found everything satisfactory. Dim took some pleasure in watching his astonishment. He clung to his composure only because, in his sort of business, he'd had long training in it.

When Galt was called to the phone before Freeman had left, the catering officer bowed to her and said, 'Ma'am, I hope you'll overlook anything in our earlier conversation which could have been interpreted as insolence or pushiness.'

She realized that he could have said worse things than that. He could have said, 'I see now what you mean by *married*.'

She noticed that instead of being frightened of that sort of moral judgement, as she would have been two months ago, she could sense her power over Captain Freeman. Half-delighted and half-frightened, she thought, 'I *am* getting like Galt. I'm not terrified if people think I'm a fornicator.'

She was beginning to relish, too, the knowledge she acquired in Galt's company and, sometimes, in his arms. She heard, for example, that the Japanese *were* actually crossing New Guinea from Buna to Port Moresby, by way of the Owen Stanley Range. There might have been thirty thousand of them, Harry Strudwick thought, and they were carrying with them all their equipment, even their cannon, up through those steamy, slimy passes. She heard that Big Drum tended to place the blame for the Japanese advance on the raw Australian militiamen who protected the trail over the mountains, the Kokoda Trail. 'It happens I think that's unfair,' Galt told her. 'But generals also blame the foot-soldiers, and there're bigger issues to argue.'

For example, Big Drum wanted to sack the Australian General Fairchild, for allowing the leap-frogging Japanese advance – one company coming forward through a defensive line made on narrow jungle tracks by another. Big Drum was thinking of sending General Billings, the Australian land forces commander, up there to sack Fairchild and to take over himself.

Even before General Billings knew what task he might soon be given, Dim had already heard. She was aware now why people such as Major Summers thought she might make a good source.

In lonelier hours in her office or her room, she understood that she was developing a taste for this sort of knowledge, and that it brought with it a primitive fear that the supply might be cut off.

She had become privy to the Big Plan too. Even now – she discovered – with things going so badly in New Guinea, Big Drum was receiving nearly daily overtures from Republican senators and congressmen, party and business leaders, to make himself available to be drafted as a Republican Presidential candidate in two years' time. Big Drum's major patron in the Republican machine was Senator Vandergrift, leader of the conservative wing of the GOP. Before Pearl Harbor, Vandergrift had been an isolationist – he had not wanted Americans to die in Europe's war. If Pearl Harbor hadn't happened, he would himself have made a popular candidate for the next Presidential elections in 1944. But anyone with an isolationist history was politically doomed these days; the Democrat President of the US would crucify them on the hustings. Vandergrift knew no one could crucify Big Drum though. He'd heard the cannon's roar.

Vandergrift and other Republicans were working to get repealed a War Department ruling forbidding military officers to stand for elections. This ruling, said Galt, was a Chaumont gang strategy to hamper Big Drum's Presidential ambitions.

'Vandergrift and the others – there's a powerful Congressional leader called Thornton Downes in there too – they keep commissioning polls in all the magazines – there's close to eighty per cent approval rating for Big Drum in the US. Vandergrift and Downes want to keep preparing the ground and then draft him at the Republican convention in mid-'44. You see, they don't want him to have to go through the indignity of politicking his way through the primaries. Imagine it: a Republican convention unable to choose between the political hacks like Fryer and Wagner, a tormented convention, and Vandergrift – who controls hundreds of delegates anyhow – rises and announces Big Drum is available. The General becomes the Republican candidate by acclamation! As it should be.'

The more Galt spoke, the more she understood the strange American political process and was excited by the oblique mechanisms by which Americans pursued their supposed democracy.

One night there was another guest for dinner in Galt's quarters. It was Brigadier-General Bryant Gibbs, whom Dim had met the very first night she'd dined with Galt. He seemed, here in Lennon's, less robust than he'd been in Melbourne. His skin was discoloured from the anti-malarial drugs he'd been taking. Big Drum had sent him off with an engineering officer to have a look at the track over the New Guinea mountains along which the Japanese were coming towards Port Moresby; on which the Australians were dying – in a thousand foul little tussles – in an attempt to stop them.

'I don't know, Galt,' said Bryant. 'If my boys and I are ordered up there, you know we'll do what we can. But the terrain is awful. Steep. One slope after another, all compounded of mud and slime. You just can't see anything either. The Aussies dig in, but the Japanese outflank them, using the jungle as a screen. Everything is rotting – the stink of decomposition is everywhere, Galt. And then there's chiggers, and leeches which go for a man's private parts. There are men dying of bayonet and bullet wounds, of snake bite and amoebic dysentery and cerebral malaria.'

'What are you telling us, Bryant?' Galt asked leniently.

'Look, Galt, you know I'm no Nervous Nelly. Big Drum sent me up there because he knew I'd give an honest answer, and my honest answer is that I wonder if troops of European descent can survive there.'

'That's an honest answer, Bryant,' Galt remarked, making a sour mouth.

'If in Big Drum's eyes that makes me unfit to command a brigade in battle, I'm damn sorry but I have to speak according to my conscience.'

Galt murmured reassurances. There was no way Big Drum would sack him for speaking his mind.

Dim felt a wild surge of hope. She wanted it to be true. She wanted Galt to be the sort of man to whom a friend could speak in confidence, she didn't want all Galt's conversations to be devices, part of some great but inhuman strategy. She was reassured to see the trust between these two men, their easy frankness. She knew Galt didn't have a reputation for such qualities, yet here they were. She knew better things about him than the world did.

Later though, when the Brigadier-General had gone, she avoided questioning Galt about it. The question itself would be a kind of insult.

Then, after they'd made love, he himself began to speak like a Gibbs, like a decent fellow with doubts. She kissed his forehead as he talked, but he seemed too troubled to notice.

'He's been shivering a lot lately, trembling.' He meant Big Drum. 'When he's faced with the maps and with Harry Strudwick's reports. You see, there's a glimmer of something now, but he doesn't quite know how to pursue it, or if the Chaumont gang will let him. It's nothing but bad news from New Guinea, but I keep assuring him New Guinea is hell for the Japanese too. We've got a funny attitude to the Japanese – we think they're superhuman, we're weakened by thinking that. Big Drum always advises us not to think like that – it'll make us feel powerless. But he thinks like that himself, in the privacy of his heart.

'And yet today he had a press conference for more than fifty journalists, Australians and our guys, and he announced to them he intended to hold Moresby at all costs. And he chewed his cigarette-holder and gestured and thrust his jaw out, and I found I believed him absolutely, even though I knew it was some kind of trick, and so did those journalists too. A real performance! He wasn't trembling any more, and he said the Japanese had dragged their line of communications taut behind them, like a great elastic strand, and soon it would either snap or recoil, jerking them backwards over the Owen Stanleys back to Buna again. And when he said that, not only did they all applaud. *I did.*

'Now here are men who have seen the Japanese attempt everything and succeed at most of it. They've seen them take Malaya and Singapore and the Philippines and the Dutch East Indies, all in a short season. Yet when Big Drum declares, *We'll defend Australia and New Guinea both*! they all believe him. And their cynical eyes fill with tears of gratitude. He's an astounding man, Dim. An astounding man.'

A Post Office telegram appeared on Dim's desk at the new version of Bataan in Brisbane: EXPECTED ARRIVAL BRISBANE THIS FRIDAY LONGING TO SEE YOU LOVE ALLAN.

He must have arrived in North Queensland by train and be making his way down that fifteen-hundred-mile coast, train by train. It was news which she knew had to come in the end, but it brought a strange remorse to her. She thought, this is why the Bible forbids adultery. It diminishes people. It brings on a squalid kind of stress.

Galt Sandforth, whom she thought of as a true spouse, would have to be told.

Galt had flown north to visit Marauder squadrons in north Queensland. She did not see him again therefore until the night before Allan had said he was arriving. The news seemed to make Galt thoughtful too.

'What will you do?' he asked.

'I don't know,' she admitted. 'I'll have to make a decision, take a line. You know. And stick to it.'

'Will you sleep with him?'

'If I did,' she said, 'nothing would happen.'

'Body would touch body,' he said. There was an unfeigned shudder. Seeing that, she felt a second's anger.

'I shouldn't say that, should I?' Galt admitted. 'When it comes down to it, I haven't offered to divorce Sandy. I don't know, Dim. I always foresee we'll lie together, Sandy and I, in some loamy Virginian hill. Spouse by spouse. Turning to dust and acid together. All to keep our children happy.'

Visibly he remembered that one of his children was vanished. But she guessed he was thinking of his daughter Sandy, the actress. She was the one whose opinion he was most frightened of.

Dim shook her head. 'That's the point, isn't it? I've got three choices. To take him in as if nothing had happened. To fob him off second by second. Or to ask him for a divorce.'

Galt Sandforth put the back of his hand against her cheek, letting it linger there. 'You can't divorce him, Dim. The story would get out. He'd tell his buddies. Journalists would get on to it. It would be used to hurt Big Drum. I wouldn't be forgiven. But more importantly, the tale would be used by American scandal sheets to separate Big Drum from his obvious future. You know, the Presidency.'

She thought about this. She had never wanted to influence history. All she had ever wanted to be until recently was a lawyer's or squatter's wife in north-eastern Victoria. She was being told, however, that her demeanour towards Allan could affect the American future.

'Will there ever be a time?' she asked.

'Yes, I know what you mean. Will there be a time when we can be together without compromise? I intend there will be. But what can I promise? We don't know whether we'll still have our heads in six months' time.' He shook his head. 'I don't like any of this. But I can't say do this with Allan, and don't do that. I'm not entitled. All I can say is, try to put him off. You've got grounds for that. You know . . . his impotence. Try to put him off, for God's sake. Or maybe more exactly, for mine.'

There was something in her which wished he would make a demand. *Don't see him! Send him packing! I'll have him sent on urgently to Melbourne, and you kiss him on his way*!

Galt took her in his arms. 'I'm sorry. You ought to be as two-faced as me. But obviously you can't be.'

This was the crisis. She doubted Galt. But meanwhile she went through the dutiful motions of a wife whose husband is coming back from the jungle.

She telephoned the Allied Officers' Club and made a dinner reservation, acting as if she was Captain Lewis's secretary; reticent about using her own name. She asked the front desk also whether the Club had rooms free, in case the captain was not able to find hotel accommodation.

'We can put him on the list, miss, but rooms are pretty scarce. Officers can get billeting at the army camp at Indooroopilly. Or I could put him on the list.'

She tried to imagine her chances, after a fairly good dinner at the officers' club, of getting him on to a train out to Indooroopilly, or trying to talk the Bataan motor pool into providing a car to take him out there. It just wasn't a believable image.

'No,' she said. 'Captain Lewis is having dinner in the dining room tomorrow night but I don't think I'll bother putting him down on the waiting list for a room. Thank you.'

The next day a further telegram arrived, giving a train arrival time. Dim *did* then call the motor pool and organize a vehicle, and was waiting at the barrier with a young driver in US private's uniform when Allan emerged from the train. It was quarter to six on a Friday night and you could tell as you saw him come towards you, with his atebrin-yellow, tanned eagerness, that he was delighted with himself and with this homecoming. He swept her up and kissed her – it wasn't a full kiss on the lips, but he was aware of the young American looking, and his bush sense of propriety held him back. It was so strange though. Because despite the perfunctory kiss, he held so avidly. She knew there was no point to his hunger though.

'My God, Dim!' he said, after the embrace. 'You've got a car? You've got more military pull than I have, my darling. I suppose that's what comes of living at Lennon's Hotel.'

When they were inside the car, Allan, whose hand was around her shoulders, leaned close to her face. 'The most wonderful things have happened, Dim. You wouldn't believe half of it. Can we get rid of this Yank?'

Dim felt a moment of panic, before she understood that he did not mean Galton Sandforth. He was nodding to the boy behind the steering wheel.

They walked into the front door of the Allied Officers' club, a former temperance hotel which had been taken over for the duration of the war. The head waiter in the dining room was an old English-butler type of man wearing World War I campaign ribbons and a white coat with sergeant's chevrons.

'Oh, Captain Lewis,' he said. 'The front desk wanted me to let you know that by happy chance there *does* happen to be a room for you here tonight.'

Allan was confused. 'Oh, I didn't ask for a . . . did I ask for a room, Dim? Or did someone ask for one for me?'

'It might be a different Captain Lewis,' Dim ventured.

'Captain Allan Lewis,' said the elderly head waiter.

'No, no,' Allan told the man. 'I shall be staying with my wife tonight. There must be some mix-up.'

'Well, sir,' said the head waiter, almost indulgently, but not exactly so, 'I'm sure there are a dozen gentlemen in this dining room tonight who will be very pleased to take the room.'

Allan and Dim were seated, and Allan ordered a bottle of claret and they had soup. Everything seemed normal, but Allan eyed his glass for a time and asked, 'What was that stuff about the room, Dim?' He looked directly at her. 'Did you order a room for me?'

She looked at her own glass and thought of lying. But there would never be such a chance as this again.

'I simply inquired, that was all. I didn't *book* a room, Allan. I just thought . . . well, it's obvious what I thought. That there'd be less pressure on you here. I didn't know whether . . . '

Allan grabbed her by the wrist and he smiled and his eyes were alight in his yellow-tanned face, a campaigner's face, the face of a man delivered.

'That's just it, Dim. You won't believe me. I wouldn't blame you for wanting me to take a separate room. But that's over. Honestly. It's over.'

And he smiled even more broadly, reassuringly, lovingly. From being bored and tremulous a little earlier, she now became actively afraid. Something had changed in him.

He leaned forward over the table, speaking in an intense whisper. 'I don't know how to tell you this, Dim. Because it involves something that will never happen again between us. I might as well say it. It involves a sort of *infidelity*.'

This word produced in her hope and dread at the same time. 'Really?' she asked.

'Listen. We've all been stuck somewhere – the group I'm with, I mean. In a particular place. Don't ask me where, because I told you too much last time. But I'm sure you can guess that it's somewhere in this region.'

'Well, I know it wasn't Norway,' said Dim, suppressing an urge to tell him that she knew exactly anyway.

'And unaccountably,' Allan went on, 'after we'd finished what we'd been sent there for, they kept us waiting around. Oh, we were quite safe. An occasional Japanese air raid. Actually two or three air raids a day. But it's amazing how you get used to that stuff. Honestly. I would never have thought . . . '

She could see once more that in his way he loved the war. Really *loved* it.

'We were just about the only troops in the whole area with time on our hands. We were totally dependent on parties the Yanks threw for entertainment, and there weren't too many of those.

'Well, one of the chaps I was with had a problem. On this last trip of ours, he'd suddenly developed piles. Really bad. Must have been a dietary thing, I don't know. But I mean, it was going to put the kibosh on him for future operations. One of the things about Special Reconnaissance, you've got to be medically perfect. I told you that before, didn't I. So he couldn't shake this problem . . . the chap I'm talking about couldn't. And, as I say, he had plenty of time to think about it.

'And then one of the smart Yanks who escorted us around everywhere, he pointed out there was an army psychologist up there in Port Moresby who was using hypnotism to help men who were bomb-happy, shell-shocked, you know. He told us that this psychologist didn't have to be told what was wrong with you. He apparently argued that if a patient tells a doctor what's wrong with him, all the doctor has to do is agree, and *that* doesn't take any cleverness to speak of. The psychologist found out from *you* what was wrong with you, but only after he'd put you under.'

Allan took a sip of wine but swallowed it quickly, wanting to continue the tale.

'So the fellow I was with, the one with piles, must have taken all this palaver in. Because one night when we were drinking, he called the Yank officer who looked after us over to our tent and demanded that he take him down to the hospital area to see the hypnotist he'd talked about. We all went along in the truck for the ride. Past the warehouses . . . they were burning from Japanese incendiaries. And we waited outside the doctor's hut as the operator took our friend inside, and it was all a great laughing matter! But after two hours or more, our friend came out, very groggy – he'd been drinking in any case – and very sleepy, and asked us to take him home.

'Now the curious thing is – and it might be the power of suggestion, I don't know – that his problem began to disappear within the next day or so. I've never seen a man happier. I mean, he considered his military career had been saved. And I began to think . . . well, what's to lose. You know my big fear with actually *telling* a doctor, you know, and being self-conscious about it.'

'So one night, with a few stiff drinks, I got our friend the Yank officer to one side and asked him to take *me* down to the hypnotist. Our escort said, OK, we could go down, but not in a crowd. The psychologist hadn't liked that aspect of our last visit. I didn't want to go in a crowd, anyhow.'

Allan had begun to sweat now, as if a fever was coming up to the surface of his skin. He had lowered his eyes as well, so that it was hard to hear him. In that posture he looked very handsome, very boyish, very forgivable.

'Of course we didn't know if the man would be too busy or tired to deal with me. He wasn't. He was smoking a pipe and writing reports by the light of a hurricane lamp. A little man, about forty years of age. I really don't have a clear idea of what happened, Dim. The man looked in my eyes. That was all. No stage props; not like in the pictures.

'When he brought me round, he said casually, you ought to go to one of the clean native girls.'

Allan's face had gone a strange boyish pink now. 'I had to

see, Dim. I was sure the curse had lifted. So I did it. I'm sorry, Dim. But not entirely. Nothing like that will ever happen again. Between now and the grave. But a man can get desperate . . . '

He looked up at her now. She could see his lips trembling. There was a great weariness in her. What a fantastical tale! What a ridiculous one. He'd gone mad up there, that was obvious. Some parasite was boring into his brain.

There was the other question of what her reaction ought to be. Did she pretend to be offended? Should she carry on as a wife was supposed to? A girl from north-eastern Victoria ought at least be shocked when her husband sleeps with a native woman. She didn't want to be forgiving to a suspicious degree.

Blessedly, tears came to her eyes. He put his hand on her wrist.

'She didn't have anything, Dim. I had myself checked by the doctors. It meant nothing to me, and yet it liberated us for a proper life together. Please, Dim. Darling.'

Dim was nonetheless able to use up some time being equivocal about her husband having slept with a New Guinean native. And though she *was* ambivalent, she found it wasn't out of jealousy. She was trying to find, behind Allan's new and overpowering reason for spending the night with her as his wife, a means she could use to prevent him.

Yet that was so unfair to him. He didn't *have* any sense of guilt, anyhow, so it wasn't much use pretending that he ought to. In the end, in a daze, she let him take her back to Lennon's Hotel and her room. And it was apparent that *something* had happened in New Guinea, because he made love quite competently, and took such pleasure in the fact that he was successful.

At the end she felt nothing but old-fashioned sexual shame. She made a quite routine trip to the bathroom at the end of the hall and wept for a time in there. She had not *given* much indication that she enjoyed it, and that was shocking. She had *not* enjoyed it anyhow, and that was shameful too. She could not even pretend to rejoice with Allan.

And then she was further ashamed because she knew now that even if Allan had been a potent husband from the start, she would still have been easily seduced by General Sandforth. For the first time in her life, she understood certain mysterious cases where the seemingly happy wives of successful pastoralists in north-east Victoria had shut themselves in bathrooms, in the midst of all their plenty, and cut their wrists or swallowed poison.

She delayed in this cramped room at the end of the corridor as long as she could, sitting on the rim of the bath whose use she shared with various middle-grade American officers. When she returned to her room at last, Allan was asleep, a serene look on his face. His breath washed in and out of him quite gently, as if he were a long-distance runner operating well within the boundaries of his endurance. She wanted to wake him and say, 'For Christ's sake, Allan! Don't you know that on top of the heap in which you struggle, in which you do brave things in the tropics, the generals shuffle and manoeuvre and follow strategies you can't even guess at?'

She put herself into the bed beside him, being careful not to touch him in any way. She went gratefully into a miserable sleep, one of those sleeps you'd be happy not to wake from.

When she woke up, Allan was standing by the window, looking down at the children's playground across the street and drinking tea. He wore a plaid dressing gown, this descendant of Scottish warriors. He turned to her and smiled. But there was pain in the smile. He came and sat on the bed. *Oh, God, no!* she thought. *Not again.*

He held up a telegram in front of his face. 'It's awful. I have to go down to Melbourne urgently.'

She felt such a surge of gratitude to Galt. She had no doubt he had arranged this.

'But don't fret about it, Dim. I think it might be the thing I've be waiting for all my life. I don't know. I can't say much. But I think it is. And after that we'll be together for good.'

At least she was able to hold him and weep, and he thought her tears were uncomplicated loss. Curiously though – as she noticed – he made no overtures for a last, quick love-making. She was grateful for that, too, but it made her wonder if he was as cured as he thought.

It was no wonder he believed the Allied cause and destiny waited upon his departure for the airfield! There was a special car to take him to Archerfield. As the vehicle pulled out, Allan waving from the back seat, it occurred to Dim as it rarely had before that she really might never see him again.

The man in Sandforth's office wore a flying jacket just like the one Big Drum always wore. His crumpled Irish face, the face of a bus driver or a railroad porter, was blotched unevenly with red. He was obviously a man who by nature would have kicked doors in and thumped tables, but he had that under control now: that was the way he had risen from being a corporal-air observer in the US Army Flying Corps fighting Pancho Villa in Mexico's Chihuahua province in 1915 to become a pilot in France in World War I, and finally a general commanding an air army, the Fifth. He was newly arrived at Bataan to replace the hapless Pendle.

'General Sandforth,' he began, not waiting to be asked to sit down, 'today I tried to put twenty B-17s over Rabaul in a single attack. I found I had only seventeen B-17s available, however. Five others had been sent off earlier on your order to bomb Buna on the north New Guinea coast.'

Galt tried to present a judicious face, swallowed slowly, and dug in behind the mask. It was an old trick, a trick of breeding. Never be quick to respond. Whereas this man – Major-General Buck Clancy – had had to learn all his tricks since boyhood, had not had them instilled in him, had needed to overcome a brawling, working-class tradition.

'I routinely send five bombers to attack Buna,' Galt explained, as if it were a matter open to any of his colleagues' reasonable inquiry.

If only this Irish NCO, this tenuously reformed bar-room brawler, could yield to his deepest instincts and begin throwing punches and breaking things! Self-betrayed, he would then be able to be neatly slotted back in under Galt's general command. Waiting for it to happen, Sandforth felt what he'd been experiencing all morning, a relentless throb of loss and jealousy over Allan and Dim Lewis, and an equally relentless fear that something reckless had happened there, that out of moral probity Dim had confessed to her husband. Or worse, that they'd had a reconciliation.

And there was a pulse of guilt too, of a kind Galt had never felt in his years with Teresa Chung. It was guilt for both those children, the Lewises, more than twenty years younger than he was. If this gnarled, stocky Irish pirate had known any of this, he would be able to use it to advantage. But Galt Sandforth understood that his own gift was not to let any of it show at all on the Sandforth family mask.

'General Pendle never had any complaints,' Galt Sandforth murmured smoothly. 'I regularly scheduled raids when he was in command. In fact, he understood the overall operational necessity of them.'

Pendle had been the one who had messed up Big Drum's air transportation and who had never been forgiven for it.

Sadly, Galt noticed, Clancy was keeping cool too – he must have observed his superiors studiously and practised their manners. 'Let me tell you something,' Buck Clancy said, 'I consider Pendle had no choice about that. There'd been a lot of nasty things whispered to senior people about my poor friend Pendle, who's a good man but found himself in an intolerable fix. No one has started whispering to anyone about me yet, and so I won't put up with such a fix. Bare fact is, Galt, you must desist from doing any more operational scheduling for me.'

Sandforth really resented that *Galt*. He collected himself and stroked his jaw sagely. 'Look, General Clancy, I'm sure you're very competent. But I have overall administrative *and* operational control.'

'Based,' cried Clancy, 'on what your various sections tell you. Now General Strudwick's intelligence section tells us that the Japanese are too well dug in at Buna for bombing raids to do much good. This information surely indicates that our air effort should be against large convoys on their way from Rabaul, or on Rabaul itself, where there are all those ships in the harbour and plentiful other military targets as well.'

'General Strudwick's intelligence,' Galt remarked, 'though as good as anyone else's, has not always been of a high enough calibre to justify slavish belief.'

Clancy advanced, uniformly red in the face now. Galt's hopes increased. A yeller, a screamer, a puncher always ended up losing influence, on any staff. Maybe Clancy would try to land a punch, which would be a superb result for Galt. But at least there should be a lot of good shouting and furniture-pounding!

Unhappily, all Clancy did was grab a sheet of paper from the front of the desk, and a pencil out of Galt's pencil cup. Then he made one dot on the paper.

'That damn dot represents what you know about the deployment of air power. The rest of the sheet represents what I know about it. Do you still want to schedule missions? For a start, we need to keep hitting the airfields in Rabaul as often as we can with as many planes as we have. Because that's where the bombing raids on our positions in Moresby are coming from. In Buna they're just dug in. To hell with Buna!'

Galt said, 'Nothing is proved by a dot on a paper. It's just a parable, and I'm a modern soldier. Unlike you Irish, I don't talk in parables. You seem to forget we're fighting a land war, too. Buna is my enemy's main base on the north coast of New Guinea.'

Galt noticed Clancy hadn't liked that slur on his Irish-Catholic origins. He stood up. He tossed the sheet of paper across the desk in Galt's direction. Galt let it flutter to the ground. 'Look, I'm not going to argue about this thing, about who's supposed to be running the goddamn air force. Let's go in and ask Big Drum what he thinks about this. About who should be issuing operational orders to the Fifth Air Force.'

This offer was alarming. A Big Drum showdown! Galt thought about it. He knew that he could not win such a confrontation. During Pendle's declining days, and after Pendle was sacked, Big Drum had been happy to have Galt scheduling operations. But there wasn't any way that he was going to say that his new air chief, Clancy, shouldn't have control of the air force. Big Drum would be forced to speak in the abstract – in the best of circumstances an air chief *should* have absolute control of the air force. The normal forms wouldn't let him say anything else. And

Clancy would then seize this abstract statement to take absolute control, as he now intended to.

'You have any doubts the validity of the intelligence we get,' Clancy said, sniffing victory, 'and you just share them with me, Galt. You'll find me receptive. But for the moment, until someone pours poison about me into Big Drum's ear, I expect to receive no more surprises. No operational orders coming from your desk and fed into my machinery.'

This man, Galt could see, was tough-minded, and therefore you could almost like him. 'Just the same,' said Galt, 'I reserve the right to make operational recommendations and orders to you. In strategic overall tactical terms, I mean. I'm quite happy to leave the daily operations to you. I've put in long enough hours here as it is.'

Clancy's squashed, pug face again showed a slight hint of knowing the battle was won. 'Yes, Galt, I don't think any creature should work harder than they need to.'

A silence grew. Galt Sandforth considered his own hands. 'Listen, Clancy, for the time being, please don't call me Galt. You don't know me well enough, and I outrank you. If you expect me to operate by the strict rules, then you can too. Call me General.'

'As you like, General,' said Clancy, beaming in a middle version of impudence.

'Perhaps we could review all this in a month or so.'

'I would be happy to do that,' said Clancy.

Big Drum called him *Buck* and *Pirate*. You could see why.

Her eyes looked bruised when he got there that night. He caressed her but she seemed wooden, and at last they sat down facing each other.

'Are you going to ask me how Allan's visit was?' she asked.

He shook his head. 'I don't want to know. I lack a right.'

'Oh yes. And too painful, eh? Too painful? How do you think it was for me?'

'I arranged for him to move on as soon as I could,' said Galt. 'But I couldn't deprive him of a last chance to see his wife. That would have been criminal.'

'Oh, it's all criminal, cobber!' she said, crossing her legs and staring furiously into the middle distance.

'Look, Dim! He's your *husband*.'

'No. You're my only husband. As you know.'

This was very painful, Galt found to his surprise. And very exciting. After a lifetime of relationships-of-convenience, to be declared the transcendent lover. 'Dim, I hate it too. The way we're hostages to Big Drum's political ambitions.'

'And to yours, for Jesus' sake. To yours as well.'

He felt an old man's sigh escaping from him. The sound of it frightened him. 'We think the world is bright and broad. But in fact it's a series of tunnels in the air.'

He remembered the tunnel of Malinta in the Philippines, being crowded in there with the rest of the staff, with Filipino politicians, with the radio operators, the wounded, the doctors and nurses; with Mrs Wraith and Corporal Little Drum.

He was reminded, too, of a file he'd seen that very afternoon. The idea behind the file had first come to Galt's desk some months ago, from a joint British-Australian-American operational planning body attached to Special Reconnaissance and located in Melbourne. The Japanese could be convinced that Big Drum intended merely to hold them in New Guinea and strike elsewhere, further to the west. Specifically, that he intended to strike through Timor, and so fight his war up the long chain of the Dutch East Indies. It was a wonderful suggestion – to convince the Japanese War Ministry to divert Japanese troops away from New Guinea, concentrate them in Timor, the tail end of the Indonesian chain. From these islands the Japanese fleet and air force got most of its oil. Timor was credible as a point of attack.

But there were aspects of the plan which had shocked even Galton Sandforth, who thought he was a hardened military man. To convince the Japanese that Timor was the planned Step 1, it would be necessary to send Australian and British operatives in with instructions to make contact with the Timorese Resistance. The operatives' orders would be to seek out, with the help of these anti-Japanese rebels, suitable beaches for amphibious landings. They would also plot the location of Japanese depots and airstrips, details of all of which they were to radio back to Australia.

These men themselves would be operating under the intense danger of betrayal and ambush, and it would be necessary for them to believe that their work was a prelude to a definite US and Australian invasion. Inevitably, they would be captured by the Japanese. There were ways to *ensure* that they were captured. The news could be leaked to a known Timorese double agent who supplied information to the Japanese. Or the men could be ordered to transmit their messages from Timor in a code the Japanese had already cracked. By the references the operatives would make in their radio transmissions, it would be possible for the Japanese to close in on where they were. The operatives would, of course, be brave men and would put up a resistance under torture, and that would convince the Japanese all the more that what they ultimately confessed to was a true indicator of things to come. Then they would be turned and begin transmitting mis-information on the enemy's behalf, to Australia, using the transmission procedures and codes only they would know and so evincing responses from Melbourne. The responses would further confirm the idea that Timor was high on the Allied agenda.

Sandforth had recognized this from the start as a typical planner's brain-wave, the sort of thing men who haven't been in the field or dealt locally with ordinary soldiers tended to produce without being at all ashamed. In this case at least two good, arduously trained, confident men who trusted their superiors would be thrown away, tortured, perhaps killed, at best committed to imprisonment for the duration of the war, which even if the Allies won it, could go on for ten years or more. And afterwards, even if they lived, they would come home with the belief they had cracked, and betrayed themselves and their brothers in arms. It was an inhuman proposal, but like a lot of inhuman proposals, it would work very well on a practical level.

That very day a more advanced version of the plan had arrived on his desk, sent by the group in Melbourne; a more refined stage of the proposal. With General Wraith's approval, training of personnel for the operation should begin at once, and the director of Special Reconnaissance, who would himself not be let into the secret, had been asked to set aside a party of six officers as the group from which the final two or perhaps three would be taken.

The names included that of Allan Lewis, as well as that of a British commander called Gordon Runcie, of whom Galt had heard through Dim's anecdote about the commander's domestic knife-throwing. So two of the men on the list were not faceless men to Galton Sandforth, and he had delayed all day passing the documents on to Big Drum. He had the primitive fear, which he despised but which nonetheless had him by the throat, that if he signed such a document, with those names on it, and passed it through to Big Drum for final approval, that the names of those two men would somehow stay in his body like a cancer. They would put poison between himself and Dim.

And yet there was no military reason why he should not sign the thing. Apart from the fact that it was murder, in the way that most war was murder. The committee's original plan, the one submitted in raw form some months past, had in any case been approved by the brigadier in charge of Galt's planning section, who had passed it on to Galt expecting him to sign it as a matter of course, which he'd done. And then Big Drum had signed it, meaning that the guilt – if there was to be guilt – was Big Drum's. And in this new version, with the names attached, the chain would be the same, and the planning brigadier would be justifiably mystified, if not annoyed, if Galt Sandforth did not sign without demur.

Not that he'd create too much of a fuss, Galt had to admit. For he'd know from experience that Galt Sandforth didn't approve of displays of temperament and anger amongst his own staff.

There was another interesting thing about these planning documents. If they were not signed and filed and done with soon, it was quite possible that some young officer who would have to frame the order telling the Melbourne committee the plan wasn't going to go ahead, might see the file and make the connection between the Captain Allan Lewis of the plan and the Lieutenant Dimity Lewis who seemed frequently to dine with General Sandforth.

Altogether, this had been one of the worst days, with Clancy standing on the letter of the law, these doubts and all this anguish about Dim, and all afternoon the murderous file about the island of Timor on his desk unsigned!

He said to Dim, 'You mentioned my political ambition. It's certainly there, Dim. It's certainly alive. I suppose I even run the staff like some political boss running things. I draw exactly the sort of hate, and all the scared loyalty, which is the best a political boss can hope for in his juniors. After running Bataan, running the US Department of Defense would be a cinch. But none of that matters much really.

'I was just thinking this afternoon, for instance, how long this war might go on – that is, if we get on top in the first place. At some stage Big Drum will move us all much closer to the front, and anything can happen there, even to a Chief of Staff. You know the term *stray shell*! Well, believe me, there are enough of those in battle zones to make every individual's survival a matter of chance.'

He noticed that concern had entered her face. She had forgotten her misery. Her love for him was miraculous, he thought.

'Now I'm not asking you to let me off this hook because I might be shot,' he said quickly. 'We both know it's more likely that Allan will be shot. What I'm saying is that I have a different view of things now. That first night I came to your flat in Melbourne you must have thought I was an absolute sonofabitch. I stood there and told you that I had the sort of life which could not afford to permit any little tremble of scandal. Somehow or another, you didn't tell me to clear out. What do the Australian troops say? To *piss off*! And you didn't do that. You forgave me that crassness of mine.

'You know what I've been thinking perhaps a dozen times a day ever since Galt Junior was lost? I've been thinking that Galt will never get to know what it's like to be an old General in love with a young woman. He'll never know the fear, he'll never know the excitement, he'll never know the unutterable joy. Beside that, a political ambition isn't worth two cents.'

'It's worth more than that,' she said. 'It's worth a great deal.'

He waved that aside. 'As I said earlier, I can't tell Big Drum

I think this way. So what this long speech comes down to is, Dim, I want you to marry me, and I'll try to stay spry and not end up in a wheelchair, because beautiful women can waste their years pushing the wheelchairs of older men.

'The only thing is, if you *are* willing to marry me, we must wait until the war turns, until Big Drum has so many victories to his name that his nomination by the Republicans is a mere formality. Point is, if you accept me, will you let me attend to my duty to Big Drum first?'

Dim felt all the tense cords in her stomach loosen and release. This astounded her. That he was as far in love as she was. She was humbled by him, by his unexpected decency and humility. 'Of course,' she said. 'Of course. My God, Galt, I never meant to . . . '

He held his hand up. 'You haven't forced the pace. You've been wonderful, Dim. Your husband's time here . . . of course it would upset you.'

'But your wife, Galt.'

'Oh, my wife,' he admitted. 'I swear to you, Dim, on whatever we hold sacred, including if you like ultimate victory and Big Drum for President, that my wife won't really miss me. It will be a social discomfort, not a discomfort of the heart. She has her horses. That's what counts with her. That's the simple truth, and you should understand it, Dim.

'There's one thing though. I mentioned the chance we might move Bataan on to another place later. The fact is, Big Drum wants to move us further along again, up to Port Moresby within two or three weeks. It had to happen once your boys started pushing the Japs back over the mountains. Although I'm not supposed to say that in front of Big Drum, that it was the Aussies' doing. It was *Allied troops*, and it was Big Drum's brilliance, and the fact that the Japanese supply line ran thin. Anyhow, it'll be a temporary separation again. But I'll get you up there as soon as I can.'

'And I'll come,' she said.

'You'll be needed in any case, Dim. Lewis South Seas Productions!'

She stood up and went to his window. It looked out on the

same park as hers did. 'Galt, what does Big Drum think about us?'

'He probably knows something. He doesn't know how things are between us though. If he did, he would take me aside for paternal talks. Dim, he probably thinks it's like a long-running friendship I had with a woman in the Philippines.'

'What woman?' asked Dim. She was simultaneously frowning and smiling.

He told her.

The next morning Galt, as his first act of the day, signed his approval to operational plan DX5372/D39/DSR.

Then he sent it on routinely to Big Drum for signature.

PART TWO

Tropical

Chapter 8

The Entertainment Officer

GENERAL BUCK CLANCY, Big Drum's new air force chief, had fitted out a C-47 especially for Big Drum. Transport planes like this were still scarce, but Clancy wasn't going to make the mistake Pendle had and fail to provide Big Drum with the type of well-appointed plane which was his due. On this one there were upholstered banquettes, a sleeping compartment for Big Drum, and another for Galt Sandforth or any officer to whom he would permit its use. There was a kitchen as well, and a drinks steward, though no officer was foolish enough to drink a lot near Big Drum.

On the flight from Townsville in North Queensland to Port Moresby in Papua-New Guinea, Big Drum slept for more than three hours, during which time all the staff, better rested than he, drank modest amounts of bourbon and became quite fraternal. This was a common enough phenomenon, Galt knew. They were going closer to the enemy. Most of them had known shelling and bombing on Corregidor, and they were going back to it again, going back to more. They would hear bombs fall. You could tell that some of them were saying to themselves, 'We're too old for this.' Even though *this* was all they had been born and trained for. They wondered how it would all be, and each man felt the need for warmth of spirit. A tentative generosity operated between them, Harry Strudwick even asking Galt to describe an incident in 1939. At the end of a July 4th ball in Manila, some young officers had for some reason never fully explained and still a mystery to Galt put a barely domesticated boar into Galt's bedroom at the Hotel Manila before he came home. Only a quick diagonal dash to the bathroom had enabled Galt and his mistress, Teresa Chung, to save themselves. They were there till dawn, locked in, until military police became aware of Galt's predicament, entered the room, shot the boar which bled copiously on the carpet, and liberated the couple from the bathroom – all the while keeping studiously sober faces.

Inevitably, as people during the flight became more spacious, General Ernie Sasser the part-Cherokee engineer had to play his trick again, the one he'd played that night at Mrs Wraith's table, planting a name in her head by telepathy.

'Why don't we give you a real challenge, Ernie?' said the medical chief of staff, Sam Winton. 'Who would you say were the two most tough-minded and least suggestible sonsofbitches on the staff?'

'Jesus,' said Ernie. 'I don't now. Harry here? What about our new friend, General Clancy?' He smiled slyly. 'And then of course, there's Galt.'

Galt chose to laugh with the rest. A chorus of voices confirmed Galt was the popular choice. He was touched, in a way, because there was a certain affection and amusement in the way they nominated him.

Even so, he was surprised Clancy had not won the competition. In the weeks past he had by force of character emerged as the star of the staff. Big Drum had been very worried these past weeks that now the three infantry divisions of his were ready for New Guinea, many of them would be lost in Japanese submarine attacks on their ships. Clancy had argued for transporting them by air. Nothing as big as this had been tried by air before, but within the past few weeks the staff had got used to hearing figures of great quantities of men airborne to New Guinea; of earth-moving equipment, dismantled in Australia, taken on board and reassembled in New Guinea; and even six-ton trucks, their chassis separated into two sections with welding torches, travelling by C-47 and being united again by welding torch in Moresby.

'I'm just glad they didn't have to cut me into pieces to get me up there,' said the hulking Quartermaster-General Russell Morgan, a rare witticism from a churchwarden of a man.

'Do you think you're able to resist me mentally?' Ernie asked Galt.

'I don't think I have a chance,' said Galt. But secretly he couldn't wait to take Ernie on and win.

Even Ernie seemed to be able to sense this determination. 'Mind you, it has to be someone world-famous you think of and write down, Galt. Anyone world-famous. Excluding Big Drum, of course.'

The normal things were done: two sheets of paper were produced from people's notebooks. Ernie wrote a name on a sheet and passed it to the officer sitting beside him. A blank sheet and a pencil remained in front of Galt. 'Let your mind go blank,' Ernie ordered Galt. But Galt was determined to resist.

'Write a name whenever you're ready,' Ernie asked him.

Galt deliberately chose an unexpected name, not an American one. It was the name of Molotov, Stalin's Foreign Minister. He waited a little longer, then wrote the name and passed it across to Winton. At Ernie's order, Winton unfolded the sheet of paper and read the name: 'Molotov.'

Ernie asked the officer beside him to unfold his own sheet and state what was on it. 'This says Molotov too,' read the officer.

There was predictable applause and no one could argue Ernie hadn't earned it. Galt felt a flush of well-concealed anger. He had been bred to react in that way, and simultaneously to hide it.

'For God's sake, Ernie, how do you do that?' he asked, in a manner which must have seemed bewildered, as it brought on more laughter and more applause.

Galt was thinking how, if Ernie could get into *his* mind for flippant reasons, maybe he could get into Big Drum's for serious ones. But that had never happened. Either it was beyond Ernie's powers, or else Ernie refrained for moral reasons. Or maybe Big Drum's mind was impervious.

Ernie seemed content anyhow to sustain his skill on a party-trick level. Might it always be so.

The new version of Bataan, Big Drum's headquarters, lay above the lagoon-like harbour of Port Moresby. It was called the 'Administration villa' and had been the house of a series of Australian civilian administrators of Papua-New Guinea. Predictably, it looked fairly Somerset Maughamish, with wide verandahs, large windows, high ceilings across which large geckos made their way, upside down, secured by their suction paws.

Only three staff officers shared the house with Big Drum and his servants. One was Clancy, the new favourite, the man whose visions of moving armies by air had so excited Big Drum; the second was Harry, to whom Big Drum still showed loyalty based on their long association in the Philippines; and the third was Galt. Other officers were in Quonset huts scattered around the luxuriant gardens.

Big Drum liked the verandah. He began to hold his conferences there, pacing with the entire staff and playing as always with his cigarette holder. During the first such conference, Galt's second afternoon in Moresby, Mitsubishi bombers came raging down out of the sky in which clouds were massing already for the afternoon downpour. Scarlet-saronged native policemen, who had charge, along with the US MPs, of Big Drum's safety, all had the luxury of being allowed to run for slit trenches in the garden. But Big Drum simply ignored the bombers, as he had done on Corregidor.

At that almost forgotten yet intimately remembered sound of bombs and diving aircraft, Galt felt that peculiar, bitter dryness of the mouth. Bombs began to land and explode in the Australian compound further down towards the harbour, the headquarters from which the Australian General Billings was running the land counter-attack for Big Drum. The Japanese obviously had the Australian headquarters location pinpointed, but Billings had surrounded it with batteries of anti-aircraft guns, and one of the bombers exploded in mid-air a mile away with an impact Galt could feel in his spine. Galt did not think of bombs themselves at that second. He thought of the young men in the plane, blown to burned fragments, who would never know anything now and had probably died without finding their equivalent of Dim Lewis.

Big Drum talked on through the raid, pointing to various officers as he strode along, appointing tasks.

Amidst the shocking detonations of bombs, Harry reported how his intelligence from hidden Australian coast watchers and from reconnaissance planes indicated that Buna, when the Australians and Americans got over the mountains and down to it, would be lightly defended. 'I think General Adachi,' said Harry, 'understands now that even the Buna coast is not a feasible position for him. That he's stretched the line of supply too thin.'

How was it that Big Drum kept him on, when he'd made this sort of pronouncement so often, even the day after Pearl Harbor, when the Japanese had come ashore on the beaches of northern Luzon? 'They can't take Manila,' Harry had promised, and had given credible reasons about lines of communication. It was surprising how such an unjolly, almost stage-Germanic man as Harry could be so consistently and murderously optimistic. And so wrong.

Galt feared that the reason Big Drum kept Harry on, besides his mysterious affection for the man, was a guilty secret they shared from Philippine days. They both had participated in what Washington – if it knew about it – would consider a grave impropriety. Maybe Big Drum understood that if he had Harry recalled to Washington, Harry might stumble around the capital, giving away embittered hints.

So Harry kept on pushing his idea that the Japanese General Adachi would pull out his troops from Buna, move them further up the north coast of New Guinea, and leave only a screen for the Americans and Australians to push through. There were probably people in the staff who agreed with him, but by the extra bunching of Clancy's pug-Irish face, it was obvious that Clancy himself was not one of them.

Meanwhile Galt noticed gratefully that the bulk of the Japanese bombing raid seemed aimed at the warehouses and at destroyers and transports in the harbour.

He hated all that stuff, the explosions and the peril. He could *stand* it, sure, unlike perhaps ten per cent of men at any time under bombardment, who went to jelly or grew irrational, sometimes for the rest of their lives. He could stand it because he came from that sort of family, because he'd inherited what he supposed was called a cool head. Or at least he'd been told that since childhood, so perhaps he had taken it so much for granted it had become the truth. But out of his cool head he abominated the hideous blasts, the inhuman size of the detonations.

He blinked at a large explosion closer to the Administration vi lla, so vast a bang that it deafened him for a time. And yet Big Drum went on talking. Galt could see him prodding in the direction of Ernie's chest with his cigarette holder, asking him something – Ernie was working very close with Clancy these days – and getting an answer back.

Do I want Dim to be here, surrounded by these explosions? Galt asked himself. Isn't it just selfish to want her company in a place like this?

It turned out that some of Clancy's P-38 fighters, which had been circling out over the ocean, took up the pursuit of the Japanese aircraft as they withdrew and brought down six of them for no losses. When Galt, in his office in the bungalow, read this, it seemed like a hopeful omen to him. At the end of a long telephone conversation with Captain Duncan, he mentioned the entertainment officer again, how she should be moved up from Brisbane at all reasonable speed.

With her orders in the breast pocket of her lightweight, tropical uniform, Dim took off for Port Moresby from quaint, stilt-housed and tropical Townsville on the Australian mainland. The journey fascinated her from the very point of take-off. North of Townsville it was all green-blue coral shoals and small islands, apparently vacant. Growing up in Victoria, she had had no idea her nation held these riches. And all this space was ripe for the picking, you would have thought. Although she supposed that whoever picked these particular islands would soon be blasted by General Clancy's growing Fifth Air Force.

Her luggage allowance was considered generous by the standards of wartime. It consisted of a suitcase – what they used to call 'a port' at boarding school – and a kitbag. She had brought along light cotton dresses to wear during dinners with Galt, and even one off-the-shoulder black silk number which her father had bought her for a cocktail party at Government House, Melbourne, two years back, in the pre-life, before she knew Galt.

Seated sideways on a primitive bench in the belly of an unadorned C-47, she was flying north with Australian and American officers and a party of journalists. She could see the wonders below her only by twisting in her seat and crooking her left leg up on the canvas-covered bench along which everyone sat. Yet that was the way she sat, and none of the other passengers paid her much attention as she gawked out of the window.

It was only when they were out over the immense Coral Sea, and when its fierce, vast blue began to hurt her eyes and make her head ache, that she turned her attention back to the interior of the plane. A tall man with his slouch hat slung over his shoulder, wearing no badges of rank, only a war correspondent's patch, made his way down the shuddering plane and stood above her. He was lean-faced and his skin was yellowed with atebrin, the anti-malarial drug which stained everyone yellow. She had been taking hers for only a few weeks, so she was still a normal colour. But she presumed the same thing would happen to her in the end.

'Excuse me,' the tall man said. His voice sounded low, but he would have had to be shouting to be heard above the engines. 'My name's Paul Stacey. *Melbourne Examiner*. I know your husband, Lieutenant Lewis. Spent time with him in Port Moresby.'

The memory made him smile. Good old Allan!

She smiled in return and with an uneasy generosity moved to make room for the correspondent to sit. Against the noise of the engines, their conversation made some progress. He spoke out of a pleasant combination of shyness and directness, and with the same slow smile with which he had earlier announced his friendship with Allan. It came to her that this must be a son of the Stacey newspaper family of Melbourne, who had founded the *Examiner* in the 1860s and whose successive patriarchs had been knighted, probably at the behest of various politicians they had served well. Although, looking at Paul Stacey and his genial boyishness, it was impossible to think too badly of the Stacey clan. With the abstract, aesthetic approval of someone whose affections are totally taken up, she found him an appealing man.

He'd been on leave in Melbourne, he said. She realized she'd read some of his pieces syndicated in the Brisbane papers. He'd described the Kokoda Trail, how young Australian militiamen made lame with malaria and tropical ulcers clawed their way up embankments of green slime to hurl themselves at the Japanese or to receive a devastating fire in the face.

She remembered that once, reading him, she had suffered a momentary pang: *What am I doing here, in the midst of an alien headquarters*? Except that Galt wasn't an alien. He was her nation and her husband. Far more than the Australians were her nation, or Allan her husband.

'Allan and his friend,' yelled Paul Stacey. 'What's that Englishman's name? Runcie? Commander Runcie. Characters. Brave men.' He shook his head for emphasis. 'You still with the Americans? Big Drum? Allan told me. He's very proud of you.'

She had to stop herself flinching. 'Yes,' she said. She made a mouth. 'Film and entertainment officer. Not very flash. Not very brave.'

'But welcome,' he yelled, smiling with a sudden sadness. 'If they've got time for pictures and songs, we must be winning.'

A message from the pilot was shouted aft that Moresby had a bombing raid, and they would circle around the Gulf of Papua until it was over. Dim felt an anxious sweat on her throat and forearms. She was alarmed to notice that Stacey – though he tried to hide it – had become distracted now. The shouted conversation sputtered. Everyone in the body of the plane seemed tense. It was clear that one Japanese fighter, detaching itself from the air battle, might spot them and descend on them like a hawk. And what made Dim fearful was that it was the experienced ones like Stacey who were the most edgy, even though they tried to hide it. After half an hour of circling Dim began to press her fingers either side of the bridge of her nose, to repress the panic growing there. But when she lowered her hands she felt Stacey's long fingers encircle her wrist with a comforting tightness.

'I think we're going to be all right,' he said, confidential though he was shouting. 'I mean, the fuel-tanks of the newest Japanese fighter-bombers give them only a half hour or so over Moresby. They're going to have to head back to Rabaul pretty soon!'

He went on holding her wrist, and she was grateful for it, until after ten minutes the plane straightened and lunged itself at a lower, thicker layer of air, and began to descend. Stacey sat back in the primitive seat with a brotherly smile and relinquished his hold on her. Dim could see people breathing in a different sort of way. Men with a future.

As the plane came in to land, she got a glimpse, by peering over her shoulder and out of the porthole, of a cargo ship belching an evil, crimson flame, and of smouldering warehouses.

'This has been a bad one,' she heard Stacey shout.

Dim had her own quarters, a cubicle in a Quonset hut in the garden of Big Drum's villa. This was nothing like Lennon's Hotel in Brisbane. She could not really go visiting Galt, for Galt did not have a suite in the villa. Even Big Drum had no more than his own bedroom and a dressing room. He shared a bath with Galt and with Clancy, while Harry Strudwick and all the other section chiefs had to share another bathroom.

So if Galt and Dim met, it had to be in her room. There, no sooner was the burden of desire released than they became aware of the smothering weight of each other's body and of the unbearable sweat in which they existed.

It was sweetness, just the same. Dim knew that beside what young men along the Kokoda Trail and over in the Kunai grass flats on the north side of New Guinea were suffering, all this was barely a discomfort. She sometimes felt there was actually a shrew inside her who nonetheless postponed complaint until the war was won.

This sense of a sort of fishwife growing in her, someone who was suspending her demands for the moment, frightened her. She wondered whether it was being in love with an imperial figure like Galt which had made her like this. Or the tendency might have been in her own background, in the demands for luxury her grandparents had made upon the Australian environment once they were securely settled on it, safe behind their walls of shorn wool.

For whatever reason then, she put up with the churning fan in the Quonset hut, with the almost putrescent sweetness of the tropical plants beyond her propped-open window, and with the mosquitoes so numerous it was no use swatting one, since a million a day swarmed in to feed on your blood.

She took her atebrin as she was required to and, looking in

the mirror, saw her skin turn gradually more sallow and yellow. But malaria was worse, they said. Malaria was hell, a dream from the netherworld.

Once a week she drove out to the airport between air raids to welcome in the entertainers – hula bands and vocalists from Hawaii; radio stars from Sydney and Melbourne, comedians and comediennes and quizmasters, names from her childhood. You had to give them credit – all of them, even stars in their forties, seemed to want to be up here with the boys. It just showed that people had developed a sense of a great crusade in the Pacific; that talented men and women were willing to give their services at terrible rates in a zone where at least two air raids occurred a day and where they had to live in tents in a general's garden.

They would perform at night to sailors and American pilots and anti-aircraft men. They would visit the field hospitals and chat to the skeletal boys with beri-beri or septicaemic wounds. It might have been a cliché – a joke or two, a song in the tropic afternoon in the field hospitals. And some boys who had seen the worst horror face to face in the Owen Stanleys were too ill or deranged to get much from it. But by and large you could see it doing soldiers good.

She now had a slack-jawed US corporal called Hutchinson working for her. Hutchinson was a Southerner and qualified for the job by having been an usher in an Atlanta cinema. With his help she was distributing film, flown in in steel canisters, around the encampments of Moresby, even amongst the destroyers who patrolled the Coral Sea. She was sending them too in transport planes over the mountains to where the decisive battles around Buna were being fought.

Big Drum himself didn't watch films any more. Galt commented on this to Dim. Big Drum, having found the library in the Administration villa, devoted himself to letters these days. He'd now decided he didn't like talkies anyhow. The last cowboy he'd admired – so he'd told Galt – was Tom Mix. He hated the new kind of cowboys like Gene Autrey, the ones who crooned and yodelled. He'd grown up in army forts in the American West, and he knew cowboys didn't croon and yodel in that glib, scrubbed-face way.

*

One afternoon when Dim was out at the airfield early to meet a party of entertainers, she went to an open-sided, camouflaged tent which operated as an officers' canteen and picked up a mug of sweet tea. Tea was wonderful in the tropics – it brought you out in a delicious sweat, a very different sweat from the normal dampness in which you lived.

These days, she wore her hair brushed up under her cap, and – like all women serving in the tropics other than nurses – army pants tucked into loosely strapped gaiters. She knew that she could pass therefore as a fresh-faced boy, and it may have been for that reason Paul Stacey, the war correspondent, who was also drinking tea in the canteen, did not at first recognize her.

He was with a party of three other correspondents. They were all young or youngish men. Obviously they were waiting for air transport – over the mountains to the war front. Dim took her slouch hat off so that Stacey could see who she was. As soon as he noticed, he stubbed out a cigarette and came over to see her.

'I'm sorry,' he said, half-amused at her jungle disguise. 'I didn't recognize you. Forgive me, but you look just about as yellow as the rest of us.'

She was aware now that he'd lost his easy, casual manner. There was a certain tension in him, the same kind of tension he'd shown in the aircraft two weeks before as they'd circled above the sea and waited for a safe entry.

'Look, Mrs Lewis,' he said. 'I'd been meaning to ask you for a drink at our villa. It's not far from the Australian headquarters – a big bungalow and they've got about three dozen of us crammed in there, Australian and American pressmen. A lot of them know Allan from when he was up here. But I delayed and . . . well, here we are!'

'That would have been nice,' she said. 'Why didn't you ask me?' She was surprised to hear her old, teasing self in that question, the self who had undergone a sea change as Galt Sandforth's lover.

'I thought you might have misinterpreted it,' he said.

He gave his familiar grin again, but it was a sort of courtly shyness that was making him tense; that and the uncertainties of the coming flight over the Owen Stanleys. 'I can tell you that now I'm going up the road again, I'm sorry I didn't.'

Lazily at first, all the airfield sirens began to sound. Then they increased in urgency and degree of alarm. 'Quick,' he told her. They ran across a few yards of open ground and dropped into a slit trench with a sandbag parapet. Landing in its muggy depths, she could smell the generations of leaf mould into which the trench had been dug. She could smell its walls. It was the first time in her Port Moresby experience that she had had to take to a slit trench.

Is this really me here? she asked. *In this melodramatic trench*? She had witnessed earlier air raids on the port and the airfield from Big Drum's high hill, and both the anti-aircraft fire and the noise of bombs had seemed surprisingly remote. But now she could feel the reverberations of cannon through the walls of the slit trench, and in her spine. There was one enormous detonation which dragged the air out of the trench and made her bite her tongue. There were two more of equal force. She knew she was crouching with her hands faced outward, paw-like, in front of her face, and Stacey seemed to stand more or less around her, tall, bowed over, his shoulders towering over hers, his hands embowering but scarcely touching her. He did not want to be misinterpreted once the bombing ceased, if it ever would. She wished he would hold her closer still but there was no way of conveying that. She wished that anyone would hold her closer.

There was an age of this experience of detonation, of the smell of rot and dust which the bombardment unleashed, of the sucking up of air out of the pit.

Later she would discover that within a few hundred yards of Dim's trench, squadron offices had been flattened, a fuel dump on the perimeter blown up, and two gun crews killed by bomb blast. But it happened too that Clancy's American and Australian fighters were already in the air, waiting in ambush off shore. Though Dim still crouched and wailed soundlessly for Galt, the Japanese were now driven slowly across the sky northwards, restricted in manoeuvre by the limitations of their fuel.

Stacey lifted her to the rim of the slit trench and then climbed out himself.

'I always want to go to sleep after something like that,' Stacey said. 'I wonder why?'

Dim was astounded to be able to hear him. He did not seem to be shouting either.

'But then,' he continued, 'when I lie down, all I can think of are the questions I should have asked the survivors.'

Dim wondered how it would be to live with that much noise day and night, as the combatants did.

'You've come through it all right?' Stacey asked her, looking confidingly into her face, his eyes crinkling.

'Yes,' she said. But still her ears were ringing, and she hated the smell of rot that seemed to be everywhere, to have been accentuated by the bombing and to be inescapable.

'So will you come some time or other, Lieutenant Lewis, when I arrive back in Moresby, and visit the gentlemen of the press gallery?'

'Of course I will. Of course.'

Secretly she hoped she would not be asked. Why should she be exposed like that to so many correspondents, so many professional inquirers? That was the problem, she saw. He thought she was a girl. He thought her life was simple.

And as for being young, Galt had made her ageless. She found herself another mug of tea – the Japanese had not got the canteen – and as she sipped it the fact came to her with a slow but unfathomable joy that she *would* see Galt again. He would still the air around her.

Amongst a scrum of entertainers arriving in Moresby one steamy evening was Ray Harris, an American vaudevillian who had come to Australia in the mid-1930s and become a radio star there. His very voice, falsely thespian as he bent to shake Dim's hand, brought back the nights in the long summer holidays as she sprawled half naked beneath her parents' radio console in the great living room in Maneering.

That evening in New Guinea Ray was sweating bravely beneath a toupee, heavy and thick, the colour of a red setter's coat.

'*Enchanté*, madame,' he announced to Dim in an overly

articulated voice. All the other singers, dancers, and comics knew he was the star of the group and let him talk for them.

Dim saw what you could not quite perceive through radio: that he seemed to have modelled himself on W.C. Fields.

In the back of the truck on the way to the entertainers' billets, which were under canvas near what people called the 'Australian headquarters' – that is, the headquarters of big, jovial General Billings, Land Forces Commander – Ray sat a little closer to Dim.

'My dear,' he said, 'I don't want there to be any misunderstanding. What is your job precisely?'

'I'm an Entertainment Officer.'

'And what precisely does that mean?'

'I'm in charge of the distribution of films, and I look after people such as yourself who are kind enough to perform for the troops.'

'Ah, yes,' he said, sighing. 'Again, I didn't want any misconception. It's just that some places I go, I am given a girl assistant, if you take my meaning. And she may have many descriptions. *Entertainment Officer* might well be one of them.' His hand sought her wrist. 'Some pretty little thing like you perhaps.'

Dim pulled her wrist away. A perverse joy could attach itself to being desired even by someone as overdone as Ray Harris. What offended her though was that he devalued her job title. Suddenly it sounded a mean description. *Entertainment Officer*. And a euphemism.

He did not know that she had got prints of *The Maltese Falcon* all the way to within five hundred yards of the front trenches at Buna!

She tried not to sound brisk. A childhood awe for his voice still had its influence on her. 'No, I haven't been assigned to you personally, Mr Harris. I assure you I have the whole range of entertainment in Papua-New Guinea to look after. My orders come from US Headquarters, and they mentioned no special arrangements for you.'

Then her anger was cooled a little.

'I'm sure,' she continued, 'a man of your wit and charm will have no trouble attracting assistants.'

Ray Harris spread his hands spaciously in front of him, as if to reassure her. 'No, no, madame. In any case I am not asking for special favours. I simply wanted to know – as the curious phrase has it – where I stood. Your response leaves me, I might say, utterly desolate. But I live with desolation!'

She laughed and then thanked him. It seemed to be the best thing to do.

When Ray Harris and his people put on their show at a bearable hour of the night, beneath a glittering sky, Dim was charmed. For there was an enchantment about live performance, one missing from radio and film.

Dim had planned a party for afterwards – deliciously iced Australian beer. The ice had been brought up here to General Billings's headquarters on the hill from that half of the Port Moresby iceworks which hadn't been bombed, and put in tubs by Hutchinson.

As the party ended, Hutchinson was waiting with a jeep to take Dim home. Even though she could easily have walked, she piled in the back gratefully. 'Ma'am,' he said, 'you look all tuckered out.'

'That's exactly what I am,' she agreed. She was finding it difficult, in these dense, humid nights, to shake off an anxiety which had been with her since the bombing raid; a childlike yearning to find Galt again and be held by him. Yet she had not told him about her experience at the airstrip. She knew it would make him wonder whether she shouldn't be returned to Brisbane.

She bathed in a basin of water in the Quonset hut. At a quarter to eleven, Galt arrived. The radiance, the unquestioning delight with which he was greeted humbled and amazed him.

Above her, Galt levered himself upright with his elbows and hands.

'There's someone,' he told her. He was frowning. It was as if he were accusing her of infidelity.

'Someone? There's no one.'

Her room was in darkness, but by shafts of moonlight one could see the mosquitoes wheel in the air.

'There's someone,' said Galt.

Now she understood he meant there was someone outside the hut, some invader of their intimacy. He launched himself then, straight at the window. He did not hesitate. He did not behave like a lawyer or a sheep farmer. He behaved like a warrior. He didn't mind if he lost fragments of skin. He vaulted out into the night, wanting to see the violator's face and impose some damage on it.

She pulled on a kimono and left by her front door, meaning to intercept whoever-it-was. She saw the athletic, near-naked Galt chasing a shadow through the gardens. He caught the shadow by one of the hundreds of sickeningly fragrant hibiscus bushes. Dim saw the toupee roll off Ray Harris's head as Galt brought him down. Ray was grotesquely dressed in army boots and a bathrobe.

From Big Drum's villa, the big Melanesian New Guinea police began to call gently. They shone their torches down the pathway which led to where Galt, Dim and Ray Harris hid in the bushes. Galt's hand clamped over Harris's mouth.

After finding nothing, Big Drum's jovial guardians withdrew.

Galt said to Dim. 'You go.'

'Are you sure?' asked Dim.

'Yes, you go. It's important.'

That meant that it had to do with everything – with Big Drum as a future President, with Galt as a future Secretary of Defense. With the future of Galt and Dim. All that was what *it's important* stood for.

Somehow Ray Harris found breath and space to say, 'I just thought . . . ' But Galt covered his mouth again.

Galt said to Dim, as an afterthought. 'You could bring me my uniform and my boots and my gun belt.' He wore a pistol everywhere, nothing obvious. Not the big six-shooter some of the officers affected. Something more modest, a Smith and Wesson.

She went and got all this and brought it to him. And then, as ordered, she went back to her room. She was becoming a junior staff officer at least in that respect. She did what the Chief of Staff said.

In a large tent in a remote corner of the Administrator's garden,

Ray Harris was handcuffed to an iron bedframe. There weren't too many of those in New Guinea, but Captain Mike Karpinsky of the Military Police had somehow acquired one, probably specifically to have something to handcuff people to.

Karpinsky was an ethnic broth – half-Irish, half-Polish, a former lieutenant of police from Chicago. His face was meatily handsome and his eyes shone with a whimsical canniness. If you were his prisoner he would look very mean indeed. In 1940, Karpinsky, as Galt had found out almost by accident, or at least through the process of reading as many routine documents as possible, had taken a broad array of kickbacks in cash and kind from bordellos in Manila. Galt had called him in for a chat, and the result was that the charges to do with these violations, mere peccadilloes by Chicago standards, were dropped. Karpinsky had seemed quite happy to serve Lieutenant-General Galton Sandforth on a confidential basis anyhow, without any pressure having to be applied. Karpinsky's good fortune had been that he had been transferred to Hawaii in November 1940, and he seemed to think Galt was somehow connected to that lucky posting.

Galt had not used him in the matter of the Australian major, since the Brigadier-General who'd run the entire Military Police in the Southeastern Australian area had been available to help. But here in the mean tropics, when you wanted someone to scare a prisoner, you couldn't do better than Karpinsky.

By 2300 hours he had already terrorized Ray Harris out of the claim that he had been merely trying to visit a girl. He made a big show, and had just about convinced Harris himself of the fact, that the old vaudevillian and antipodean radio star had been found prowling like a saboteur in the vicinity of Big Drum's bungalow.

'I demand to see General Billings,' Ray said at one stage. 'Billings is a friend of mine.'

It was certain to be the truth, Galt knew. Yet the loss of his toupee, which had been kicked into a corner, seemed to have knocked the starch and the resistance out of Ray, and he was frightened. He was frightened by Karpinsky's lack of humour, and by the lack of ice his Australian renown cut here, in Karpinsky's office-tent. Karpinsky genuinely didn't give a damn whether Ray lived or died, and that was apparent to Ray himself.

Galt, who had stood beyond the circle of light and just within the tent flap throughout the interrogation, now stepped forward. Ray looked at him with a kind of gratitude. No one could be *more* dangerous than Karpinsky.

Galt asked Karpinsky and his men to leave. They obeyed, sidling out in exactly the right way, a way which said, '*You might be the General, but we're the enforcers. We're waiting round for the pieces you throw us.*

Staring him in the eye in that practised way, Galt stood before the performer. Harris, not accustomed to such looks, flinched.

'I am not the sort of man who hits a shackled prisoner,' said Galt.

'Just let me talk to General Billings. Please, sir. He'll vouch for me.'

'The Australians can't help you, Mr Harris. What did you see when you were prowling?'

'I didn't see anything,' Ray Harris claimed.

'You're either a traitor or a voyeur, Mr Harris. A Peeping Tom. At the very least.'

'What d'you mean?'

'Or as Karpinsky says, a spy or an assassin.'

'You must be joking . . . '

Galt took Ray Harris's jaw one-handed and squeezed the cheeks. 'God won't let you interfere with Big Drum. I won't let you. You saw me, didn't you? *Didn't you?*'

'I couldn't see clearly, for Christ's sake. I'd only just got there.'

'Where?'

'At the window, for Christ's sake.'

'You saw nothing! Do you understand, friend Harris? Do you understand what we can do to you? You like being a star in Australia? We can have you deported to the United States. Right now! A transport plane from here. The Prime Minister of Australia would agree to it, because he's our friend. Two cavalrymen to guard you all the way to Hawaii and then on to California.'

'But for Christ's sake, my wife's in Sydney!'

Galt felt obscurely ashamed as he turned the screw. He

wouldn't want Dim to know anything about what he was doing here. 'You want to be able to watch women being fucked, do you, Ray? Voyeur Ray?'

Ray Harris was consumed with fury but also a kind of shame.

'Not only can I have you held and questioned in San Diego. I can give your name to the Propaganda Office in Washington. I can get you blacklisted by the Entertainment Liaison Office. Just one word about your loyalty to them, and it would be the close of everything for you. No theatrical management, no radio station, no film studio would touch you. And why should they anyhow? You're a disgusting little fake.'

It was working superbly. Harris was not a fool, but you could see him calculating the risks of defiance and forswearing them. And the more he forswore them, the less likely he was to take a line like, 'Yes, and when I'm interrogated I'll tell them I saw you screwing a young Australian woman.'

And the more unadventurous and undefiant he became, the more likely he was to accept any concession from Galt with irrational gratitude.

'Captain Karpinsky!' yelled Galt; and Karpinsky entered the tent, the feral intelligence gleaming in his eyes.

'Release him,' said Galt. 'Take him back to his tent. Keep him under watch for another twenty-four hours and let him perform tomorrow night. Then fly the sonofabitch home. But if you hear a suspicious word from him, we'll fly him out for the States under guard. He's on probation.'

'General,' said Karpinsky. He acted out apparent disappointment. He began to unlock the performer from the bedframe.

'Oh,' said Galt. 'I also want you to report him to the Australian authorities, so that they can keep him under surveillance for the duration and deport him if they think it fit. You understand?'

'Yessir,' said Karpinsky enthusiastically.

'Drag him out of here,' ordered Galt.

Galt was almost sickened by the ease with which he had managed all this. Karpinsky undid Harris's cuffs and led him to the door. Harris, being a performer, wanted to retrieve something from the ashes, and so he baulked grandly in his dressing gown and said, 'Sir, I swear you have no reason to be worried about me. No reason to put any authorities on my trail.'

'Go to hell!' said Galt.

The thing was, he didn't want to be a secret lover. He wanted to be her husband. He wanted an arrangement where it wasn't necessary to use the skills of threat which he'd built up in his military career. For the first time, he actually wanted love and peace.

Chapter 9

The Buna Longueurs

THE AIRSTRIP, STEAMING in the afternoon sun and fringed with tall kunai grass, seemed abandoned. From the air, it had occurred to Galt and, it seemed, to the Australian pilot who had just landed him and his party there that some sudden disaster might have struck, that the Japanese had maybe forced two American divisions and all the Australians back into the mountains. But the pilot's radio communication with the ground told them it *was* safe to land. As they circled and then aligned themselves with the runway, some threads of camp smoke could be seen wheeling upwards in the heavy air, as if the tall grass was peopled with hidden soldiers cooking lunch.

This strip was called Dobadura. The strangeness of it was that it was one of the lesser sites the party Allan Lewis belonged to had surveyed. The main strip the Runcie/Lewis group had surveyed, about twenty miles north and near the coast, was a forward strike base for the Japanese.

Big Drum was dissatisfied not only with that fact but with the conduct of the American troops over here on New Guinea's north side. He was particularly displeased with the hapless corps commander, General Stevens, who seemed to have dug in tenuously and to be now waiting for Buck Clancy to perform some miracle of logistics, on the basis of which he would feel competent to gain a little ground.

The plane landed and rolled up to the edge of the enormous tracts of kunai grass. It had orders to stay on the ground only long enough to let Galt and Captain Duncan, together with an Australian general and his aide, leave it and reach the edge of the kunai. It also had some mail, which bare-chested Aussie cargo-handlers dropped in a pile for collection some thirty or forty paces from Galt and the others. They then sprinted back for their plane, not even bothering to salute their own general. Galt would have remarked on that to his Australian colleague, but though the Aussies were not great saluters they were fighting wonderfully on General Stevens's left flank and being let down by him. Slack American units were not keeping pace, were leaving their flanks exposed to the terrible enfilading fire of the Nambu machine-gun, the weapon of the Japanese marine divisions. But General Stevens, whom Galt still had to find somewhere in this swampy mess, was the problem. This general sent up here to see what was happening and report to his chief, General Billings, knew that. Galt was in no position to reflect on the etiquette of Aussie cargo-handlers.

Unapologetically, the plane took off again, straining for height and the safety of the thunderheads which lay over the mountains.

Duncan and the young Australian aide nervously parted the razor-edged kunai with their hands. This is grotesque, thought Galt. This is Vera Cruz, 1915 all over. Except that now I'm no longer brave or strong, and I know what death is. Death is the end of the caresses of Dim Lewis.

'Through here, General,' said Duncan, who had found the source of the white smoke they had seen from the air.

Galt and the Australian general stepped through into the strange world of the kunai. *I would not like to fight in here*, thought Galt at once. Enclosed and hot and impossible to assess.

But there was a population in here. In small spaces cut out of the kunai with machetes, young men with muddied faces slept on ponchos. Some smoked and looked out of grime-rimmed eyes at Galt. They all looked very informal and very thin. The nearest smoke was rising from a fire of dried grass. Over it a tripod had been placed, and a pot dangled from it by a chain. A cook was stirring the pot. He was the only man who seemed to be doing something positive in the whole scene. For many of the young soldiers were simply staring. Others drowsed and slept on ponchos awkwardly spread amongst the grassroots. As Galt drew closer, he could see eagle insignia on the man's shoulders. A colonel? A colonel doing the cooking? In a crowd of beaten young men! This was not command. It was a nightmare.

Slowly the colonel noticed Galt and the Australian general and sprang to as much attention as he could manage.

Galt felt furious at the man. A professional, so called. He had let his men get into this state.

'My God,' the colonel said. 'General.'

'Colonel,' said Galt, 'what are you doing? Don't you have an orderly?'

'General, my orderly has malaria.' The man's voice rose. 'My boys have been getting by on a third of a C ration per day. This is their first hot meal in seventeen days.'

The man was hysterical. He seemed to be authorizing his men to despair. An instinct of command told Galt to raise his foot and kick the tripod. When he did it, stew splashed out across kunai grass and sleeping youths. The colonel looked appalled.

'What are you, colonel?' he asked. 'Are you a warrior or a fucking chef? Whatever you are, it's too late for you to change trains now!'

In the cold astringent half-shame of having destroyed the stew, Galt knew one thing. *He* would never have acted like this in the colonel's position. He *knew* it. If you're a soldier, you're a soldier and you face that destiny. And if your boys have had only a third of a C ration for seventeen days, then join the queue, the long line of complaint which stretched from Alexander's army to Hannibal's to Napoleon's to Lee's to this forest of kunai.

'Do you have a radio, colonel?' Galt asked.

The colonel's response was sharper now. It just showed you, there was only one way to run things. The old way. Fear, shouting, relentless questioning. The tried methods.

'Yes, General.'

'I want you to call forward for General Stevens. He's to come back here and then escort us forward. I am Lieutenant-General Galton Sandforth, General Wraith's Chief of Staff. If he wonders whether it's an inspection or not, put the sonofabitch out of his misery. Tell him it is.'

Through this, the Australians stood by. Even though their General Billings was land commander, it was well recognized that Big Drum was Big Drum and *his* chief of staff was *the* chief of staff.

Now, Galt noticed, there were tears in the colonel's grimy eyes. 'Sir,' he said in a lowered voice, 'my regiment took three hundred casualties as part of Warren Force. We've been sent back here to Dobadura to rest and have a hot meal. It was very harrowing for these kids.'

'There are no circumstances,' Galt told him, 'where a colonel stirs the stew. Do you understand? There are none.'

Galt noticed that one of the colonel's boy-soldiers calmly picked up chunks of stew from the ground and put them pensively in his mouth.

'I want you to radio forward for General Stevens to send a truck back here for us,' Galt reiterated, since nothing was happening.

The colonel's eyes wavered. 'Our signal section drowned in a swamp. Our radios are there, sir. In the swamp.'

Galt swallowed. The implied invitation was for him to go and dig them out. There was no point in raging. And sure, kicking over the stew had been army-barbarous. Except that this man needed that to happen, needed it as a deliverance and a cure. It was almost a kindness towards a man who had so far forgotten himself as to become his men's butler amongst the kunai!

'Give me your best NCO then,' said Galt. 'I want to go forward to the nearest unit with a radio.'

'That's three miles down the duckboards, General. It's a truck maintenance depot.'

'Get your man to take us there,' said Galt.

It was a bitch of a day for a walk amongst the kunai. The sun penetrated the cloth of shirts and bit into the shoulders. Artillery could be heard – the cannon and tank guns which the Australians had sneaked into shore under cover of night.

What people like Stevens, general officer of the US IX Infantry Corps, did not understand was the cosmic scale of what they were engaged upon. Senator Vandergrift, distinguished leader of the Republican machine and of the conservative wing in the Senate, had a program organized for Big Drum. The program was geared to Big Drum's drafting as Presidential candidate by the Republican convention in some eighteen months' time.

Galt was aware that he himself was doing what was necessary.

He had drafted plans for amphibious landings along the New Guinea coast, landings to bypass strong-points. Landings aimed at giving Clancy's aircraft fields from which they could strike a further two thousand miles into the Japanese lines.

But before that could happen there had to be results from the Americans here. People were getting wise to press releases which said: 'Allied troops today captured . . . ' They knew that 'Allied troops' meant that the Australians had borne most of the heat.

To fill in the time on the way to see General Stevens, Galt talked to the young NCO who had been assigned to guide them to the truck repair depot.

'So, how's it been, sergeant?'

'They're dug in real good, General. We was told they wouldn't be dug in. But they're dug in *real* good. Bunkers. You take one and you find there are three behind you, shooting at your ass. And you can't ever work out where anyone else is. You just got your own clump of mud.'

'Sounds difficult,' said Galt. You could sympathize with sergeants as you never could with colonels.

'At night they sing to us, General. They sing in English and they sing in Japanese. They call out, "Joe, my buddy's already in your trench. He just put his bayonet in your buddy . . . "'

Galt let him talk on. The boy was – in a possessed way – near hysteria.

When at last he stopped, Galt said, 'We're going to fix it, son. You tell all your pals. We're going to fix it.'

Big Drum had put an embargo on the use of the term GI. But the bewildered boys who lounged beside the trail, up which Galt and Captain Duncan and the Australians ultimately travelled by jeep that afternoon to meet General Stevens, looked like Government Issue, Government Issue which had been expended, used up, hollowed out.

The atmosphere at Stevens's headquarters was frazzled. General Stevens himself, when they found him in his communications tent, seemed distracted, as if he did not understand that he was receiving the most crucial visitors of his career. There was some of the air of the colonel-chef about him too. Yet he was a man with a highly intelligent face, a reliable-looking guy.

Galt found himself shocked by the numbers of corpses who lay around the base hospital nearby covered with blankets, awaiting a quick and shallow burial in mud. The numbers were all the more alarming since *these* boys must have died of wounds to be back here, at the base hospital. God knew how many dead lay in the coastal jungle and swamps up ahead.

Night was coming on and what looked like visible evil was steaming up under the palm trees. There was a continual noise of machine-guns and mortars and cannon.

Stevens led Galt and the Australian General into his headquarters tent and showed them the map of the Buna coast.

'I've got no exact idea, I'm sorry, General Sandforth. Every unit seems to have lost their radios. They're too bulky for this terrain.'

Galt felt an awe and a sorrow to hear that last sentence. For it disqualified Stevens for command. The only eyes he had in this terrain were radio eyes. And yet radios had been lost or jettisoned because they were too heavy. Stevens was blaming the loss of a thousand lives so far and the taking of no objectives on the weight of his radios.

'If there's no radio communication, why were you in the communications tent.'

'Well, some units still have their radios. I'm talking as a generality when I say we're out of contact. We do get a partial picture.'

Steven's intelligence officer stood by mutely. He had nothing to say. The engineer on Stevens's staff was – as Stevens had already told them – in a nearby tent trembling with malaria.

To his own amazement Galt spoke softly. He understood somehow there was nothing to be gained by speaking harshly. The standard army thing was to kick over the tripod – which he *had* managed to do – and to scream at the helpless, which in the case of General Stevens he found himself not doing at all.

'I want to see your quartermaster, General Stevens,' was all he said.

So the man was sent for. When he arrived, he looked professorial, about forty, with an unlit pipe in his teeth.

'We landed at the airstrip at Dobadura,' Galt told him after salutes were finished with. 'All we saw were hungry troops. All we've seen all the way are hungry troops. Where are the supplies?'

'Sir, they're over at Soputa strip.'

Another Lewis-reconnoitred strip.

'Why are men starving here?'

'General, I don't have the manpower to bring adequate supplies up here. We can't use trucks . . . '

'Why not?'

'The jungle tracks aren't fit for large vehicular traffic.'

Galt turned to Stevens. 'Don't you have an engineer on staff?'

'He's ill, General.'

'I know. But doesn't he have a goddamn deputy?'

The professor said, 'I don't think you understand the problems, General Sandforth.'

'I understand from reports that the Australians have laid down viable roads in their sector.'

'But they're used to it,' said the pitiable Stevens, not even aware how thoroughly he was condemning himself. 'It's their sort of terrain.'

So, we fight a battle without supplies and radios, thought Galt. There was an unreality, a madness, that overtakes some commanders in the field, and it was entrenched here, with Stevens, who tolerated a man who sucked a pipe and said nothing was possible.

Galt found Soputa on the map spread across Stevens's table. 'Five miles,' he said. 'That's all? Adequate supplies are five miles back?'

He was even vaguely and perversely disappointed. If the supplies hadn't been there, he would have been able to knock a little of the wind out of Clancy's billowing reputation as an air chief with a gift for logistics. But Clancy was by the pipe-sucker's own admission delivering the stuff. Which was good; for it was best for the timetable anyhow, the Big Plan, that Clancy should be efficient.

Galt took the time therefore to speak to the professorial quartermaster in a passionate tone of voice, like a man appealing to reason. That he ought to get the supplies up by one means or another, even if it meant taking men out of the line to do it. The quartermaster seemed surprised by this firm line and by this revolutionary proposal. Let a screen of infantry hold a perimeter while the rest ran the supplies? It seemed to strike the quartermaster as an heretical idea, a barbarous one. It appeared that he and Stevens had caught a form of jungle madness from each other.

In a tent supplied by General Stevens, Galt spent a chaotic night trying to sleep and missing Dim, feeling that he had derived from his life with her a new gift for handling people like Stevens, feeling he needed to get back and check her features against the contours of what had happened here. He was grateful when dawn came, so that they could roll back to Dobadura in a jeep and rendezvous with their plane for Port Moresby.

Big Drum paced the long verandah. He was a man of prodigious fitness. Yet he was a depressed old-young man today. That didn't really show either, except in a certain fixedness of the eyes. 'Well,' said Big Drum, 'well . . . drat the whole thing!'

He wasn't a curser or blasphemer. His mother had raised him strictly as a non-cusser in the profane Western forts he'd grown up in.

'Channing and that Chaumont gang will use this, Galt! They'll use Stevens's laxity. For the normal purposes: starve me of resources, whittle my power. They'll be delighted at the lack of news from Buna, that crowd.'

As was his habit, he put his long, cigarette-less holder in his mouth and spoke around it. 'Given this mess, Galt, what do you suggest?'

Though he already knew the answer, Galt pretended to consider this question painfully and tentatively. 'I know Bryant Gibbs is a friend of mine,' he began. The very name of Major-General Gibbs carried the redolence of that first night he'd had Dim to dinner, when Gibbs, then only a Brigadier-General, had been the protective colouring for Galt's overtures to Dim. Since then Gibbs had risen to divisional rank and was acting commander of a corps in Queensland. He had shown administrative ability, and was good at training programs. But then that's what had been said about Stevens. It was no guarantee.

The General had begun to grin around the cigarette-holder. 'Well, I don't consider friendship with you to be a disqualification, Galt. I'm your friend, I believe. And I hope that doesn't disqualify me from higher office.'

'I hope so too, General,' murmured Galt, trying to imagine the day he would announce Dim's existence to Big Drum. 'Gibbs has a good reputation, anyhow. He was a combat company commander in France, and his reports were excellent. Stevens never was. You know, General, the old argument about how if a man can run a company well, he can run an army. I don't know much about the validity of that proposition. But my instinct is, he won't fall to pieces like Stevens has.'

Big Drum took the holder from his mouth and squinted down through the town of Port Moresby and out over the hard glitter of the harbour in which sunken freighters raised forlorn prows and warehouses still smoked.

'Summon him,' said Big Drum. In the imperial manner.

It was a small but lush garden. The banana trees grew as you watched them. And all the normal fragrances were there, the sweetness of frangipani and bougainvillea, a sweetness on the edge of decay. The place had only two bedrooms. Its furniture was sparse, some of it left there by the Australian official who had once occupied the place, before the Japanese threatened Moresby. The rest – tables, chairs, two camp beds – had been made up out of general issue and installed by Ernie Sasser's engineers.

'Look,' said Galt, pointing to a bookcase. 'A little library.'

He led Dim over to it. The titles were not as distinguished as those in the Administrator's villa which was now occupied by Big Drum. They were mainly detective novels. Galt could visualize some middle-aged, mediocre civil servant sitting here half soused with Scotch and reading whodunnits.

'It's big, Galt,' she said, putting her hand on his upper arm. 'Really kind of you. I'll rattle around in here.'

'That's what the army does to you. It takes away your sense

of proper space. This isn't a proper space for a woman of your talent and beauty, Dim. One day we'll share an appropriate space, and then you'll know the difference.'

'Won't this draw envious glances? A villa to myself?'

'I want to think about that, Dim. Maybe put in a captain of nurses, if she can be trusted? In any case, you wrote me that letter, and the letter's my justification.'

At his own suggestion, she had sat down and composed a complaint to the Chief of Staff, to Galt himself, about molestation and peeping toms back there at Bataan, Big Drum's headquarters. There was already a complaint on file, with MPs to back the complaint. And since Dim and the chief of nursing staff were the only headquarters women, special accommodation arrangements now seemed justified.

Meanwhile, Dim and Galt had the place to themselves for a week. When the nurse moved in, she proved to be a plain, no-nonsense woman of about forty who went to bed early from pure exhaustion and who had that air of discretion about her which comes from having to cover up for the sins of physicians.

Two anti-aircraft guns protected the small hill on which Dim's villa sat.

Galt had a desk set up on Big Drum's verandah, where he worked with the Generalissimo throughout the morning. Seated behind it, he was working on the future, the draft instructions for a plan for an amphibious landing in the Admiralty Islands, where airstrips were located which Clancy coveted for future operations. The question was, would Big Drum hit these islands, called Manus and Los Negros, or would he try for a frontal attack on the great Japanese base at Rabaul, the heart of things.

The answer seemed in some ways apparent. Until Washington allocated more to him, Big Drum couldn't possibly assault Rabaul by landing troops there. Yet the dream, and even the Washington Joint Chiefs' *demand* that it be captured seemed to hang over Bataan/Moresby even now, at a stage when the two US divisions already in place on the north coast under General Stevens couldn't even take Buna.

About mid-morning Galt saw – from his place on the verandah

– Gibbs and his Chief of Staff ascending the stairs. Tough little Bryant paused in the shade of the verandah and looked at Galt with a hard yet excited glitter in his eye. He knew that something out of the ordinary was behind his being brought up here from Queensland in a bomber and with a P-38 squadron for escort. Such panoply did not usually accompany the movements of general officers. Galt could testify they hadn't accompanied his movement to Buna and back.

Galt rose and saluted and shook hands, but dispassionately, in a way that said, *This has nothing to do with our friendship up to this point. This is really big.* He saw both men to cane chairs and went to fetch Big Drum.

There were certainly no jollities when Big Drum emerged on to the verandah. He wasn't much of a handshaker or a backslapper, certainly not before a task was achieved. Gibbs and his chief of staff both felt a certain sense of awe as Big Drum sat down and got out that damn cigarette holder and jammed it in the corner of his mouth and looked at them with his august eye.

'Tell these gentlemen about Dobadura and Buna, Galt,' Big Drum ordered in a still, barely audible voice. 'Fill them in.'

Galt played along. He spoke low and in awe as well. But then, he had felt awed by the fiasco in Buna. 'It's a disaster, Bryant, and it could sink our front. The men are exhausted and sick and ill-managed and – in my opinion – damn poorly trained. Stevens and most of his battalion commanders are dithering. The communications system is gone completely. Our troops are letting the Australians down. There it is. That's the bluntest way to put it. *Our troops* are letting the Australians down. We're looking foolish to our allies, and if news about this got back to Washington, we'd all be militarily dead.'

He paused to gauge effect.

'As well as that, the supply situation has been bungled. Not from this end. Not from Clancy's end. But there. No one is effective. Supplies just sit in the sun at Soputa and no one moves them in the quantities needed.'

Galt and Big Drum between them and by instinct conspired to let a silence grow then.

At last Big Drum took his empty cigarette-holder out of his

mouth to make a pronouncement. 'Bryant, I'm putting you in command at Buna. Relieve Stevens and send him back here, where after a curt greeting we'll dispatch him Stateside. As well as relieving Stevens, Bryant, I want you to sack all officers who won't do their job or who won't fight. I mean, right down to regimental and battalion commanders. If necessary, put sergeants in charge of battalions and corporals in charge of companies – anyone who will fight. Sack the quartermaster and bring in someone you can trust. Sack the intelligence chief, too. Bring in an engineer you know will make a track from the air supply strips to the fighting troops. Time is of the essence, Bryant. The enemy may land reinforcements at Buna and Gona any night.'

Then Big Drum went striding down the verandah and looked out into the teeth of the glare off the harbour of Port Moresby. He spoke softly now, but just loud enough for Galt and Gibbs and his Chief of Staff to hear. 'Those boys up there in front of Buna are from Michigan and Wisconsin. National Guardsmen. They aren't used to that climate. But imagine how I feel, General Gibbs, when the Australian, General Billings, draws to my attention the fact that last Tuesday the Australians got to within sixty yards of the Japanese airstrip at Buna, and then had to withdraw because they found themselves outflanked. Where there should have been an American battalion, a battalion with a proud record since the War between the States, the 128th Battalion, there was instead the *enemy*. Our boys had, not to put too fine a point on it, *lit out*. They had thrown their weapons and other equipment away, the better to flee.'

He turned around, did one further lap of the spacious verandah, turned again and fixed Gibbs with his avian eye.

'Bryant, I want you to take Buna or not come back alive.' He pointed also to Gibbs's Chief of Staff, but without looking at the man, still keeping his gaze fixed on Gibbs. 'And that goes for your Chief of Staff, too. You have no purpose but the taking of Buna. If ever you were men who gave excuses, let me tell you you have uttered your last one. It is either Buna or your body! I hope you understand?'

Bryant Gibbs pushed his jaw around somewhat, readjusting it as if he had just been struck a blow.

'I understand, General,' he said.

'Let's go and have some mangoes for breakfast,' said Big Drum.

After a mango and some coffee in the dining room, Big Drum stopped in front of the place where Gibbs was eating a heartier breakfast of scrambled eggs. Now he was ready for gestures of friendship. He put a hand affectionately on Gibbs's shoulder. 'If you take Buna, Bryant, I'll give you a Distinguished Service Cross and recommend you for the highest British decoration as well. Also, I shall release your name for newspaper publication. You'll become as famous as General Bradley.'

Gibbs allowed himself a half-smile in Galt's direction. *That*, thought Galt, was the reason Bryant would do the job. If Big Drum couldn't overawe him, the Japanese might have a diminished chance.

'Why thank you, General,' said Gibbs.

Broadly smiling now. As if to say, Big Drum must really be serious.

His moans woke her in the small hours. She felt sweaty; the night air was dense with humidity. The dark was smothering. In the near-panic she had frequently suffered since the air raid took her breath away, she searched for her torch beside the bed, found it and switched it on, panting in relief to find there was still light in the world.

Galt was seated on the edge of the bed, his hand in front of his face as if there was something there too tender to touch.

'One of my molars, Dim,' he said in a swollen-tongued way. 'The nerve feels like it's totally exposed.'

He rose and crossed the room to a small table by the window where a bottle of Scotch stood. He poured himself a small amount and rinsed it around his mouth. He swallowed hurriedly. 'Ach!' he said, grimacing. 'That's not the solution, Dim.'

In the end, the pain was so sharp that Dim went and woke the American nurse in the other room. The nurse had a medical kit. She searched for the phial of cocaine drops which was included in it.

At three in the morning, Galt and the nurse and Dim sat

together in the kitchen, the nurse and Dim in their nightdresses, Galt in his uniform pants. The women drank tea, and Galt waited for the Novocaine, which he had poured on to a swab of cotton wool and held wadded against his screaming tooth, to take effect.

It was a new and not totally comfortable experience to be so frank with Dim's housemate. She was used to seeing Galt around the house, but it was the first time she had encountered him in terms which stated frankly that he spent entire nights with Dim. Dim noticed, however, that the nurse took it all with great aplomb. Again, a woman who'd seen everything and could wryly forgive.

'There are two field dental units here in Moresby,' she told Galt familiarly, a sister talking good sense. 'I don't know though . . . to be honest . . . if you ought to trust this to them unless you have to.'

She did not call him *General*. She did not call him *sir*. This kitchen table conversation was innocent of titles.

'My dental records are in Brisbane,' said Galt. 'I'll probably have to fly down there. Goddammit!'

It was not the first time Dim had noticed that Americans were painstaking and even fussy about their health. In north-eastern Victoria, for example, the men who worked on her father's sheep station, even her father as well, took toothache on an ache-by-ache basis. They did not see a problem with one tooth as affecting the whole realm of the mouth. They did not need dental charts. They needed only some bush practitioner, preferably but not necessarily a dentist, to rip the offending tooth out by its roots and then rinse the socket with rum or antiseptic. It was characteristic of American thoroughness – she didn't want to think, for the moment, that it represented self-centredness – that they should not want a tooth drawn without a dental chart to sail by. An entire geography, a blueprint was involved.

She realized she intended to marry into this strangeness, but it would never become native to her.

Galt reached out and held her hand in both of his. 'I'm sorry, Dim,' he told her. 'I'll only be gone three days. Maximum.'

'You don't have to ask my permission,' she said, smiling. Here he was, masterminding Big Drum's war, Big Drum's march to the Presidency, and he was begging the pardon of an Entertainment Officer because he wanted three days off!

'That tooth will really hurt when you're airborne,' the nurse warned him.

'I know,' he said. He turned to Dim. 'I'll bring you back a floral dress.'

Two days after Galt flew off to Brisbane, she was surprised to find Paul Stacey in her office.

'I thought you were over in Buna,' she said.

He stood before her desk. He was very tall. Clearly he would not sit until invited to.

'I was,' he said.

'Please, sit down.' He did, arranging his long legs in a way which struck her as disconsolate.

'Thank you for saving my mind that day out at the airstrip.'

'Did I save your mind?'

'I think I would have gone crazy if I didn't have a friend there.'

She noticed he did not seem to welcome these compliments. He was still frowning. 'They've pulled me out, Dim. Those American bastards!' Surprisingly, he did not apologize for this profanity, as the Stacey she'd met earlier almost certainly would have. 'They didn't like a piece I sent back. They said it was bad for morale.'

He drifted off into thinking about this for a while. He seemed dismally aggrieved, as if his probity had been questioned. In every likelihood, it *had*.

'Who pulled you out?'

'Big Drum's press office. In their neat uniforms. God, you ought to see the US sector of the front. The troops are hungry and in tatters, and they don't have cigarettes and vitamin pills like the jokers in Big Drum's press office. The jungle terrifies them. They can't tell where anyone is. General Gibbs is trying to untangle everything, to set up a chain of command. But the men have lost heart. They're wearing long beards. They won't patrol, even though it's the only thing that can protect them from ambush. They just go to sleep in the mud and hope that God will make it all pass.

'So I was silly enough to write what I would call a very sympathetic piece about their sufferings, and Big Drum's headquarters intercepted it when I radioed it through, and I was ordered out. Like a miscreant, a bloody schoolboy found smoking.'

He looked Dim straight in the eye, something he did not do with people generally, since he was a man of shy niceties. 'Big Drum's press office are bloody tyrants. The Yanks are supposed to believe in freedom of speech. Well, that's gone by the board. That's completely down the drain! My father's put in a formal protest. But what's Big Drum so paranoid about?'

Dim could have told him what it meant – Big Drum was to be emperor, and all press releases had to be honed to that objective. She felt sympathy for Stacey, but she thought him naïve. He did not know the Big Plan.

Dim wondered if he had come simply to tell her this, or if he had another purpose as well. Because he still had the manner of a man working up to something. What it was soon surfaced. 'I wonder would you like to come to a party?' he asked then, as if that was the hard part of this conversation and all the rest had been prelude. 'Up at Château Stacey, Lieutenant Lewis? The press villa. It's my welcome back, you see. A celebration of my distress. Mainly Aussies. A few of the enemy just for colour.'

'The *enemy*?'

'The Americans.'

The idea of a party, an event in which she could simply be one other officer, appealed to her.

'I would like that very much. I'm not sure if I can find the press villa in the dark though.'

Stacey stood and leaned, gangling, over her desk. 'Don't worry about that. You'll be collected by jeep. 07.00 hours. If I were you, Mrs Lewis, I'd have a siesta this afternoon, in preparation. I intend to.'

And he gave that old, shy, oblique smile again, which showed that Big Drum's press office hadn't quite taken his youth away from him.

Chapter 10

Jealousy which lasts till Christmas

SUSPECTING SHE MIGHT need the safety of numbers, Dim took along to the party at the press villa that evening three girl vocalists from Melbourne, the Brontë Sisters, who – like Ray Harris in his time – had come to Moresby to entertain the troops. The Brontë Sisters seemed to be tough but generous-hearted girls in their late twenties. They wore their blonde-to-reddish hair bouffant-style, and in their act often perched a patriotic forage cap up on top. They were an antipodean version of the famous American Andrews Sisters.

In any case, everyone at the press villa seemed delighted to see them. Particularly so, a group of young officers from Big Drum's press office. One of them, a dark young lieutenant with a cowboy accent, took a particular liking to the youngest of the three singers. So, too, did a friend of Stacey's, a fellow correspondent for a rival Melbourne paper. Feeling so profoundly wed to Galt, Dim saw herself as an observer at this party and took some amusement in the increasingly drunken rivalry which developed between the Australian and the American.

Later she would not easily forgive herself for forgetting that harmless rivalry could quickly move on from *Ignore what he says*! to *Shut up*! to *Who's going to make me*?

Perhaps it was because she and Stacey were chatting together at the time: distracting each other from taking part in what looked like the usual, banal, boastful contest across the room between the Australian war correspondent and the American press officer. The other thing that allayed Dim's concern was that the youngest Brontë sister seemed quite happy to have generated a competition between the two men. So Dim had no need to interfere to protect her entertainer.

'You invited the "enemy"?' she asked Stacey, ironically nodding to all the young Americans in the room.

'They're just the office boys,' said Stacey. 'Besides, we can show we're not intimidated, I suppose.'

'Advance Australia!' said Dim.

'Poor bloody Australia. There's seven million of us in a continent the size of the United States! Those two facts are the determinants of our existence, Dim. For one thing, they make us history's bridesmaids.'

'It doesn't matter. Our time will come.'

'Do you believe that?'

For some reason, Dim thought of her father. Whenever anyone inquired into the nature of Australians and whether they had talent, she always thought of him. Did this mean she still had a ten-year-old's view of the world? If so, she might as well be unapologetic about it. She nodded. 'Yes. It might take time. But we *are* a remarkable people.'

Stacey spoke confidentially. 'You know who the remarkable people are? The really remarkable people? The remarkable people are the Japanese.'

Stacey's drunken friend began making a loud, angry speech. The anger saved it from incoherence. 'You people are all bloody liars. Lies reach a professional bloody level with you jokers. That's when you're not out-and-out bloody cowards. You go to this base hospital here in Moresby and look at the men who've just been brought in! OK. They're from the Australian Second Battalion. One poor bastard is a stockman from the Northern Territory, and he's been wounded in five places. And why? Because bloody craven bastards in your Civic Force buggered off and left the Second Battalion exposed. Not only do you lie about the results, you're bloody craven bastards as well. So why should any Australian girl want to speak to you?'

The dark-complexioned young American officer remained admirably composed through all this, and bravely argued – for the sake of the youngest Brontë sister who couldn't really have given a damn – that Stacey's friend was talking about ancient history. General Gibbs had taken over up there now. General Gibbs was personally leading Civic Force against the bunkers of

Buna. 'From now on, you guys are mere auxiliaries,' said the young officer dangerously, and Stacey's mad-eyed friend listened for the moment. 'You guys are the pipsqueaks of the Pacific. You think this is all about goddamn hayseed bravery, when it's all about numbers! Nothing but numbers. And in the end, we'll bring numbers to bear that'll make your goddamn head spin, hayseed!'

It was as if the American had been listening to Stacey's earlier conversation with Dim, had picked up a sense of the Australian sensitivities and where to probe them.

There was a tussle then, because the Australian tried to hit the American. People moved in to separate the antagonists. When Stacey's drunken friend seemed pacified, the peacemakers let go of him. In the next second he managed one clean, graceful punch which landed so flush that the dark-complexioned boy dropped legless with an awful suddenness.

Now that someone had fallen, there was a primal scrimmage, but Stacey and a second wave of coolheads calmed it down and separated the combatants. In the aftermath, the American's friends tried to rouse him, shaking him by the shoulder, tapping his cheekbone, but avoiding his jaw which was distended. Stacey and others stood by contritely for a time. Then Dim saw Stacey move away from the group, take another war correspondent by the arm, and whisper to him. The man Stacey had spoken to led the culprit, the young man who'd landed the punch, out of the room, down the verandah, helped him into a jeep and drove him away.

Soon an ambulance and a detachment of MPs arrived. A young medic said he believed the American press officer's jaw was broken. He was suffering also a severe concussion.

A lieutenant of the US Military Police began to collect witnesses' names. 'Who hit Lieutenant Signorelli?' he asked Stacey.

Stacey tried to argue that it was confused, and the MP officer ordered him to quit bullshitting. Stacey insisted that it had been a scuffle, and a number of fair-minded Americans spoke up and said that there had been equal blame for the brawl. But the MP officer kept insisting, and at last Stacey said that the man who'd landed the punch had been taken home. He wasn't sure what his name was. He was a blow-in. A correspondent? asked the officer.

Yes, said Stacey, a correspondent. Well, said the MP officer, we'll just have to interview every Aussie scribe.

Amongst the names he took were those of the Brontë Sisters and of Dim Lewis.

The next day, in her office at Bataan, Dim would find herself presented with a summons to appear at a court of military inquiry into the grievous bodily harm done Lieutenant Signorelli of Southwest Pacific Zone Headquarters Press Office.

Stacey drove Dim and the chastened Brontë Sisters home. First he dropped the Brontë Sisters at their tent quarters in the Australian compound, and then turned the jeep towards Dim's villa. When he drew the jeep up outside Dim's place, the night seemed very dark and the burring sounds of insects could be heard even with the engine running.

For a second, while Dim mentally prepared a small speech of thanks, they both sat still.

Stacey said, 'It didn't turn out too well, did it? I'm sorry, Mrs Lewis.'

'You were calling me Dim earlier this evening.'

'Isn't there some other name?' he asked. 'Dim isn't the word for you.'

'I'm stuck with it. It's better than Dimity. Dimity sounds like something crocheted you put down on a dining room table under the teapot. As I explain to everyone, it's my Scottish grandmother's name.'

'All right then. *Dim.*' He breathed in and raised his eyes for a while to the canopy of foliage overhead. 'I hope that Lieutenant Signorelli doesn't die. Both for his own sake and for ours. That American MP was really looking for blood.'

'Can they court-martial your friend? After all, he's not a member of the armed forces.'

'I don't know how the law stands,' said Paul Stacey, not seeming to care much for the moment either.

'It was a nice night apart from Lieutenant Signorelli. Thanks for letting me bring the Brontë Sisters.'

He laughed. 'It's a long way from Wuthering Heights,' he said.

She began to get out of the jeep, but he grabbed her gently by the upper arm. His face looked absolutely stricken, as if he was overtaken by sudden pain.

'Dim, I'm sorry. I know you're a hero's wife. But I love you. You're beautiful. You're the most exquisite woman I've ever set eyes on, and you're lively and generous and nobody's fool. I'm not asking you to do anything about it. I wouldn't be an absolute bastard like that. I mean, your husband . . . I admire those fellows. But if he were here now I'd try to take you away from him. I just had to tell you that. I want you to know that.'

Dim felt a strange shame. Firstly, it was a boy's speech. Secondly, she was married indeed, utterly and in spirit, but not to the brave man whom Stacey admired.

She began to mutter the normal things that applied at embarrassing moments like this – how flattered she was and so forth. But even as she said it, she knew how much it had taken for Stacey to make his declaration like this.

'I'm sorry,' he said. 'You should go.'

Her body crepitating with embarrassment, she said goodnight yet again and got down from the jeep.

'Dim,' he called.

She turned briefly.

'I'm ashamed,' he said. 'But I'm glad too.'

She told him not to worry about it. She hoped she was so offhand that he would never contact her again.

Galt returned within three days. The tooth had had to be pulled. The socket was still apparently draining. There was a sourness on his breath. 'Your toothless old man is home,' he told her. As she would remark later in the evening, he still had some bite.

He had brought her a yellow and white dress, apologizing that it had been impossible to find silk in Brisbane. This was the best he could manage, he said.

She was delighted with it. It was obvious, from his report of what the saleswoman had said to him that he had bought it himself and not merely sent an aide out.

This was like a homecoming for two homeless children.

The next visit from him, however, he was polite in a glacial sort of way. He sat drinking his Scotch and water and projecting a sort of thoughtful reproach. She wondered had he heard some garbled story about her going to Stacey's party.

'Come on,' said Dim. 'I don't like bloody mysteries. Tell me what it is?'

He thought some more but then he began to tell her. 'This Signorelli business has come across my desk. There's going to be a court of inquiry. There has to be. Signorelli's only just woken up, and half his tongue's paralysed, and his left arm as well. Fortunately, the doctor says he'll get better. Dim, I just wonder. What in the hell were you doing at that party?'

'I was being sociable,' she said at once, combatively. She knew she couldn't give him an inch in a matter like this. 'I was giving the Brontë Sisters a night out.'

'Your name is on the list of potential witnesses, for Christ's sake. At least I was able to cross it out.'

'Why shouldn't I give evidence if they want me?' she asked. 'I'm not ashamed of being there.'

'Who asked you to go there though?' he asked, taking a sip of his drink. 'It was what you'd call male personnel, wasn't it?'

'Not exactly personnel. A war correspondent. An Australian. A friend of my husband's. His name is Paul Stacey. You wouldn't know him.'

Galt laughed in a way she considered unworthy of him. Men thought women were self-dramatizing. But that laugh was self-dramatizing to the limit. It said, *She considers me a fool. She's deliberately toying with me.* 'I know the sonofabitch, Dim. We threw him out of Buna.'

'You're proud of that, are you? That you threw him out for trying to tell us what's really happening over the mountains?'

Galt continued laughing in the offensively smart, superior way of a man who considers himself to have been hurt. 'It is expedient for the sake of the people that one man should be prevented from being a know-it-all and telling a little bit of the truth. There are people who have envied Big Drum since he commanded a brigade in the Ardennes a quarter of a century ago. There are lesser humans, and they have no destiny. They would fall with great glee on the fragment of truth – if that's what you call it – which your friend Stacey wanted to give the world.'

Dim was all at once a little chastened. She believed in Big Drum too. In Galt's arms, she had assented to the Big Plan. But, of course, the Big Plan and its validity wasn't really Galt's point. His point was individual jealousy. She wasn't going to give it room.

She said, 'If you were away again, and if he asked me again, I'd go. Like many a woman, Galt, I like an outing. That's all there is to say.'

'All?' he asked. 'You want me to believe that, do you, Dim?'

'I do. Only because I said it. Only because I wouldn't have said it if it wasn't the truth.'

He stood up and began to pace the living room of the little villa. Thank God the nursing officer wasn't there to see this show of rancour. 'It just seems it didn't take you long, Dim. I'm gone in the morning, and by that evening you're at a party. How come you got to know this goddamn hack Stacey so quickly?'

'As I told you, I already knew him. We came on the same plane to Moresby. Galt, I warn you. Don't be like this.'

'How am I supposed to be? Am I supposed to be the silent, cuckolded Chief of Staff? Am I to be the old rooster? Is Stacey the young rooster? You tell me. How am I supposed to be?'

'Galt, I'm warning you. It's so unjust.'

'A witness has already told the MPs they saw Stacey drive off with you. This was after Signorelli was knocked flat.'

'For God's sake, Galt. The Brontë Sisters were with us too!'

'OK. OK. Just look me in the eye, Dim, and tell me that he dropped you off first. Come on, look me in the eye and tell me that.'

She couldn't tell him that, of course. So she refused to answer. She walked to the chair where he'd been sitting and picked his campaign cap up from the floor.

'I was once a young man myself, Dim,' he was loudly proclaiming. 'I know what young men are like. They don't ask you to parties and they don't drive you home because their mothers told them to do it. They're being kind for their own sakes. They want something from you. So the question arises, doesn't it, Dim? The big question arises.'

Dim took his cap, stamped out across the wide verandah and hurled it into the bushes. Then she turned. He was standing at the double doors. 'Get out!' she told him.

'I'm not the one here on sufferance,' he said. 'You're the one who's on sufferance.'

'Right-oh,' she told him. 'I'll move out tomorrow morning.'

'Don't be fucking stupid,' he said. 'I'll get out of your way. No doubt you'll want to go over to the Aussie press villa.'

She turned and hit him hard on the upper arm. 'Don't slander me, bugger-it-all!'

His lips were pursed in a hateful way she somehow thought of as patrician. He turned and went straight away down the steps into the garden. He parted bushes and found his cap, clamped it on his head, and walked out to his jeep.

She spoke low so that he would not hear. The tears were running freely now. 'Bugger you, Galt! I love you, can't you bloody see?'

He stayed away for a week. It was the worst week she had ever endured, matching for human misery her bewildered first week at boarding school in Melbourne at the age of ten. She spent pensive, miserable nights with the nursing officer, who did not press her for information or exceed the boundaries of ordinary sisterly talk. Except once – the final cup of tea of the evening, and both of them in their kimonos, ready for bed.

'I don't know,' said the nurse. 'I just take one look at your face and I know what I've always known. Love isn't worth the pain. Work is a girl's best friend. It was always that way.'

Dim stared into the middle distance. She tried to gauge her suitability for a life of loveless efficiency.

'Of course,' said the nurse then. 'I have to say I like the look of that young Aussie correspondent who came here to collect you the other night. Please.' And she held her hand up. 'I'm not trying to interfere. It could be though that he's more your age and type.' The nurse gulped her tea nervously. 'I suppose I've said too much.'

'No. You're right. If God knew what he was doing, I'd be in

love with the Australian. Not with an American General more than fifty years old.'

Christmas was coming. No one really believed that you could do more than *attempt* Christmas up here, in this steamy port. Shell-shocked young men arrived by plane from the front, or else were carried out, wounds crawling with jungle bugs. The atmosphere wasn't right for big Christian festivals.

A future with Allan Lewis, who might be anywhere this Christmas, and a future without Galt seemed equally desperate.

Three days before Christmas, Galt turned up in his jeep at the gate. He strolled up the path amongst the bougainvillaeas, a bound volume in his hand. When he knocked on the front door, Dim – who could see him through the double windows of her bedroom – let the nurse answer it.

'Hallo, captain,' Galt told the nurse. 'Is Lieutenant Lewis in?'

'I'll go and see,' said the nurse, with the firmness of an older sister anxious for the happiness of a younger one.

'I'll have to see him,' Dim muttered as soon as the nurse entered her bedroom.

'You give him hell, honey,' said the nurse.

Dim went out into the living room, where Galt was sitting in a rattan chair. He stood up, the bound volume in his hand.

'Dim,' he said, 'I'll tell you everything you'll need to know. The idea of young men desiring you makes me crazy. I know I have to do something about it, I have to stop letting myself think like that. But I don't know how to. I'll do my best.'

He looked at the floor and up again. 'Second, I've stayed away all this time out of bloody stupid Virginian pride. It's done me no good. I've been in hell. I mean, how could I have caused you pain like that?'

'I don't know,' she said. 'I don't intend to go through it on a regular basis.'

He laughed in a simple, grateful way. 'My Dim,' he said. 'Look, I've brought you the only present I could find. Forgive me. Forgive me, Dim.'

He came towards her and pushed the book he was holding into her hands. She looked at the gold lettering on its spine: *A*

History of Sheep Farming in the Colony of Victoria. She heard him start to laugh again. 'I stole it out of Big Drum's library. Your grandfather, so I notice, gets a mention in it.'

Dim took possession of the volume. She turned the pages. Tracks of mould ran across the old photographs of championship rams and proud breeders. She had a sense that the world of men was fundamentally innocent – it dealt with the unimportant things like the best ram and the best way to reduce Buna, and there was a continuity between her grandfather, the sheep king, and her lover, the king of operational planning.

'Is this for Christmas?' she asked in a voice which insisted on breaking.

'No. No, Dim. There'll be other presents.'

She could barely speak, but she managed to wave her hand. 'There's no need for them,' she said.

Galt then dropped to his knees on the floor of the villa. 'I'll manage this crazy jealousy, Dim. You deserve better.'

She had a sense of this being excessive, unreal, baroque. 'Get up, Galt,' she said. 'This isn't Shakespeare, you ratbag!'

Though he didn't bother burdening Dim with the knowledge, Galt had received a letter from Senator Vandergrift suggesting that if possible there should be an announcement of a victory round about the Christmas/New Year period. The Navy and the Marines seemed to be holding on in Guadalcanal, and it was important that they should not steal Big Drum's thunder by trying to hog the Christmas glad tidings. The Allies were announcing successes in North Africa as well. Big Drum's old enemy, General Channing, would be delighted to find that by the beginning of the new year, 1943, Big Drum had no glories to display. Senator Vandergrift said he understood that victories couldn't be made to order, but even if the Buna campaign had reached a conclusive stage by the start of the new year, perhaps *that* could be dressed up to look like the real item, something like a triumph.

That, said the letter, was the thinking not only of Senator Vandergrift but of Senators Coulter and Greenidge, and of the Congressional Republican leader Thornton Downes. It would be helpful if, despite Big Drum's criminal lack of resources –

criminal, that is, on the part of General Channing and the President – Big Drum stamped the new year as his own.

Through the party machine, Senator Vandergrift's group had the resources to disseminate throughout the press the slogan, *You Can't Beat Big Drum.* And when, as planned, the Republican convention drafted Big Drum in 1944, that slogan would already have come to dominate the public imagination and become the battle cry of Big Drum's drive towards the Presidency.

Vandergrift said he knew that Galt was the man to talk to Big Drum about this. Big Drum was an honest fellow. But he sometimes, like any human being, had a boyish urge to colour the facts his way, and that was a worthwhile tendency in a politician. He who does not toot his own horn, the same shall not be tooted. It would be a matter of Galt passing on the political news to Big Drum and planting the idea in the terms Vandergrift had already stated: *if* the campaign around Buna had reached a conclusive stage, then . . .

If Bryant Gibbs was getting control over there in the swamps and the kunai, it was not yet quite clear at Moresby. But at least there were hopeful signs that the Japanese were suffering attrition. Radio signals – and Bryant had established radio links with all his units – spoke of an increasing number of suicidal enemy charges against enfilading fire. That seemed significant. Until now, the enemy had been masters of the enfilade.

Based on these straws in the wind, and in preparation for a possible announcement of the kind Vandergrift's letter had suggested, Galt went, spoke to the chief press officer and told him to leak word to the journalists in the field and the news organizations in the US of an important announcement likely to be made over the next few weeks. It seemed to serve well to create an atmosphere of anticipation in the press office, even though, up to now, there had been little to be too anticipatory about; apart, of course, from the Battle of the Coral Sea and the part of Big Drum's B-17s in it; the Australian (Allied) victory at Milne Bay, and the Australian (Allied) repulsing of the Japanese over the Owen Stanley mountains and back to Buna.

While Galt busily attended to all this ground work with the press office, he felt a pulse of regret. He would not go to the

White House himself. He would by then have filed for divorce, and that would have made him an unsuitable Secretary of Defense. And though he intended everything he'd promised Dim; though he couldn't imagine a life separate from her, just the same he needed to employ a different set of underused imaginative cells to picture Big Drum in the White House without him. He had till now in his life been half-amused by the tests society set men who wanted public office. The Democrat President had a mistress who travelled with him and performed services limited only by the man's parlous health condition. But that was OK, because he remained staunchly married to the First Lady. Let him, however, acknowledge that his marriage was a sepulchre, let him proclaim love for his mistress publicly, and the great tree of his political support would wither overnight. That the American system should depend on a man's public pretence that his dead marriage was vibrantly alive seemed no longer a joke to Galt, but an American tragedy.

Big Drum himself disrupted the idea of anything developing before Christmas by flying back to Brisbane. He had a particular Indian suit and a very fancy model car with a beeper horn, both put away at a Brisbane department store and reserved for Little Drum's Christmas.

The absence of Big Drum enabled Dim and Galt to spend the whole of Christmas together. Clancy's transports had brought in a limited number of turkeys, and Dim and Galt and the nursing officer spent the morning preparing one of them in the kitchen of Dim's villa. Dim and Galt had earlier, separately, attended the Episcopalian Christmas service over at the Administration villa, Dim well back in the wide-open-windowed wooden church ringed by slit trenches in case of air attack, and Galt representing the United States itself on the threshold of the altar. The chaplain of a nearby artillery unit gave the sermon, in which he said that Jesus had come even to redeem the enemy. Indeed if the Japanese had before now listened to Jesus's message, this whole savage conflict might not have got under way.

Back at the bungalow, before they ate the turkey, as a sort of ceremonial reading, and in imitation of the gunners' chaplain,

Galt read from *A History of Sheep Farming in the Colony of Victoria* the piece which concerned Dim's grandfather:

'In 1843, my dear brothers and sisters, the highest price ever paid for wool in the history of the world up to that time was reached when the factors and representatives of the great woollen mills of Bradford, Leeds and Huddersfield paid thirteen pence a pound for a wool clip which came principally from the merino stud station of Angus Sinclair MacRobertson. MacRobertson, dearly beloved brethren, was a native of Fife who had managed to purchase on preferential terms, arranged with the inadequately informed Governor of New South Wales Sir Henry Gipps, a large holding between the Ovens and King Rivers. This land had previously been granted the North-East Grazing Company by the Colonial Secretary of Great Britain. But a six-month delay in correspondence between Britain and Australia meant that MacRobertson was able to make good his title over the disputed grazing land through a court case which lasted three years.'

That court case had been the subject of anecdotes and legends in Maneering during Dim's own childhood, nearly a hundred years after the case was fought. How strange now to hear the details read out of a dry book by an American general.

'The wool clips of this and successive years would bring MacRobertson substantial returns, my brethren. Yea verily, was MacRobertson a pirate? No!' (And here Galt returned to the real text.) 'Still, though already wealthier than most British landlords, he was – like most of the squatters of the region – forced to live in fairly primitive slab timber accommodation. These rudimentary structures would of course be crowded with William IV furniture, pianofortes, Staffordshire and Meissen pottery all shipped out from Britain. It would not be until the discovery of gold brought hundreds of thousands of prospectors to Victoria, many of them excellent craftsmen, and all of them providing as superlative a market for MacRobertson's mutton as the woollen mills of Britain did for his wool, that he was able to build his fine house, Thanet . . . '

Galt regarded her severely. 'Is that where you grew up, young lady?'

Dim, who had never known her grandfather, nonetheless remembered Thanet – what a big place it was, and how cold. It went to a lot of trouble to shut out the Australian light, too. To make everything as dim and overcast and sepulchral as old Angus MacRobertson's childhood home in Scotland was, or at least as dark as the homes of the gentry he had envied as a boy.

Her parents had built their own house, ten miles from Thanet. It was rambling and had wide verandahs, and she'd often felt grateful as a child that it was here and not in her grandfather's old pile that she lived.

She explained all this to Galt and the nurse, who listened avidly, Galt because he was in love, the nurse because she was getting information about a foreign land which she had seen only briefly, during a two-week transit in north Queensland.

Dim noticed Galt growing thoughtful as Christmas lunch ended. She could tell he was thinking of his son. Galt had said privately to her, even while the cooking was going on, 'Either now he's part of the sea, or else he's in some prison hospital in Italy or Tunisia, not knowing who the hell he is.'

So it was a mixed Christmas for Galt. But he thought wistfully too of his daughters, Abbey the language whiz, Sandy the actress, and of his wife back in Virginia, feeling an uxorious and normal compassion for her, for what she must be wondering, for the sad vigil she must be keeping. Dim understood all this and knew she would never claim these memories, and shouldn't even try.

Anyhow, he had received warm letters from both his daughters, and that had made him feel better.

Then, late that night, he confessed something else that was making him pensive.

'They're all going to meet in Quebec next March. There'll be Churchill, the President, Channing, Admiral Kremnitz, Mountbatten, all the commanders from the European sphere. And they're going to sort out the order of business. Who gets what priority. Big Drum wants me to go.'

'Well, my congratulations,' said Dim, brushing her hand across his forehead and the top of his head. 'He obviously thinks you're a clever boy.'

'Yes, and maybe he's mistaken. Everyone else, including his

old enemy, Channing, think he's too influenced by me. Half the goddamn staff here think so too! But he doesn't realize that. He doesn't realize everything I say in Quebec will be discounted.' This sort of self-doubt was very rarely visible in Galt. But he was tired and a little hung over. She was surprised to find how much she liked the doubtful General Sandforth as against the severe administrative version.

Galt said, 'I urged him to go himself, but he said he's not leaving this zone till it's all over. He asked Channing, why couldn't they hold the meeting in Brisbane? He doesn't like meeting other people on the turf of their choosing. He's got quite a thing about that.'

'I know, I absolutely *know*, you'll be first-class.'

'I'll be gone nearly two weeks – nearly a whole week for flying, and nearly a whole other one for the talks. Now I acknowledge you're entitled to your own social life . . . I just worry like hell about younger men, Dim.'

She wondered should she be angry or lenient. She decided to be soft. 'You have nothing to worry about, for God's sake, Galt, you lunatic.'

'I know this sort of thing only makes you angry . . . '

'It only makes me angry, Galt, because I can't do anything about it. I can't make you as young as most of those people at the party I went to. If you were as young as that, you wouldn't bloody well be Chief of Staff to Big Drum.'

He laughed at that, but then he went solemn around the corners of the mouth again and said, 'I just want to make sure you know what's working on me. If I ever go all Italian and jealous again, I mean. I don't want you to write me off. I don't want you to use my stupidity as the excuse for looking for someone else. Do you understand that, Dim? Does that make sense?'

The explanation had creaked forth. It used emotional machinery which he had not employed for most of his middle age.

'I understand,' she said. 'I'll be as cranky as hell, but I *will* give you a chance to come back and explain yourself.'

He said, 'I wonder did my son ever have a woman like you?

Jesus Christ, I hope so. No one should go into the darkness without that . . . '

And then he began to hiccup with grief, and she opened her arms to a lost boy nearly a foot taller and twenty-seven years older than herself.

A few days after New Year, the Australians captured Gona, and Bryant Gibbs's troops had the Japanese hardcore pushed nearly back onto the beach at Buna mission. The sinister development was that the enemy had landed fifteen thousand first-class troops from Rabaul a little further up the coast at Sananada, so that position, too, was going to require a major battle. The bypassing methods based on Orange Plan Hucker would not apply there, for Buna, which was the start of the way back, could not be held while Sananada threatened it.

Galt had told Big Drum all about Senator Vandergrift's letter, and it was obvious that every day Big Drum scanned the news from Buna for justification for declaring a year's end victory. The Australians' success at Gona was the only definite item Big Drum had to hand, so rather than wait and hope, which was not General Wraith's style, a communiqué went out from Big Drum's press office announcing that Gona had fallen to 'Allied troops', that the Japanese in Buna were within a hair's breadth of defeat, of succumbing to gallant General Gibbs, and that therefore all was over except the mopping up.

This created an ecstatic press at home. It was seen as the first great reversal of the enemy on land. The name Sananada, and the problem it would present Bryant Gibbs, received no mention. Big Drum had seized a victory before Kremnitz had over in Guadalcanal.

At the end of the first week of 1943, Bryant Gibbs flew over the mountains from Buna for a conference with Galt.

'Jesus, Galt,' said the little man as the two of them sat at Galt's desk on the verandah. He had lost weight, and looked profoundly yellow, as if even when he stopped taking the anti-malarials he would never come back to his normal colour. 'What's this fucking mopping up the American press is talking about?'

'Well, Bryant,' Galt spread his hands dispassionately and with apparent apology, 'this is how it is. We do have Gona, Buna's about to fall, and that will outflank the enemy in Sananada. It adds up. And your name's been released to the American papers, just like Big Drum promised.'

Bryant dropped his voice. 'You know what, Galt? I don't understand who's fooling who. Is the press office jerking Big Drum around, or is Big Drum jerking the American public?'

'You're a big-time general now, Bryant.' A feature on General Gibbs had already appeared in *Life*. 'Perhaps you could decide the question for yourself.'

'Yes, but what the fuck do I tell my troops? *Mopping up*. Is it a good enough frigging term to die for?'

As he did a hundred times a day and did now to defend himself from Bryant's just anger, Galt looked out over the harbour. It had been nearly two days since the last air raid. That could mean either that the Japanese bombers were stretched thin, or else that they were saving themselves to support another landing somewhere over on the north coast. General Clancy, the air force man, believed the latter, the less optimistic of the two possibilities. Next time there was bad weather up there, the Japanese would sneak another fifteen thousand men in from Rabaul, and then the bombers and fighters would come in in support. If that happened, Bryant Gibbs would be most likely to fulfil Big Drum's order and die leading his men at Sananada. The Australians were worried anyhow that he already spent too much time far forward. He had managed to win their respect, this little chunk of a man.

Galt, too, appreciated the guts Bryant had shown. Here was a man of perhaps forty-nine, fifty, fifty-one years of age. And he had more than his career at stake. He had invested his very life in a campaign. That gave him the authority to get something like an answer from Galt.

Returning his eyes from their consideration of the harbour, Galt said; 'If you ever quote me, I'll deny we had this conversation. Let me talk straight to you, Bryant. As you know, the President and the Chaumont gang who run the Joint Chiefs are all terrified of Big Drum's success. You don't need a program to know why that's so. It was essential to announce a victory at this time, that's all. So that Big Drum's whole zone doesn't end up starved of supplies. If the Navy have their way, they'll drive on from where they are in the Solomons and leave us as a mere fringe activity. You would feel that, Bryant, hard and sharp, up where you are.'

The eyes in Bryant's solemn face gave a few flickers of appeasement.

Galt seized on them. 'I suggest you tell your men everything depends on Sananda. After that, there'll be more supplies and a different order of doing things.'

'I don't want to be hearing this same tune in a year's time, Galt,' murmured Bryant.

'You do me an injustice, Bryant.'

'OK. I'll fight it Big Drum's way for the moment.'

'Come on, Bryant. Big Drum's way is your path to glory, my boy.'

'I've seen baby soldiers coughing up bubbles of blood and bits of lung, Galt. And what I say is, fuck glory!'

But he smiled.

Chapter 11

Statesmen, Generals and Daughters

IT WAS COLD at the Palais de Justice in Quebec, particularly for Galt and Admiral Kremnitz and their aides who had all spent months in the tropics. A baronial log fire burned at either end of the great *salle*, but their warmth was felt mainly by the junior officers at one end of the table, and by the President and Churchill and their staffs at the other. Galt and Captain Duncan, with Admiral Kremnitz, General Eisenhower, General Montgomery, General Bradley and their respective aides, occupied mid-table. Further up, closer to Churchill and the President, sat the strong but slightly horse-faced Vice-Admiral, Lord Louis Mountbatten.

For the first time in years, Galt wore a winter-weight uniform, specially provided for him by the US Military Mission in Ottawa. He would have liked to have been able to wear his greatcoat in this great, chilly hall, but that wouldn't be diplomatic. During the long, cold stages of the conference, his mind kept drifting too, off to the question of how he could excuse himself from visiting his wife Sandy in Virginia. He wished at the same time to be able to get down to New York and visit his daughter, Sandy the younger, who was acting in a Sherwood Anderson play on Broadway. He might even, if he was lucky, get to see the play. But he did not want to face the stranger who had mothered his vanished son. It had been hard enough at the beginning of the conference, when General Bradley offered his condolences, and declared how he knew that when men went missing it was worse than definite news.

Galt could not share condolences politely with that now remote woman down in Charlottesville. He intended to send her a signal – even to get a staff officer from Central Atlantic Command to call round and tell her – about how her husband regretted that as improbable as it might sound, events in the Southwest Pacific demanded his immediate return to that zone, even though he had been attending a conference in Quebec. He was uncomfortable though to think she might find out from his daughter that he had had time to visit New York. If his daughter were insensitive enough to tell her. His memory was that his daughter had a dark and punishing affection for him. He had after all been a largely absent father.

The first day of the conference had concerned the North African campaign and the question of forces available for a lunge at Europe. Churchill had spoken at great length in his honking, British voice. Did my ancestors really speak like that? Galt wondered.

After coffee on the second morning, the discussion turned to the Pacific, but even then Churchill would not be silent. He went on haranguing the table about the limited forces and *matériel* available in the West. He had spoken of the factors governing the continued strength of purpose and resistance to the Germans demonstrated by the man he called 'Mr Stalin', pronouncing it *Stahl-een*. He had been very eloquent and even amusing during the first day of the conference in describing 'Mr Stahl-een's' demand for a second front to take the pressure off the Russians. But now, with the apparent connivance of the US President, he was hijacking the discussion on the Pacific and making it yet another discussion about European logistics.

'I wish to make it clear if I have not already done so that I agree with my friend Joseph Stahl-een,' huffed Churchill. 'We need at least another thirty American divisions before a new front can be contemplated. And we need the great armouries of the United States to devote most of their manufacture to the needs of the European theatre. The threat of Nippon has now been contained. Even General Wraith has reported victory in New Guinea in the past few months . . . '

Though, as Galt could have told him, Bryant Gibbs lost three thousand lives taking Sanananda. 'Mopping up.'

'I urge upon the President of the United States,' Churchill ground on, 'in the most fraternal manner, linked in the comradeship of arms and of right, that the United States Navy in the

Central Pacific and General Wraith in the Southwest Pacific be asked to hold the line with the resources they already possess, while we destroy the Germans and then outflank the Japanese by crushing Nazism in Europe. Let me put it frankly . . . and I know my friend the President will forgive my frankness. Of the twelve US Army Air Forces now training in the United States, we need the entire dozen. We'd take a baker's dozen, if it were available. Of the ten thousand tanks a month leaving your great manufacturies, we need eleven thousand.

'I know I need remind no one at *this* table that if the Russians cease to fight, then our cause is emasculated. And cease to fight they will unless we can devote ourselves to the opening of a Second Front in Europe. For Joseph Stahl-een is sadly not motivated by the same principles as motivate my friend the President and me. Divine guidance plays no part in Mr Stahl-een's motives. He will realign himself according to his convenience. Suffice it to say, the world is therefore in the balance not in the Pacific, but in Europe.'

There was, even on this second day, an enormous swell of approval around the table for Churchill's position. Galt suffered a curious memory of Teresa Chung. Of all the Filipinos he had known. Of the faces of Filipino soldiers on the road out of Manila and on Corregidor. The seductive appeal of Churchill's request was that it dealt with the question of the 'real' people, the people who spoke European languages and shared 'our' values. Galt saw General Bradley seemed impressed. So were General Eisenhower and even Mountbatten, who was supposed to be concerned with the re-taking of Singapore. But, of course, that could wait.

What was most alarming was that even Admiral Kremnitz seemed pleased. For Kremnitz could make a better argument for moving his aircraft-carriers forward in the Pacific than Galt could for moving armies across the impermeable jungles.

When it came to his turn, towards lunchtime on the second day, that was exactly what Kremnitz said. 'The road to the mainland of Japan lies through the Solomons by way of the Marshalls and Marianas to Iwo Jima. We can use our Navy and the dominance it has established to move our aircraft-carriers forward. They are, in effect, islands with airstrips ready built on them, islands we have not had to lose thousands of infantrymen to secure. Wherever the Marines land, they will do so under the screen of our naval artillery and our naval air wings. What we passionately urge, Mr President and Mr Prime Minister, is that we be allowed to go forward across the Central Pacific while General Wraith holds down the enemy left in New Guinea and New Britain. In that way, some hundreds of thousands of Japanese forces will be immobilized by General Wraith's forces, an objective which I am sure General Wraith would applaud as enthusiastically as anyone else.'

Galt felt a great rage moving in him. *Yes*, he wanted to yell. *Sideline Big Drum. Help the Russians out, and then when you've done that, watch them turn eastwards, turn on the Japanese, grab territory in Asia.* The plausible injustice of making Big Drum's war a side-show came close to unhinging him. But he was not, he knew, very good at speaking in anger. He remembered his old regimental commander at Fort Duchesne, Utah, in 1923, who said to him after an officers' meeting, 'Galt, don't talk when you feel heated. Any fool can do that. You scare the shit out of the sonsofbitches when you talk cool.'

So he waited for the fury to pass, for his anger to anneal to something harder. Luncheon was pressing. Aides were already whispering to the President about it. But the President knew it would appear a slight to Big Drum if Galt were not permitted to speak in the same session as Kremnitz. So, at last and more or less at the bottom of the line, he called on Galt to make his comments.

All at once terrified, Galt gathered himself. He let a silence grow. To hell with the appetites of these old men! 'Mr President,' he said, 'and Mr Prime Minster, thank you for the chance to speak on behalf of my superior, General Wraith. With the greatest respect, I have to say for a start that certain assumptions have gone unchallenged at this table, assumptions at which I myself – coming to this meeting from that distant Southwest Pacific Admiral Kremnitz has already mentioned – find it difficult to hide my incredulity. For example, unlike the Admiral, I do not believe it is possible to stand still in the Southwest Pacific area, for reasons which I have set down in the report I've circulated to all the parties at this table. The war in Europe may well run another ten years. You are proposing that for that time the enemy be allowed to occupy the Dutch East Indies – both Java and Sumatra – as well as Singapore, Malaya, Thailand, Formosa and the Philippines, with all their natural wealth, all their supplies of rubber and oil. You are suggesting that General Clancy's heavy bombers, which cannot operate from aircraft-carriers, be restricted to the present line, that new airfields should not be captured for them, even though their bombing range is so much greater than anything the Navy's planes can provide . . . '

Now he was well launched, and he knew it. He began to speak of the enemy air forces which would be left with secure bases of operation if Big Drum was held down. He cast up examples of the Japanese capacity and expertise in moving troops from one zone to another. In a few nights they had landed at Sananda fifteen thousand men from Rabaul. They were not an enemy who would be content to be held down in great numbers on one wing while the Navy made its end run up the Central Pacific.

'Above all,' he announced, 'the idea of this war as a war which can limp, a war which can be fought fully on one front and partially on the other, is a notion which General Wraith believes is based on fallacy. We are fighting an Axis, gentlemen, and what happens on one front will inevitably be reflected in what happens on another.'

He knew he must sound like something more than a mere spokesman. But to hell with it, this was so important. With that smiling Democrat President at the head of the table, so anxious to see Big Drum relegated, dead-ended, how else should he speak?

He took the ultimate risk then. 'I would even say this, Mr President and Mr Prime Minister and colleagues – that the American people would be extremely dissatisfied if General Wraith were not supplied equally when compared with generals in other areas. The American people, by all opinion polls, consider him the man who can best repulse the enemy. *Time* Magazine this very week, gentlemen, has expressed alarm at the fact that such a national icon has been relegated to command of what the magazine itself sees as a "secondary front". They consider that he should be supported to the hilt, and that his secondary front be made the front of major thrust in the Pacific. They would certainly not be happy to contemplate a situation in which his front was actually reduced to a mere line of defence.'

He could tell he had them now. He had at least shocked them, at best galvanized them, with his invoking of *Time* Magazine.

'General Wraith sympathizes with the Prime Minister of Great Britain and his Atlantic concerns. But no American administration should forget that *we* are also a Pacific nation as well as an Atlantic one.

'Lastly, I remind you that there are some thirty or forty million Filipinos who expect us to fulfil our pledge to return and deliver them from this Asiatic tyranny. If we forget that particular pledge, I suggest, with the greatest respect, we will be high and dry in the Pacific when the war comes to an end. We will be considered a nation whose word is worthless. It is from this fate that General Wraith looks to deliver America.'

George Channing looked like a very ordinary man. He had the sober face and the receding lower features which Galt associated with those of a Methodist preacher. His hair was not so much thin as threadbare. He made a very prosaic-looking Chairman of the Joint Chiefs of Staff.

This was the man who now summoned Galt to the fifth floor of the Hotel Montmireil, where the Joint Chiefs and their staffs were billeted. The generals and admirals from the different war zones had been accommodated in various suites on the third and fourth floor, and so Galt did not have far to travel that evening after his speech at the Quebec Conference, to face General Channing. Channing was well established in Galt's map of the military earth as Big Drum's old enemy. He had once watched with joy Big Drum's loud and bitter reprimand at the hands of General Pershing about the state of Brigadier-General Wraith's combat troops during World War I.

Galt took the stairs instead of the elevator. He was asked to wait in the anteroom of Channing's suite, an indignity he passed off by reading through a *New Yorker*. The *New Yorker* was its old self, he noticed. It did carry a few scholarly pieces on this or that campaign, but they were generally to do with news which was old by now. A few of their cartoons made reference to the fact that so much of America's manhood, and womanhood for that matter, was involved in the services. But by and large, the magazine kept its old, pre-World War II whimsy and seemed confident that there would be a life for it after the inconvenience of the cataclysm had passed.

It was the sort of magazine his daughters loved – Abbey the linguist and Alexandra the actress. He couldn't see why, but if he had more time, as he one day hoped to, perhaps he would apply himself to it.

At last a secretary – a colonel no less, but then all the Joint Chiefs' errand runners were colonels – came to lead him in to Channing's office.

Channing didn't waste time shaking hands or exchanging salutes. He was looking distractedly at some report, a slab of someone's condensed wisdom round about five hundred pages in length. 'Sit down, General Sandforth,' he said absently.

Thinking what a hackneyed device this was, Galt sat down. He couldn't be bothered feeling disgruntled, but he did feel suddenly nervous. Earlier he had felt so confident, so willing to shake any tree and beard any lion. Now he suffered with neurotic rather than notional impact the fear of having to go back to Big Drum with the order merely to hold the line, not take battle to the enemy. Though Big Drum would blame not Sandforth himself if this was the result from Quebec, though Big Drum would happily blame Channing and the President, Galt urgently wanted the boldness of his speech in the conference to bear fruit. He knew too that to be told to stand still would be intimately damaging to Big Drum, would unman him, put him into a terminal despair and certainly influence his Presidential chances.

Channing looked up from the report then and even smiled. 'Are you well, Galt? You look well. Very tanned, but a bit yellow as well.'

'It's the malaria pills they make us all take, General Channing.'

Channing nodded and signalled an end to the pleasantries by

thrusting his lips forward in a way which said, *This will be painful.*

'The President was not much amused, General Sandforth, by your invoking the press and the public in your speech today.'

'I regret that, General Channing.' But secretly, Galt was delighted to have shocked the President. This President.

'And to say the President was not amused is to give only a poor picture of how Mr Churchill felt,' George Channing continued. 'He has never – before this day – heard a general bring these elements into a discussion of world strategy.'

'And yet the public pays for all our strategies, General Channing. They sacrifice their sons.'

'That's a very democratic approach for you to take, Galt. I didn't think that around General Wraith such democratic concepts were favoured.'

'The democratic concept of liberating the Philippines is favoured very much, General Channing.'

Channing looked for a second as if he had heartburn. A sourness crossed his homely face. 'I hope you're not implying, Galt, that the Philippines have a low value amongst the Joint Chiefs.'

'We were always confident,' said Galt, 'that if the Joint Chiefs had the facts presented to them, they would support General Wraith's efforts in the Southwest Pacific. And that they would do their best to persuade the politicians that way.'

'Do you *really* feel that way, General Sandforth? It doesn't seem to me that a general who was confident in his superiors would, in making submissions to them, draw their attention to an article in *Time* Magazine of all things. *Time* Magazine is an excellent journal, General Sandforth. But it's a damn-awful basis for planning global campaigns.'

Galt permitted himself a penitent sigh.

'I'm sure you understand, General Channing, that I must be quite fatigued, since I have had further to travel to this conference than anyone else at the table. I have already expressed my regret if I was guilty of an indiscretion in my speech. I'm sure I needn't tell you how much I would appreciate now a clear indication of the policies the President and Mr Churchill settled on as a result of your advice.'

'Very well,' said Channing with a half smile. He didn't mind forthrightness. Everyone said it was his greatest strength. 'Mr Churchill and the President have been persuaded – and I needn't tell you it was a difficult job of persuasion when it came to Mr Churchill – that there should be a continuation of effort in both the Central Pacific and the Southwest Pacific Zone. General Wraith and Admiral Kremnitz will continue to receive an equal share of resources and material. The orders we first issued a year ago, including the order to recapture the Philippines, stands. No brake will be put upon General Wraith.'

Galt spread his hands a little and shook his head in a dumb-show of gratitude.

'Let me say another thing, General Sandforth. You must be aware that General Wraith and I have never been friends, and probably never will be. It's a temperamental thing. I would argue also that it's based on General Wraith's misreading of some of my actions in the past. But then, he would argue that he'd read me accurately. So the enmity's of too long a standing to mess with. But I want the man to be healthy and to have a clear head. And so I'm telling you this: he has nothing to fear from me. There will *never* be a Joint Chiefs' policy to deprive him of men and supplies. There never has been. We are, after all – the lot of us – professionals. The President's communiqués to General Wraith during the Philippines campaign were misleading. They promised reinforcements, and they shouldn't have. Because the reinforcements simply weren't there, and if we'd sent those divisions you now have in Australia and the Southwest Pacific into the Philippines débâcle, they would have been ground beef.

'A second thing to tell you: you know the decision to apply ourselves primarily to the war in Europe. We can keep the British and the Russians fighting hard only by *doing* that, giving them those assurances and then proving our intent. There is no way *that* policy will be reversed. No way. And you and General Wraith and I – we all have to live by that reality. That's not a Chaumont gang stratagem. It's what Churchill came here for and what we're bound to give him. Things could have been vastly worse: if he'd *really* had his way, the whole of the Pacific could go to hell.'

Channing shook his head. He was smiling quite disarmingly. Despite himself, Galt found him formidably so.

'Now I know that Big Drum respects your judgement, General Sandforth. So I want you to help lever him away from unreality, from his fears about me and the other Joint Chiefs, and so free up his enormous creative abilities. Mistrust is killing, when you're over sixty. Like sex and whisky, it's an indulgence of young men. Believe me. I want General Wraith to be still campaigning in ten years' time. And I want him acting on real issues, not on imagined ones. Is that clear to you?'

Galt declared it was. Only later, when he was downstairs drinking scotch with Captain Duncan, did suspicion set in. The Chaumont gang feared Big Drum would be President one day. When that happened, their names would be wiped off honour rolls, army camps and airstrips. They would become forgotten men. They didn't want to be.

This confirmation of Big Drum's destiny excited Galt, and he felt a few seconds' regret that as big a part as he would have in setting up Big Drum's Presidency, he himself would not take part in the power sharing.

But then, he would have Dim, and Dim was essential to him. He knew it. Surely.

It had been nearly ten years since he had last visited New York and he found it a little bewildering, even with everything provided – vehicles, a suite at the Biltmore, a folder supplied by Northeast Atlantic Command with maps and advice on everything from the use of the subway to the qualities of bars. After all his years in the Philippines and in small Australian cities, the crowds and the hubbub seemed enormous. Brisbane and Melbourne, he realized, had made him something of a provincial. He found himself daydreaming about the prospect of bringing Dim here when the war ended, of showing her this immense antheap and all its admitted wonders and eccentricities.

He had tickets to his daughter Sandy's play that night, provided by Sandy herself.

A wistful note from his daughter Abbey had been waiting for him. She said that she could not get up from Washington, where she worked now, and pleaded with him to come down there. It was a dilemma. If he came to Washington he would be so close to Charlottesville that everyone in the family would rightly take it as very remiss, close to callous, if he did not go the extra distance and see his wife.

At four o'clock in the afternoon, he was puzzling over this family dilemma when the reception desk called.

'General, your daughter is here,' the respectful reception clerk announced.

'My *daughter*?' For he knew tht Sandy had a matinée that afternoon.

'Your daughter, Miss Abbey Sandforth, General.'

He was all at once tingling with parental anticipation. Sweet Abbey. Who demanded little of him but kindness and an occasional sighting. 'Please send her up.'

Abbey was tall, perhaps an inch taller than him. She had his wife's angular look, and superb features. Unlike her sister, who had an earthier beauty. She was wearing a plain overcoat over a good suit, and she looked tired, patches of blue exhaustion under her young, but very wise eyes.

After they embraced they both began speaking at once. But at last he was able to say clearly, 'But you look as though you need a rest, Abbey. They're working you very hard down there, aren't they?'

'You know how it is, father. There's an awful lot of material coming in.'

He supposed she was involved in the translation of Japanese radio intercepts, both those in plain and those in code. A New Zealand destroyer had recently captured a complete set of Japanese cipher codes from a sinking Japanese submarine off the north coast of New Guinea. That meant that Big Drum and Washington would be able to find out a great amount about future Japanese movements, would not have to depend solely on endless reconnaissance missions of the kind which had found the Japanese carriers during the Battle of the Coral Sea.

But the price his daughter was paying for all this seemed a

little high. The Sandforths were suffering in this war. And both his son and his daughter had suffered more than he.

'I had that note from you. It was waiting here at the hotel. Young Sandy told you where I was staying?'

'Yes. You could have told me too.' But her reproach was a smiling one.

'I didn't want to disappoint you. I'm only here in New York because the conference ended half a day early.'

'What's Churchill like?'

'Stubborn,' said Galt.

'And the President?'

'He doesn't like me. He thought I was trying to push Big Drum's barrow too much.'

'He's a remarkable President, father.'

'Don't tell me you're turning Democrat before my eyes!'

'I'm just saying, I'm pleased we have him at the moment. Big Drum . . . Big Drum will be fine when he comes too.'

'Are people talking about that? I mean, people in Washington. Do they take it for granted? That Big Drum is on his way?'

'Of course they do. Not as a certainty. But as a likelihood.'

'And what do people think of that? The people you meet in your work, and socially?'

Abbey smiled. It was such a delightful smile, so full of quiet irony. Some fortunate man would take on that smile for life. He hoped the man would be better at everything than he had been with her mother. 'Most of my friends say that if we have to have a Republican some day, it might as well be Big Drum.'

Galt laughed at that. 'Very damn kind of them,' he said.

'Mind you,' she cautioned him, 'some of them see streaks of autocracy in him.'

'They're right,' Galt laughed. 'I see those selfsame streaks every day.'

They called for tea and coffee. Abbey thirstily drank tea and it seemed to relax her. Galt took a telephone call from Captain Duncan about the timetable of their journey back to Port Moresby. They would travel by one of the new B-23s to California, where they would be transferred to a second plane for the flight to Hawaii. There arrangements would be made for the

Hawaii-New Guinea leg, since that would require a fighter escort.

While Galt was on the phone, Abbey simply fell asleep in her chair. The call over, Galt went to her, took her hand and roused her very gently, so that she wouldn't wake fully. 'Come along,' he told her. 'It's bedtime for you.'

'Oh, I'm really sorry,' she said. She smiled. 'Fancy coming to see your father, whom you haven't seen for two and a half years, and then falling asleep.'

He put his arm around her shoulder and pulled her upright. 'You're going to sleep a little longer now, my young friend. We'll have plenty of time to talk at the theatre, and afterwards at supper.'

He led her into his bedroom and pulled the covers back on the bed.

'You're too tired to take your clothes off,' he told her, and she sat down like a small child and let him take her shoes off. He was ecstatic to be at these paternal tasks. He built the pillows up and then pushed her backwards. She lay there blinking, his daughter the Japanese translator, and he smiled at her and then went and drew the drapes.

He woke her two hours later, and she got ready quickly without fuss. She was like *his* mother that way – tasks to do with beauty and decoration were swiftly fulfilled.

They had martinis brought to them from the bar downstairs. At a quarter past seven, their car was ready for them. It took them across town and a little way up, to West 45th, to the Barrymore. Seeing the men and women in overcoats outside the theatre door, under the marquee, gave him an unexpected feeling of excitement. This was *his* daughter they were coming to see. It was astonishing. A child who, when he had first been appointed to Big Drum's staff in 1937, had been a pimply, smouldering adolescent, who had not then been able to find her voice or her authority. They had come to be enchanted by *her*.

She played a young schoolteacher in a small town, in an America somewhere before the war, where there was peace but tedium, poverty and meanness as well. She was driven for company to crass local men – a salesman, a garage proprietor. Older, sour women misjudged her. It was a hypnotic play – at least Galt thought so – about the situation of those who do not so much sell themselves short as have no other option. At the play's end, she was arrested for an attempted murder of the garage proprietor, and was taken away catatonic while older women, still handsome but with their age weighing on them, crowed in chorus, discovering, though, that her fall has really done nothing for them.

It was a strange play to be a hit at such a time, in the midst of war and separation. But perhaps half its charm, as Abbey had said to him in the interval, was that there were worse things, things more narrow, than the war.

The applause and the curtain calls brought unexpected tears to his eyes. He wanted Dim to be here to see this, he wanted young Galt too.

Escorting Abbey backstage afterwards, he had to make a way for them through a mêlée of people at the stage door and in corridors.

Sandy's dressing room was even more of a crush. At the core, a twinkly little man in horn-rimmed glasses was haranguing Sandy, who sat at her dressing table and didn't seem to mind. She was laughing.

'They call it psychological warfare,' he was telling Sandy. 'So does that make me a psychological warrior? I ask you that, and maybe you can answer. I have a feeling, darling Alex, that when this madness is over, the motion pictures people will look at will be the ones not made to fit some little general's idea of what Americans should watch here and now.' Suddenly, Galt recognized the man as the renowned studio founder and head, Sam Schweitzer.

Sandy saw Galt, exclaimed theatrically but with warmth, and rose to embrace him. She did the same to her scholarly sister. Galt found he was excited – almost despite himself – to shake hands with Sam Schweitzer. There was some primitive magic in the movies which rendered people deliciously flustered by contact with anyone involved in that great industry of illusion.

'You are the father of this magnificent girl?' asked Schweitzer. 'General, you will soon deserve the world's gratitude.'

Sandy smiled, and he rejoiced to see, was quite pleased with herself. 'Mr Schweitzer wants me to contract myself to his studios for two films.' She turned to the producer. 'Will you be sweet to me, Mr Schweitzer, once the contract ink is dry?'

'Darling, to all the beautiful and talented women at the Schweitzer studios. I play no favourites.'

'I don't want to find myself a movie serf,' said Sandy.

'Darling, you're talking to the son of serfs. I treat my people very well, and all the better for my memories of Russia. Who is of course our beloved ally . . . !'

The film mogul tried to make Galt and his two daughters change their plans, so they could attend a party which he himself was due to attend that night.

'I have to talk to my father while I can,' said Sandy.

'I'll forgive you just this one time,' said Schweitzer, 'because – despite the rumours – I have a heart. When I have you under contract, of course . . . I can be tough as I like then, and make you come to parties.' He winked at Galt Sandforth. 'Joking, of course, my dear general.'

Schweitzer went. There were some other celebrities crowding around whom Galt and Abbey were introduced to, and at last Sandy excused herself to change. Then they fought their way out of the stage door. There were young men and women, in and out of uniform, their faces avid to see Sandy. There was something fresh and clean in their enthusiasm for the theatre. Their contemporaries were dying in mud and shit in New Guinea and the Solomons.

Sandy took them on a short walk to Sardi's, the theatrical restaurant. With a great deal of Italian fuss, they were ushered to a prime banquette in a corner.

Sandy ordered a 1927 Dom Pérignon. She was very commanding in the way she did this, organized the taking of food orders, and then dispatched the waiters to the edge of the room. Presumably so that she could talk.

'Oh,' she said when asked about Schweitzer. 'I may do a two-film contract with him. With a good writer and a good leading man.'

Abbey made an extraordinarily risqué grunting noise, and said, 'Make it Paul Henried.'

Sandy smiled. 'The intellectual's sex object, eh?'

'I'm shocked by the way you girls talk,' said Galt Sandforth, like a father who had been around them along enough to be routinely shocked, who was shocked at breakfast and lunch and dinner on a daily basis. They both smiled broadly and permitted him that fantasy. The fantasy of being a regular parent.

'If you're not actually enslaved to the studio,' said Sandy, 'then they pay you better. And you can tell them what publicity you will and won't do. That's the way I want to take, whether it's good for my career in films or not. The theatre is what is most important.'

Both Galt and Abbey took their time telling her that she was marvellous. And she smiled, yet with a remoteness, Galt thought. He had a sense that she was standing back a little from him.

The real business of the evening began with the arrival of their poached salmon, their pasta and their veal. Sandy regarded her meal as if she found it unsatisfactory and raised her eyes then to Galt's. 'What about mother?' she asked.

Galt took a breath. 'Sandy, I just won't have time to go down there. Things are really pressing in New Guinea. Between you and me, Big Drum has only barely survived as a commander in any meaningful sense. They wanted to strip him back to token activity. We all know why.'

'I don't think it's a plot,' said Sandy coldly, beginning to eat. 'We *are* Europeans. Our greatest responsibility is to Europe. News is coming through that the Nazis are actually exterminating Jews. Not the occasional pogrom. Something more systematic. It's almost as if we – the Americans – have to deliver Europe from itself.'

'We have a promise in place to the people of the Philippines as well,' he protested. But then he gave up. He was sick of the arguments. And it wasn't tonight's real argument anyhow.

'Look, please, Dad,' said Sandy. 'Abbey and I know what the truth is. You don't want to see mother. You could have brought her up here – I think the army has enough planes for that. I mean, you've put Abbey and me in a dreadful situation. Are we supposed to keep it a secret that we've seen you?'

'Well, perhaps you could tell a tactful lie,' said Galt, feeling very uncomfortable now. 'No, it's not a lie anyhow. I don't have the time to visit with her, I don't have the space left over from my job. But if you refuse to believe that, you could just say I wanted to go down there but found it impossible.'

'I won't tell lies for you,' said Sandy, very gruff now, her mouth drawn tight. 'She's lost a son too, you know.'

It was the first time any of them had mentioned Galt Junior. He saw Abbey's face begin to flutter with grief. She deserved a happier time than this.

'OK. Listen. I ask you to believe me when I say that's the problem. I can't handle a reunion. I don't know what to say to her or how to touch her.'

'Is this because you've got some woman down there in the Pacific?' asked the unappeased Sandy.

'You should find the time, father,' Abbey urged. 'The war against Japan might last another twelve years. Surely you can spare a day for your wife?'

He was almost grateful to Abbey for dragging the subject away from Sandy's hard-nosed question.

'I'm under orders,' said Galt. 'I swear to you I am. Now let's drop it. I think your mother and I are best left alone to our solitary grief. Seeing each other will only raise a lot of other regrets on top of the grief for Galt Junior. Besides, you know, it *is* the truth that my plane's standing by. You don't seem to believe me, but I need to report to General Wraith as a matter of urgency.'

'There's another woman,' said Sandy sagely to Abbey. There was a communication between them, Abbey's wise, bruised eyes meeting the unnegotiable fire of Sandy's.

'If there were . . . ' said Galt. 'If there were, that would be my problem and my business. My failure to visit Charlottesville has nothing to do with anything like that. Nothing.'

Abbey put out her hand and touched his wrist and began to weep. Galt passed a vast handkerchief of his to her and put his arm around her shoulder. She cried neatly and discreetly. Sandy, still frowning, filled up her wine glass and put it to Abbey's lips.

'If Galt Junior was still alive,' Abbey said, 'we'd still be a family.'

'Possibly,' said Galt. 'But none of it's your fault, darling Abbey. Or yours, Sandy. It's your mother and I who are strangers to each other.'

Sandy said, 'I can't ever respect you if you won't face Mother. I mean that. You forfeit my respect.'

'Don't set me tasks,' he said, reasonably but in a tone which he hoped didn't give her false hope. 'It's unfair to set people tasks like that. I would go if I could. And I could have arranged things better, I know. But as matters stand, I'm due to fly out in less than twelve hours. What can I do about that?'

He reached out his right hand to Sandy. 'You two have all my love. And all my pride's invested in you too.'

Sandy tossed her head. 'I would like to believe you.' Now she began to blink back tears. 'Don't you ever do anything like this again. Do you understand? Don't do it!'

Abbey was recovering. Sandy's method of pulling herself together was obviously to sweep off to the women's room, which she did now.

'She doesn't mean it,' said Abbey. 'She's having a difficult time herself.'

'Not professionally,' remarked Galt.

'No. But in another way. She's in love with the director, Rowan Styles. You've heard of him, I'm sure. He tells her he's going to divorce his wife for her, and I suppose in a way he means it. But he keeps backsliding. And she forgives him. That's why I know she'll forgive you, no matter what she says. She's beginning to doubt that anything will ever happen with Mr Styles though.'

Galt felt a surge of anxiety for Sandy, combined with anger. He had not lied to the girls, not strictly speaking. Big Drum did want him back. And if there was some prevarication to it, they saw through it anyhow. But he could not respect men who deliberately lied to women. He was not aware of having consciously lied to Dim, not even at the start. Yet his child was in the hands of someone who might lie recklessly. He wondered if he should call this Rowan Styles and speak to him. But then he knew Sandy really *wouldn't* ever forgive that.

Sandy returned from the powder room and kissed him as if she wanted really to punish him.

'Anyway,' she said, 'you're not going down to Charlottesville, you've made damn sure you can't. So let's forget it and enjoy ourselves.'

For the rest of the dinner there was polite but engaging conversation. Then Galt and Abbey, even though it was fifteen blocks and he and Abbey would have to return almost the same distance to the Biltmore, insisted on walking Sandy home to her Park Avenue apartment through the cold.

When they got there, they even walked her into the lobby. She wrapped Galt in a sudden, desperate embrace.

'I'm sorry,' he said. 'You know what I mean.'

'Are you in any danger down there?' she asked.

'We're pretty safe. The occasional air raid . . .'

'If anything goes wrong with you,' said Sandy passionately, 'I'll put a curse on God. And he knows it!'

Outside again, both he and Abbey felt a relief to have settled down Abbey's turbulent younger sister for the night.

Galt said, 'I want you to sleep on in the morning. I'll be gone by five, I'm sorry to say.'

'But you'll knock on my door,' said Abbey. 'I want you to kiss me goodbye.'

'OK,' he said, smiling.

They began to walk, crossing the great wind canyon of Park Avenue and making for the comparative cosiness of Madison. All the way, Abbey hugged his arm to her. He wished he could tell her about Dim, but the time wasn't right. There was something wrong with telling Abbey such a thing before her mother knew.

For a moment he had a mental picture of what rage his daughter Sandy would feel when at last it was safe for him to announce his intention about Dim Lewis.

'Do you know what I remember about you as a child?' he asked Abbey now.

'No,' said Abbey, instantly agog.

'You never believed in emotional vendettas. When your mother and I, or Sandy and your mother had an argument, you couldn't rest until it was settled, until everyone was reconciled. You were a force for peace.'

On her lean but well-made features a simple delight spread. 'I think that's just about the best thing anyone ever said to me.'

'Surely your intelligence officer compliments you.'

'He's a mathematician,' she said, as if it explained something.

'Please don't think I'm setting you up to treat me kindly in future.'

'I'll always treat you kindly,' she said, leaning closer. She obviously thought that no one would presume that a woman her age and a man his age were anything but father and daughter. 'You know I will. I can't help it.'

The next day, when the B-23 bomber which was serving him as transport was high above the snowy farmlands of Illinois, he sat at the shaky navigation table and wrote a letter to his younger daughter.

> *Darling Sandy, I want you to know that I took to heart everything you said to me last night. I agree with you that my behaviour and my plan-making could have been better done, and if I had this visit over again I would try to do more to win your approval.*

He was very pleased that there was no chance that he would have to measure up to any such pledge. He was safely on his way back to the world he knew, in which the poles were Big Drum and Dim.

> *One thing better planning on my part would have done would be to give me a greater right to write you now. A friend of mine tells me that you have become a close companion of a quite famous married man. The fame isn't a disqualification. I am delighted to know that you are*

famous too, and that long after I have disappeared from the ranks of ole army, you will still be a famous actress.

And I don't necessarily disapprove, at least in any heavy handed way, of the association. I just want to make sure you know about the dangers. I'm going to write things which no doubt your friends have already said to you, but I hope they might have greater authority because of my love, and because warnings from the mouths of sinners often have greater authority than those which come from the virtuous.

I believe, for example, that this man has promised you he will divorce his wife and marry you. If that is what you want, and it then happens, I will be very happy for you. Just realize, darling Sandy, that the greater love is not always the one which triumphs. Marrige is a very strong institution. It is possible for a man to fear the judgement of his children. I showed when we met that I feared yours. *And it is possible for him also to be frightened of the disruption and the scenes and the fact that half the acquaintances his wife and he share will side with* her *and never fully forgive* him.

I think it's worth pursuing love at just about any cost – you never thought I'd write that, did you? I just want this man to be straight and honest with you, to fulfil his undertakings, and not to use you. Demand a decision of him, darling Sandy, because you're worth that much.

I am looking forward to seeing my daughter in the movies.

I'm signing off with all my love.

Your proud father, Galt.

He gave it to one of the Air Force stewards aboard. 'Just make sure that it's posted,' he called to the young man above the noise of the engines. 'Will you do that for me?' The young man's face became sullen. There was no way the letter *wouldn't* be efficiently posted.

Below them Illinois gave way to Missouri as the Mississippi, a glacial grey meander, was crossed. *This is the America I'm fighting for*, thought Galt. *And yet I'm a stranger to it. No sooner returned home than I flee.*

But he would rediscover America with Dim.

12

The Pro-Big Drum Movement

GALT HAD ALREADY been to seem Dim in her little bungalow, and had given her a silk scarf he'd bought in Beverly Hills, during a dash into town while his aircraft was being refuelled at Long Beach. He would return to her later in the evening, but now he was fulfilling the other half of his life's work, conferring with Big Drum on the enormous verandahs of the Administration villa. Big Drum had invited General Clancy to join them for this stroll in the mosquito-and-fragrance-laden evening. Galt had to confess that it made sense to have Clancy there. Clancy controlled the air arm, and the air arm was the key. That was the fact of life. And the way that Big Drum's ideas and his own had been coming together, the way those ideas were pitching themselves to what had happened in Quebec, made Clancy an almost essential companion for their discussions.

Galt had been astounded and pleased at the same time to find that Big Drum had not been downcast by the news from Quebec. But then Galt himself knew that the news could have been worse still, that the 'neutralization' of Big Drum as a commander had been on the agenda of a number of parties in the Palais de Justice. And at least that had been avoided. But Galt had expected that the pledge Churchill and the President and Channing had given – that the level of supply would remain as it had been – would have been likely to send Big Drum into a state of melancholy.

Far from it. It seemed to clarify his thinking. Indeed Galt had the exhilarating sense that the discussions taking place that night were crucial, that there was a special weight to them. That no one anywhere else was talking turkey the way Big Drum and Clancy and he were that night. Though Churchill and the President and all the sentimental *Europe-firsters* had driven them to this, Big Drum and Buck and Galt were fraternally and creatively pleased that it was so.

The atmosphere of this strolling conference was helped by the news of that day. Based on good intelligence from Harry Strudwick, Big Drum had sent in Australian airborne troops to grab the airport at Wau, inland from Salamaua. According to Japanese messages intercepted and decoded in Washington, the orders for the seizing of Wau by fresh Japanese troops came all the way from Mr Sugiyama, the Japanese War Minister. The Japanese troops chosen to seize Wau had been specially shipped from Rabaul under cover of night, men of the 51st Division, veterans of the capture of Shanghai and of French Indo-China. But the Australians had stopped them within a mile of the airfield and, in the end, driven them back over the Bulolo River to the coast. The Australian command at Wau had that very day told Big Drum that the Japanese had abandoned the entire Wau sector. Another version of Buna had thereby been forstalled, and Australian aircraft and Clancy's air force had another advanced airstrip from which to hammer the Japanese.

This too had elated Big Drum, as had further news from Senator Vandergrift concerning the development of a pro-Big Drum movement, kept secret for the moment, amongst Republicans from California to Maine.

'Airstrips are the key,' Big Drum kept telling Galt and Clancy that night. It was like a repeated verse, like something reiterated by monks to focus their minds. Both Galt and Clancy subscribed to that principle anyhow. And Ernie Sasser's engineers were already on their way to Wau to pave the airstrip there.

'The P-40s have a range of nearly three thousand miles,' Clancy murmured, spinning possibilities in front of Big Drum's eyes. 'This means, General, that they can fly at least a thousand miles north or west and cover an amphibious landing . . . '

'Which,' said Big Drum, 'doesn't have to be against a strong point. Just a place that has an airstrip . . . '

' . . . or the possibility of an airstrip,' said Clancy.

Six months ago it would have been incredible to believe that they would have been able to speak like this, like the one person. Galt wanted to sound a note of caution. He remembered the disaster of Clark Field near Manila. 'We have to keep squadrons of pursuit planes in reserve, to make sure that the Japanese don't come in from the flank and cut the line.'

But there was an approving silence at this. Both Big Drum and Clancy understood this already. They were three men making sure that they *all* understood the first principles.

Big Drum said, 'Buck, the enemy will be trying to bring in more men from Rabaul next time there's cyclonic weather . . . that's the time to watch for them. I think 1943 is going to be a better year than the last one. Why don't we all have some tea in the library?'

That night, Clancy excused himself early. It was partly etiquette – to allow Big Drum and his chief of staff to exchange final words. But rumour amongst the staff had it that Buck Clancy, in any case, had evening duties – that he had promised his dying Irish mother, twenty years past, that he would say the Rosary for her every night before retiring, and that he still religiously did it.

Somewhere in the Connecticut suburbs Buck had a similarly devout wife and a litter of pug-faced offspring who would probably expect, as of right, places at West Point or Yale. As if to prove his worthiness to inject his children into the centres of American power, Buck never had any scandals attached to his name. The only scandal was his abnormal chastity. He poured everything into the Fifth Air Force, working a sixteen to eighteen-hour day, saying the Rosary, and then sleeping the sleep of the mysteriously fulfilled.

After Buck Clancy had gone off to his prayers and his narrow bed, Big Drum began to ask Galt questions at greater length about Quebec, especially about the demeanour of Admiral Kremnitz and General Channing, and that of the President.

Big Drum became distracted then. He looked up to the books in the glass-fronted cabinets all around the room. He was becoming an expert on eighteenth-century literature by reading this scholar's library late into the night. He seemed to be selecting a title to take to bed with him. Still considering the spines of the books, his head tilted so that his gaze was nearly over his right shoulder, Big Drum murmured, 'Just one small thing, Galt. I know you'll forgive me for mentioning it. Friend to friend . . . '

'Of course,' said Galt, though he was in dread.

'I hear you see a young woman. An Australian. That's perfectly fine and understandable. When I say perfectly fine, Galt, I mean almost an army practice. Sadly so . . . '

He gestured, he seemed to be inviting Galt to feel better, to take account of the extenuating fact that he himself, Big Drum, had in the years before he met Mrs Wraith, maintained a handsome Eurasian woman in an apartment in Washington and had even helped her discreetly with the setting-up of a fashion house. The leniently implied difference, though, was that Big Drum had been between marriages then and had not met the little Southerner to whom he was now married.

Whereas Galt was already married, so that questions to do with that still had to be asked. Because there was no doubt that having started this conversation, Big Drum *would* ask them.

So Galt sat, trying to look as relaxed as he could, and simply waited.

'It's your business, Galt. But there's no question of this being a . . . forgive me . . . a *grande passion*, say? Is there?'

Galt knew that he should answer at once to be convincing, but he couldn't.

So Big Drum generously restated the question. 'No chance of this leading to a press scandal, say? Or a divorce?'

Galt felt a flush of anger. He wished he could have walked out, demanding that he be left to his own privacy. The question was unfair because Big Drum should have known that Galt would not manage any affair in a way which would hurt the Big Plan.

'I ask the General to trust me,' he said. 'I'm aware of how destiny beckons you, General, and I swear to you I will do nothing to give comfort to your enemies.'

Big Drum looked piercingly at Galt for a second and then – like a character in one of the eighteenth-century novels he'd been reading – remarked, 'Handsomely said, Galt. The subject is closed as far as I am concerned.'

It had been a warning, just the same.

Galt spent an uneasy night. He had in strict terms deceived Big Drum. Yet in practical terms he hadn't. He *would* ensure that Big Drum's enemies got no comfort. He was devoted to Big Drum's chances of becoming President.

Knowing the meeting with Big Drum and Clancy would go on till late, Galt had told Dim he would not visit her that evening. He needed a solid sleep anyhow, uninterrupted by ardour. The slow ceiling fan, which in some cases seemed as comforting as a heart beat, grated now above his head. He could hear the companionable metal friction in the thing.

He knew he risked losing Big Drum's friendship in the end. He risked what he hoped would be the temporary anger of his daughter, the Broadway star. The grief of all this rankled with him; but he saw beyond that area of risk to a sunny America which he occupied with Dim. The options seemed prodigious. Santa Barbara. Palm Springs. Santa Fe. What a climate for an ageing military man.

In the end the promise of all this overcame the intermediate uncertainty and sadness. He looked at the ceiling and reflected – it was a revelation and he'd never known it before – that life wasn't a low-priced item.

The thought was extraordinarily sedative and put him to sleep. In his not unhappy dreams, he felt a certain security. Harry Strudwick and Ernie Sasser and the others could no longer, even if they chose to, hold the mere fact of Dim's existence over him as a threat. Big Drum already knew about the young woman. If Harry or Ernie had let him know as a stratagem, then it had failed. Big Drum was, for the time being, secure in Galt's assurances, in Galt's white lies which, some time in the future, Big Drum would surely forgive.

Galt was grateful that Dim didn't seem to remember the US VI Corps, the one that the Australian blackmailer, Major Summers, had mentioned to her the winter before in Melbourne. For Big Drum *had* assigned it special tasks and made its new commander, Hal Metzger, another of the German-born prodigies like Harry Strudwick, directly answerable to himself and not to the Australian General Billings. Galt did not talk to Billings much, but the report was he had not been happy to know that there would be a large independent corps – one intended ultimately to become an army in its own right – acting with his forces but not subject to his orders.

Galt knew that Dim had not seen Paul Stacey in his absence. The reason was simple. Galt had himself directed the press office to readmit Stacey to the battle zone, as long as the young Australian newspaperman gave certain assurances.

The feelings of contentment Galt had developed falling asleep under his fan were soon enhanced by events. The monsoon season was nearing an end, and Big Drum flew back to Brisbane to visit his wife and Corporal Little Drum and to inspect Hal Metzger's VI Corps, in their training camps in the Queensland rainforest. Soon these men would be committed to amphibious landings – perhaps along the New Guinea coast, perhaps north of New Guinea in what Captain Cook had named the Admiralty Islands.

In his chief's absence, Galt and Dim spent leisurely evenings together, and Galt's fears about the semi-truths he had told Big Drum were soothed.

On an overcast afternoon when Galt was working on the verandah, Buck Clancy marched up to his desk with that rebellious smile on his face.

'One of my big bombers, the B-24s, has sighted a large convoy steaming through Dampier Strait, across the Bismarck Sea to Lae,' he whispered to Galt. Lae, westwards up the New Guinea north coast, was where the Japanese forces were now concentrated. Clancy looked exultant.

'Have you signalled Big Drum?'

'Does a bear shit in the woods?' asked Clancy. 'All we've got to do is stop Harry Strudwick from convincing Big Drum they're sailing for Los Angeles.'

Galt laughed at that. Harry seemed to have a mental block about picking the objective of particular convoys. He rarely believed that they were heading where they appeared to be heading.

Galt was sure it was raining all over New Guinea, but it turned out that an Australian Catalina flying-boat was able to follow the convoy until darkness came down. Clancy's bombers and Australian Beaufighters were ready to go at dawn. If this weather lasted, some of them would be lost, but the feelings at Moresby, Galt noticed as if he were a stranger, were all in favour of a small sacrifice to bring about a much-desired end.

The next day, the Beaufighters and B-17s, B-23s and B-25s pounded the Japanese convoy, dropping on them from the cover of one cyclonic squall after another. There was elation at the Administration villa. A Japanese radio intercept told Galt, Strudwick and Clancy that the convoy of sixteen ships was carrying new elements of the Japanese 51st Division. The convoy was protected by four destroyers and a larger ship of some kind, hard to distinguish in the tropic overcast. Many planes reported hits. The reports were chaotic though.

Again by dawn the next thundery morning, Clancy's planes were out, looking not only for the convoy but patrolling its line of retreat. It could not turn back though. Its commanders must have realized that. Their best chance was weather cover. Weather around the Huon Peninsula near Lae was very heavy. The Japanese must have hoped that it would have been heavy enough to see them safe to harbour back in Rabaul.

But by mid-morning, while Clancy, Strudwick and Galt crowded into a communications room in a Quonset hut in the garden, it became apparent that the weather over the convoy itself was improving. Wonderful, exhilarating reports proliferated – planes reported great flashes of fire aboard the convoy vessels. By a little after noon, all four destroyers had been sunk. The fifth warship was listing. Life-boats from the transports were making for the Trobriand Islands, where American garrisons would hunt them down.

The euphoria which came from being part of this extraordinary triumph, this turning of the Japanese thrust back upon itself, intoxicated everyone in Bataan, Moresby. Galt and Buck spoke to Big Drum on a special telephone line to Brisbane, and Big Drum was himself as elevated in spirits as the staff were. It had been an extraordinary day. Big Drum said, 'Galt, I want you to frame a special communiqué as soon as the figures are in. I want you to give a special credit to the work of the bombers.

I want the communiqué to say that the age of the bomber has come. That very phrase. I want our Navy friends to understand that this has been achieved practically without them. You and Buck Clancy have put paid to the idea that we should be subsidiary to the Navy. God bless you for that, Galt. God bless you.'

Late that night when reliable figures showed that eight transports had been sunk along with the four destroyers, Galt drafted the communiqué Big Drum had requested and transmitted it to him in Brisbane for approval. Within thirty-six hours it was headlines in American papers. Admiral Kremnitz wrote to Bataan in protest, disputing the figures for sinkings. Carrier-based planes had in any case sunk some of the Japanese vessels. 'I don't give a damn *who* sank them,' raged that good Irish-Catholic Buck Clancy. 'And neither should those panty-waisted sailors.'

Galt's operational plans section had placed another document before him for signature. It was time for a particular plan to be put into operation. Big Drum's advance against the Japanese had been mainly westward. The Japanese must have been asking themselves whether it would continue westward or it would strike out north. North seemed likely, but west was credible – that he would want to consolidate the island of Timor, part of the Dutch East Indies archipelago. That Special Reconnaissance plan again – put some brave men into Timor, give them tasks which made them look pre-runners of an invasion, let them be captured, let them yield up under torture their false version of what was to happen, a version in which they themselves nonetheless believed passionately and were willing to suffer all things, even death, to protect.

This time, Galt signed the document as quickly as he could and got rid of it. It made sense. If, in 1915, when he had gone inland from Vera Cruz in the Bay of Campeche looking for rolling stock with Big Drum he, too, had been part of a feint, an act of deceit planned by General Gaines on the coast, then as little as he would have liked to die, his ghost would have understood. Perhaps better than Galt Junior's ghost, wherever it was, confusedly dead or confusedly alive.

So, in the fervour and excitement of having isolated the enemy from his reinforcements, Galt signed the authorization for the plan to be put into effect. The personnel for the great Timor defeat had not yet been finally chosen from the six officers who had been trained for the mission. That fact added a saving hint of indefiniteness to the plan.

Surprisingly, the intoxication of the big Bismarck Sea victory went out of Galt about midway through the afternoon. It was an unlikely trigger which brought him back to his ordinary humanity. It was a message from Churchill to Big Drum, congratulating him on the destruction he had wrought in the Bismarck Sea. It arrived just as Harry's intelligence section produced estimates that at least fifteen hundred of the Japanese pitched into the sea by Clancy's bombers and the Australian Beaufighters had been devoured alive by sharks. The contrast between that statistic and Churchill's grand message sobered Galt.

The second focusing event of the afternoon was the arrival in the midst of a thunderstorm towards dusk of a rear-admiral from Kremnitz's staff. He came up the Administration villa driveway in a perfectly white Navy jeep, advanced up the stairs accompanied by a junior officer carrying a blue folder.

The rear-admiral was dressed splendidly in tropical mess uniform, and his aide seemed to be even better tailored still. They saluted Galt as Galt stood.

The rear-admiral said, 'I have a formal letter of protest from Admiral Kremnitz, Central Pacific Area Command, for General Wraith, Commander of the Southwest Pacific Zone. Admiral Kremnitz has instructed me to hand it to General Wraith in person.'

'That will be difficult,' said Galt. He pitied the man his task as messenger, envoy of chagrin. The man himself must be feeling the unreality of his mission. Galt decided to pile on the unreality. 'General Wraith is in Brisbane. I am willing to arrange transportation for you if you wish to see him in person.'

Even as Galt adopted this deliberately conciliatory tone, even enjoying it, knowing it was not what the rear-admiral would have expected, not what Kremnitz would be expecting to hear, the thought came that these were insubstantial and unworthy games. He would have enjoyed them uncritically once.

The rear-admiral put his hand out, so that his aide could open the blue folder, extract a letter, and place it in his superior's hand. 'In General Wraith's absence, I deliver the letter to you then.'

But he sounded dubious about that, as if Galt might throw it in the latrine.

'I shall transmit the full contents of the letter to General Wraith at once,' Galt pledged. 'May I inquire – on an informal basis – what the contents are?'

The rear-admiral pursed his lips and considered for a while. 'Admiral Kremnitz,' he said, 'asked me to pass on my respects to you, General Sandforth, and to convey to you his disappointment in the communiqué issued by your press office three days ago. That communiqué is the substance of Admiral Kremnitz's letter to General Wraith. Basically, sir, Admiral Kremnitz protests that your communiqué not only ignores the part of the Navy in the obliteration of the recent Japanese convoy. It actually proposes that the Navy is now obsolete and that only the bomber counts. It is a communiqué which does an injustice to all the brave men, aviators, destroyer personnel, who took part in operations on the eastern side of the enemy convoy's route. Admiral Kremnitz does not know what policy is being pursued by a communiqué of the type which issued from this place, but he is certain that it is one which can be very harmful to the Navy and – since you need the Navy – to your proposed operations as well.'

Galt said, 'I doubt the General intended to pre-empt the Navy's task. Please, perhaps we could talk less formally.'

He took the rear-admiral and his aide into the library and had them served drinks. He could not say to them that the communiqué wasn't intended to state *precisely* how things had gone in the Battle of the Bismarck Sea. It was designed to reverberate in American politics. It was nonetheless true that the bomber, handled by Buck Clancy, was in many ways superseding the Navy, though it would have been impolite that humid, rainy afternoon to press the point. Galt maintained the polite, unblinking, sober demeanour needed to reassure the rear-admiral that here in Moresby there was no barbarous under-appreciation of the Navy. He knew he was good at that sort of thing. It was his special strength in the spectrum of military arts, these powers of appeasement or, when appeasement failed, control. He was able to do it all without thinking.

But what his mind was really on was the fact that both Buck Clancy and Harry Strudwick were dining at Australian headquarters that night, and that he could have Dim to dinner in the large Administration villa dining room, after which, when all the staff had gone away and while the New Guinea native policemen in their red sarongs patrolled the perimeter, he and Dim could make leisurely love.

But as Galt should have known by that stage of his life, you can't really make the idyllic and the happy occur by planning. When she arrived by jeep, he had a sense that Dim was distracted or not at her ease. He asked her about it, but she gave the normal reassurances, not like a woman who is holding out, but more like one who cannot quite define what's distressing her.

Though she couldn't talk about it, though there wasn't *any point* in talking about it, what depressed her about dinner at the Administration villa was that it made her aware that her life in a small office in a Quonset hut in the garden, and the quarters she shared in the little bungalow with the nursing officer, made her feel marginal and secretive, and she didn't like that feeling. She didn't know how to put that to Galt without seeming to demand more than she was entitled to by her rank. But she knew she occupied this greater space now – the dining room at the Administration villa, and Galt's large bedroom – only by accident and for the night. She felt an anger rankling in her throat, certain complaints itching to be made. She didn't want to be consigned after tonight back to the crevices in which she lived. She believed in and honoured the Big Plan, but a night at the Administration villa showed her what a cramped life she'd been living for it.

Sleeping badly, Dim rose from Galt's bed in the mauve light before dawn. She had taken to sleeping in one of his long-tailed shirts since in the tropics bare flesh, where it touched another body or where it touched bed linen, became so instantly clammy. She moved off, taking care to open and close the bedroom door with stealth, and crept down the corridor to the communal lavatory which Galt shared with Harry Strudwick and Buck Clancy. She made it to the end of the long corridor, locked herself in, gathered up the shirt tails in her arm, sat on the seat and relieved herself. Above the bath, she noticed, one of those large but harmless spiders, of the kind they even had in Maneering, was hanging almost companionably.

She let herself back out into the corridor, taking as much care with the bathroom door as she had earlier, with the bedroom. Harry Strudwick might have insomnia and inquire after any random noise she made. The fact that she was taking so much care, that she was willingly doing it, somehow fitted in with the discontent she'd felt the night before. She could hear birds beginning to wake in the garden, and far away there were shouted orders – you couldn't tell in which accent – as the headquarters troops of Bataan and of the Australian compound began their morning parade.

Then a door into the hallway opened. It was opened by someone who thought he belonged there and was going about the normal business of this house and this corridor. It was Clancy who emerged. He was wearing nothing but an old pair of khaki pants and a pair of slippers, but he carried various toiletries with him, including an ivory-handled razor. His tough little agate eyes fixed on her. What worried her, and pleased her at the same time, was that there was no surprise in his glance. Naked beneath the shirt, she strained not to go red under his gaze. He did not leer at her as General Strudwick would have. She was grateful now for Buck Clancy's much-gossiped-about tendencies towards prudishness. He said only one word: '*Mademoiselle*.'

Why that word? she asked herself even then. There were hidden meanings to it, she was certain of that.

When she had got herself back into Galt's room, she found herself panting for breath. That meeting with Clancy had clinched the intentions which had been building in her since the evening before.

She sat on the side of the bed, waiting for Galt to awake. When he did, slowly surfacing, going back under for a minute at a time, but not able to hold on to unconsciousness either because Dim was there in her army shirt – a form of apparel he seemed to find desirable – or because of the steamy day which was breaking; or perhaps because of both.

He smiled at her but as he reached out, quickly saw she was looking confused.

'I went to the lavatory,' she told him, 'and on the way back I met Buck Clancy.'

'Oh,' he said. It was a long, considered *oh*. 'Well, Buck would not approve. But he isn't dangerous like Harry and the others.'

She played with the hem of her shirt. 'He called me *Mademoiselle*. Why do you think he called me that?'

'I don't know, Dim.'

'Isn't that what all the troops, yours and ours, called prostitutes in World War I? "*Mademoiselle from Armentières*"?'

Galt sat up and reached out again for her, but it already felt too hot for the showing of much affection.

'I want to live more publicly. I don't want any honour from them. I get enough from you. But I don't want to hide any more. I don't want anyone calling me Mademoiselle. I want to be honest. I want to look them in the eye.'

'It isn't possible, Dim.'

'Big Drum knows about me.'

'Yes. But he doesn't know that you're my life. He doesn't know yet that I won't go on to Washington with him. There's no need for him to know. It would be positively harmful. If he saw us together all the time, he'd gauge it. He's like that.'

'Strudwick and Sasser know,' she insisted.

'They might know I visit you. But again, they don't know the truth. How serious it is. If they did, it would be leaked to the press, Dim. They would rather see Big Drum forced to acquire a new Chief of Staff, with all the disruption that would entail, than see Big Drum achieve the White House.'

'But you keep on telling me you can control Strudwick and Sasser.' She was speaking solemnly and without complaint, with all the soberness of a seriously aggrieved and very determined child. She was lovely. She was an honest kid.

'I do have something on them.'

'What is it?'

'Not now, Dim,' he begged. 'Not in this house. It's something from the Filipino days.'

Dim took thought, then she said, 'I don't want to live the sort of secret life I've been living. I would rather be known outright as your mistress. I would rather encounter them, I'd rather meet them – Buck Clancy and the rest – full on, instead of creeping around like I was this morning. I despise myself the way I was this morning.' Tears broke through on to her lashes, but she suppressed them. He knew why. She knew that once she began to weep she would be too easy to reassure. She wanted results.

'I love you more than anything,' he told her. 'Let me think about it. Please let me think. Please be patient.'

'I don't want anyone calling me *Mademoiselle*. I want to be in a position where I can say to someone like Clancy, *Hey, mister, cut that out!*'

When it was time for her to go, she insisted she wanted to walk rather than be driven home in a jeep by a corporal. She said it was for her health, that she needed a walk. But he knew she wanted *him* to drive her, openly in the morning light. She knew he wasn't ready for it, and so she walked, her steel helmet carried on her shoulder.

More than Galt knew, she still feared air raids.

That Sunday evening he was at her bungalow by dusk. The nurse was out and Dim made him tea in the kitchen and brought it through into the living room.

He took his cup from her. She had trained him to drink it strongly black, after the fashion of Australian sheep stations. 'I want what you want,' he told her. 'I'm not ashamed of you or of myself.'

'I know that. That's my point.'

He noticed she was still in the same intense, dogged mood as she had been in that morning. 'I have to tell you this,' he said. 'I'm fifty-four and I'm terrified of Big Drum. I'm terrified of his disapproval.'

She said nothing. That wasn't *her* problem.

'There's something else too. It might be vanity, but I'm Big Drum's *best* lieutenant. If he falls out with me, he really won't find a substitute to match me.'

'Then take your time over it. To bring him around. I've always agreed with that. It's part of the scheme. I just don't want to live in secret. I don't want to creep along in secrecy, like I've been doing. I want them to know and see my face, so that they won't insult me to it.'

'Dim, Buck Clancy meant nothing by that *Mademoiselle* bullshit.'

'No, he meant everything,' she said, still frowning. She poured him another cup of tea from the capacious pot which had come from the bungalow. She seemed to be saying, *Here you are; this might help you with your decision.*

Galt said, 'Even if we're more open about things, they're still going to resent us and talk behind our backs.'

'I've never noticed that people talking behind your back worried you.'

'OK.' He made a deep, conclusive sigh. 'Look, all this depends on events. But as we keep pushing westward in New Guinea, it's very likely that we'll move Bataan further forward. With the radio and the telephone, Big Drum does not need to move forward with us. He needs to join us for conferences, or have us join him. But he'll want to stay in Moresby, far enough forward but not so far he can't get down to Brisbane to see Mrs Wraith and Little Drum. I know it's despicable to talk like this, but it's going to make it all easier for us. The sort of life you speak about will be possible. That's what I want, Dim, to make it possible.'

'But if we don't move forward?' she asked. 'Are you saying that coming out of hiding will be possible only if our troops keep pushing ahead at a good clip?'

He thought about this and, delaying, took a mouthful of tea.

'No, you will have a visible life with me, Dim. I swear. Just bear with me, and you'll be in a position to tell me soon whether things are better or not.'

And it came to him in any case. That he had certainty. They all had certainty. He, Buck Clancy, Big Drum.

'Besides, we'll keep winning,' he assured her. 'We've got the formula, Dim.' She looked away, shook her head and relented.

'I hope so,' she said with a half-smile. 'For everyone's sake.'

He considered approaching Buck Clancy, man to man. *Look, Buck, this isn't some floozy. I really love this girl . . .* There was, he believed, an eighty per cent chance that Buck would respond properly, even utter a genuine apology.

He was unaccustomed though to take that sort of risk. In any case, an approach like that would give Buck the feeling at best that he was being admitted to intimate friendship; at worst the sense that he had an advantage.

Last of all, it would remove the chance of making him pay ultimately for that small slight in the corridor. Small slight? A massive one for Dim.

But how could you make him pay in any significant way? The man was doing dazzling work. Galt did not doubt that if he himself couldn't be Big Drum's Secretary of Defense, Clancy would become the all-too-apparent candidate. In the Pentagon, there would actually be an Irish Catholic, saying the Rosary and giving no cause for scandal.

That week the names which preoccupied discussions between Big Drum and Clancy and Galt included that of Bougainville. As a result of the Japanese collapse in the Solomons, a whole naval group had been liberated to Big Drum's use, and its commander was Admiral Peter Andrews, a talented operational leader of whom Big Drum said, 'He's a *reasonable* Navy man. And he can take a joke.'

From the island of Bougainville, Clancy's bombers could hit Rabaul according to a new and highly regular schedule. To Galt Bougainville had a fragrance. He tried to pronounce it in the French manner. Clancy did not try. He announced it as if it were a stop on the Trenton line. He pronounced it as he would have pronounced '*Mademoiselle*'.

There was another name preoccupying Galt that week. *Lynx.* That was the name of a British submarine which had been refitting in Fremantle, Western Australia. He knew, because he was keeping track of the matter, that Commander Runcie and Captain Lewis were due to embark on *Lynx* at the end of that week. With them they would bring their radios, collapsible canoes, jungle knives, rations. They would check their gear endlessly and at sea by night they would practise deployment of their canoes from the blacked-out deck of the ship. In the wardroom, they would consult their maps by the hour in good faith. The *Lynx* would enjoy a comfortable running-in period up along the long Western Australian coast and would drop the two Special Reconnaissance operatives off Timor on the night of either the following Tuesday or Wednesday. After dropping them, the submarine would take up station in the South China Sea, preying on the approaches to Singapore.

How long would it take the Japanese to find Lewis and Runcie? Two young men who now, as they stowed their gear aboard the *Lynx*, must have hoped and assured themselves internally that they were off on the central adventure of their lives, the enterprise that would shed value on everything that would happen to them in the future.

There was no melodramatically constituted court in an afterlife where public men had their crimes read out. But that didn't mean there *wasn't* any sort of tribunal at all. Everyone who wasn't utterly mad and brutal knew there was; he could feel its breath on his face. Palpable judgement hung in the air above Galt. In the face of that judgement, Galt would argue, 'But I didn't choose to send him. I chose a stratagem before I knew his name was attached. I did not attach it myself.'

He knew in his blood, however, that a defence like that would not avail him.

The name *Lynx* was soon swallowed up in the welter of events of that notable military season. To the name Bougainville, for example, Peter Andrews – in conference – added that of New Georgia. The staff already had plans drawn up for an amphibious landing on New Georgia in any case.

Galt remembered Peter Andrews, a lanky, studious man, as a running back in the Navy teams just before World War I, about 1912 or so. But he was one of those students whose gifts transcended mere athletics. He could quote classical Greek and Shakespeare. When Galt and Big Drum flew down to Brisbane to meet him just after Easter that year, he took Galt aside and spoke warmly of a performance of *As You Like It* in which he'd seen young Sandy play Rosalind. He wanted the airport named Munda on New Georgia as a naval depot for *his* operations against Bougainville, that long island to the east of Rabaul. But though he was not theatrical himself, though he relayed his plans in an undramatic voice, his ideas, and his whole manner, delighted Big Drum. 'We will do wonderful things together,' Galt heard Big Drum say to Peter Andrews. 'Together we'll make Farragut seem like a weekend yachtsman.'

Though Big Drum's flamboyance was on the increase, it did not affect Andrews, who simply nodded, like a man accepting the offer of a fresh cup of coffee.

At that meeting with Andrews, Galt had raised his concern that there were ten thousand Japanese dug in on New Georgia, and that not far behind the beaches, the terrain became mountainous. But Andrews pushed the need for the airstrip. Without it, he would lose far more men when the landings went in at Bougainville.

This argument fitted in with the way Big Drum and Galt and Buck Clancy were thinking: expand by outflanking, and get the planes further and further forward. So at the time, everyone accepted Andrews's contention that the mountains of New Georgia were no argument against the need to take it. Later though, when one of Gibbs's divisions became bogged down on the seeping slopes of New Georgia, Galt would wonder if he should have argued harder.

Yet every omen seemed to drive events forward and justify the daring proposals of Big Drum and Clancy, and to encourage enthusiasm for daring in Galt himself. It was during these days of the first conversations with Peter Andrews, for example, that the plane of Admiral Yamamoto, commander of the Combined Imperial Fleet was intercepted by American fighters during a visit to his troops in Bougainville and shot down. Like a Roman emperor, Big Drum accepted all such favours of the gods gratefully, cementing them into place to make the wall of conviction he needed to have behind his back. This time last year the wall had been rubble. Now it was growing apace.

The time between the death of Yamamoto and the end of June 1943 was taken up for Galt in conferences, with the making of operational plans, with getting information from all the departments of staff and then handing out concerted instructions. The paperwork which built up or washed across his desk was prodigious. It seemed to him to be something akin to the other excesses of this region, the limitless coral reefs, the astounding rainstorms, the effulgent vegetation.

Big Drum was often absent for days at a time during this period. Galt made sure that Dim was invited to staff cocktail parties. She spent time talking to the junior staff, particularly to Captain Duncan, whom – Galt noticed, not without some ambiguity – she seemed to like. Galt was pleased to schedule these parties during Big Drum's absences, so that Dim could be there somewhat more frequently than most of the junior staff were. People such as Harry Strudwick and Ernie Sasser and Buck Clancy exchanged no more than a few words with her, but they got used to the look of her, of the way she carried herself. She was no longer such a stranger to them. He believed they couldn't make easy judgements about her anymore.

Dim confessed to feeling happier. 'At least,' she told him, 'I don't feel any more that I'm living in the outer edge of the universe.'

At the end of June, Hal Metzger's VI Corps landed on Kiriwina and Woodlark Island off New Guinea and occupied them with ease. The building of airfields for Clancy, according to plans drawn up by Sasser, started at once. From these bases even Clancy's short-range fighters could operate against the Rabaul garrison.

The Australians were landed near Salamaua. This was to be one of many risky but successful landings on the Huon Peninsula of New Guinea over the months to come. And Peter Andrews began his New Georgia expedition by easily putting six thousand Americans ashore on Rendova Island, just across from New Georgia and its airstrip at Munda. Within days he would land three other forces on the south side of New Georgia. Things looked potentially very good. Big Drum was consistently exhilarated.

And everything seemed to go well, although through Andrews's plan a thousand of Bryant's men were lost on New Georgia. The figures came to Port Moresby like production figures or statistics coming to head office from a subsidiary in a distant region. Andrews had no problem admitting in conversations with Galt and Big Drum that he understood now it would have been better to bypass the place and find some island to the north of it, and build an airstrip there. Way up in the Arctic islands off Alaska, in the Aleutians, the Americans under General Gates had attacked not the heavily defended island of Kiska but the more lightly garrisoned Attu to the west. That had caused the withdrawal of the entire Japanese garrison from Kiska. 'If I had it to do again,' Andrews said philosophically, 'I'd use the Attu and Kiska method.'

Big Drum told him not to worry. It had been an enormous success anyhow – though as Galt reflected, there were a thousand families in the United States who would not be too pleased with that success; who would be the ones to keep the name New Georgia in the front of their minds long after Andrews and Big Drum had reduced its memory to no more than an intermediate lesson on the techniques of victory.

'The trouble is,' said Big Drum at breakfast in the Administration villa one morning, 'if you take on *this* enemy frontally, he'll fight you to the absolute limit. At a stage where our boys would with honour and all good reasons surrender, *he* will still be fighting. He has no sense of personal value. There's a lack of Christian and democratic values there . . . '

Big Drum was delivering such lectures to all the staff these days, not that his diagnosis wasn't exact. It was a sign of the greater spaciousness of his life, that he had time to reflect in this way.

Clancy was arguing for a division to be sent to a place called Nadzab, on the northern foothills of New Guinea and well to the west of Salamaua. Again, the idea was to seize an airstrip:

all part of a plan to fill the air with Flying Fortresses as they arrived from US manufactories in all their upgraded forms.

The seizure of Nadzab had to be initiated with a well-trained parachute regiment, but the regiment best fitted happened to be one fresh from Queensland. These young men had never seen action before. At a staff meeting the afternoon before these boys were to be dropped Clancy mentioned to Big Drum that he wanted to fly into the drop site with them. Galt noticed this proposal had made Big Drum thoughtful – not in a melancholy way, more in a speculative one.

Galt was getting ready for bed that night when Captain Duncan knocked on his door and said that the General would like to see him.

'On the verandah?' asked Galt.

'No, General. He wants you to go to his bedroom.'

Galt quickly dressed in the rudiments of uniform and went and knocked on Big Drum's bedroom door, which was ajar. Entering at Big Drum's shouted order, he saw the General wearing extremely natty silk pyjamas and striding up and down by the widely opened window and wielding his empty cigarette-holder in a way which conveyed he was in the full flood of thought and decision-making.

'Sorry to do this to you, Galt,' he said. 'I haven't been able to sleep. I want to go with Clancy, too. I want those kids to know I'm in the lead plane. I want them to know I'm watching them.'

Galt frowned. If Big Drum did what he threatened, it would be the first time he'd gone north of the mountains. Galt thought at once about the possibility of air ambush. P-38s had ambushed Yamamoto. He felt a quick, astringent sweat of fear – for his sake as for Big Drum's. What must it be like to be in the belly of a slow transport when Mitsubishi fighters latched on to you?

'General, have you spoken to Clancy himself about this?'

'Not yet. I wanted to know if you'd come with me, Galt?'

Galt felt the sweat cool and a steady pulsing dread overtake him. He still had painful memories of his journey to Dobadura in the bad old days, before Bryant Gibbs took over and made something of the Buna mess.

Besides, it was a gratuitous piece of bravado on the part of

Big Drum to want these particular boys to know he was *there*. Thousands of kids had gone into battle presuming Big Drum was not watching them and was never likely to. What was so special about these paratroopers?

But Galt felt he could not argue this way, that it would only encourage Big Drum more. But he essayed an equivalent level of daring argument instead. 'It could be rash, General. Without flattering you, you're the only one who can take us back to the places we were driven out of. To be frank, I don't think you should take the risk – as Commander-in-Chief in this region – that some five-dollar-a-month Japanese aviator will blow a hole in you.'

Big Drum laughed, but he was shaking his head and his cigarette holder at the one time. 'No, there's no risk of ambush. Buck will look after that. We'll have fighters and pursuit planes nursemaiding us all the way. What worries me is that I might pass out when we're going over the Owen Stanleys. Or maybe I'll be sick in front of the boys. That possibility has given me plenty of pause in the past, Galt.'

Galt said, 'The boys would forgive you. That's not the point. If I might say so, General, the risk is the point.'

Big Drum was still thoughtful, but was barely listening to Galt now. 'I don't want the story to get round that Big Drum can't cross mountains with paratroopers.' He clapped Galt on the shoulder. 'The orderly's waking me at 0350. I'll have him rouse you at the same time.'

In the half dark of the Moresby airstrip, the paratroopers of the 503rd Parachute Regiment could be heard muttering as Galt and the General got near. 'Fuck, it's Big Drum!' Galt heard a dozen times. 'Shiiit!'

Big Drum proceeded down the lines of young faces marked by excitement and fixity of will and bemusement. He chatted to some of them. Many of them sounded to Galt like West Virginians or maybe Ohians. To hear that twang, remembered from his own childhood, reassured him. A tidewater aristocrat like himself had not been raised to have much respect for the Appalachian folk, and yet it was always taken for granted they were tough and wiry and full of a slack-mouthed determination. There were some from Ohio and Kentucky too. They had never heard in all their rough rural schooling of Nadzab or the Huon Peninsula or any of all of this.

When the moment came for him to make a little speech to them, Big Drum studiedly restricted himself to three brisk sentences, as if he knew that these were no bullshit boys. 'We are going to take an airstrip from the enemy,' the General announced. 'I am with you, and the God of battles is with you too. No men ever jumped out from a moving plane for a better purpose.'

Galt was distressed that he had not had a chance to tell Dim that he was going on a morning adventure. An old man wary of his life, he felt shamed by these young men so willing at this moment to hurl theirs out into the air above the jungle.

Big Drum climbed aboard the B-17 which would be first to take off. Galt still remembered the layout of these planes so intimately from the time he and Big Drum and all the others fled the Philippines an age ago. The well of this morning's plane had however been fitted with facing canvas and metal benches on which the paratroopers could sit, facing each other, on their last uncomfortable ride prior to their supreme moment. For those who lived, and Galt hoped it was most of them, this would be remembered as the most significant morning of their lives, and every detail of this cramped aircraft would be with them until they were old men.

Big Drum and Clancy insisted on sitting in the well with the paratroopers, even though the navigator would have made room for them on the slightly more comfortable flight deck. Here was Big Drum in his sixties, contemplating a flight without oxygen over mountains fourteen thousand feet high. Even as the B-17 taxied for take-off, Galt was feeling disoriented and wondered about how he himself would perform, locking his will into place to ensure that in no circumstances would he faint, topple to the metal floor and become the subject of an anecdote for the paratroopers.

Rudimentary conversations were possible over the roar of engines. Galt found himself talking to a young captain. The man was a former National Guardsman, engaged to a woman in North Carolina. In answer to Galt's shouted questions, he admitted further that he was a junior from Ohio State University and he intended to graduate as an agronomist and work amidst what he called with a smile, 'the great American horn of plenty.'

From the port behind him, Galt got an occasional view of other B-17s and even an occasional escorting fighter. The exhilaration of the event was taking hold of him, as it did of ordinary soldiers, inducing a sense of confidence, of predestined success.

Then, when they were high but still climbing, there was a change in the noise of the engines. Clancy blinked and looked around him and began to speak as quietly as he could in Big Drum's ear. Galt's attitude towards this space in which they all sat now changed back to what it had been before take-off. He had *known* that all this was ill advised. One of the two pilots came back, too, climbed down the ladder from the flight deck, began talking with a slight frown, just like Clancy.

Big Drum was keeping nothing secret. He called cheerily to as many as could hear, 'An engine gone.'

'We ought to turn back,' Clancy cried to Galt, almost as if trying to enlist him to talk sense to Big Drum.

Big Drum still seemed amused. 'Back to the controls, young man,' he yelled to the pilot. 'Keep flying this thing.'

Clancy shook his head.

'Buck, you know as well as I do that one engine doesn't mean a thing. This crate can fly as well on three as on four.' And he made a fist and affectionately punched the metal above his head. 'I want to see these boys take their jump.'

Galt shut out of his imagination an image of the B-17, straining for altitude, clipping some unspeakable peak. It *was* true, everyone said so. Three are as good as four. He exchanged a smile with the young man from Ohio State.

'The boys couldn't have taken turning back, General,' the young captain cried out to Galt.

Galt smiled and nodded, as if he too, like all these young men, had been primed for this moment.

As the aircraft crested the Owen Stanleys, breaking through the high cloud which weighed on the summits, Galt felt some dizziness. Occasionally he would inhale and there would be no air there. Big Drum must surely have been feeling the same effects. Yet he went on talking with Buck. At one stage he turned to Galt and yelled with a grin, 'No airsickness!'

The plane descended towards the coast. Big Drum, Buck and Galt stood aft, behind the door the boys would jump from. The door was opened. All the paratroopers were standing. They shuffled aft in a robot-like manner and hurled themselves without hesitation into the air. Galt saw the young man from Ohio State fly out the door. Does he think his woman is out there? Galt wondered. Or is it his woman he's jumping away from?

The two NCOs who brought up the tail of the line looked ageless with their chinstraps on. They grinned at the generals with a bad-cowboy smirk they might have picked up from the movies. The sky, Galt could see by looking slantwise through the angle of the door, was suddenly full of the blossoms of their silk.

'Wow!' said Big Drum.

Once the B-17 had crossed the Owen Stanleys again without being attacked and was well on its way back to Port Moresby, Galt too began to feel some of Big Drum's exultation. Signals were already coming in by radio. The airstrip at Nadzab had been barely defended and had been secured within an hour of the drop. It belonged now to Buck Clancy and the paratroopers.

Events continued to match Big Drum's buoyancy. By late September the Australians and the Americans had Salamaua and had finally captured the Japanese base at Lae. As the first Christmas cards arrived, Hal Metzger landed on the southwest coast of New Britain, the island at whose far eastern end lay Rabaul. The Marines went ashore at Cape Gloucester. In Bougainville, Peter Andrews had got some thirty-three thousand men ashore beneath the island's great volcano in Empress Augusta Bay. It was clear the Japanese did not understand any more what was a feint and what a main attack. Rabaul was more or less encircled now and expected frontal assault. Intelligence reports came in of enormous preparations and of the garrison of more than a hundred thousand men getting ready their thousand-stitch belts, which when put on committed the warrior to die in battle or else by his own hand.

'We're going to have to disappoint them,' said Big Drum, at the peak of his form.

Now Clancy's bombers were pounding the new Japanese headquarters at Wewak, far up the coast from Lae.

Amongst all the other data to do with the enemy's confusion which came to Galt's desk on the verandah of the Administration villa in Port Moresby, was one not exactly dramatic yet nonetheless significant detail.

The Japanese 7th Air Division was moved out of Rabaul and across to the Celebes, north of Timor. They would not be needed there, but the enemy did not know that. Someone had convinced them that Timor was in danger. What could be deduced was that under torture Captain Lewis and Commander Runcie had convinced them of this. The planning committee in Melbourne emphasized, in documents destined for the desks of Galt and Big Drum, that the movement of the 7th Air Division justified this cruel strategy. The Japanese were using Lewis and Runcie to transmit properly coded false material to Australia, and in return, the Allies were transmitting a mass of false material to Runcie and Lewis. Shamed and tormented, those two young men must have been sustained alive by the Japanese only adequately to ensure that they went on broadcasting. For the Japanese believed they had a bargain in these two.

No veterans' organization could ever make up to Runcie and Lewis for what they were going through now. No general would ever pin a medal on them. No official history would honour their brave fallibility or say that their torment was necessary.

As much as he could, Galt suppressed the thought of them. Sometimes he would utter to himself the pious hope that the Japanese, when they were finished with them, would end their misery with some fast and humane method of execution.

Throughout what would have been in the US a fall of greater hope than any other during the last ten years of depression and threat, Senator Vandergrift wrote regularly to Galt and Big Drum:

Dear General Sandforth,
I am writing to you once more as someone who has influence over our admired friend. I believe it is important for him to understand fully the meaning he has for our side of politics. The new weapons of war have meant that we have become in a sense – though I would not once have used such a term – one world. *The Senate has passed the preliminary draft for American participation in a United Nations. In Bretton Woods, New Hampshire, diplomats from half a dozen nations have produced agreements which will lead to the creation of a world bank. This suits our facile friend, Wendell Fryer, who will again try to corner the Republican nomination. It is as if what our side of politics needs is a thin version of the present Democrat incumbent of the White House. If by some unhappy accident, he did receive the Republican nomination and were elected, he would be just as reckless as any Democrat President in dragging us into foreign messes, political, diplomatic and economic. As for Mr Wagner, our other front runner for Republican nomination, he runs in terror of the left-wing press. They want us bonded to the Soviets like Siamese twins, and he will do it.*

For our side of politics, only Big Drum can combine the demands of this new world with the essential requirement that Communism does not enter the pores of our body politic, that we remain American. It is obvious that although there are signs of military success, we still have a great way to travel. Yet the more we succeed militarily, the greater will American anxiety grow that we will lose ourselves in the world.

Please convey my warmest regards to our friend, and tell him not to take unnecessary risks. We all need him.

Yours sincerely,
H.G. Vandergrift
US Senator

Dim now had three enlisted men working for her. The most recent films were shown to Hal Metzger's 1st Cavalry Division at Cape Gloucester, or to the paratroopers and the Australians at Lae: *This Above All*, *Double Indemnity*, *For Whom the Bell Tolls*, *Woman of the Year*, *Saratoga Trunk*, *Lifeboat*. Occasionally she might go to an Australian or American camp in Moresby to see one of them, but generally she had no personal enthusiasm for her merchandise.

She wrote an occasional, pleasant letter to Allan Lewis, closing with, '*With all my affection*.' She felt that wasn't a lie, and since Allan had never found her a demonstrative woman, she hoped he would be happy with that.

But she received no letters back. She presumed it meant that he was somewhere unreachable. Living in the jungle, observing Japanese movements and, no doubt, learning from Runcie how to throw the jungle knife accurately. At least she hoped that was the extent of their perils.

She occasionally felt the impulse to ask Galt where he was, but it always passed. He was safe, quite clearly. She would have heard if anything had happened to him.

But at last a letter arrived from Honor Runcie which forced her hand. As a document, it grew in intensity from minor grievances to the central one. '*I can't tell you how dismal a winter it has been in Melbourne. Really, I don't want to live here after the war. It isn't the city for me. Rangoon, here I come!*'

Then she dealt with the various illnesses her daughter had had, including a version of pneumonia. '*Yet if it wasn't for my daughter, I would go quite mad.*'

She went on: '*I haven't heard a single word from Gordon since July. That's four months without a word. I know these things are not abnormal, and I'm not complaining. I just thought that you might have contacts there. I don't want to know anything secret. I just want to get an indication. They say no news is good news, but you and I must know that isn't quite the case. I have the most dreadful dreams about Gordon, and I miss him so. Sometimes I think that if I could simply have a visit from one of those terrible people in South Yarra, those stuffed shirts with their tailored suits and their polished Sam Brownes, and if they said, "Shut up and stop complaining. He's* well *and* somewhere, *but we can't tell you where", then I'd be happy. I wouldn't mind being told off as a slacker and complainer.*

'*But it's as if Gordon's disappeared into a hole, and in a sense my daughter and I are in a hole too. In an oubliette, a pit they drop you into and then walk away and forget.*

'*I wouldn't ask you if I wasn't confident you knew what I was going through. Because you're going through it too. This is a real bugger of a war . . .*'

Dim had always consoled herself that if anything bad happened to Gordon or Allan, then Honor would hear about it promptly. But now it was clear that wasn't so.

'*I think it's rotten,*' Honor's letter to Dim concluded, '*to leave a woman languishing in a little flat in South Yarra with an infant and tell her nothing.*'

When Dim showed him the letter, it caused Galt some thought. He could not seem to know too much about Runcie and Lewis. He understood too clearly that if it ever came out where Allan Lewis was and had been, and what had been done to him, he wanted to be able to claim ignorance. That would be the central and only lie of his life with Dim.

'I'll find out what I can,' Galt told her. The imputation he wanted to create was that he would look, as a special favour, into the health and whereabouts of two men lost in obscure endeavours.

A few days later, like a man returning from having made what could be called extensive inquiries, he told her to write a letter of reassurance to Honor Runcie. Her husband could not be reached, but he was alive. They knew he was alive because he was transmitting properly, bravely feeding coded warnings into his transmission trying to let the people in Melbourne and Brisbane know that he had been captured and turned. That side of the thing Galt did not mention to Dim.

'Are our letters getting through to them?' Dim asked.

Galt flinched and then decided to take Dim into his confidence. 'No, they're not receiving your letters. They can't. They're beyond the range of the postman. But don't tell Mrs Runcie that. It's best for her to be able to write regularly.'

*

At breakfast Big Drum, eating his scrambled eggs, told Galt that the President's wife wanted to come to Moresby. 'I can't have it,' he said jovially. He cast his eyes up. 'This is far too dangerous an area.' And then he winked. 'Do you know what I think she's coming for? In her little Red Cross uniform? Visiting the boys? She wants to ask whether I intend to run? She wants to get her picture taken with me too. That would be something for the Democrats to make capital of, wouldn't you say?' And he laughed broadly.

The Democratic and Republican conventions were less than a year away, and in the past few weeks Big Drum was beginning to speak openly about his Presidential prospects. There was somehow an unspoken rule however that neither Galt nor Harry Strudwick nor Buck Clancy were to make uninvited comments about this. The only appropriate reaction from them was a knowing and supportive grin. It was fascinating how these rules existed, how good Big Drum was at making them up, at letting others know of their existence without saying a word.

'Thank God Andrews is down there, and I'm going to send your friend Gibbs down there as well. He can take her to dinner and show her the kangaroos.'

Then, 'Buck,' Big Drum said reflectively in the middle of his coffee. 'Just so the President won't be offended by any refusal of mine to greet his beloved spouse here, could you mobilize some of your squadrons in expectation of a heavy air assault? And issue a communiqué to that effect? The peril, I need hardly say, can be completely fictitious.'

And he twirled his fork. To be a naughty boy on such a scale delighted him.

Galt reflected that it was a fortunate thing for Big Drum that he happened to be in Moresby, not Brisbane, at this moment of the First Lady's visit. Or perhaps it was simply good management.

Despite Big Drum's flippancy, everyone on the staff respected the First Lady. She had been travelling at some personal danger throughout the Central and Southwest Pacific, talking to the wounded and the disgruntled. Her actions went far beyond the narrow consideration of political benefit. Her courage and goodwill probably had more to do with a desire to make a constructive life for herself in view of her husband's long affair with one of his aides than it did with any Democratic political strategy.

From reading what they call the Pony editions of magazines, reduced in format, carrying no advertising and printed especially for the soldiers, Galt could tell that the campaign for and against Big Drum's candidacy had already begun. Leonard Parrish, a journalist and author who had lived in the Philippines in the late 1930s and been an acquaintance of Big Drum's, had produced a glowing biography which was on the bestseller lists. On the other hand, the normal journals of the Left – *Year, Republic, Mercury* – were producing hostile analyses of how a Big Drum candidacy and Presidency might proceed. They kept stressing that he was anti-British – as if this had not once been an American virtue – and an enemy of their own Navy. They even went so far as to imply that it was anti-European xenophobia which caused Big Drum to seek the means to polish off the Japanese with some dispatch. These writers argued that a Big Drum Presidency would see a reversal of priorities, and a deterioration in the relationship between the United States and the Soviet Union. A Big Drum Presidency would have as its aim the pursuit of some arcadian, isolated America which no longer existed. In trying to recover its own inaccurate mythology, America would lose its management of the free world.

In *Time* magazine, Democratic Senator Griffen of California was quoted as saying that, distinguished a soldier as Big Drum was, his main political support would be amongst the leavings of rural isolationism. This sort of thing made Big Drum rub his hands. 'How amusing that he feels bound to acknowledge I'm Napoleon,' Big Drum chortled. 'Even if he thinks my politics stink.'

So it appeared that he was amused by these pieces and took the distinguished nature of the names which were attached to the articles as a sign that the Democrats were beginning to get scared.

In any case, Vandergrift demonstrated his own influence and the power of Big Drum's name by getting equally distinguished writers to produce sober essays in *Harper's* and *Saturday Evening Post* on Big Drum's political nature and prospects.

Bryant Gibbs came back from Brisbane quite charmed by the First Lady and told Galt and Big Drum an amusing story of a dinner Mrs Wraith had given for the First Lady in Lennon's Hotel in Brisbane. She'd invited some Australian socialite, a woman who knew nothing about American politics. The woman had at some stage of the evening breathed all over the First Lady and said, 'Isn't it wonderful that General Wraith is going to become President? Things will really move along then.'

Mrs Wraith and the First Lady had actually smiled at each other and between them had edged the conversation along from that point of potential social danger.

Telling the tale, Gibbs winked at Galt. 'I think the First Lady and Admiral Andrews got on well together. I think our friend Andrews may actually be a closet Democrat.'

Big Drum said, 'Very well, Bryant. You captured Buna for me. Now for your next job, you have to turn Pete Andrews back into a decent Republican.'

The Australian Prime Minister was, however, welcome in Port Moresby, and towards Christmas 1943 he arrived to visit Big Drum. He was near the start of a long flight to Washington to see the President. Already he looked poorly. Even discounting the influence of the malaria tablets, his skin looked sallow, and his eyes were red from sleeplessness.

Galt noticed, however, that the Australian guard of honour who met their leader at the airport burst into a spontaneous, affectionate cheer at the sight of him, and threw their slouch hats in the air. He did not beam at this, but gave merely a watery grin. For he was a sensitive man in a way that Big Drum *should* never be. The fighting of war as the pacifist Prime Minister of a small nation had hollowed him out. And it was not only the pursuit of war. Galt was aware he had had battles on the home front. Against the bitter opposition of some of his fellow Labor people, he had introduced conscription, so that Australians could be drafted and sent throughout the Southwest Pacific. Old friends had called him a class-traitor for his trouble.

Big Drum laid on a dinner at the Administration villa for him, and Gibbs and Metzger, as well as the Australian General Billings, were all in Port Moresby for it. Gibbs's corps was routinely campaigning in the Huon Peninsula of New Guinea, and Metzger's troops, including the renowned 1st Cavalry Division, were holding the western end of New Britain.

Once, when Gibbs was tired and a little depressed at the inaccurate nature of communiqués Big Drum sent the American press, he predicted that Big Drum wouldn't be in a position to launch an assault on the Philippines until the end of the decade. But there was none of that atmosphere at the table for the Australian Prime Minister's dinner. Everyone was very much in favour of hopeful timetables, and very complimentary about the Australians. Except for such special events, it was not normal to praise the Australians around Big Drum. It was still too recently that their superior expertise had been something of an embarrassment to him. But tonight that was all OK. The Australians who were fighting their way down jungle trails towards the port of Madang, those lean boys with slouch hats and Owen guns, were fit subjects for public praise tonight. And so they should have been, thought Galt, a minor Australian nationalist by association with Dim. Many of those who were now defeating the Japanese were veterans of the fighting against Rommel in the Western Desert. That was more than any American unit could claim.

But it was not just the public tributes to the Australians which both amused and took away the breath of the staff and other visitors that evening. It was Big Drum's daring use of a man he had often called his friend, and for whom he had often expressed to Galt a genuine affection.

'Mr Prime Minister,' Big Drum was booming, 'you might have heard that the President has acquired this notion that I want to be nominated for the Republican candidacy in the next Presidential election.'

The Prime Minister smiled sadly. There were far worse ghosts on his back. 'I've been worried about that myself, General,' he said. 'It might be a good thing for the American people, but I wonder what we'd do without you?'

'In that regard,' said Big Drum, to this man who was a good practical politician, despite his sadness, a man who should have been able to sniff out a lie, 'in that regard, if the matter comes up during your discussion with the President, you could tell him that you heard me say that I don't seek the candidacy.'

The Prime Minister raised an eyebrow. He had a working-class face, like Buck Clancy's, but his was different. Buck's was the face of a saloon owner, a fight manager. The Prime Minister's was the face of a disappointed but canny priest.

At this sign of scepticism, Big Drum smiled with utter frankness. This was his gift. To create in other people the idea that they were seeing to the pit of his soul, whereas – as Galt knew – they were seeing only a thin tactic brilliantly executed. 'I'll say it again, my friend, so that you can tell him you've heard me say it more than once.' There was laughter around the table. 'I do not seek the Republican candidacy.'

'But if you were offered it?' asked the Prime Minister.

'As you correctly say, Mr Prime Minister, we have so many things to do here.' And Big Drum pounded the table a number of times with his empty cigarette-holder.

The Prime Minister was still smiling knowingly. At last he said, 'I shall tell the President I've heard you say that. It will encourage him to supply you more generously.'

'Exactly,' said Big Drum with an absolutely seraphic smile now. 'Besides, it's the truth.'

The Prime Minister went to bed early. Exhausted by the long flight from Canberra, he still had to face the flight from Port Moresby to Hawaii to Los Angeles to Washington. Big Drum also retired, in very good spirits. Harry Strudwick, Ernie Sasser, Sam Winton, General Billings, Bryant Gibbs, Hal Metzger and Galt all sat out on the verandah drinking gin and tonics or beer. One by one they too went off to bed. General Billings passed out in his wicker chair. It was not only that he was an Australian which made him different from the others. He was also not a professional soldier – again, the Australian passion for citizen soldiers had been demonstrated in his appointment. He was a former police chief of Melbourne, and had a traditional police chief's taste for fleshpots. He was a skilled commander and a man of lively intelligence, but every night he wiped himself out with Scotch whisky.

At last all that was left of the party were Galt, Bryant, Hal and the comatose Australian general.

Bryant began to talk about the dinner. 'Sometimes I think Big Drum runs the risk of being too cute. And that doesn't worry me. He can be cute all he likes. He's getting the results.'

'Well, what's the problem then?' asked Galt, who had himself been made uneasy by Big Drum's ploys at dinner.

'I'm worried that he'll set himself up for a political disappointment. None of us want him disappointed, do we?'

'But surely he could handle a disappointment, Bryant? And come back the next time round.'

'Remember McClellan, during the War between the States?' Bryant invited him. '*There* was a general who was loved by the people, and because he was loved by the people *as* a general, he thought that he would be loved as a leader. But it's never been that way with the Americans.' Bryant held up a hand as if he didn't want to be misinterpreted. 'If the American people want Big Drum, I'll be as delighted about it as anyone. I mean, there's a big difference between McClellan and Big Drum. McClellan never delivered as a general, and Big Drum *is* delivering. Though not always in exactly the terms the press office would have us believe.'

'The press office is all showbiz,' conceded Hal Metzger, as if he was happy to leave it that way.

Bryant, however, was frowning. He had never been content with the way the press office worked, or the way the chimera of the presidency impacted on what the press office said about the fighting on the north coast of New Guinea. 'I'm with our friend the Aussie Prime Minister. I want Big Drum *here*. When we capture Manila, he'll be such a national hero that he can take the Presidency then. He'll be able to walk across the Pacific on water and step ashore at Los Angeles to the adulation of the people. And that'll suit me fine.'

Galt thought of this eventuality. After all, it was a likely one.

But it wouldn't suit him fine. He wanted the thing settled early – so he could declare to the world where he stood with Dim. So he could *legitimize* things. No more than Dim did he want to keep his love underground until 1948.

But Bryant Gibbs's sincerity could not be doubted, his lack of self-interest. It was very likely that if Big Drum went off to fight a Presidential campaign, Gibbs would be appointed supremo in the Southwest Pacific. The good thing about Bryant was that he wouldn't have objected to that; and it wasn't that he couldn't do it. It was that, in spite of his reasonable objections to the methods of Big Drum's press office, the possibility had no impact on his inner life. He was happy to fight the battle appointed to him, but capable of fighting bigger battles too.

He was thus – Galt thought – the best sort of soldier. Therefore his doubts about Big Drum's military-based candidacy were spoken without malice or artifice. For that reason they had weight.

'We'll see,' said Galt. But he wasn't really worried about it. Even apart from the fact that he had never won battles, McClellan had been a different case. He had got Napoleonic ideas because he had never triumphed in the field and, instead, blamed it all on Washington. Whereas Big Drum's ambition, by contrast, was to be not emperor, in any strict sense, but simply President within the limits of the US Constitution.

Yet Bryant's idea was not just interesting. In a strange and uncomfortable way, Galt would remember it whenever the question of the candidacy arose at table.

Perhaps he needed another fortifying letter from Senator Vandergrift.

She had all but forgotten Stacey, but the week before Christmas, he appeared in her office again, without appointment, a genuine civilian calling by. He looked leaner still and somehow older, less than ever the young man in the jeep who had told her with awful embarrassment that he loved her.

'If I promise not to make speeches,' he said, 'will you let me sit down?'

She noticed he wasn't even smiling as he said it. No deprecation there. He was uttering a serious promise.

She told him to sit down, but he shook his head. 'I'm flying back to Melbourne. My father is very ill. It's something to do with his heart and high blood pressure. He's been working twenty-hour days and he's had this fight with the government over censorship – they surrounded the printworks with troops a month or two ago. All because he printed an edition without reference to the military censors.'

'So, it runs in the family,' said Dim with a smile. 'I hope he recovers well and goes on being a thorn in their sides.'

Stacey took it the right way and laughed. But there was a fragility to him which made her wonder whether he *would* take things the right way.

'How have you been yourself?' she asked him.

'I've had the happiest time of my life so far,' Stacey told her, staring straight ahead with hollow eyes.

'Oh?' she said.

'Yes. I spent a month in the field with an infantry section. Australian, of course. Got to know them like brothers, and all that sort of thing. You see, I want to write a book. All I can say, Dim, is that if men can behave in peace the way they do up there on the Huon Peninsula, then a golden age is coming. Do you have anything to drink, Dim?'

A tear had spiked his left eye. It wasn't hard to speculate why. Obviously one of his 'brothers' had died up there.

She got the bottle of scotch she kept for visitors. 'And how are you?' he asked, unnaturally loudly, while she poured him a glass.

'I'm fine. Very busy.'

'You know that night, what I said to you. It embarrasses me now. I'd always remember that when I was very tired, you know up there near Salamaua. I'd remember it whenever I woke up in the night to go for a piss.' He laughed. 'You must have thought I was pretty ridiculous, Dim. So I was.'

'No. I didn't think anything, except that I was touched. Women enjoy hearing speeches like that, in a peculiar way . . . And for God's sake, Paul, I know something about infatuation. I had my first infatuation at fourteen.'

He shook his head and drank a large gulp of the spirit. 'You know I'm engaged to a girl in Melbourne. I suppose it will be all all right when I go to see her this time. I mean, maybe then I'll know if it's like you say. *Infatuation*. Now that's a word we usen't to use, did we? We got it out of American pictures.'

He looked at her significantly. She didn't know whether it was battle strain or a kind of accusation. Surely any rumours about herself and Galt were restricted to the staff.

He said nothing more to give her a clue. The conversation drifted. Again, like a sentiment uttered as a parting summation, he apologized if he had embarrassed her that night when he'd told her he loved her.

By then he had drunk at least a tumbler of scotch. It had evened out his voice, and he seemed more serene.

'Here,' she said, offering him the bottle. 'Take this with you, in your haversack.'

'No,' he said. 'That stuff's too expensive.'

'In show business it's standard issue,' she insisted. Taking the bottle from her, he tapped its side lovingly.

'You're a great girl, Dim.'

'Don't drink it all at once,' she advised him.

She found it so hard to believe that a year had passed since that first Moresby Christmas, the reconciliation Christmas, the one for which Galt had given her a present of the history of sheep farming in Victoria, a pilfered gift from Big Drum's library.

Her good friend the nursing officer had now been flown north, to administer a hospital in Lae, and a slightly younger, even more tightly lipped and fairly unhumorous woman had taken over the Port Moresby job and shared Dim's bungalow. Since she was colourless and had no vices, she could have been hand-picked by Galt, and indeed perhaps she was.

This year Galt's present was a kimono Buck Clancy had bought back from Brisbane with him. Buck had not been under any misapprehension as to who it was for when Galt had asked him to fetch it back . . . and so in a way it made good that slighting word *mademoiselle* which he had uttered in the Administration villa corridor some months before.

There was a second present as well. Galt presented her with a small cardboard box which when opened was seen to contain a captain's six metal pips, Australian Army style, and two highly polished AUSTRALIA badges to support them. The sight of them reminded her at once of Allan. She had been thinking of him for days. What sort of Christmas would he spend? Behind the enemy lines, exchanging wry gifts with Gordon Runcie? Happy? Thinking how he would write a book?

'Your work has not gone without notice, Dim,' said Galt. 'This is not my doing. It's the work of Ernie Sasser's department. That's what you come under, in case you wondered. They intend to elevate you to captain. You know, I made captain at the same age you have. I think you might have a wonderful career.'

The idea amused her, distracted her from the painful speculation about Allan. She didn't want to burden Galt with all that today in any case.

'This is extraordinary,' she said. 'Two years ago I was a private.' There was an unspoken accusation in what she said. She found she intended that there should be.

'Dim, I have nothing to do with this. OK, it means you won't have to meet the second class artists at the airport – you need only meet the first class ones. But again that's not my doing. I wouldn't arrange that. I don't want to lose you by interfering too much.'

'I must seem an ungrateful cow,' conceded Dim, smiling broadly. But she realized, not for the first time, that everything was ambiguous if you loved Big Drum's right-hand man.

'I have something for you, of course,' she told him then. She left the living room. She moved freely through the house. For this year they were not sharing Christmas dinner with the nursing officer. She had chosen to join her fellow nurses at the Port Moresby base hospital.

She came back holding a square imitation-leather bag with a handle, and opened it to show that it contained two reels of film in metal canisters. The canisters had tags attached which proclaimed, '*Winter of Content*'.

'What is this?' Galt asked.

'It's your daughter's first film. I've been exchanging telegrams with the distributors. It won't be released in the United States until January 7th. I've arranged a private screening for you at five o'clock in the open air cinema in Port Moresby. There's been a report in *Time* magazine – I'm surprised you didn't see it – which says that she's dazzling.'

He had never seen Dim as such an orchestrator of events. It was as if she was proving at once that her captain's pips were indeed earned. And he was touched. Had anyone ever gone to such trouble for him before? He couldn't remember.

After turkey and cranberry sauce and wine, Corporal Hutchinson, the former film theatre usher who now worked for Dim, drove them down to the cinema and they watched the extraordinary reels. Alexandra Sandforth had found a screenplay worthy of her. It concerned a young woman who worked as a riveter in a bomber factory and whose husband had been killed in the South Pacific. It covered the people she met – the wolf, the honourable and tubercular young shop floor supervisor, the older woman, the parents of the dead boy, and finally another young war widow, one with a child this time. Because it was not overtly propagandistic, the film worked superbly.

Dim could herself imagine it being a kind of comfort to many women. Even taking into account the shadows of her own situation, the fact that her husband, whom she no longer desired, was in a sort of continuous peril, a professional hero, a member of a unit so brave and so secret that it never recommended anyone for decorations.

When the show was finished, and only the white-blue projector light was still flickering on the screen, Galt looked away, wanting to keep silent for at least ten seconds. A minute would have been better. And as if she understood, Dim said nothing. The time stretched. At last he was composed enough to speak.

'Is that damn good, or is it only because I'm her father?'

'It's damn good,' said Dim.

He looked at Dim's well made, worshipped features. The irony was that if his daughter could have known that her future stepmother had gone to this trouble, had wheedled reels out of a distributor just so that in a thick tropical dusk her father could get a foretaste of her coming fame, then she might be appeased, might understand and relent.

'Do you envy her, Dim? That's a fine young man she was acting with.' He asked that though only to hide his deeper feelings. He was no longer tormented by fear that Dim was thinking always of younger men. Not today anyhow.

'Don't be a bloody ratbag,' said Dim. It was his favourite Aussie term of abuse, and he laughed.

'Until I served in Mexico as a young man, I always thought it had to snow to be a perfect Christmas. *This* is the most perfect Christmas.'

Mosquitoes were biting them. There was no mosquito here that wasn't a carrier and a donor of malaria. Their anti-malarial pills were more or less proof against the fury of the insects.

This most perfect Christmas.

Chapter 13

Beach Walks

'WHAT CAN I help you with, Galt?' asked Surgeon-General Winton, settling himself companionably into the chair across from Galt's desk on the verandah. He was used to doing the staff favours, giving them painkillers, dispensing benzedrine – the Australians called them 'wakey-wakey' pills – for all-night work sessions, and perhaps even arranging abortions for their girlfriends. Maybe he thought that that was what Galt would ask him for today. Galt had often thought of a child, of what a seal that would make between him and Dim, and though he had not discussed it with her, he was hopeful that if it ever happened she would want to keep the child rather than look for unofficial help from Winton. In any case, nothing like that had happened and Galt had entirely different matters to raise.

'I hope you found your family well?' he asked the surgeon, for Winton had just flown back from a home leave. His family lived in Rhode Island.

'Sure. My son's at sea, somewhere off North Africa. But the womenfolk are fine. We went up to Vermont, to my brother's lodge. It was superb up there. Even did some skiing. I felt the cold though. I mean, all that snow. Vermont's not even on the same planet as Port Moresby.'

Galt did not answer. It would have been fatuous for him to have done so. 'You gave an interview to the north-east correspondent of the *New York Times* while you were there?'

'Yes.' Winton shrugged. He hoped perhaps he wasn't going to be accused of seeking publicity. 'Yes. In Providence. Before we went skiing. He knew I was on Big Drum's staff. Big Drum's enormous news back there, you know.'

'I've got the clipping here,' said Galt. 'When the man asked you about Big Drum and the Republican nomination, you're quoted as saying, "No, I've actually heard him assure the Australian Prime Minister a number of times that he doesn't want it. He is a soldier and wants to march all the way to Tokyo." '

Winton nodded. He seemed quite pleased with himself for having made that clear, yet he was uneasy too. 'I thought that was the impression we wanted to spread. So the Democrats would be persuaded to keep supplying us here.'

'Did Big Drum's press office authorize you to make a statement like that?'

Winton was frowning for the first time in the interview. 'No. But I heard Big Drum say it twice at that dinner.'

'And when he said it, Surgeon Winton, was he telling the Australian Prime Minister to pass his remarks on to the press?'

'No. He was probably telling him to pass the news on in talks with the President himself.'

'Well,' said Galt. 'I'm sure you can see the difference between telling the President and telling the press. You did the latter. You took away Big Drum's freedom to manoeuvre.'

'Sure, Galt, but . . . '

'Now he can't change his mind about the nomination at some future date without the Democrats using this denial, from your own mouth, as ammunition.'

'Oh Jesus,' said Winton. He put a hand to his forehead. 'I had no idea . . . I mean, everything I see of Big Drum . . . I mean, I'm never in the central deliberations. I'm on the sidelines in the major planning conferences. And for Christ's sake, haven't I done some good work? Especially with the forward hospitals and the transportation of the wounded?'

'You've done a very good job,' said Galt. He kept the severe Sandforth tone in place, and even though he found he no longer enjoyed being Big Drum's hatchet man, he hoped no one would be able to tell that from his demeanour. 'The good job you've done isn't the question. You're being transferred to Washington.'

Winton looked all at once sick. He was a decent fellow, and he must have held a hope that if he played his cards right he would be Big Drum's Secretary of Health or at least a Surgeon-General of the United States, whenever Big Drum *did* decide to run for the White House. But now he was about to be dispatched into oblivion.

'Jesus, don't just drop me in a hole, Galt. Let me talk to Big Drum.'

'I'm acting on Big Drum's orders. You know that. Don't be naive. Besides you're being upped to Deputy Chairman. The Warfront Medical and Surgical Supplies Sub-Committee. European Theater of Operations, Department of Defense. WAMSSSE-TODD to those who do business with it. I have your orders here.'

Galt took up the envelope with Winton's orders in them and passed them over the table.

'At least you can do plenty of skiing,' he told Winton. Afterwards, he was ashamed of that tawdry parting shot. But the strain of the task habitually brought out the cheapness in him. He was mutely grateful Dim never saw him at these moments.

He had never understood the meaning of bosuns' whistles. But there seemed to be too great a number of them providing a shrill descant to the cheers of sailors as Big Drum led his staff up the gangplank of the light cruiser *Tucson*. It was a Sunday afternoon in Milne Bay, predictably humid, thunder clouds massing as always at the top of the coastal mountains. On the upper deck of the cruiser, hundreds of sailors and Marines were screaming their approval of Big Drum, invoking a messianic wave from him. The fury of their approval for the man reminded Galt of how easily the opposite response, the passionate jeers of the world, would be evoked if Big Drum's planned big operation failed, if in coming days these sailors, covered with grit and blood, had to go in to the beach again and again to rescue troops they had earlier landed.

That was Harry Strudwick's frankly expressed fear, anyhow. He'd advised against this operation.

To join his staff abroad *Tucson*, Big Drum had flown straight on to Milne Bay from Brisbane, and had not passed through Port Moresby at all. So that the night before, in the Administration villa, Dim and Galt had been able to sleep spaciously together. Now however Galt was shown to a narrow cabin off the wardroom. Ships had always given him a feeling of claustrophobia, and this cabin with its minute portholes was a cell. He stashed his gear joylessly and took the enormous folder labelled *Reconnaissance-in-Force, Admiralty Islands* with him out to the wardroom for the evening conference. As he went he could hear the bosuns' whistles sounding again. Probably Admiral Peter Andrews coming aboard.

The staff all sat round the table with sober expressions. Galt wished Buck were there, but he was far away on the north coast, organizing the air support for the Admiralty Islands landings. Without him, there was a tendency for Strudwick to set the tone in a subtle way Big Drum didn't seem to notice, and the tone this afternoon was apprehensive. But Hal Metzger, commander of VI Corps, seemed depressed too. As Galt entered, he was in the process of handing Big Drum a number of G2 (Intelligence) reports. When Galt was settled in at the General's side, Big Drum passed them on to him. They were reconnaissance reports from a number of sources – reconnaissance planes, radio intercepts – which showed that Los Negros island was being reinforced by night.

When Galt looked up from them, he was aware of Harry Strudwick's mournful eyes on him.

It had been Big Drum's confident aim to land troops in the Admiralty Islands two hundred miles north of the New Guinea coast. The largest island of the group was Manus – Harry Strudwick's reports said that it was garrisoned by twenty-five thousand Japanese troops. Like a calf whale on its eastern flank sat the island of Los Negros, where, according to Harry, there were eight thousand enemy troops, though Hal Metzger offered a more conservative figure of four thousand. But now the Los Negros garrison had received reinforcements.

The planned amphibious landing of Metzger's troops in Hyane Harbour, Los Negros, would involve a first wave of fifteen hundred men of the 1st Cavalry Division. If the entire garrison was concentrated against the first wave, they would be killed in the water – a few would survive to die a later death on the beach.

Big Drum's studies of the habits of Japanese commanders in the Pacific in the past eight months, a study organized for him by Galt, indicated that the Japanese troops would almost certainly *not* be committed to repelling the landing. The commander on Los Negros would be in doubt as to whether the Hyane Harbour landing was a feint, and would have to keep at least half his force ready to counter-attack a landing on some other part of the island. That other landing wasn't due for another ten days, but the commander wouldn't know that.

Big Drum was radiant with confidence, even tonight in the wardroom of the *Tucson*. His idea was that Manus would fall once Los Negros was in his hands. Why? Because Los Negros had an airstrip which Ernie Sasser's boys could pave and extend. Once the Fortresses and the Liberators came in, the enemy on Manus would be pounded into a condition of impotence.

Galt was largely on Big Drum's side in this. It was the great strategy that he and Buck and Big Drum had arrived at after Quebec. Yet tonight, on this steel tube of hot air in a tropical sea, it seemed less viable. Or else Galt dreaded that events would prove that it was a false dream, like all the other dreams, like Big Drum's confident prediction in 1939 that the Japanese couldn't take the Philippines. Similarly, the objections of Harry Strudwick seemed more credible tonight, as the fans churned above everyone's head in the wardroom of *Tucson* but gave no real relief from the oppressive climate of this steel tub. The closest resupply depot for Los Negros was at Finschhafen, which was on the New Guinea coastline, and more than three hundred miles away from the place the troops would land. That's OK, Big Drum had argued, I'll reinforce Los Negros by air.

But, Harry suggested, that's assuming that the troops who land in the first wave capture the airstrip, which is a mile behind the landing beaches.

'They'll capture it,' Big Drum had serenely announced. 'It will be their first order of business.'

'But I think we have to wonder,' objected Harry, 'what happens if they don't. And even if they do, can General Clancy supply adequately by air?'

Buck Clancy had always been a member of Big Drum's expansionist school however. 'There'll be no problem,' he asserted. 'There'll be transports and Fortresses packed with men shuttling between Finschhafen and Los Negros continually. For ten days. Then there'll be the second landing.'

But now Los Negros, chosen by Big Drum as the enemy's weak link in the Admiralties, was being strengthened.

Galt gave the reports back to Big Drum. Big Drum dropped his voice. 'What do you think?' he asked.

Galt had in that second the chance to ally himself with Strudwick's caution and save the disaster he half-expected and certainly dreaded. Everything in him cried out to do that, and as far as he was conscious of what he was doing, he was conscious that he was now going to utter words of caution. Why take the risk? The advance so far had been gradual and worthwhile. Why go for a prize which might on the one hand allow you to jump your line far forward beyond your dreams, but on the other hand could turn into an American tropical Dunkirk?

But there was another side to Galt, suppressed perhaps by his having to be Big Drum's organizer and right-hand sonofabitch. It was what his mother had once called the 'Stonewall Jackson side of your nature'. If Big Drum did this once, this giant upping of the stakes, and it worked, then he could keep doing it at an increasingly accelerated pace. The date Buck Clancy had mentioned on the verandah before Christmas – Manila by 1950 – could be advanced by years.

'These intelligence reports,' he heard himself say, 'indicate nothing more than a reinforcement in battalion strength on a nightly basis from Manus itself. This isn't a case of thousands of men being shipped in from Rabaul. These, I would suggest, are simply routine movements.'

There was enormous silence in the room, Galt noticed, except from the fan, which kept on with its manic business of sharing out the scalding air. He heard Big Drum speak. 'You know what? I agree with Galt. We'll continue as planned, gentlemen.'

Harry Strudwick looked sick, victim of a terrible pallor. Galt was sure that he himself looked just like that. But Big Drum was tapping the table with his cigarette holder, a sign he had not finished his commentaries on the decision. 'Another thing,' said Big Drum, '*we're* going to have to land with the boys. We must show them we have the courage of our decision. We're going ashore, gentlemen.'

Now there was an aghast silence again. Hal Metzger stirred in his seat. 'General,' he said, 'I urge you to reconsider that. Both at Cape Gloucester and Aitape, you forbade me to accompany the landing forces. Again, quite rightly, you feared that if anything happened to me my troops and my chain of command would be thrown into disarray and the entire landing jeopardized. That was in my opinion a wise decision. But now you wish to expose yourself in this way? It doesn't make sense. Landing craft can be entirely engulfed and vanish with all hands. If that happened in this case, there could be chaos amongst the landing force.'

Through Hal's answer, Big Drum had nodded a number of times, and Galt hoped this meant his statement of an intention to land was mere flamboyance and now obviously ill considered.

Instead, he said, 'Well that all makes a lot of sense, Hal. A lot of things make a lot of sense. I suppose it makes a lot of sense not even to be here, and not even to have planned the operation to start with. But the Japanese got down here in the first place not by sense but by inspiration. I've just got to go. That's my command. I'm going. And so is the staff.'

In his so-called cabin that night Galt felt a terrible restlessness. *Tucson* was steaming north-west along a shoal coast with Buna, Gona and Salamaua somewhere far to port. Galt had an ugly heat rash on his legs, and the one thing worse than not scratching it was yielding to the temptation to do so. A second's relief brought an aftermath of creeping, itching torment. Sam Winton would have known what to do, but he was on his way back to Washington.

At one stage Galt might have got as much as forty minutes' sleep before waking itchily and dressing and going on deck. He found himself below and aft of the bridge, looking out at the rich, creamy trench of water the *Tucson* was leaving in its wake. Dampier Strait, between New Britain and New Guinea, named after a British buccaneer, lay ahead, but little was visible except the vivid froth of the wake.

On the wing of the bridge stood Big Drum, wearing his battered campaign hat. The officer of the watch and sundry yeomen came and went, busy up there. But Big Drum was fixed in place. Galt hoped that he would get some sleep. If he didn't, he might become very nervous or else very rash.

Galt went back to his bunk. At last he fell asleep. He felt regretful and scared when a steward woke him before five with a cup of black coffee. On his way to join Big Drum on the bridge, he heard the anchor go down. Immediately all *Tucson*'s main armament and the guns of all the ships in company, broke out in an intolerable ruckus. The air shuddered and the ship rolled to port. The seaman who was leading him up the companionway glanced around to see if he was all right. He did his best to seem to be accustomed to such shocks and waved, as if he wanted the boy to go on.

Big Drum was on the starboard side of the bridge, the side facing the shore. He was with Peter Andrews, but Harry Strudwick had not yet arrived.

Big Drum was very composed. He watched the shore through binoculars and let Andrews point out features of the landscape to him. Already gaps of flame were rising in the semi-circle of shore which enclosed them, and not all of them were points where the cruiser's shells had landed. Some of the flashes were from replying artillery. Galt was aware of the stillness in the instant before a shell raged over the top of the bridge and landed behind them. It was succeeded by the shriek of another which landed in the water three hundred yards inshore. Galt watched the naval officers who seemed very wan. The sailors were twitching. They expected that the next round from the shore battery would split the difference and land on *Tucson*. But Andrews turned with a calm, congratulatory smile to Big Drum as half the shoreline seemed to erupt. It seemed *Tucson*'s salvoes had wiped out the threat in time.

The anchorage all around was at once full not only of gushes of water thrown up by enemy artillery, but also of Higgins boats, the landing craft. Big Drum turned round to Galt and clapped him on the shoulder, as if Galt were personally responsible for all this and should take a bow. Young men could be seen crouching in the narrow waists of the landing craft, which looked ridiculously narrow and fragile. Their front flap had a narrow sheet of armoured metal as protection, but the rest was astoundingly vulnerable. Galt could very nearly see the platoons in the closer boats, as they went by, hunched down, working mentally on the odds. Yet none of the landing craft seemed to be hit.

'They're rushing to the beach like piglets to the sow,' roared Big Drum delightedly.

Whatever those damn things were – boats, landing craft, barges – that's what Big Drum and the staff would have to go ashore in later in the day.

Enemy fire from the shore seemed to be decreasing. After what Galt found to his amazement was not the longest but the shortest two hours of his life, even the *Tucson* ceased fire. Remotely, from the beach, could be heard small-arms, machine-gun and mortar fire, but those sounds struck Galt as minute and almost homely in this huge harbour. A message arrived on the bridge that the 93rd Regiment was establishing regimental headquarters nearly half a mile inland from the beach. Next, a signal came that its neighbour battalion, the 203rd, was plunging up a road towards the airstrip, and its commander was consolidating his position under heavy fire.

'That's good enough,' said Big Drum, clapping his hands as if the landing was secured. 'Let's all have breakfast.'

After two helpings of scrambled eggs, Big Drum was ready to rest. He slept an hour or two while the staff stayed on in the wardroom and received further occasional radio signals. They were hopeful signals, even jaunty. They included estimates of enemy losses. But the airstrip was still in the enemy's hands.

Big Drum had left orders to be aroused at 11.00 hours. It looked as if he and the staff would go ashore in the heat of noon.

On the deck it was raining in that peculiarly soft and insidious monsoonal manner, and everyone wore a rain slicker. Galt carried his steel helmet, but he noticed that Big Drum hadn't even brought one with him. At least they didn't have to climb down a grappling net to enter the deep well of the Higgins boat. The *Tucson* had let its steps down to water-level.

The high-gunwaled Higgins boat seemed to its passengers to move at hectic speed. It was a brisk run into the beach therefore, but the rain increased. Explosions could be heard, too, above the row of the engines. By the time the boat nudged the beach, the sounds of the battle inland, and not so far inland, had increased in volume.

The ramp of the Higgins boat descended into the shallows on a beach of ground-up coral, and Big Drum strode ashore in his tropic-weight raincoat and his battered hat. Galt kept to his right side, getting seawater in his boots. The coral sand was uneven, and impossible to walk quickly on, and the rifle fire seemed to be being exchanged only just ahead, in the first fringe of foliage. Galt could see palm branches, struck by some projectile or other, falling to the ground.

One of Pete Andrews's officers met them and there was a conversation. The major who had led the first wave was just over there on the edge of the jungle, crouched down with his men in reserve now, in the position they had taken soon after landing. The General and Galt and Pete Andrews and everyone strolled over there. All the young men here were wearing jungle camouflage and were lying low, but a few of them got up and saluted. Bullets could be heard thwacking and thudding into the meat of palm trees seemingly a few steps away. Big Drum extracted a medal from his breast pocket. Galt could see that it was the Distinguished Service Cross, which Galt himself had won in the Meuse sector in France in the last days of World War I. The tough-looking young major so honoured saluted in gratitude, but smiled when Big Drum shook his hand. Army photographers appointed by Big Drum's press office were everywhere now. They had been ordered to come on and record this death walk.

Galt now expected Big Drum to head down the length of the beach, perhaps to visit the nearest field surgical unit, and then return to the Higgins boat and *Tucson*. But without warning he turned inland. Galt found himself battling to keep up, but so were the rest of the staff.

'He's gone crazy,' muttered Harry Strudwick. 'Someone ought to stop him.'

Yet Galt felt certain nothing evil would befall Big Drum, even though it might befall one of the staff.

The rain had, if anything, worsened. But they were in amongst the palms, and Galt took his raincoat off. How could anyone romanticize the South Seas? The smell of rot was everywhere. Yet the bullets which Galt had heard earlier whacking into tree trunks didn't seem to be here. It was as if Big Drum moved in a portable zone of security.

Stretcher-bearers passed carrying heavily bandaged lumps, this morning's infantrymen. They lived outside the zone of security. The stretcher-bearers didn't seem to notice Big Drum, nor he them.

Next, they came across half-naked and barefooted Japanese corpses strewn everywhere, but Big Drum ploughed on. Galt was fascinated for a few seconds by the feet of the dead. Surely souvenir hunters couldn't have been here already, taking the shoes from the Japanese corpses, that curious footwear in which the big toe was separate from the rest?

Now Big Drum's party reached a junction in the trail. Here, Galt felt, the General's invisible wall of safety simply dropped away. There was that terrible frenetic sound of rapid fire. Tropical verdure flapped as bullets struck it and passed on. Worst was the sense that the air was full of projectiles. His eyesight speckled by all this ballistic traffic before him, Galt had an impulse to drop, like all the GIs around about, who were hugging the cover amongst the trees. But Big Drum considered the trail junction, whether to turn left, like a man on a Sunday walk. An officer came bobbing up through the fire, saluted, saw the iconic face smile at him, saluted again and said, 'Sir! You should get down. They've still got that low hill over there on the right.'

'That's the direction of the airfield, major?'

'Yes, sir.' He ducked involuntarily and actually blushed behind his atebrin-yellowed face. 'Sir, we're going to flank them on the left, and the 115th is going to sweep round them on the right towards the east side airstrip. That's my understanding, sir. Please . . . '

A Japanese mortar round decapitated a palm twenty yards away.

'Sir,' the officer persisted, 'we've only just killed two snipers down there.' He pointed in the direction Big Drum showed every indication of wanting to take. Indeed, two lifeless bundles lay along the trail, where they had fallen from the treetops. Anyone could have seen them. Big Drum did not even care to look. Instead he strode off in their direction. Galt stayed at his side. 'General,' the panic-stricken officer behind Big Drum called. 'I have to stay here to command my men.'

'Goes without saying,' Big Drum yelled over his shoulder. Galt wondered why he himself was doing this; walking into the furnace cheerily with Big Drum, dissenting only to the extent that he wore one of the steel helmets Big Drum shunned. *I am not a passive man. Neither are the others.* Such a mystery: Big Drum's power to make others move against their will. It was partly orders and partly ambition marching them along, but it was neither in total.

The photographers took shots of Big Drum and his staff inspecting the fallen snipers. Then Big Drum strode on again. Galt fought all the way the impulse to dive to the ground and keep to it. They came up behind columns of GIs working either side of this trail, going forward, firing berserkly and receiving fire in return. Amongst all the clatter of small-arms there were screams and yelled orders and the brief but frightful grunts of death-dealing. Soon Galt saw a dead GI, his rifle driven by the bayonet into the leaf mould and coral debris of the track close to his head.

Ten paces further forward sat a young American, the left side of his camouflage shirt torn away, a great pad of surgical dressing absorbing blood on his right upper breast. But a medic knelt beside him, injecting him with something. Painkiller. Something to coagulate the flow from his wound.

Big Drum bent over the wounded soldier. 'You'll be all right, son,' he advised him. 'We have the best field hospitals. Better than the enemy.'

'I was with Tommy,' said the boy, dazed.

'Is Tommy up with the others?' asked Big Drum.

'I was with Tommy,' said the boy.

Two stretcher-bearers arrived from the rear and loaded the

boy. Galt saw the sand kick evilly near the boot of one of the bearers.

They must have walked at least half a mile behind the stream of advancing infantry. Then they could see, beyond the passageway of palms, the hard glint off the open spaces of the runway. 'There it is!' said Big Drum, taking his campaign cap off and pointing towards the airstrip with it.

He made for that white glare. Amongst the undergrowth, where the tall palm trees gave out on the edge of the runway, an officer and four men were clustered around a heavy machine-gun which they were firing. The officer was very young, and glancing up and seeing this phalanx of brass emerge from the palm trees seemed for a second stupefied.

'Sir,' he yelled, a collective greeting. You didn't need to be a lip reader to see that the man who was feeding the Browning was yelling, 'Jesus Christ, it's Big Drum!'

The Browning ceased its racket.

'Sir,' called the young officer again, addressing all these generals. 'You can't come out here. The Japanese are dug all along the far perimeter and up the end there.'

'It's OK, son. We just need a brief look.'

Big Drum made his way behind the fire team and on to the open runway. The rain had eased by now, and he carried his raincoat balled in one hand. He considered the surface of the runway while the five young men in the undergrowth provided what covering fire they could. He began to kick at the crushed coral surface with the toe of his muddy shoe.

'Ernie,' he called. 'Ernie!'

Ernie Sasser bravely left the huddle of Big Drum's escorts. He stood by his General.

'Ernie, can your boys put down a decent surface on this stuff?'

'Yes, General. This is a fine surface.' Ernie cagily took advantage of this professionally sanctioned opportunity to kneel down. He dug the coral with his hand. 'Perfectly OK,' he assured Big Drum. 'Absolutely no problems! The drainage looks good.'

'Very well,' said Big Drum loudly, looking around the perimeter of the airstrip. 'The 1st Cavalry seem to have all this under control. Let's go, gentlemen.'

As the party moved back again into the jungle, they could hear the spit and fizz of shots hitting the coral surface. From the trail the group retreated along, GIs were battling northwards through the jungle, parallel to the airstrip perimeter. More wounded were coming back, but not in vast numbers. Galt could even tell by the drift of fire, by the absence of GIs now along the trail, that the thing was going well, that the strip was surrounded.

The rain began so hard it penetrated the screen of jungle and drenched everyone, making their light raincoats irrelevant. But the staff had begun to chatter with each other in a congratulatory way. Harry Strudwick suddenly had a cautious appreciation of the wisdom of this move against Los Negros, though his enthusiasm for it was, like everyone else's, probably stoked by his enthusiasm at the thought of getting back to the *USS Tucson*.

The beach was an astounding sight now. Landing craft arrived still, young men in camouflage moved competently across the coral fragments and inland, and the anchorage was full of a fleet such as it had never seen – cruisers, destroyers, troop carriers. The naval officer who was beachmaster led them to their Higgins boat, which had crunched up on to the coral of the beach, was revving its engines for a quick getaway, and looked to Galt all at once immensely more secure and desirable a shelter than it had earlier in the day.

When they were aboard, standing in the waist, Hal Metzger, who like Galt himself, had been sensibly wearing a steel helmet the whole time, stood beside Galt and murmured, 'What was he doing, Galt? What was it about?'

It was strange the way they all thought he understood Big Drum in some way they didn't.

'I think he didn't want to wait offshore for the result. He wanted to *see* it all . . . '

'You know what? That's the most outrageous afternoon I've ever goddamn spent. I don't want to spend too many more like it. We were glorying in death, Galt.'

The *Tucson*, when they returned to it, seemed a secure planet. Harry Strudwick, trying to clean the mud off his boots on a grating over a hatchway, asked Galt, 'Do you think Big Drum plans many walks like this?'

'I don't know. But his critics were wrong, weren't they?'

Harry lowered his eyebrows. Galt had been very careful to convey, by the confidentiality of his tone, that he didn't consider Harry one of the critics. But Harry was nervous. He wanted his earlier opposition to the Los Negros expedition to be forgotten.

Galt did not push the question. He had lived, and life was sweeter for him than for most men. That was enough.

Ultimately the entire staff abandoned its hopelessly muddied shoes by a companionway and went into the boardroom in stockinged feet. There, Galt found to his amazement, Big Drum and Hal Metzger were sitting together drinking strawberry malteds.

The chorus of approval for what Big Drum had pulled off at Los Negros was resounding. Everyone recognized its significance. It meant that great bounce-forward movements, as opposed to village-by-village assault, were possible. Churchill was delighted; the President said that it was a spectacular use of limited resources.

'If it hadn't worked,' said Big Drum in Port Moresby, grinning a rare pirate grin, 'he would have cut my supplies and told me to dig in.'

Even Wendell Fryer, the one-worlder Republican candidate for the Presidency, sent a hearty telegram. Big Drum had a joke about this too. 'He's telling me to stick to soldiering, but I'm so good at it he'd hate to see me change trades.'

Big Drum flew off to Brisbane to see Mrs Wraith and Little Drum. Galt threw a cocktail party for the staff – it was appropriate after all the hard work. Dim was invited, and was a quiet presence there, chatting with Captain Duncan and some of the junior staff and leaving after three-quarters of an hour.

In the United States it was getting on towards spring, and the first primaries, Democrat and Republican, were due to be held. That was OK – Big Drum wasn't intended to participate in any of this, his name was to arise at a locked convention, when the votes were split between Fryer and Wagner.

There were rafts of press speculation – 'CAN THE BIG DRUM BE BEATEN?' – supplied to him by Big Drum's press office in the garden. Senator Vandergrift and Thornton Downes, chairman of the Republican Party, both wrote to him indicating that a large mass of potential Big Drum delegates was ready to emerge at a deadlocked convention.

And then an extraordinary and unplanned political phenomenon occurred. In Wisconsin, Big Drum's state of birth, and a state which had contributed heavily to Big Drum's early divisions in the Southwest Pacific campaign, the first Republican primary of the season had got under way. A Wisconsin Republican delegate from Milwaukee, a lawyer and Big Drum enthusiast called Donner suffered a rush of Big Drum euphoria and placed the General's name on the Wisconsin Republican primary ballot paper. Donner had done what every Republican delegate had the right to do. It was just that he was part of the party undergrowth, and no one had bothered telling him that this was *not* the way the experts intended Big Drum to reach the White House.

Galt got notification from Thornton Downes and Senator Vandergrift almost at once – at least, these were messages addressed to both Galt and Big Drum. The politicians presumed that Big Drum was perpetually and heroically located in New Guinea, and were unaware that he was so frequently in Brisbane now. Big Drum's press office had worked only too well in firming up this impression. Thornton Downes said he was sending, with a young officer about to leave Chicago for Port Moresby, a document for Big Drum to sign, renouncing his nomination for the primary. Less than two weeks remained to arrange all this – but if Big Drum sent a radio message or telegram indicating that the signed paper was on its way, party officials would probably withdraw his name from the ballot paper.

As soon as he was notified, Galt sent signals in his own right, including amongst them the communications from Senator Vandergrift and Thornton Downes, to Big Drum's rear headquarters in Brisbane. The message was that Big Drum should come to Port Moresby to meet the young officer who was bringing the paper. He should also begin refusing nomination by sending a telegram to the Republican Party.

When, the following afternoon, no reply had come from Big

Drum, Galt sent further signals. They at last produced a casual answer, the next morning, from Big Drum. 'Perhaps you and the young man should bring the paper down here to Brisbane,' said Big Drum. 'At this stage my final decision in this matter has not been reached.'

The Republican Party had its power, even when it came to military transport, and the young officer, a lieutenant-commander who had a sweet job visiting war fronts and reporting to Congress, turned up in less than four days. Buck Clancy had a Flying Fortress standing by to run Galt and the boy, at an hour's notice, down the long coastline to Brisbane.

They set off at mid-afternoon and landed at Archerfield near Brisbane towards two the next morning. They got to Lennon's, where life for the rear echelon staff looked very upholstered. Galt was told that Big Drum had retired for the night. Maybe he was sleeping better now, but it was quite possible that he was still reading, and Galt felt frustrated that he wasn't able to go in and see him at once.

After a night's sleep in a room in the hotel, Galt was awoken at 7.30 by a steward who said an officer was waiting to take him to breakfast in the General's suite. Galt and the naval officer with the sinecure and the letter took the elevator two floors to Big Drum's apartments. When they were admitted to the dining room, it all looked like a family tableau. Little Drum was wearing the top half of a cowboy suit and being fed boiled egg by Ling. He had grown a lot, and Galt said so, making a fuss of the little boy, which the little boy very much liked. He had had a hard life, this child; an odd life for an infant. The Hotel Manila, Corregidor, the Malinta Tunnel, and now more than two years living with the staff in a military hotel.

Galt noticed that everything the boy said, 'Do cowboys eat boiled eggs?' or, 'Will we see Ernesto when we go back to Manila?' (Ernesto having been the butler in their suite on top of the Hotel Manila) seemed to fill Big Drum with pride and admiration.

Mrs Wraith said, 'My, you do look thoroughly tropical, Galt.'

Galt and the young naval officer sat down at the table. The naval officer, sniffing opportunity, said, 'Sir, may I say it is a great honour to be associated with you in any way. If there is anything I can ever do . . . ?'

'That's OK, son,' said Big Drum. 'I believe Senator Vandergrift has a very high opinion of you.'

The young lieutenant-commander glowed. He could hear destiny calling. 'I've tried to provide the House and Senate with useful insights, General Wraith, sir.'

'I'm sure you have. Have some coffee and orange juice.'

Galt was impatient. The young lieutenant-commander was not meant to be garnering great moments to relay to his grandchildren.

Big Drum turned, with painful politeness, to the young officer.

'Would you mind waiting outside just for a moment, commander? I have to discuss this with General Sandforth.'

Galt did not know what that meant. *Discuss this*?

The young man rose, saluted, and left at once.

'This is quite an event, Galt,' said Big Drum, grabbing his empty cigarette-holder, jamming it in his mouth and more or less whistling with incredulity through it.

'Mr Donner will have to be disciplined,' said Galt. 'I would imagine Senator Vandergrift will be attending to it straight away. In the meantime, General, we must signal the Senator, and then get that paper signed and off to him.'

Big Drum said nothing. All that could be heard was the whistle of his breath through his ridiculous amber holder.

'Perhaps this is the voice of God, Galt,' Big Drum murmured at last. 'Perhaps I'm intended to go the primary route.'

Galt shook his head. 'It's Senator Vandergrift's belief though, sir, that a locked convention is the way for you to achieve the candidacy. Even if you were to win Wisconsin, General . . . '

'Well, it's my home state. There's no way I wouldn't win it.'

Galt held his hand up. He wasn't arguing about a narrow, local victory or failure. He was getting annoyed. 'As I say, even if and when you win Wisconsin, the next primary will be in Illinois, which Wendell Fryer has sewn up.'

'I'm very strongly connected in Illinois as well, Galt,' said Big Drum with reproof.

My God, thought Galt, he means to do it. Take the pros on, round by round.

Galt said, 'Senator Vandergrift has been a Presidential candidate himself. He's an established campaigner. I think we should be guided . . . '

Big Drum raised his fists and blinked for emphasis. 'You could just as well say, Galt, that the Chaumont gang are experts, too. But I've shown them up. When we took Los Negros, it wasn't just the Japanese we were outflanking. What I'm saying is, we have to follow our noses, you and I. We have to operate by enlightened instinct. Perhaps Donner was right to make an honest candidate of me.'

A sweat had broken out on Galt's lower arms now, and across his eyebrows. This was getting very dangerous. How to tell Big Drum that he could be destroyed and humiliated in the primaries, no matter how much he was loved in Illinois or other parts of the Midwest? 'Sir, I hope you understand that I – more than any other American – want to see you in the White House . . . '

'And I want to see you, Galt, at the Pentagon.'

Galt shook this sentiment aside as brusquely as he could. It distracted him and in a way it grieved him. He would *not* be in the Pentagon. He would be a private man, living somewhere in the United States with Dim. Perhaps he could hope for an ambassadorship. But that wasn't the point. 'It is my most sincere judgement, General Wraith,' he pressed on, 'that you will not win by proceeding from one primary to another. You would need to be there. These men – Fryer and Wagner – are on the ground, they're in position for campaigning. They're able to pour shots of whiskey for voters and delegates. They're able to ask them how their wives are. On the day, it is they who will visit the polling stations. I know, you have a higher calling. You don't have to visit polling stations. You have to bring visitations upon the enemy. But in the trench warfare of primary day, that truth may be obscured. You are, if you'll forgive my saying so, General, a distant figure, something of an American god. No one disapproves of you except the envious. But at a state level, distant figures don't do so well as they do in nationwide elections. That's why I urge you out of the greatest concern for your political future to sign Thornton Downes's paper and let us shuttle it back to Wisconsin as swiftly as we can.'

Big Drum took the cigarette holder out now and punched the breakfast table emphatically with it. 'I presume I'll be permitted to make up my own mind,' he said with a hint of petulance.

'Of course, sir. But the well-being of the grand Republic depends on the judgement you make today.'

'Don't be so goddamned portentous, Galt. If I listened to you and Harry Strudwick all the time, we'd still be stuck in front of Salamaua.'

Galt felt affronted. How could he be associated with Harry Strudwick's paltry intelligence and cautious advice? He and Buck Clancy had flown as high, mentally, as Big Drum. Wingtip to wingtip. How could Big Drum lump his *mind*, whose integrity he treasured, in with that of Harry Strudwick, the non-visionary?

'I think if the General consults his memory,' said Galt, though he knew it was a mistake, 'he'll find that I gave consistent support to his bold strategies.'

'All right, Galt. I acknowledge that. But for God's sake, don't be such an old woman.'

Galt said nothing now. There was no defence to an accusation of old womanhood.

Big Drum began to check his pockets, as if he were about to go off to his desk and wanted to have all basic appurtenances of his life with him. 'Keep that young commander around till after lunch.'

'I was hoping to be back in Port Moresby at least by tomorrow morning,' said Galt.

'You will be, you will be,' groaned Big Drum. He suddenly became more fatherly. 'Don't worry, Galt. And take no notice of what I say. I'll think about this Thornton Downes letter. I will. But if I didn't sometimes go my own way, I wouldn't be anywhere.'

'In my opinion,' said Galt, bravely, because he thought it was essential to be brave again, 'in my opinion, if you go Donner's way, it will be a disaster.'

As Galt left the breakfast room, the commander in the waiting room stood. 'Can you keep yourself busy this morning, commander?' Galt asked him. He looked into the fresh, anxious features. The young political-appointee commander would do anything to be of service to Big Drum. At that second, Galt thought, how funny it was: he just understood that he himself was no longer Big Drum's servant, no longer a tender of the flame.

In the last hour Big Drum had rashly relegated Galt Sandforth from a devotee into a mere employee. If he stuck by his decision about the primaries, he would have shown himself to be just another man, capable of vanities and rashness.

Galt spent the morning at the staff surgeon's having his teeth checked. Then he filled in another half hour with a standard medical check. His blood pressure, the doctor astonished him by saying, was lower than average. That was good news to take back to Dim.

Nonetheless, Galt felt that his world was changing. Or it would if Big Drum didn't sign Downes's letter. When compared with Big Drum's peevishness, Dim's loyalty and sanity shone all the more brightly and grew in significance. These private virtues which he always secretly but not actively cherished now seemed to swamp Big Drum's public ambitions and make his own fatuous. This new understanding was sweet but also frightening. It required him to become a new kind of Galt Sandforth.

About lunchtime, and without eating, not even feeling hungry, he went back to the office they still kept vacant for him at the insurance building which had once been Bataan. He hoped he would not have to remind Big Drum that he was waiting for an answer. But anything was possible now. He didn't know where he stood with the man.

He was delighted when the ageing lieutenant-colonel who ran Big Drum's office here in Brisbane called him a little after one o'clock and said that General Wraith wanted to see him.

Galt deliberately took slow steps along the corridor. As if this were any other summons, as if what he was about to hear was not one way or another a key to the American future.

Big Drum was standing by his office window, looking towards Lennon's, where he would soon go for his afternoon siesta. Is it just what happened this morning? Galt wondered. Because in profile Big Drum looked like a sham, an aged character actor in an old-buffer part.

After some seconds, and with a small sigh, he turned fully to Galt.

'Old friend, I was unnecessarily harsh with you this morning. But this is a very hard decision.'

Again, there was no sense in not being forthright, Galt thought. 'You have only one obviously right decision to make, sir.'

Big Drum held his hand up. 'No. No, Galt, if you'll forgive me for saying so. No, there are no obvious solutions and don't tell me there are. The question is, was Donner's chance nomination of me an inspired event?'

Galt was beginning to wonder if military success was affecting Big Drum's mental stability.

'Might I ask, General . . . inspired by whom?'

'Don't be naive, Galt. By a force larger than any of us.'

'I don't know about forces as great as that, sir. I doubt they work on the politics of Wisconsin.'

'Very humorous, Galt. But it's no use telling me it'll all be a disaster. Disasters are continually converting themselves into triumphs all the time, particularly in this phase of history. We are in the furnace. The temperatures are so high that false judgements get annealed into judgements of steel and rectitude and divine inspiration.'

Galt thought, *he* has *lost some of his mind. He's forbidden me to say Donner is a mistake because he believes that all mistakes are victories wearing a divine mask.*

'I'm going to run in Wisconsin, Galt. It's my birth state. I know I can win it. I can certainly win Illinois.'

'Not against Wendell Fryer. Vandergrift says there isn't a chance.'

'He's a party machine man, Vandergrift. Their thinking is limited. My press office will issue a communiqué on the matter this afternoon. I shall run for the candidacy and for the Presidency *in absentia*. I intend to have captured Manila and be in command of the bulk of the Philippines before my Inauguration Day next year. I hope I can look to you for every assistance.'

What Galt thought about were the years he'd wasted in fantasies about a Big Drum Presidency: the fact he'd imposed the fantasy on Dim as well.

'Of course you can rely on me, General. Although, I don't think you will need much political assistance after Wisconsin.'

Big Drum chose to laugh. At least *that* was good. He wasn't as paranoid as usual. 'Well,' said the General, 'if you're wrong, you can buy Little Drum another cowboy suit by way of reparation. I trust you Galt. Wish me luck.'

Galt thrust his hand out. He smiled despite himself as he shook the General's hand. OK, he thought, maybe just not an employee. Perhaps a devoted friend. But certainly, no longer a disciple.

Without Big Drum's signed renunciation of the Wisconsin ballot, Galt returned empty-handed then in the belly of the B-17, and he slept shallowly and had the usual distorted dreams about Republican primaries and Dim and marriage and Sandy senior and Sandy junior.

The plane landed in Port Moresby in the small hours. Galt commandeered a jeep and drove himself immediately to Dim's bungalow. So that her starchy housemate, the nurse, would not be aroused, Galt threw coins at Dim's window. At last Dim roused herself and looked out. She saw him amongst the bougainvillaeas.

'This is no way for a general to behave,' she said, with that loving leniency. He had not had anything as valuable from Big Drum. He had only had a sort of mad gaiety.

'I'll open the front door for you,' said Dim. 'If that's not too civilized a form of entry for you.'

He was home with Dim. Home. The Charlottesville estate was a grand, dominating, demanding sort of place, and though Sandy seemed to enjoy its demands, it had never been home, and neither had any base he'd ever served on. But now he'd found his place, here against the shoulder of a compact Australian girl.

'I've had another letter from Honor Runcie,' Dim told him as they lay together.

'Oh, God!' he said, forgetting himself, expressing his abhorence for what had befallen Runcie and Lewis, his fear too that Dim might one day blame him for this circus – if ever anyone found out about it.

'Just asking if I've heard any more,' she continued.

'Dim,' he said, gathering himself, 'Special Reconnaissance is of its nature secret. It doesn't tell us everything. But I asked them to let us know if there was any change in what was happening with Runcie and Allan, and they said they would. That's all I can tell you.'

'I suppose you think that this is a kind of residual wifeliness,' Dim asked. 'But I don't exactly harp on it, do I?'

He waved a hand in the dark. 'No, no. You're entitled to be told these things.'

'As long as Allan's happy . . . ' she said.

He was back at the Administration villa in time for breakfast, although Buck Clancy was the only one who showed up at table. Buck asked some questions about Big Drum, but Galt didn't feel like committing himself. He was somehow ashamed to admit that Big Drum hadn't signed the paper the senior Republicans had sent him. It was a pity, Galt thought, that he hadn't taken Buck Clancy with him – the General valued his advice. In any case Buck seemed distracted.

'Listen,' he admitted over his coffee. 'I'm worried about Metzger. He hasn't been the same since that Los Negros business. I mean, the walk. He takes the death of every GI very personally. Too damned personally. And he keeps on talking to me about Big Drum's methods. He thinks Big Drum is putting VI Corps out on a limb, pushing them forward. He believes that the Japanese will dart in from the north-east and cut our line of communication somehow. I give him the facts. I tell him that's impossible while ever I've got airstrips both sides of the Bismarck Sea and control of the air above it. But the way he talks you wouldn't think Big Drum had been light on casualties. You'd think he'd been a goddamn butcher.'

'Kremnitz is the butcher,' said Galt. 'He didn't need to land on Tarawa and kill all those Marines.'

'My exact sentiments,' said Buck. 'But Metzger believes we can push forward a mile at a time and not suffer as much.'

'Doesn't he remember World War I?'

'Sure he does. But he's learned damn all from it.'

'What can I do?' Galt asked.

'Well, I'll tell you, Galt. The corps is being reinforced and will become an army. Same with Bryant's corps. We're talking about armies of 150,000 to 180,000. I don't think Metzger is fit to command what will be Sixth Army when we hit the Philippines – and if all goes well, we'll hit them some time this year. I want you commanding them. Your protégé Gibbs has come on vastly, and I think you and he in combination would be wonderful. If I plant the idea with Big Drum, would you consider it?'

Galt thought about it. He'd always seen himself as by nature and forever Chief of Staff. He had never liked field work, at least as a junior officer. But if he won renown in a real command, he could become a man as highly regarded by the American people as Patton and Bradley and even Bryant Gibbs were. This would mean that his divorce and his passion for a younger woman might be quite rightly forgiven.

It would mean also that his close, and now claustrophobic, connection to Big Drum would be altered. He would not be daily in Big Drum's service, dealing with Big Drum's mind and continually serving the flame. He would have a star of his own to follow.

And then the challenge. Handling an army in the face of the Japanese. He was suddenly quite excited. 'I wouldn't be against that, Buck. If you keep up the air cover over my head, I think I can handle a few corps adequately.'

'I know you could,' said Buck.

This frank declaration of confidence from Buck Clancy made Galt feel something should be given in return. 'Buck,' he said, 'that letter from Thornton Downes?'

'So Big Drum signed it, eh?'

'Not exactly,' said Galt. 'He's decided to fight the primaries.'

'But he'll be killed?'

'Exactly. I assure you, I fought like hell. I've probably come close to straining my friendship with him.'

'I have to talk to him,' said Buck Clancy. His Irish, working-class face was flushed with the urgency. Surprisingly, Galt himself did not feel that same urgency. He had grown such a distance from Big Drum since this time yesterday.

'Do what you can, Buck. I'll be delighted if you succeed.'

Galt saw Buck again at dinner that night. Buck's face was still suffused with the dread Galt had seen there when they parted that morning. 'He told me no, Galt. He says he wants to run. It's a signal from God. He even got aggressive with me. Dear God, Galt, what are we going to do?'

'We're going to continue to be soldiers,' said Galt with a smile. 'For at least another four years.'

'And abandon the country to the Democrats?'

'Probably. But you know, how can we tell Big Drum *isn't* right? Nothing would surprise me any more.'

'We *know* he's not right,' growled Buck.

Galt felt he knew him well enough to say, 'I thought you Irish were all Democrats, anyhow?'

Buck grinned like a cracked jug. 'America's changing,' he said.

It was St Patrick's Day. Buck Clancy wore a little flap of green ribbon beside the stars on his collar. He attended Mass in the garden with all the other Irish, amongst whom he was counted some sort of Celtic hero.

Moresby time was ahead of time in America, where it was the evening before the Wisconsin primaries.

Joining Galt and Harry Strudwick for a meeting over breakfast, Buck confessed, 'I'm wearing this green for Big Drum's sake. I hope it's the green of political reality. And – to use Big Drum's favourite word – triumph.'

The professional talk that morning was about a place called Wewak, a port and fortified town along the north New Guinea coast. The Joint Chiefs had ordered Big Drum to attack and capture Wewak, and it looked like the next step according to military orthodoxy. It was thought that – before an amphibious landing there – Buck would be able to wallop the place from his airstrips on the Huon Peninsula and up in the Admiralty Islands.

But Big Drum, martially if not politically gifted, had asked

Harry to monitor reports of Japanese troop movements along the coast, and he obviously doubted the wisdom of landing at Wewak, since it was heavily garrisoned – the estimates went as high as a hundred thousand troops. The place Big Drum wanted to hit was Hollandia, a cape some two hundred miles further along the coast than Wewak. All Harry's Intelligence indicated that Hollandia was thinly manned – two brigades had recently been shipped overnight from Hollandia to Wewak to strengthen the garrison there for the expected frontal attack, the one the Joint Chiefs wanted.

Like the attack on the Admiralty Islands, the taking of Hollandia by amphibious landing would increase the pace of Big Drum's program in the Southwest Pacific, bringing forward events by months if not by years – if it succeeded. The corps commanders, Bryant Gibbs and Hal Metzger, had specifically not been invited to this breakfast, since everyone feared Hal Metzger would argue interminably against it. Harry Strudwick himself was only marginally for it. Hollandia was too far forward, said Harry. Buck Clancy – with the best will in the world – couldn't supply air cover.

'There are three airstrips at Hollandia,' said Buck. 'If the troops take them for me, that's the end of our air cover concerns.'

'If, if,' interrupted Harry, in his Germanic mode.

Both Galt and Buck wondered what influence a political defeat this St Patrick's Day would have on Big Drum's military daring.

Harry Strudwick was also by now privy to Big Drum's decision. He was also wondering how it would affect Big Drum's behaviour. 'If Big Drum does insist on this operation, then I wonder will we all have to land again and go walking with him.'

Buck Clancy laughed. 'Wouldn't you like that, Harry?' asked Buck. 'I'd love it myself.'

He knew they knew he was kidding.

'I don't have the same guarantees of immortality as Big Drum has,' said Harry.

It was the truth. If Big Drum persisted with the Hollandia idea, they would again be involved in a dangerous trek. That could be one of the benefits of becoming an army commander. An army commander decided for himself – at least most of the time – what degree of risk he would expose himself to. But as a member of Big Drum's staff, you were subject all the time to Big Drum's spates of inspirational military daring, which might become more frequent if he lost the Wisconsin primary.

Although Galt spent a busy day, and then had Dim over for dinner in the evening, he was restless all that night. Long before dawn the next day he had dressed and crept out to the press office in the garden. A number of Big Drum's press boys had stayed up all night. They were sweaty and bug-eyed and stank of Scotch. They were depressed as well. With two-thirds of the votes in, Big Drum looked like finishing third or fourth, behind Wendell Fryer and Senator Stokes of Wisconsin, and perhaps even behind Wagner. The petty political commentators were queueing to say that this was a tragedy for Big Drum, but Vandergrift was bravely arguing on shortwave radio that that wasn't necessarily so. Indications were that Big Drum *would* win in Illinois. The thing was though that Wendell Fryer wasn't going to be bothered with Illinois. He said he didn't want to run against 'nonentities', by which he meant not Big Drum but the other two or three Illinois politicians on the primary ballot paper there. Fryer knew that in the end, the Illinois delegates would have to come to him, since no one else on the ballot paper other than Big Drum was a credible candidate.

Despite Senator Vandergrift's brave denial that Big Drum was finished politically for the year, he sent a signal to Galt which arrived later that morning. 'I have to state in the plainest terms that the General's candidacy has now perished, as we feared it would. Big Drum should cancel his participation in all future primaries. There is no sense in his continuing to be humiliated. Please use your influence.'

Big Drum himself sent an almost manic communication: *Not what I expected in Wisconsin, but I suppose we're in process of warming voters up. Expect to triumph in Illinois. Will arrive Bataan-Moresby Thursday noon. Please arrange for immediate staff meeting.*

On Wednesday the Illinois primary was held. Again Galt rose early and went to the press office on Thursday morning. Big Drum had garnered sixty per cent of the vote in Illinois, but since the other names on the ballot were barely known, this success was called, by at least one commentator, a 'humiliation'.

In the circumstances, Galt thought he should go out to the airport to meet Big Drum's aircraft. As the steps were wheeled out to the newly arrived plane and Big Drum descended them, it was with the same imperial gait and wave as ever. He shook Galt's hand warmly and threw himself into the back of the jeep. As Galt got in beside him he said, 'Well, Galt. The news from Illinois and Wisconsin would seem to validate your earlier judgement.'

'That gives me no pleasure, General.'

'It gives me precious little either. It's very mysterious. The Americans don't always vote for generals they love.'

Galt could remember Bryant Gibbs saying something like that.

'The good thing is,' said Big Drum, 'if we want to take a day off and not get to Manila until the day after Inauguration next January, then we can. Gentlemen of leisure, Galt!'

Galt was relieved at the sound of this, the apparent sanity of it. 'This means that you haven't been nominated for any further primaries, General?'

'I may sometimes be wrong in hearing the voice of God amidst the voices of fools, Galt. But I don't enjoy punishment.'

They rolled through the town. Once it had been the forward station, the extent of what they tenuously held. Now it was almost like a cross between a normal town in the tropics and a great peacetime military base. The Japanese air force was fully occupied with Buck Clancy's men some hundreds of miles away from here.

'I want to come back again in '48, Galt,' Big Drum suddenly confided. 'I want to take a train across America and speak to people from the back platform of it, like that Democrat charlatan does. Will you be with me, Galt?'

Galt felt a prickly discomfort. 'I shall do what I can, General.'

'Galt, if we took Hollandia at a stroke, they wouldn't be able to deny us a thing any more. They wouldn't dare. It would be political death. So we can get our way militarily this year, and politically in '48. You don't think the age of sixty-six years is too old for a President?'

'There are some sixty-six-year-olds for whom it would be too old,' said Galt. 'But not you, General.' And yet there was that doubt as to whether Big Drum *was* fit for the Presidency. He had made this howling error in Wisconsin. He had seen destiny where there was only chaos and humiliation. Such tendencies generally increased with age.

'Galt, I want you to visit the Joint Chiefs in Washington. I want you to tell them we're going to bypass Wewak and go for Hollandia. I want them to know that that's happening. If they express any doubts, remind them of Los Negros. Will you do that?'

'Of course I will, General.'

It would have one side-effect – he would not have to go ashore in a Higgins boat at Hollandia and go tramping with the General. On the other hand though, a visit to Sandy, his wife, would be inescapable.

He was pleased that Big Drum didn't seem distressed by the political débâcle. Big Drum paced the Administration villa verandah with the old vigour and hammered away at the idea of Hollandia. Hal Metzger was anxious, and Harry Strudwick advised caution. But his own data seemed to support Big Drum.

Through all this, the question was: was it a sign of greatness to be able to forget the Wisconsin loss so easily and turn himself to a new and adventurous plan? Or did it mean that his intentions had become erratic?

No sign of the latter though, Galt thought, striding in Big Drum's wake on the verandah. No sign.

14

Joint Chiefs

He had a feeling now that his long-established affair with Dim was about to enter a new phase. Just as it had a year past, when Buck Clancy had called Dim *Mademoiselle* and Dim had made a reasonable demand not to have to live beneath rock. He seemed to have dealt with that adequately to serve and balance out those two poles of his life, Dim and Big Drum. But he knew, as he felt the *frisson* of fear in her when he mentioned his imminent journey to talk to the Joint Chiefs, there would be a further compass change now. The point was that she knew as well as he did that this time he'd have to visit his wife.

He decided to be frank about it. 'I'll have to, Dim. I got into trouble with my movie star daughter for not going last time. I don't want to hurt my daughters unnecessarily. Or lose their affection, to be honest. And I don't want to offend my wife either. I don't consider her an enemy.'

He noticed that since Big Drum's loss in Wisconsin and average showing in Illinois, Dim had lost bearings as much as he had. Or at least she'd acquired new ones. The alteration to Big Drum's destiny and Galt's own potential future had depressed rather than elated her.

Dim was not good at stating her terror. She knew she never had been. But she thought of her parents, and got little positive comfort from it. If her father, as unimaginable as it might be, had been involved with another woman and had come home to Maneering to tell her mother that a thirty-year-old marriage was finished, she was certain that her mother would have it in her power to make him change his mind. She would use as a lever the thirty years of secret pleasures and griefs.

Galt at least had an accumulation of intense experience with herself, with Dim Lewis. It seemed immemorial, but it was only two years old.

And the simple and frightening truth was that men found out who they were by going home, and by encountering that half-forgotten self which waited there like a barely remembered suit of clothes but which carried a musk declaring, *This is you, and you can't escape it.*

'I can't be sure you'll come back,' she said.

'Come back? To Moresby?'

'Of course you'll come back *here*. I mean come back to me.'

'Don't be ridiculous. What is it you say? *A ratbag*. Don't be one.'

'You might find out things that you'd forgotten. You might see her and remember how good it all was when you were mere kids together, or when the children were small.'

'Those memories . . . They're there. But they don't compel me now, Dim. Really.'

'You say that. But you won't know anyhow until you're home. You won't know anything till then. You can't make any promises.'

'But I've already made promises, Dim. And I'll keep them.'

She clung to him. 'Please do come back,' she said.

He found himself mentally redefining their lives. It had to be done. The big plan no longer existed. It did in Big Drum's mind – he now considered himself a certainty for 1948. But Senator Vandergrift seemed to think the General's political credit was blown for good. In any case, the idea that Big Drum would be inaugurated as President in 1945 and that Galt himself would become simultaneously Secretary of Defense was now gone.

As for Dim, two weeks ago she had been in love with a man who was willing to give up a grand public future for her. She didn't like it that he had to pay such a price, she even spent hours dreaming up means of making it possible for him to pursue a public career. The chance of that career had been a wonderful thing to have there, a dominant and exciting feature in their landscape; and above all, there was his willingness to give all that up, to apologize to Big Drum his demi-god, and walk away.

Now all that fixed landscape of the future had vanished. It couldn't happen anyhow.

'Listen, Dim,' he told her, confused that she couldn't see that *he* was the dependent one, the one who had to come back, just for the oxygen he believed to be in her presence if for nothing else. 'This is how things stand. We're going to try a big jump soon. It will advance the whole program.' Because if Hollandia fell, then the next step would be the Moluccas and then the Philippines themselves. 'We could be in Manila within eighteen months. Once that's happened, once we're back where Big Drum and I began with each other, then I'm leaving him. I'm ready for it. I'm going, and the thought gives me nothing but simple joy.'

She said, 'I hate it. The fact you feel bound to make these crappy little timetables.'

'Well,' he told her, 'they're not crappy to me. You know, I've been toying with the possibility of a diplomatic career . . . '

He paused, swallowed, and then wondered again if he should utter the next sentiment which was forming at the base of his tongue. And for some reason he did not want to tell her about Clancy, and Clancy's desire that he should take over VI Corps or Sixth Army. Surely that was too problematic an idea to introduce yet, and too confusing. As for the rest, could he be absolutely certain he was telling her the truth? Was it settled yet that Big Drum and he were now mere professional associates and no longer soulmates?

But Big Drum seemed to have lightly destroyed his own chances of the White House, and Galt could not lightly forgive him that. So he coughed and said it. 'Fact is, Dim, the time will come for me to stop being Big Drum's acolyte. I don't think it's a healthy relationship for a man my age.'

He was surprised that she seemed a little shocked and confused by this. 'You know,' she reminded him, 'there are men who would murder for the chance of working with Big Drum.'

'There are always men who have unreal estimations of the glory of others. Big Drum won't be there forever you know. He's a phenomenon, a clever and kindly autocrat. And he's fighting a cunning war. But I won't give him my soul, Dim. That belongs to you.'

At that second, an instinct told him to let the subject drop. He could see that as far as she was concerned Big Drum was solidly and eternally in the Pantheon.

'Anyhow,' he concluded as she frowned at him, 'I'm coming back. That's certain.'

For Galt it was a tentative and wistful leavetaking. Even though he was going to the Joint Chiefs to get permission for a huge expansion of Big Drum's military sphere, even though the Joint Chiefs would now approve any strategy of Big Drum's for which reasonable arguments could be given, the world itself seemed to Galt to have shrunk. The stupidity of that recent day in Brisbane had brought that about.

With Captain Duncan for company, he travelled overnight towards Hawaii in a Super Fortress. A bunk had been set up for him amidships, and he had a small overhead light to read by. Unable to sleep, he got through a John P. Marquand novel, reading a few paragraphs at a time and then dreaming off into uneasy and shallow sleep. By dawn he had not slept continuously for more than twenty minutes at a time. The more he was awake, the more the fear of reunion with Sandy oppressed him.

He found himself trying to imagine the life Allan Lewis was leading now too, and visions of imprisonment, slurred dreams of Dim's husband trapped in a bamboo cage, further exhausted him. He was sorry he hadn't brought a bottle with him as well as a book. The more tired he got, the more he felt the burden of the murder-of-spirit to which Dim's husband and his English companion had been subjected.

At Hickam Field in Hawaii the next afternoon, he was delighted to find that what was waiting for him was not another bomber but one of the newest and fastest transport planes, fitted out like a commercial airliner. Inside it was all settees, banquettes and curtained sleeping compartments. Stewards attended him. He had taken a double Scotch and was already in a bunk even before take off. He felt grateful for whatever accidents of aircraft allocation had appointed him to this palace in the sky.

He was awakened thirteen hours later by a steward with a tray laden with a superb breakfast and coffee. The steward told him that Catalina Island, off the Southern Californian coast, was coming up on the starboard side. Galt looked out and saw the arid mountains of Catalina and then, ahead, the dim coast of California rising up to the clarity of the Sierras behind.

The steward said, 'We were to land at San Diego, sir, but the pilot sends his respects and says we've been diverted to Long Beach.'

Galt nodded. He did not see this news as having any special weight.

This plane was to take Galt and Duncan right across to Washington, as Captain Duncan himself was happy to announce to Galt. While it was refuelling, said Duncan, there was a special lounge provided for the general's use.

The plane touched down smoothly, the propellers shut off and the steward opened the door and rolled the steps down. Galt could have confidently expected to be met by the station commander. But instead, what he saw as he walked down on to the sunny Californian runway, was a host of men and women, civilian and military, bearing down on him from a nearby hangar, and a limousine wheeling towards him from the blind side of his aircraft. Galt turned to Duncan. He felt very angry to be under this unscheduled assault.

'What's happening, Captain Duncan?'

'I don't know, sir. We've had no notification . . . '

Galt saw the eagerness with which both the civilians and soldiers, some of them carrying cine and flash cameras, were coming on. They looked like a rabble, but one which knew its object clearly.

'I suggest you goddamn find out, captain!' said Galt in a voice which – he hoped – conveyed that Duncan's career depended on it. On a calmer level, Galt wondered why this mob so affronted and angered him. He looked to the limousine, which had now parked under the wing.

Duncan had advanced to throw his body, if necessary, in front of the crowd. 'Who's in charge here?' he barked with some efficacy. Most of the crowd halted. A few on the flank kept pressing forward. But Duncan pointed a finger at them and yelled, 'You!'

A handsome major emerged from the ruck in a tailored uniform. He saluted sloppily, in a manner favoured in the movies. 'Captain, would you convey to the General that my name is Major Baldock of the Army Press Office, and that I was instructed to arrange this photographic session for him?'

'Who arranged it?' asked Galt.

'Sir,' said the smart alec major. 'Why, General Wraith's own press office in the Southwest Pacific.'

Galt cried, 'Well they didn't tell me! Advise these clowns there'll be no photographic session. Any civilian in my sight in a minute's time will be arrested. Any of the military here I see with a flash camera or a film camera will be thrown in the block house. Do you understand?'

'Sir, with respect,' said Major Baldock, 'I would like to ask if that applies to your daughter as well.'

Then he pointed to the limousine. Its door had been opened by an aged chauffeur, and Sandy Sandforth the younger was emerging, followed by Mr Schweitzer himself. Schweitzer was yelling, 'My dear General. Did I tell you we would look after your daughter in Hollywood? Or did I tell you?'

There was no controlling the flashbulbs and the whirring of cine cameras. Sandy looked remarkable in a wide-brimmed straw hat and a pastel dress. Her legs were bare. A lot of movie stars went bare legged to try to encourage ordinary American girls not to desire nylons. It was apparent that Sandy had turned up in good faith. She thought she was helping her father in some way. It would be ungracious to be negative about all this snapping and whirring, but before Sandy reached him Galt had time to say to Duncan, 'Get on the phone and find out if this is authorized. And if it is, tell them they can expect a protest from me.'

Duncan saluted and marched off across the tarmac.

The other thing that was apparent now was that he was incidental to this event. It was his daughter who had primacy in the scene. They all called to her, 'Please, over here, Miss Sandforth. Miss Sandforth, over here. Alexandra, look over this way.

Thank you! Thank you!' She was the siren and the goddess in this scene.

Strangely, that fact exhilarated Galt. It was like a long awaited permission to be his own man. To become the private man he wanted to be.

Sandy kissed him with genuine affection, which of course generated a further flurry of shutter snapping. 'Aren't these awful, these events? A real meat market. But once I knew General Wraith wanted it, and Schweitzer certainly wanted it, I felt even a Democrat like myself should agree.'

'That's very generous of you, my dear,' said Galt, beaming suddenly in a way which must have confused the press photographers. But to hell with them!

'You're so famous,' he said with what he hoped she could tell was unalloyed delight.

She hugged him. 'Yes. And a lot of the time it's enjoyable. But sometimes it's like cannibalism. Not the eating side of cannibalism either, the missionary side.'

'And what about your friend? The producer? You didn't mind that letter I wrote you, did you?'

She rubbed her hand up and down his upper arm, reassuringly. 'Of course not. It was a wise letter.'

'Did he leave his wife?'

'The question is still open that he might,' she said, looking him straight in the eye. 'Since you've interrogated me to this extent, I'll tell you further that I've met another fellow.'

'One without complications?'

'That's right. He's a playwright. He works with Sherwood Anderson for the President. His name's Wellman.'

'You really are deep in with the Democrats, aren't you?'

'If anyone else said that, I would look for the *double entendre*. But I don't with you, because you're my very proper father.'

'I never claim to be proper, Sandy.'

'No, but you can't help *being* that way. And by the way, do me a favour and call me Alexandra. I don't want the whole of America calling me Sandy. Sounds like the name of a fox terrier.'

The journalists moved in and began to ask questions. 'Is your daughter a bit hit in the South Pacific?' 'What does Big Drum think of her?' 'What was she like as a kid?'

'She was a serious kid,' said Galt, smiling. 'And she always scared me.'

Everyone laughed but they were writing away. It was obviously quotable.

'I too am scared,' Schweitzer claimed, looking very *gemütlich* about it.

'Are you going to see Mother?' Sandy asked in a hiatus in the questioning, when the celluloid merchants had taken over again and the journalists were running away with their newly captured copy.

'Well, I certainly hope to see Abbey.'

But he was careful to say that with a teasing smile.

'But will you see Mother?'

'Of course.'

A press man was yelling, 'Look this way, pops, and smile.' Galt had never thought of himself as pops and was stunned by the irreverence. Nonetheless, he *was* frightened of his daughter and he played along. 'One more *pops* from you, sir, and you're off this base.'

Having so recently left an unsmiling general, Captain Duncan was confused to return to a smiling but equally besieged one.

'Sir, they're apologetic. But they say they only thought of it after we'd left Port Moresby. They asked General Wraith whether he thought you'd mind, sir, and he said no. He thought it was a great idea, they say.'

Sandy was murmuring at his side. 'When the war ends, do you intend to live with Mother?'

Galt, beset, shook his head. 'I have to draw breath before I know those things, Sandy. Please don't harry me.'

Sandy bridled, just as she used to when she was an adolescent. 'I'm not harrying you, for God's sake.'

'OK.' He flashed a concessive smile. 'Look, you take care of yourself. I hope that playwright works out.'

'I think they'll bring him in as a screenwriter on my next movie, so I can have him handy. Keep my eye on him.'

'Your second movie?'

'No.' His unworldliness amused her. 'I've done a second one, didn't you know? It's about to be released. I'm on a new contract now. Schweitzer dealt honestly with me, and while he keeps it up, I find the work invigorating. I actually *like* the long hours. Compared to this the theatre seems a little bit dilettante.'

She stayed talking until the plane's engines began to churn. He watched her from one of the ports as she made her way in the choppy wind from the propellers over to the limo. Even buffeted she looked regal. You could, he thought with some joy, imagine her becoming queen of the cinema.

With this wonderful new plane, it would be necessary only to make one stop in the journey across the continental United States. That was to be somewhere near Kansas City. By now Galt was running two days early, so at some Air Force base in Missouri, where the aircraft landed, Galt was shown to a senior officers' suite. He fell asleep with the sense that he had done his job according to the demands both of Big Drum and of Hollywood.

Waking the next morning, he began making interpretative notes on the hundred-and-twenty-page plan for the Hollandia operation he was to present to the Joint Chiefs.

Towards evening, he and Duncan took off again. It still worried Galt that Big Drum had so calmly committed him to a newspaper and newsreel circus of the kind which had descended upon him at Long Beach. It was a minor and yet significant betrayal, a further item of disenchantment, of falling out of love with destiny.

He telephoned his wife – 'Mrs General Sandforth' as she sometimes wryly called herself – that morning, immediately he touched down at National and before going to the Pentagon. He said he hoped to be finished with business by lunchtime the next day, and he was hoping he could find some nice little reconnaissance plane or other to drop him down to Charlottesville. If he did, could she meet him at the airport?

He listened to the way she spoke. She had a rich, friendly, faintly accented Southern voice, and all its nuances seemed at the same time foreign to him – the intonations of a stranger –

and yet to be keys to the sort of intimate memories whose impact Dim had feared. 'I'm just in from morning exercise,' she said. She meant the horses, not herself. 'And I opened the *Richmond Examiner*, and I see on page three a photograph of yourself and my famous daughter. Galt, you both look so handsome. Do you think you could get me a copy of that picture?'

'Why don't you ask Sandy Junior yourself?'

'Well . . . we had a little disagreement. You know how Sandy is. She'll get over it.'

Galt did not ask what the disagreement was about, but he could not think of anything else to say so the question hung there.

His wife said, 'It was about whether I was to blame for everything or not.'

'To blame? How could you be to blame?'

'She argues I should have been with you in the Philippines and then in Australia. For a movie star, she's very old-fashioned about these things.'

'Oh, Jesus.'

'You know, Galt, I don't want to open up that Pandora's box. But I did say to her, why don't you ask your father if he wanted me there?'

'Oh, Jesus,' said Galt again. 'That's all tender stuff, Sandy.'

'Yes,' she said. 'So let's not talk about it.'

He was glad to have survived that conversation, and to have got it over early, on the phone. Because it would have been less pleasant face to face.

He wondered if he should raise the other painful subject. She did, but simultaneously shelved it for the time being. 'Come down, Galt, and we'll have a drink and dinner and we can shed some conjugal tears for the loss of our wonderful son.'

The tears came to him anyway, then, and he could detect them in her voice too. 'Yes, we'll do that,' said Galt. 'I'll have Duncan let you know the exact time.'

'Do you want to stay overnight?'

'No,' he told her. 'I would love to. But Big Drum will be waiting.'

It was not really the truth. He did not have to rejoin Big Drum urgently. If the Joint Chiefs agreed, Big Drum would simply swing the plan for Hollandia into place. By the time Galt got back to Moresby, the staff would already be on its way to join Big Drum and the amphibious forces.

The first time he had been to the Pentagon, it had seemed cavernous, barely filled with personnel and perhaps a wasteful monument. But now its corridors teemed with people. It was full of noise, typewriters, teleprinters, even radio static and fragments of transmissions in all languages.

On arrival at the core of the building, he was shown into the Joint Chiefs' conference room within half a minute: a good sign. But as old General Channing led him to his seat, he found the atmosphere in the room not as genial as he would have expected. General Channing, Big Drum's old perceived enemy but self-declared friend, had shaken Galt's hand warmly, but in the case of others, particularly Admiral Cotter, friend of that Admiral Kremnitz who in Quebec had wanted Big Drum relegated to a defensive role, there was a reluctance in the handshake and a cool expression in the face. General Burger, the air force member of the Joint Chiefs, asked a number of carping questions as Galt sat directing the attention of the Joint Chiefs as a body to the various main ends of the planned attack on Hollandia. How Admiral Andrews's Task Force would feint north-west past the Admiralty Islands before turning back towards its destination. The Australians and some of Hal Metzger's VI Corps would land at Aitape, half-way between Wewak and Hollandia. General Adachi and his troops in Wewak would have to retreat, forcing their way through the jungles to march all the hundreds of miles around the Allied positions, before they could count themselves half-way safe. Buck Clancy's plan was to destroy four hundred aircraft on the ground. Meanwhile General Gibbs's corps would land on either side of Hollandia in Humboldt and Tanahmerah Bays.

'This is an adventurous bound,' said General Burger in a tone which attempted to equate *adventurous* with *lunatic*.

Galt said, 'The truth is, two more adventurous bounds of this nature will put the enemy positions in the Philippines within reach of Buck Clancy's air force.'

He could see Burger frowning in a particular way. He hadn't liked Galt repeating that adjective, trying to turn it back. I suppose, thought Galt with regret, a man like Burger would consider this an item of typical Sandforth hubris.

Admiral Cotter said, 'I think it's only proper that you and General Wraith should understand one thing. That is that the Joint Chiefs will give no automatic go-ahead for an assault on the Philippines.'

'I don't understand.'

'It's clear enough, General Sandforth. The Chinese Nationalists are fighting some tough battles on the Chinese mainland, and their fortunes could be helped if we could capture Formosa and get our new B-29s operating from there.'

'You see,' another General at the table, a Marine called Brotherton, stated, 'General Wraith has shown us the benefits which come from sidestepping and bypassing. It must be obvious to him and to you that there is no reason at all why on the road to Tokyo the Philippines should not be bypassed and Formosa hit instead.'

The idea brought an unaccustomed sweat to Galt. The retaking of the Philippines was a fundamental principle to him as to Big Drum. 'But General Wraith has promised to liberate the Philippines! If we renege on that promise, if we leave the Filipinos there languishing, suffering the enemy's atrocities, what credit will the United States have in Asia?'

Besides that, a Formosa landing will be handled by the Navy and the Marines. He had thought until this morning that any move to cut Big Drum out of the game had by now been reduced to the status of a mere fantasy entertained by a vengeful rump of the Joint Chiefs. But here was the plot again, in robust flower.

He was relieved when George Channing broke into the conversation in a more conciliatory way.

'It *is* true that as Admiral Cotter and General Burger say, the Chinese are under a lot of pressure. But it has also to be said that Formosa is one option, no more. It is nonetheless under active discussion. Anything that you or General Wraith say on the matter, any argument you put forward, will be taken seriously.'

'I'm sure General Wraith will be pleased to hear it,' said Galt. Internally, he was surprised at himself, in the sense that he was arguing for the people of the Philippines now. He was not arguing for Big Drum.

In Quebec some months earlier, it had been the reverse.

Admiral Cotter wasn't finished pushing the Formosa barrow yet. 'Formosa and mainland China had been a source of reinforcements to the Southwest Pacific. That's why taking Formosa and hammering the mainland would be of benefit to you as well, you know.'

Galt decided not to laugh at this argument. Two years ago he would have, perhaps openly, losing Burger and his faction for life. Is it Dim who has altered me? he wondered. Or is it disenchantment with Big Drum?

Galt chose, however, to risk offending Burger and Cotter to the extent of directing all his remarks from now on to the Chairman, George Channing. 'What we know in Moresby is that enemy reinforcements from China are being regularly sunk by our submarines, or else intercepted by Admiral Andrews's surface vessels or Buck Clancy's bombers. We would get no benefit from a Formosa invasion. The United States would earn itself incalculable damage.'

Channing, after closing his eyes, murmured something about how the Joint Chiefs always understood there were losses – political and military – inherent in every option the Joint Chiefs took. 'Balance,' he said. 'There's got to be balance.'

But then, as if to make a gesture of goodwill, Channing called for a vote authorizing the Hollandia expedition with Galt still right there in the conference room. The vote was unanimous. At least for the moment, they couldn't afford to vote against a winner. They could afford only to undermine him.

Afterwards, Channing asked Galt to join him for morning coffee. Galt was half expecting that the other members of the Joint Chiefs would be present, but he found it was just himself and Channing standing in a suite attached to his office and adequate for holding a small cocktail party.

Channing dismissed the orderly who had poured their coffee and got straight to business. 'OK, Galt. Kremnitz and Cotter want to blockade the Philippines instead of retaking it by amphibious landing. They want to starve the Japanese garrison out.'

'But that would starve the Filipinos as well.'

'Exactly,' said Channing. 'Look, I want to tell you something, which if you repeat it to anyone other than Big Drum I shall deny vehemently having ever uttered. A very powerful man wants to visit the Southwest Pacific, probably in July. This very powerful man lives in a house which is white. He wants his picture taken with Big Drum. He wants Big Drum to meet him, probably in Hawaii, along with Kremnitz, to discuss the final drive to the Japanese mainland. Via Formosa, or via the Philippines. Now to reiterate, the famous man wants to be photographed smiling with Big Drum. He wants America to look at himself and Big Drum smiling together and approving of each other. For Big Drum may have lost the primaries in Wisconsin and Illinois, but he still has extraordinary political force.'

Channing took a gulp of coffee and looked away. He looked older than he had in Quebec. He was probably exhausted, and he looked like a man with a health problem.

'Perhaps,' he said, 'there could be a tacit arrangement between Big Drum and the very powerful man. To put it in its basest terms, the meeting and the photograph in exchange for the right to liberate the Philippines. I leave it to you and Big Drum himself to arrange how this tacit contract could be made.'

Galt was astonished by this generous gift of intelligence. He wondered – on the basis of changes in himself – if Channing had changed. Or – heretical thought – maybe Big Drum had always been wrong about him.

In the midst of considering this, Galt was confused by Channing's next remark.

'I'm sorry about the Sixth Army, Galt.'

There was no reason Galt could think of why General Channing should be sorry about Hal Metzger's corps.

'I don't quite understand what you mean, General.'

Channing himself looked confused. 'But Big Drum must have told you?'

'I . . . I'm not quite on to what you're saying, General?'

'Well, look . . . I think you ought to have a conversation with Big Drum about this when you get back.'

'But about what, sir?'

'Well, between us . . . OK. Between us. I don't want Big Drum thinking I spread dissension.'

'I'll be discreet, sir.'

'OK. I was getting a lot of confidential and private letters from friends of yours saying that Hal Metzger should be replaced, and you should be put in command of his force. Big Drum must have told you, for Christ's sake. I spoke to him about it. He said you'd make a fine Sixth Army field commander. But that he needed you, and he didn't want to break in another Chief of Staff. He said, "Galt's absolutely essential to me." I said to him, "Then you'd better tell him that you feel like that. Otherwise, when rumours of this get out, he might misunderstand the reasons he was never offered the command." So he said he'd consult with you. Jesus, I don't like saying any of this. You're a good team, you and the Drum. Why don't you talk to him about it?'

Automatically, Galt tried to regain lost ground. 'I think he did mention something about it, General Channing. You know about Big Drum. He's a bit of a Delphic oracle. You have to listen all the time while you're around him.'

Then Channing did something for which Galt felt gratitude towards him. He dropped the subject, wrung his hand, and escorted him personally to the Pentagon lobby.

Flying south to Charlottesville in an artillery-spotting plane, Galt felt a lasting bewilderment at Big Drum's oversight. He wondered had it been wilful, or had a senile forgetfulness set in? The latter didn't seem likely.

He felt a cool anger too. He might have gone on expecting the offer of the Sixth Army, and wondering why it wasn't ever tendered to him. He was flattered at Big Drum's paternal desire to retain him at his side, but it was hard to say what sort of paternal emotion was operating: jealousy, lack of trust, the fear of losing one's main support in life.

The plane juddered down over the kindly hills outside Charlottesville. It slewed across the sky to align itself with the airstrip. Even from two hundred feet up, he could see Sandy waiting in open-necked shirt and jeans by the airfield gate.

She strolled out towards the plane after it had touched down. Dressed like that, and in her check shirt, she could have been a well-to-do farmer's wife. By the late 1930s she had stopped wearing make-up by daytime, even though that was against the rules for her type of hand-reared and arduously *finished* Southern woman, and this did not diminish her good looks but gave them an interesting rawness.

'Galt,' she said, smiling honestly. 'It's so wonderful to see you.' She put her arms comprehensively but loosely around him and kissed his cheek, not his lips. He held her similarly. He had been wondering how this would all go, and he was relieved that there wasn't any clutching or clinging.

Just so that she knew he was not staying for the night, he turned and called to the pilot, 'OK, captain. It's back here, any time from 22.30 hours onwards.'

The young pilot saluted. 'I'll be here, General.'

'Could we give you a lift into town?' Sandy asked the pilot. Perhaps she wanted the time to pass easily as much as he did.

'Thank you, ma'am. I have to call base and do some paperwork.'

They turned towards Sandy's station wagon. 'And how's the stud farm?' he asked.

'Marvellous, Galt. People are already buying mounts for the 1948 Olympics, wherever they will be. Everyone's pretty sure the Games will be held somewhere. But you don't want to hear any of that. For a military man, you were never interested in horses.'

They climbed in the wagon, and Sandy drove, turning westwards away from the town, into the hills where Sorrento was, the Sandforth mansion Galt had spent his life avoiding.

'They haven't found our boy, have they, Galt?'

Galt found it difficult to speak. 'No. I think we should face they may never.'

'Sometimes I think you military people might know something about all that, might have found him, and decided it was all too horrible to tell me. That George Channing might have told you something . . . '

'No. No, that never happens, Sandy.' He reached out and patted her thigh. 'I swear they've found nothing.'

'God,' she said. 'How have you dealt with it, Galt?'

'By keeping busy. That's easy around Big Drum.'

'With me it's been the same. But I also joined a group of women who go round and visit the mothers of boys who've been killed. I mean, in one sense Galt Junior was uniquely gifted, and his death is an utter obscenity. But it's strange – the fact that there are so many of them. I often take out his year book, and maybe forty per cent of that class is gone. A lot of them were in the Army Air Force. I suppose that explains it. It shouldn't be a comfort, it's wrong that it is. But I can't deny it. That's how I feel.'

'I feel that way too,' he told her. 'It's ridiculous, I know, but there you are.'

They were rolling through the family property now. It was bordered on both sides by high whitewashed palings.

Sandy said, 'Sometimes we go as far away as Richmond, visiting bereaved mothers and young widows. Some of them are so poor you wonder what possessed the boys to go and get killed.'

'It's not always a matter of choice,' said Galt, remembering Los Negros.

'But they have so little, Galt. Men working in the war plants get so much, but the families of some of the soldiers are the true poor. You can't work out how they could have considered what they have worth dying for.'

'That's a very radical opinion,' said Galt, genially reproving.

She laughed. 'Maybe I'm becoming a Democrat like our movie star daughter.'

She parked the wagon by the stables. They spent the afternoon pleasantly, visiting the stalls and corrals, looking at the yearlings. Sandy ran it all superbly. She was no dilettante.

Staring at a black handler who was putting an Arabian through its paces, she said, 'I hope you don't mind but I thought you might have appreciated company tonight. I've invited the Sharptons.'

The Sharptons were friends from his thirties. Max Sharpton was a steel merchant and had no doubt done superbly from the war.

'That will be very pleasant,' said Galt.

'Galt, do you have a woman down there in the Pacific?'

He could have evaded things by saying, 'The Pacific is a big place.' But Sandy was worth better than that.

'Yes.'

'Who is she?'

'She's an Australian.'

'Young?'

'Yes. About the same age as our famous daughter.'

Sandy inclined her head a little and considered this. 'Funny how with men it's always someone younger.'

'Yes,' said Galt. 'I don't understand it myself. But it's not a cheap affair. This case is different, Sandy.'

They strolled on together, passed some more elderly grooms and handlers, who waved and nodded – Sandy seemed to have a good working relationship with them.

'So, Galt, after all this time, you're going to divorce me?'

There were great dangers in answering her. Yet again, she deserved the truth. 'I intend to stay beside Big Drum until we're in Manila again. Then I'll retire, and my present intention is to seek a divorce, Sandy. I'm sorry.'

Sandy trailed a hand along a railing. 'Do you know, my life is strangely full. I wonder if yours will be, Galt. The scandal won't hurt me. But are you prepared for how it will hurt you?'

'Yes,' said Galt. 'That's why I'll resign.'

'My God. So you've found someone you *really* love.'

There was penetrating truth and great reproach in that sentence. He hoped he would be able to get away without answering it. Fortunately she did not press the matter.

'Please don't worry, Galt. There will be no scenes. Of course, the divorce will attract all the more attention not just because you're Big Drum's Chief of Staff. Being Sandy's father will itself give the thing prominence. You're ready for that?'

'I'm ready for the press to do what they want. What worries me is whether young Sandy will forgive me.'

'So, you presume Abbey will?'

'I hope so.'

'Abbey might surprise you. Not that I intend to enlist her on my side. I don't mean that.'

'I know you don't.'

Sandy stopped and began to shudder. Then the tears came. 'I wish I had my son,' she whimpered. 'Everything would be all right if I had my boy.'

Galt held her close, and she started to bite back the tears, as girls of her background were supposed to. She coughed.

'Even though we had three children,' she said, 'I think we could both tell there was something at fault. But then there so often is in marriages, and not all of them end like this.'

They got back to the house. Sandy excused herself early, saying that she was going to dress for dinner. An elderly black servant called Eugene served Galt coffee. Then he went walking through the house, bravely and gingerly, as if the ghost of Galt Junior was still there, though ghost was hardly appropriate in the case of a boy who had not yet been officially listed as dead. Nothing had been altered in his room. All the clichés of boyhood enthusiasm were there, even the Ty Cobb, Babe Ruth posters, and a picture of the old Washington Senators, *circa* 1932. Bats, tennis racquets, a pitcher's mitt, a VMI track and field team photograph were all in evidence.

In case the subtle curse could somehow be transferred from brother and sister, he did not visit the girls' rooms. He found the library. There were extraordinary treasures in here, vellum-bound psalteries of the sixteenth century, Vesalius's *Anatomy*, a Monticello cookbook signed by Mrs Jefferson, all the classics in the original Greek and Latin, and the Bible in all its versions, Hebrew, Greek, Vulgate Latin, English. When he was a child, before his mother's death, he'd imagined himself here, a great reader, a Southern sage, lost for hours in Hesiod or Tacitus. In his adult life, however, he had probably spent as little as ten hours contemplatively reading in this place.

He pulled down Edward Gibbon's *Decline and Fall* and began to read a volume that was somehow familiar to him. It concerned the excesses of the Emperor Heliogabalus. He remembered in a flood then that he used to come here sometimes as an adolescent boy and read not about the noble emperors – Hadrian or Marcus Aurelius – but about the decadent ones. Heliogabalus, who used to make naked Nubian women wrestle to the death with naked German women had been a favourite emperor of young Galt.

He began to read the section in which Heliogabalus, whose degradations had appalled even the Praetorian guard, was assassinated by archers.

The winter's day closed in. And the house seemed to him to be silent. It was not age which seemed to make it mute, but the weight of Sandy's grief. Another five or six hours, he thought, and I will be safe in that little spotter plane. The sound of propellers would stupefy him and drown the memory of her voice. Soon, after shaving and showering, he was downstairs greeting the Sharptons.

The pilot ran into a bank of high cloud above the Chesapeake, and the spotter aircraft tumbled round in a way which pleasantly confused Galt. He had drunk a lot before and during dinner. He and Sandy had displayed a brittle vivacity at dinner, to an extent which he knew was confusing their guests. But to hell with that. To hell with Mr Max Sharpton and his war contracts and his *pro bono publico* service, a dollar a year, on various statutory bodies. The Sharptons of the world were the ones the war had not changed. The war had been merely a great trigger for business.

The turbulence got suddenly less severe and visibility became crystalline as the Potomac came up. The little spotter aircraft followed the glint of the river into Washington. During the descent Galt put on headphones and listened to the radio traffic. A B-27 flown by a young Southerner led them into National, where his fancy transport plane awaited him.

From the airfield office, he tried to call Abbey, who had been sent to Ottawa on some intelligence task. She was not home, however. He hoped she was out, having dinner, rather than working all night.

Before take-off, he wrote her a letter. He did not mention the proposed divorce.

In the sense that there were no staff there with him (they were all on their way to Hollandia, to take their little beach walks with Big Drum), Galt was on his own in the Administration villa, sharing its amenities with Dim. It was three days before significant reports began to come through from Hollandia. Both the beachhead in Humboldt and Tanahmerah Bays had been secured without any loss of life at all. Bryant Gibbs's now seasoned troops had found some fourteen thousand rear administration Japanese soldiers opposing them and had brushed them aside. Down the coast Hal Metzger's men and the Australians took Aitape and its airstrip. It looked like another Big Drum triumph.

Galt began at once studying plans for the invasion of the Philippines. Buck Clancy's long-range bombers were already visiting those islands. Harry Strudwick had obeyed the instructions all passed on from Big Drum more than two years ago to provide information on every beach and tidal variation between Melbourne and Tokyo.

At last Galt spoke on the telephone with Big Drum, who thanked him for persuading the Joint Chiefs to allow this great advance. Galt told him what Channing had said about the President requiring a meeting in Hawaii with his great South Pacific general and his most distinguished Central Pacific admiral.

Galt said nothing, however, about the Sixth Army. There was no way he could introduce such a topic. He felt strange, like a man lying to a spouse, veiling secret agendas. If he had been Big Drum's *éminence grise* he wasn't any more. Big Drum would not be able to tell any difference from the old Galt, however. It was just that the old Galt would feel he had a greater mental freedom and moral amplitude than before. Big Drum was no longer entitled to unambiguous truth. Galt would leave Big

Drum according to his own timetable, not according to the schedules of that 'destiny' which Big Drum was always referring to, which Big Drum's staff could not prevent themselves jabbering away about.

Galt also spoke by telephone to Peter Andrews. The staff, along with Bryant and Hal Metzger, *had* suffered a little anxiety at Hollandia. They had gone ashore in the Higgins boat from the USS *Chattanooga.* They had been heading ashore in Tanahmerah Bay when they received a radio message from the *Chattanooga* – a Japanese fighter was strafing landing craft. Andrews had ordered the Higgins boat commander to take it in under the protection of the guns of a nearby US warship and to shelter there until the threat passed. But Big Drum had demanded to know what the deviation was all about and, when told, demanded that they press on to the beach.

'We were three hours ashore,' Peter Andrews told Galt. 'The nearest of the three airstrips Buck Clancy wanted was on the itinerary of course. It wasn't a matter of flying lead, like on Los Negros. The airstrip fell easily. But the heat was enormous. Ernie Sasser had to be revived with re-hydration salts.'

'I'm glad I missed all that,' said Galt. It seemed a banal and pious expression of gratitude to his good luck. It was more than that. There was no longer much percentage for him in going into the teeth of things with Big Drum.

Andrews said then, 'Do you know, Big Drum wants to move headquarters up here to Hollandia.'

'Is that right?'

'It's a beautiful place, Galt.'

That night Galt and Dim celebrated with a bottle of Californian champagne somehow acquired by the villa staff. If headquarters were moved to Hollandia, Big Drum would visit only occasionally. To a greater degree than ever, Galt would be his own man. Though he had not told Dim what he had discovered from Channing, she could tell somehow that he was ready for a little more remoteness between himself and Big Drum. She had recovered now from the news that Sandy knew about her, knew about the divorce which waited only upon a successful Philippines campaign. There is a shock for all parties, Galt was aware, when matters take a definite turn, when intentions are locked into place. Dim didn't quite believe either that Sandy had taken it so philosophically.

'She didn't even call you a heartless bastard?'

'The time for that accusation is some years past now, Dim. I mean, we treated each other like two mourners at a funeral. And so we were. But you have to have passion to have crimes of passion. The glands that would cause people to hurl a bitter insult, or a knife for that matter, have ossified in Sandy and me.'

'I hope you'll de-ossify them for my sake,' said Dim with a half-smile, yet still she did not believe it. That the plan to divorce had been uttered and had produced so little punishment other than the subtle ones of remorse and memory and guilt.

Dim had in any case been looking askance at the sort of life she lived now. She'd given to her lieutenant, who liked the job, the task of collecting, entertaining and shipping onwards the talent which arrived from Australia and from other battle fronts and rear areas of the Pacific. She spent all her days on administration, filling out requisitions, sending signals, writing letters to the film distribution companies in Australia. One day, when a WAC in the typing pool had succumbed to malaria, Dim had approached a typewriter and typed her own letters. So the shibboleths of a genteel bush upbringing were shattered. Her requirements were simple. She wanted to be treated kindly by people when she met them. She didn't want to be called *Mademoiselle*. She didn't want the staff being snide about her, though she knew there was no chance they wouldn't be, at least in secret.

But apart from those desires, she had no great wish to meet people. She feared she was becoming strange, a recluse here in the midst of a great military campaign. Life in Hollandia, where Galt would be the supremo during Big Drum's absences, would – she hoped – bring her out of herself.

She was having increasing numbers of dreams about Allan. He struggled through mangroves and called out to her.

But she had heard no bad news. Galt would have told her if there were anything. Surely she would see him within a few months. She would tell him about Galt. Apart from that aspect, she was almost looking forward to it.

15

The New Bataan

THE PLACE WHICH Big Drum, or more exactly Ernie Sasser's engineers, had chosen for the new advanced version of Bataan was a ridge of jungle between Humboldt Bay and a superb, tropical, islet-filled lake called Sentani. The house was not a pre-existing colonial structure. Ernie's engineers simply ran a number of spacious prefabricated structures – they had arrived by cargo ship from Hawaii – and then furnished it, right down to reproductions of Raphaels and photographs of the cool, high, elegant Rockies.

Galt and the staff moved in in July, just as the Democratic convention re-endorsed the present White House incumbent for a fourth successive term as President.

The new Bataan looked like an enormous, rambling ranch house. When Galt first saw it from the back seat of his jeep, he said so to Admiral Andrews. 'That's overpraising it,' said Andrews. 'It's pretty basic.'

There were nonetheless fifteen bedrooms in the place.

Galt and Harry and Ernie and Buck were busy on plans for the seizure of the Wakde Island airstrip, and of Biak Island, all far to the west. Buck and Galt and Pete Andrews were still members of the optimistic school; Ernie and Harry would sometimes talk as if the Hollandia success had been a lucky accident, as if no one should presume that such luck could recur. But Big Drum had decreed Wakde and Biak; and no one, not even the Joint Chiefs, could deny him.

At the end of the first staff meeting in Hollandia, Galt asked Harry and Ernie to stay. Admiral Andrews and Buck Clancy went back to their offices.

'How do you like this place?' Galt, sitting on his desk, asked the pair of them.

'Better than the first time we came here,' said Harry, and Galt and Ernie laughed.

'Gentlemen, I know bedrooms are at a premium here in what we might call Bataan Forward. But there's a young Australian captain who organizes our entertainment services. She was harassed by some prowler in Port Moresby during her stay there. It seems appropriate to me to offer her accommodation in this household. Besides that, she's a charming woman and would be very good company. Perhaps a civilizing influence over the staff.'

He paused for the dutiful laughter.

'Now, in a way, I consider this a staff club, and you are, with me, the two most senior members of this staff. I thought it a matter of courtesy to ask you if you have any objections.'

He saw the two of them exchange glances. Will you speak or will I? But then it began to turn into something of a competition: Strudwick trying to outwait Sasser, and vice-versa. At last Harry said, 'There may be some minor resentment. Colonels will find themselves living down the hill . . . '

Ernie Sasser considered this, his head to one side. 'Of course, there are always resentments in billeting. There's always a lot of ill feeling amongst the middle-ranking staff.'

Harry nodded his head as if this truism had never occurred to him before and now clinched the argument.

'I'm not against it in principle, Galt.'

'Me neither,' said Ernie.

It probably meant that they were against it, but they were worried by Galt's powerful connection with Big Drum, by Big Drum's affectionate esteem for Galt Sandforth. Perhaps they thought, too, that he was playing into their hands.

Dim was due to arrive within the next twenty-four hours, on a transport plane which also carried some of the potentially disgruntled staff middle-rankers. The flight was without event – the terror and the claustrophobia which had characterized her first flight into Port Moresby some twenty months before no longer seemed a possibility. The air over New Guinea had been altered by Big Drum's successes.

A jeep brought Dim up from the airstrip at one end of Tanahmerah Bay to the house on the hill. The driver, a corporal, said, 'You must rank, ma'am. Living in the White House?'

'The White House?' she asked, tired and confused. Was this some subtle joke about Big Drum's Presidential hopes and Galt's place in them?

'That's what they call the headquarters, ma'am. Bataan Forward. The White House.'

A steward showed her to her room at the end of one of the White House's corridors. It was as spacious as the one she'd left behind in her bungalow in Port Moresby. An enormous electric fan hung from the roof, and there was a photograph on the wall of some of Bryant Gibbs's men landing from a Higgins boat in Humboldt Bay. And on the other side, by the window, hung a painting of the town plaza in Sante Fe.

'I'm not sure where my office will be,' she said to the steward.

'I believe it's down the hill a little ways, ma'am. But the gentlemen will no doubt acquaint you with that once they come out of their meeting.'

She lay on the bed in her combat boots and let the ceiling fan wash the damp air across her. It was a not unpleasant experience. She was getting used to the tropics.

She was awakened by a gentle knocking on the door. She hoped it was Galt, and it proved to be. Embracing him, she speculated on how she'd changed in the two or more years since she first met him. Because he had changed. There was less weariness to him. And it seemed to her he had deliberately let some of his *militariness* slip away.

'Welcome home,' he told her. He broke off the embrace to close the door. Then he let his cheek lean against the top of her head. 'I want you to treat this as your home. As much as Harry Strudwick would. I don't want you to try to dine alone. I don't want you to feel you can't converse with Buck Clancy.'

'And when Big Drum comes?' she asked.

'I want you to treat this as your home still.'

'That will take a little courage.'

'Yes. But you have it.'

Dinner was served at any time from 7 p.m., and so Dim chose what she thought of as an optimum time and went in at 7.15.

The dining room had views out to sea and gave on to a bar and a living room from which could be seen the glimmer of Lake Sentani. Galt was sitting at the head of the table, and Buck and Bryant Gibbs were there as well, together with the new Surgeon-General, called Meacham. Hal Metzger, still in command of the Sixth Army, was due in later that night. Everyone stood for her. General Clancy was particularly attentive. 'Delightful to see you again, captain,' he told her, with what seemed to be sincerity.

They amused her with tales of their amphibious landings with Big Drum. Ernie Sasser disarmed everyone by describing how on Los Negros he had grabbed his cigarette lighter from his top pocket, intending to drop it on the ground so that he could bend over and pick it up, so that he could take a few seconds to do it, a few seconds during which his upper body would not be exposed to enemy fire. That he hadn't quite had the moral courage to drop the thing then, so he kept it in his fist. Somewhere on the edge of the airstrip, where there had been an explosion, his hand opened and, without knowing it he dropped the thing. 'I've been expecting it back,' he said. 'I figured some honest infantryman would find it. It's got my initials on it. It's a gift from my favourite uncle.'

Bryant Gibbs said, 'I picked it up actually, Ernie, but if you don't mind I'll hang on to it. I'm saving it up for Big Drum's next amphibious excursion.'

Harry Strudwick came in about 8 p.m., apologizing for lateness. He asked if he could have a quick word with Galt in the living room. Dim watched the two of them move out to the large windows above the lake. She saw Galt raise his head sharply as Harry spoke, and yet if it was an emergency it wasn't a massive one, for Galt began to speak quite calmly, and the two of them reached what looked like an arrangement, and then moved back to the table. Sitting down, Galt smiled down the table, a general smile that focused nonetheless on her.

What Galt had heard from Harry was that the transmissions from the captured operatives in Timor had ceased three weeks before. It was assumed the two men had lost their apparent usefulness and been executed. But now an Australian destroyer, far out in the Arafura Sea northwest of the Australian northern base at Darwin, had met an Indonesian native prau, and found aboard the fishing vessel a ragged, ulcerated and demented British naval officer. This man had escaped Timor, with a member of the Timorese Resistance, had island-hopped a number of days, and then set off across the Arafura for north-western Australia.

As soon as the intelligence officer on the destroyer sent a signal about who the man was, Special Reconnaissance command had arranged for an order that the ship abort its patrol and bring Runcie to Darwin.

Runcie was very ill – beri-beri, malaria, malnutrition. There were doubts about his sanity. The story he told was that his companion, Captain Allan Lewis, had become too deranged in captivity to transmit any more misinformation for the Japanese. He had been beheaded. Runcie, seeing in Lewis's tragedy a foretaste of his own, made a suicidal attempt to escape, had somehow succeeded, had stumbled on members of the Timorese resistance, and been given the prau as a means of escape. He was, according to reports, very angry. He felt he and Allan Lewis had been set up for their capture, torture and misuse.

Runcie had been treated kindly and been confined in the closed wing of a mental hospital in Darwin. Intelligence bodies were still debating whether to tell his wife of his survival. It was unlikely he could be prevented from ranting at her about what had happened. For similar security reasons, it had been recommended that Captain Allan Lewis's wife should not be told the bad news.

So Galt, apparently smiling, apparently sure, apparently composed, looked into the dining room and considered the beautiful widow Lewis at the end of the table. An unencumbered woman. How could she be told? Could he let her know in confidence? But then, when later she did find out the truth about her husband's brave death, he would have to lie to her about not having had any idea.

Returning to the table, Galt, like the intelligence authorities, decided to keep it all dark, to let the news emerge later if at all.

Soon after Dim's arrival in Hollandia, Galt had to fly down the coast to Aitape to visit General Billings, the Australian Land

Forces Commander, and inspect the Australian and American positions there. General Adachi's troops from Wewak were hurling themselves against Aitape, but their situation was hopeless. The Australians and Americans were so well supplied, fed and fortified. General Adachi himself had been in command at Buna, where he had enjoyed the position of strength which Billings's and Metzger's troops now enjoyed. Except that Billings and Metzger were more copiously supplied and reinforced from the sea than Adachi had ever been, and were protected from on high by Buck Clancy's air force.

The reports of fighting in the forward positions told of bitter combat, frequently hand to hand, frequently suicidal. But the enemy had no chance of dislodging the Allies.

Galt Sandforth nonetheless had a duty to go down there to assure himself of that fact.

In the early afternoon of the day of Galt's Aitape visit, Dim, working at her office in Hollandia, began to suffer headaches and pains in the joints and a sudden febrile coldness in her chest. Within half an hour it was so insupportable that she began to walk down the corridors asking people if they had an army blanket they could lend her. She shuddered and her face was glossed with sweat when she looked in a mirror. She remembered that Galt said to call the new Surgeon-General if she needed anything in his absence.

Meacham ordered her to be driven back to the White House. He allocated her a nurse from the base hospital to sit beside her and feed her pills of synthetic quinine, something new from the American pharmacopoeia. It had been developed both for efficacy and to save Allied troops from that yellow complexion which came as a result of taking atebrin, the only drug available till then.

Dim would later remember in a confused way these ministrations of the nurse, but what she would most remember was the terrible sense of urgency which is one of the symptoms of the disease, the necessity of getting an entertainers' movement scheduled to the satisfaction of a particular green python which had Allan Lewis by the neck. She was aware, too, that Buck Clancy came into the room to inspect her condition. She couldn't say anything to him, since all her conversation was earmarked for the python. She heard him say, 'What's her temperature?'

'Accelerated, General,' said the girl. 'One hundred and four point two degrees.'

'My God. It's not the cerebral variety of the thing, is it?'

She became engrossed by the concern behind that question. This was the man who had once thought she was a tart. Yet he showed a paternal interest in not letting her temperature get too high.

Meacham himself came in also while she went on battling with the imaginary movement schedule. Her teeth were clattering in her skull and there was a spike of ice in her heart. The task of the names and times and places which had to be filled in to satisfy the python evaded her and yet was always insistently there. She was aware that the sheet over her shoulder was sodden and heavy with sweat. Meacham said, 'If her temperature doesn't begin to fall by twenty hundred hours, we'll move her.'

She slept and woke feeling hollow yet sublimely cool. The fan above her head was still turning, and the young nurse was asleep on a camp bed set in the corner. Her watch said 4 a.m. An hour later the nurse woke, took her temperature and pulse and went out to return with a quart bottle of orange juice. Dim drank perhaps half of it. 'It's a godawful thing, malaria,' the nurse told her. Meacham came in and looked at her eyes and felt her brow and began to praise the new synthetic quinine tablets. 'I'll get straight in contact with the drug company,' he told Dim. 'Yours might be the first case where they've been used to such good effect.'

The nurse went back to her quarters. By mid-morning Dim was feeling restless. She wanted to wait in the living room perhaps for Galt's return from Aitape. He had said the morning before that he might be back at lunchtime today. Pausing outside she overheard familiar voices already in the living room: Metzger, Strudwick, Sasser and Meacham. It occurred to her even then that none of them except Meacham would expect her to be up. An average attack of malaria, untreated by wonder drugs, should have kept her turning in her bed much longer than this one had. Their voices were low and conspiratorial, the normal mode around Bataan Forward, but she could make out what they were saying.

Ernie Sasser was speaking. A jovial man, full of party tricks. She liked him. She had always liked him better than Galt did. He was clearly a gifted organizer, too – his men had paved airstrips all over the Southwest Pacific and it had all been done with astounding American energy and at marvellous speed.

Now he was saying, 'So he used the old chestnut on us.' He imitated Galt's Virginian drawl. '*When she was quartered in the garden at Port Moresby, she was molested*. She doesn't seem to be too scared of molestation when it comes to Galt himself.'

There was some laughter, notably from Hal Metzger.

Harry Strudwick groaned. It seemed he had not joined in the snide laughter. But his voice was taut with an unexpected anger. Here again, she'd thought Strudwick had come to terms with Galt. But there was some impermeable bitterness there in his voice. 'I think it's an outrage that he keeps his mistress right in the heart of the staff. Everyone pretends it's not an inhibiting factor. But I think it's goddamn dangerous as well as a scandal. I don't think any military historian could find similar cases, not even amongst Napoleon's marshals. And God knows they were fabulous cocksmen.'

Metzger said, 'Of course, he flaunts her in front of all of us to show the influence he has over Big Drum.'

Ernie muttered, 'Well, screw him. I'm fed up with buttering up to him.'

Harry joined in. 'I don't want to sound too pious, gentlemen. But I almost think we'd be saving America from an evil fate if we prevented him ever becoming Secretary of Defense.'

Meacham, who had fed Dim the wonder drug asked, 'Then what are you proposing?'

There was some silence. Then Harry spoke. 'As much as we dislike the correspondents, I think we have to bring a selected few in on this. No need for the stories to appear under their bylines. They can feed the stuff to someone else in their organizations. We want the news to get out so widely across the States that even people like Senator Vandergrift are pleading with Big Drum to cut Galt Sandforth loose.'

Hal Metzger laughed. 'Big Drum isn't going to thank you for this.'

'No. But he won't know it's us. The stories will not name sources specifically. And then if Big Drum wants to run for office in 1948, he'll have outlived by then the memory of Galt Sandforth's little Hollandia scandal. He'll have a new Chief of Staff and new military successes to stand on.'

'If we fed the news out through an Australian correspondent,' said Ernie Sasser, 'Sandforth would think it was her fault. We can have the whole thing appear first in one of the Australian scandal sheets.'

She heard Metzger make a noise which characteristically was intended to convey a need for caution. 'Listen, if you guys do this, the timing's crucial. Big Drum's due to meet the President in Hawaii on Thursday week. He's coming on here on the Sunday. My guess is he'll be here at least a week. The news should start to break then. Sandforth won't be able to threaten or attempt a damage control with Big Drum here.'

It was the intensity of their resentment which transfixed Dim. Surely I haven't been as offensive as all that, she thought. I haven't tried to alter anything. I'm Galt's lover, that's all, and for some reason that's why they find him supremely hateful.

She felt the familiar ice at her heart again and began to tremble. Her forehead, and the planes of her face beneath her eyes, ran with sweat.

She could hear Harry say, 'Well, Ernie. Do you think you can line up two journalists for us? One Australian, one American.'

'For a start,' said Ernie, 'I know plenty of guys in Big Drum's press office I can trust.'

'No. Make it correspondents. Maybe people with a bad record with the press office. We can always wash our hands of them. And they'll die – if they have to – to protect their sources.'

'I hope so,' said Ernie.

'Sure they will. The story, even if it doesn't appear under their name, will make them big shots in their professions. Their editors will love them.'

There was what she took to be an assenting silence. Then,

'Oh dear Jesus!' Hal Metzger said, as if he hated this civil warfare.

'OK, Ernie,' said Harry. 'It's your job to find the two press boys.'

'I've got two in mind already.'

'You report to me, and I report to the others. None of us knows anything of this. Everything is totally deniable.'

Ernie said, 'We should have done this a long goddamn time ago.'

She wanted Galt to arrive and surprise them. Yet they seemed very secure in their deliberations, as if they knew what time he would get in, and knew also that it wasn't going to be soon. She could not ask them. She could not politely intrude, and ask *that* question. There was, however, a telephone at the end of her corridor. Perhaps from there she could call the airstrip and discover if General Sandforth's plane had touched down. She made for it, but it seemed an uphill endeavour. And so costly in terms of cold and sweat.

The cold glowered now again within her ribcage and stomach, and her face flowed with salt sweat she could taste as it hit the corners of her mouth. She fell against a doorway, and then to the floor. She knew she must not let the conspirators find her there. 'Perhaps I got up too early,' she muttered to herself by way of explanation. She did not believe that getting up again was within her powers, but she did and entered the door, and even closed it to keep the plotters out, and climbed up what seemed an enormous slope to her bed. She crawled in under the mosquito net and shivered there, freezing, dragging the dank sheets of her recent night fever towards her for warmth.

In a thunderstorm at dusk, Galt returned to the White House above Lake Sentani in Hollandia. He had had a good journey, in contrast to that miserable visit he'd made so long ago to the Buna front, where he had seen a colonel forgetting himself and cooking stew. He imagined he would reflect on all this with Dim that evening.

But when he arrived the White House seemed startlingly

empty. It was as if none of the staff except him intended to eat there that evening. No stewards were visible.

He set off down the corridor towards Dim's room. The Surgeon-General was hurrying up the hall towards him.

'Captain Lewis has a high fever and is delirious,' he announced. 'We found her just a little while ago. We thought she was over the attack she had last night.'

'Attack?'

'I've diagnosed it as cerebral malaria. Last night's fever mimicked standard malaria, but this recurrence has declared itself in its full colours.'

Meacham led Galt into Dim's room. A young nurse was there, applying facecloths to Dim's face. Dim herself, he could see even from the door, was unquietly asleep, twitching and muttering. He went over and took her hand. It was outrageously hot. Fragments of words and of protest fell from her lips.

'I was just on my way to make arrangements to transfer her to the base hospital,' said Meacham. 'She's burning up, Galt. She needs a saline drip.'

Galt felt panicked. 'And what are you giving her otherwise?'

'Synthetic quinine. But it just doesn't work against cerebral malaria the way it does against the average stuff.'

'You arrange an ambulance,' said Galt. 'I'll wait here.'

He had always imagined his own death. The gods were mauling him now for lack of imagination, for presuming she was safe.

After Meacham went, Galt felt Dim's brow, from which the nurse had for the moment taken the facecloth. 'Jesus,' said Galt. 'Nurse, have you seen many of these cases?'

'Yessir.'

'She's very hot, isn't she?'

'Her temperature is dangerously high, General.'

'This is the one they sometimes have brain damage from?' asked Galt.

'This is the one,' the young nurse agreed. 'But if we get her to the hospital . . . It's not like she's cut off somewhere in the jungle.'

Galt wondered who he could do a deal with: Big Drum or

God. He contemplated making an offer to God that he'd give her up if she could be saved. But he knew God wasn't a dealer like that, didn't accept straight something-for-something deals.

When the ambulance came and he climbed in behind her, along with Meacham and the nurse, there was still none of the staff about. It was as if they were scattered all over Hollandia, pursuing their own ends.

For two days it was a question whether that plain and forthright Australian brain, beloved of Galt Sandforth, would be damaged by its own internal heat, would be jangled for good by the fever. Meacham visited her often and took a personal interest. Galt was comforted by the concern of the staff. Harry and Ernie seemed to him almost to understand Dim's place in his map of the world and, although they probably never approved of the liaison, to feel a comradely sympathy for him now.

The part that was worst was that Dim was clearly in hell. She was haunted and harried by ghosts. It seemed to him as if she was under some crazy urgency to get what she saw as a distilled item of truth to him. But when she spoke it came out jumbled, as if it were in a kind of code. He pressed the wet cloths to her forehead himself and told her to be still and simply to rest, that nothing was a worry. That the President was meeting Big Drum in Hawaii, that Bryant Gibbs's and Hal Metzger's men would soon be ashore in Wakde Island, and after that Biak, and after that the Vogelkop Peninsula, the eagle's head of the whole great island of New Guinea; that is, he whispered to her that the order of the world was being reasserted, and that this was a hopeful omen for the coming good order of her overheated brain. But she was driven by a frightful, overbearing energy to utter fevered gibberish.

It seemed to Galt that some of the darkness of Dim's mind began to fall over the battle front too. The commander of the Japanese troops on Biak Island drew them back from the beaches and into caves and bunkers and was inflicting the highest casualty count Big Drum's soldiers had encountered since Buna and Sanananda. As Dim turned into an apparently older and scrawnier woman before his eyes, there was a peril that the war would turn from an exercise in gifted strategy to the dogged, muddy affair it had been at the start.

Amongst the names which – writhing in her sleep – she uttered, were his own and Allan Lewis's, Gordon Runcie's and Ray Harris's, the radio star. She uttered, too, Ernie Sasser's, Harry Strudwick's, Stacey's. Stacey? Oh, yes, the Australian correspondent.

She spoke of correspondents and pythons. Her anxiety to utter these words was pitiable to watch. It was as if her brain were afire, and these were sparks it gave off.

On the third night Galt felt desperate enough to say to Meacham, 'She'll just dry out. She'll die for lack of moisture. How can you stop it?'

To which Meacham replied, 'No, she's young. If the fever breaks, she'll recuperate quickly. We'll keep the synthetic quinine coming. I'm sorry about this, Galt. I now know how much she means to you.'

And Galt thought that if Dim could have heard that, how the Surgeon-General accepted the open secret, that this alone might regenerate her.

She became conscious some hours before anyone noticed. That was because it was deep into the night, and because she had no strength left, so that she could not now manage even the flutterings and writhings which her fever had so recently extracted from her. She felt a raging but not a killing thirst. A nurse who took her temperature an hour before dawn was the first to know she would recover. Dim lay still, not even asking for water. She was saving herself for the supreme business of talking to Galt.

She slept despite herself, a calm, cool sleep. He was there when she opened her eyes. 'Galt,' she said. 'Galt.'

He filled a glass from a pitcher of what turned out to be lemonade and pushed it too hard against her lips, a forgiveable clumsiness, she thought. 'Don't talk, Dim,' he advised her. He uttered all the other normal urgings of the lover who waits by the bedside of the sick beloved. 'Save your strength! Just rest!'

She part absorbed and part choked on the lemonade. Gasping, she strained to speak again. 'Galt, they want to put it in the papers. They are looking for journalists.'

'Shh!' said Galt, laying a cool cloth on her brow. He was an awful nurse. He was trying too hard.

'Listen,' she said. Her vision was speckled and she could feel consciousness going. 'Strudwick, Sasser. They want two correspondents. They want to let it all out.'

'It's all right,' he reassured her. 'You're going to be well. Everything's looked after.'

'No,' she said. 'Listen!'

He took both her hands. 'You listen, Dim. I'll sit here for the next two hours. You rest. If you wake up in two hours and want to tell me something, I'll pay attention. But don't let things confuse you. Remember that everything terrible that's happened to you was delirium.'

'No,' said Dim.

'Shh!' said Galt. 'We've got a deal.'

'Don't go,' she managed to say before plummeting into that new kind of oblivion, the cool kind, one not of terrors, but of deep, creative stillness.

Watching her sleep, watching the face relax and become as young as it should be, Galt wondered where he'd got that idea from: the idea that if she started to speak in a jangled way, it would set her brain on a jangled path. He hoped she would wake to calm, plain, meat-and-potatoes conversation, the daily bread of sane talk. On such a diet he could face any task – the operational plans for Mindanao, Leyte and Luzon, even the visit from Big Drum later in the week, when he would fly in fresh from his meeting with the President in Hawaii with further tales of limitless Democrat chicanery and of the limitless machinations of the Chaumont gang!

Yet she did not easily wake. Work awaited him. He left his campaign hat on her bedside table. She would understand a message like that. For the first time in a career which had begun in boyhood, he went out into the sun incompletely uniformed.

As he arrived at his office, he saw a tall, youngish Australian war correspondent sitting on the far side of Captain Duncan's desk. You could tell he was Australian because his great slouch hat had been placed without any particular care at his feet. He exchanged a bleak glance with Galt, one which nearly but not quite made Galt pause on his way into his office.

Captain Duncan followed Galt through and closed the door behind him.

'What's that Australian scribe doing here, captain?'

'Paul Stacey, sir, he says he has to see you.'

'Does he know that I don't give interviews? That no one gives interviews? That all the interviews are for Big Drum?'

Captain Duncan smiled at that. Galt thought, *Be cautious. You're beginning to sound like someone who's lost the faith.*

'He doesn't want an interview, General. He wants a conference.'

'Really?' Galt laughed. 'Why should he have a conference?'

Duncan gave Galt an envelope. Galt opened it and read, on a plain yellow piece of paper;

Lieutenant-General Sandforth,
I have some urgent news to give you which affects Mrs Lewis.
Paul Stacey
Australian Independent Press.

Galt didn't like that 'Mrs Lewis' instead of 'Captain Lewis'. Had this Australian found out about Timor? Did he have a source in Special Reconnaissance, someone with an outraged conscience?

Galt was fearful anyhow. He looked up at Duncan. The man was simply waiting there, his face that of a good servant. For two years Galt had been wondering would he one day turn, or be recruited by others. It was time, Galt thought, to give him the benefit of the doubt. His loyalty might be needed in the future.

'Captain Duncan, I'm recommending you for promotion to major. You've richly deserved it. I don't always express gratitude to my staff . . . '

Duncan was almost touchingly pleased. He snapped a salute. 'Thank you heartily, sir.'

'Now you have your majority, Duncan, I want you as your

first task to requisition me a campaign cap. I seem to have misplaced the other one. Just an ordinary campaign cap. Forget the braid.'

'Certainly, sir.'

'I'll need it within the hour. Show in the Aussie.'

Coming in, Paul Stacey looked disgruntled, a potentially dangerous man. Galt had sometimes seen him in press conferences in Port Moresby, had even noticed how he had gradually lost his boyishness.

Galt asked him to sit down. The way he disposed of his hat on the floor again implied rebelliousness and dissent. Holding up the letter, Galt asked, 'What's this about, Mr Stacey?'

'It's about a bloody tragedy, sir.'

Galt felt his forearms chill. An almost chemical apprehension had come over him.

'As you know,' Stacey told him, 'my relationship with Big Drum's press office hasn't always been a happy one. At one stage I was expelled from Buna for saying that the Americans weren't fighting.'

'That's a long time ago, Mr Stacey. They're fighting now. What do you want of me? An admission that the Aussies have talent as military men?'

'I just mentioned that little incident, because it might have given someone in General Sasser's office the idea that I had a grudge against you, or against Americans in general.'

'I don't know what could have given them that idea. Anyhow, let's get to the point.'

'I hear Mrs Lewis is in hospital. Is she well?'

'Yes. She's been very ill. But she's well now.'

'I'm glad about that,' said Stacey. 'In any case, someone in General Sasser's office, as I said, thought I'd get any story published as long as it seemed to reflect badly on Big Drum or you. So they came to me with the whole story. They didn't want me necessarily to write it. They wanted me to feed it to the press. It was a good story. How you had your mistress on the premises, on pretty grand premises too.'

'I warn you,' said Galt. 'You may be a civilian, but don't think you can get away with being snide.'

Yet that was a primitive reaction, he realized at once. They were after him! The *staff*, the ones who'd been so sympathetic about Dim: they were after him.

'Listen, General,' said Stacey. 'You'd better start treating me like a human being. Because I can walk out of here now. I have the story, and I know the press everywhere will love it. And while I'm at it, let me say I don't give a damn about you. You're the normal effete old man who fucks young women while young men die for him. I don't give a damn about you! I'll go now if you want!'

'No,' said Galt. 'To hell with it! Finish!'

'I happen to know Allan Lewis. Wherever he is. I happen to know and like Dim. But someone wants the story to appear not only in the Australian press but throughout the US as well. I wouldn't like to see it happen. I don't want to see Allan Lewis come back from some arsehole place and find himself an internationally acclaimed cuckold instead of an honoured hero. As for Dim, I don't want her treated like a tart. The very fact that you're her lover makes me think you might have something not immediately obvious from your shitty manner. Some quality that's never been apparent to any of the press, American or Australian, I can tell you that much.'

This young man was too worked-up for Galt to be angry with him. Besides, under any terms, he was doing him a great favour. Frightening him, yes. But doing a great favour just the same.

'I don't care on what terms you're acting. I realize I'm lucky that they picked someone who had no grievance against Dim. She deserves nobody to hold grievances, you know, Mr Stacey.'

The journalist shook his head. There was confusion there. It struck Galt then that the man desired Dim. Perhaps matters of desire were in any case at the base of this whole sorry act of treachery. Ernie envying Galt, desiring Dim.

'Did they put an embargo on this news they gave you?' asked Galt. 'Was there a time it was to be released?'

'I believe Big Drum is paying a visit. It's top secret, but for once they've let a journalist know. They suggested that next Sunday was a good time for it to appear in Australia. They even offered me a secure radio frequency to get the news to Melbourne.'

Galt whistled. Why are you whistling, he wondered? Perhaps because it was a serious plot. Professional. They'd done their research well, up to a point. 'So the scenario is, Big Drum becomes disgruntled and expels me from paradise?'

'That seems to be it,' Stacey agreed.

'All for the terrible crime of loving Dim.'

Stacey's head jerked back.

'Yes,' said Galt. 'I love her, and I intend to marry her. That's non-attributable, Mr Stacey, and will be denied for the time being.'

'You'll marry her? And take her to the States?'

'Yes. But I never said so.'

'Can you stop them?'

'They may have stopped themselves. When you said no.'

'No, that's not the case. They swore me to confidentiality. I've broken confidentiality for your sake, General. Or more accurately, for Dim's. They can throw me out of New Guinea for good. And the thing that upsets me, General, to repeat myself, is that they might think that I've done it from some sort of respect for you.'

'That would be a shameful reputation to bear, Mr Stacey,' said Galt with a half smile. 'So you think they've approached someone else?'

'I'm sure of it. It's a bloody great story. The White House itself, up there above the lake, is a great story. And as a love nest it's a godsend. I'd imagine the Democrats would be pleased as hell to read it.'

'Just in case you're wondering, Mr Stacey, Dim wants what I want. And my wife has been told.'

'So that makes you an honest man, does it? Does Allan Lewis know?'

'Not yet. Morality's very mixed in wartime.' And more mixed than even you know, he could have said. 'If I survive this, Mr Stacey, you'll be a protected species, I assure you. The fact that you're doing it for Dim increases its value for me.'

'Christ,' said Stacey, 'You're a bloody hard man to insult.'

'I wouldn't pack your bags yet if I were you.'

Galt stood and offered his hand to Stacey.

'Oh, shit,' said Stacey, 'Why not?' He shook Galt's hand. 'She's a lovely woman. Are you sure she wants to marry an old man?'

'You're a bit like her,' said Galt. 'You don't have much respect.'

'It's the only Australian virtue,' said Stacey.

'When they tried to recruit you, this personage from Ernie Sasser's office. Did they convey that there was broad support for what they were doing?'

'Sure. They mentioned General Metzger, General Strudwick.'

'General Buck Clancy?'

'No. Are you making up your hit list?'

'I hope that will be for me to do, Mr Stacey, and you perhaps to report.'

'This scene goes in my fucking memoirs,' growled Stacey.

There had never been an adequate reason up to now to bring Harry and Ernie to heel, not even over Buna, and Harry's misreading of that. It was an internally coherent error, and so Galt had not bludgeoned him. He hoped however, to do his best to bludgeon him now.

First he went back to the hospital, wearing his new, undecorated hat. Dim was still asleep. Then it struck him. She had said everything Stacey had. *Two correspondents. Sasser and Strudwick. Let it all out.* She had known that, somehow, all through her illness. It accounted for the terrible killing restlessness of her fever. Jesus, they would pay for that.

He moved his regular cap closer to her face, so that on waking she would see it. Then he marched out of the hospital in a way which might well have made passing nurses wonder what fury was driving him at this mid-phase of a successful war.

There were now two full days before Big Drum was due to arrive in Hollandia from Hawaii with news of the President and with the sanction to go back to the Philippines. On Biak Island Bryant Gibbs's men were fighting hand to hand with General Ozinawi's young Japanese die-hards. The difference between the two armies was, however, that when the bouts of savagery ceased, and the Americans rested, Buck Clancy's bombers and fighters came in to shatter the enemy's rest.

Whereas everything was composure that day at Bataan Forward; at the hottest hour of mid-afternoon, Dim woke, and Galt was already at her bedside. He saw panic suddenly overtake the languor of her eyes, and she began to splutter. 'No, Dim,' he said, 'I'll tell you what I know, and you'll tell me if it matches what you have heard.'

So he recounted what he had been told by Stacey, and she nodded.

'How did you know?' she asked.

'How did you?' he countered.

'I heard them. My fever left, and I wanted to be there when you came in, so I got up and . . .'

'Heard them. Well, I know from a spy.'

'What will we do?'

He had hold of her hand. 'They can't take this away, can they?' He meant, the connection between them.

'No. But I do think of my parents, Galt . . . And your daughter. If that story gets out. She'll hate me.'

'I will stop them, Dim. I believe I can.'

'Please, please. Can you *do* that?'

She was drifting off again. They had taken her drip away. But she needed another one. He would mention it to Meacham on the way out. Meacham the conspirator.

'Dim,' he said. 'I *do* have something potent against them. I'll tell you.'

But she was asleep before he could. He went to the door. 'Nurse,' he bellowed.

Today his powers of command ran high.

From about 5.30 that evening there were as usual drinks in the conference-living room and out on the verandah. No one seemed to have anywhere else but the White House to go on that day, the way they all had on the day Galt had returned from Aitape and Dim had collapsed. Admiral Peter Andrews was there, back from the landing at Sansapor at the north-west end of New

Guinea. He said he was grateful that Big Drum hadn't been available to go ashore there. There had been no resistance, but the terrain had been very swampy, and the heat had been withering. But then, said Pete, Big Drum didn't sweat. It was but one of his godlike qualities.

From the full complement of staff and commanders drinking at Hollandia that afternoon, only Big Drum, Bryant Gibbs and Buck Clancy were missing. It cheered Galt that his old-fashioned friendship with Bryant Gibbs had not been put to any tests. Buck Clancy, likewise, would have considered the making of scandal a mortal sin, fit matter for the confessional. Besides, unlike Harry Strudwick, he was doing too well in his own right as air commander to feel the need to strike at Galt.

After about three-quarters of an hour of martinis for some and Scotch for others, Galt asked Harry and Ernie if he could have a quiet word with them on the verandah. They went out there together, carrying their last pre-dinner drinks. They would not be interrupted here, since they would look like what they were – a conference.

In the violet twilight the islands in Lake Sentani were purple, and the waterfall which broke from the mountains at the lake's southern end made a phosphorescent dent in the surface of the lake. That waterfall would be a place to take Dim during her convalescence. Either that, or into an American exile. But he was confident in his powers this evening, and he knew that the idea of exile for him or Dim lacked credibility.

Looking out over the lake still, he said, 'I wanted to let you both know that Captain Lewis is well again.'

'Glad to hear it,' said Ernie.

'It must have been a strain for you, Galt,' said Harry.

'I believe that while she was sick, no beat was missed in implementing your plans, Ernie, or yours, Harry.'

'I don't understand what you mean,' replied Harry.

'Well, you were employing a pipeline, weren't you? And along a pipeline there are many points of connection. And at a point of connection there can be a leak. Well, gentlemen, I'm sorry for your sake that a leak has occurred.'

'Sorry?' said Ernie Sasser, child of Oklahoma settlers and

Cherokee Indians and so not easily rendered uncomfortable. 'I don't know why you have to be sorry for us.'

'Why did you find it necessary to try this? What was it about Dim that you find so offensive? What, fundamentally, is there about me?'

'You shouldn't bring your mistress into headquarters, for Christ's sake,' said Harry. 'That breaks the code.'

'What should I do?' Galt asked, falling back on a phrase of Dim's from a year past. 'Keep her under a rock?'

'It's a professional offence to us,' Harry said.

'No. Do you know what is a professional offence, Harry? The number of times you've been wrong in this fucking war, and the number of times Big Drum has forgiven you for it. That's the goddamn offence. Christ, don't you guys get laid at all? Do you have to envy a man who's in love? I suppose you do. I suppose you've got that sort of mind. I feel genuine pity for you sons of bitches.'

'Don't feel pity for us, Galt. You'll have enough trouble explaining yourself to Big Drum, *and* your wife *and* the Secretary of Defense.'

'Well, Ernie, nice of you to show some concern. But I don't think that's the way it'll run.'

'We have our men already in place,' said Harry.

'Then I suggest you might want to call them off,' Galt told him. 'I think I can give you adequate reasons why that would become a matter of priority for you. Would you like me to call the steward to freshen your drinks? You may appreciate it before I'm finished.'

'That's not necessary,' said Ernie, and he frowned at Harry. He was always less committed to folly than Harry, and more self-questioning. He was beginning to feel uneasy.

'I know,' said Galt, 'that Ernie comes from a family which has done well from Oklahoma oil. You, Harry, have made a small fortune out of steel and manufacturing stocks since this war began. But I suppose that in 1938 you may have been a little short of cash. So for you at least there was that minor extenuation.'

'Extenuation? Listen, Galt, you've got nothing you can use against me.'

'Xavier Rivez. Do you remember him in the good old days in Manila? Deputy Foreign Minister. He did a lot of running between Big Drum and the Filipino government. Something like a bagman. The Filipino parliament had an extraordinary way of voting people gifts without recording the fact in public documents. Rivez came to Big Drum's headquarters with bags full of money, didn't he? US dollars. Voted as an *ex gratia* payment in appreciation for our work. They probably noticed that some of us lived in genuinely humble circumstances – Harry did, for example – staying in officers' quarters to save money. And that went against all their principles. They think generals should live like generals. And so they made a vote in favour of all of us. $US 400,000 to Big Drum, $250,000 for me, $200,000 for you Harry, and $150,000 for Ernie. Massive sums.'

Neither Ernie or Harry had anything to say. So Galt went on.

'At the time I raised with Señor Rivez the propriety of this. I said to him that no officer was to accept such a gift unless it was reported to and approved by the Department of Defense. To which he said, "You are under Filipino jurisdiction now. The gift is made to General Wraith as a Field Marshal of the Filipino armed forces, and to you and others as valued members of his staff." I ascertained from him that Big Drum had already taken the money without reporting it to the Department of Defense. I did not begrudge that. Big Drum's family wealth is not as great as that of my family. Then, while I was still wondering about this grant, or whatever you'd call it, this highly tempting sum, I had a letter from Rivez encouraging me and saying that sensible General Strudwick and sensible Brigadier-General Sasser had also accepted their sums.'

'And you're telling us you didn't accept yours?'

'That's what I'm telling you, Harry. Not only that, I made copies of my letter to Rivez, and kept records of all my banking. I deposited them with my lawyer in Richmond. They are still there. In plain print, on official Filipino government stationery, Rivez declares that you have accepted the *ex gratia* payments voted to you without any scruples about consulting the Pentagon.'

'So what are you saying?' asked Harry.

Ernie had shaken his head. 'Jesus Christ, he's saying that if any prejudicial story appears, he will send those documents to the Secretary of Defense.'

'That's exactly what I'm damn well saying, Ernie.'

'It will create a scandal involving Big Drum.'

'Big Drum will survive. He's so genuinely big now. But you? You're just functionaries. You'll be dead. I'd say that within two weeks you will have retired and be starting to look for directorships on the boards of companies, and deciding where you're going to go fishing this fall. Oblivion awaits you, you sons of bitches! But I'm not going to wait to see if something appears. I'm going to tell my lawyers to release the documents on Friday both to the Secretary *and* to the press. I think that if anything is calculated to drive my peccadilloes off the front page, this story could well be it.'

Harry said, 'So you want an assurance by Friday?' He was tallow-coloured from shock and fury.

'That's it. Call the jackals off. But be certain of one thing, if anything *does* happen to appear, anything concerning me and Dim, then it will be quickly followed by another story. Yours.'

Ernie finished his drink. 'Then if you'll excuse me, I have some arranging to do.'

'Me too,' said Harry.

They both started to leave the verandah, but Galt called after them. 'Gentlemen, if we all survive this, through your good efforts, then I intend we shall work well together until we reach Manila. Anything else will be an indulgence.'

Ernie said, 'I resent the shit out of you, Galt. But I'll work with you. That is, if I can smother this story in time.'

'Better go and do it,' said Galt.

Harry Strudwick, leaving, said nothing.

Big Drum's B-29 from Hawaii landed at Hollandia late on Friday. Galt was at the Tanahmerah Bay airstrip to meet his chief, and was a little shocked to see how tired Big Drum looked after his flight of more than twenty-four hours.

'Couldn't sleep, Galt,' said Big Drum, twirling his customary amber cigarette-holder. 'Too full of ideas. The great times are coming, Galt. They're on their way!'

In the jeep on the way to the Hollandia White House, only the most rudimentary conversation was possible. Big Drum sat at table with his staff but ate very little. He seemed to have energy only for anecdotes.

The President had wanted a sky-blue convertible for his drive through the streets of Waikiki with Big Drum and Kremnitz. The only two available belonged to a local pineapple king and to the Chinese madame of a famous Hotel Street whorehouse. The madame's convertible was a much snazzier affair, Big Drum said, but for fear of its being recognized by the populace, the President had fallen back on the more sedate conveyance of the pineapple baron.

Big Drum also spent time explaining how he managed to board the President's cruiser *Chesapeake* later than Kremnitz. He deliberately called off at the house of the Marine General, Wrench, and took a long bath. Then he travelled to the *Chesapeake* in a vehicle with sirens atop and mounted the gangplank wearing a flying jacket given him by Buck Clancy.

Everyone at Bataan Forward seemed to love these point-scoring tales, but for the first time Galt wondered were they not a little mean-minded? Would Big Drum as President be less averse to powder-blue convertibles than the Democrats were? And did it really matter who went aboard *Chesapeake* first, or what they were wearing?

Afterwards, Big Drum dismissed everyone, telling them how tired he was. He went off to his bedroom. Galt strolled out on to the verandah to look at the lake. Ernie Sasser was out there with Hal Metzger. General Sasser broke away from Hal and came over. 'The story's been squashed, Galt. Both Harry and I have leaned on our journalists.'

'They must be very confused, Ernie.'

'Let 'em be.'

'You'd better be right about this.'

'Fuck you, Galt, I am.'

'At any stage, Ernie, I'll unleash the whirlwind on you.'

'I understand that,' said Ernie. 'I wouldn't expect better.'

'You're a good staff officer, Ernie. A damn sight better than that tight-assed Prussian friend of yours. Just keep everything going, that's all I ask.'

'Sleep tight, Galt.'

'I will. You too, Ernie.'

A steward had appeared on the verandah. 'General Sandforth, General Wraith wonders could you visit him in his room?'

When Galt knocked on Big Drum's door and was asked in, he found the General wearing a light dressing gown and reading a book. The legs that showed out of the dressing gown were astoundingly young and athletic. Big Drum's face was screwed up around the empty holder.

'You know how it is, Galt. So tired you can't sleep. Tired, but exhilarated. Grab a chair, I've got something to tell you. The President himself has guaranteed the Joint Chiefs will authorize us to hit Mindanao, Leyte and then Luzon. We've been given the green light for the Philippines. None of this blockade nonsense, Galt. We're going back. Of course, Kremnitz was all for a damned blockade, Galt. I told him all it would do was make the enemy take scarce food away from the population. Do you know, though, we sat up arguing the point, Kremnitz and the President and I, until nearly midnight? And I went to bed convinced I'd lost. Because Kremnitz was pushing all this rubbish about casualty rates. I said to the President, "He ought to know. He ran up plenty at Guadalcanal and at Saipan." '

Big Drum had so far revived that he had now swung his feet off the bed and was sitting facing Galt. 'I'd argued myself blue in the face that you couldn't take Formosa unless you already had the Philippines anyhow. In any case, I went and slept, and it came to me in a kind of dream that Kremnitz was only a stooge for Channing. That he was arguing a case he didn't have any belief in. So at breakfast I hit him again, and he gave in. And the President gave his guarantee. And so we're on our way, Galt. Definitely. I think we should be able to hit the Philippines by November. About the time of the elections. Would you believe it? There were people saying we wouldn't get back there till 1948, and I may well have been one of them. Amazing!'

Galt looked at his knees. He felt an urge to test Big Drum. He had never felt that impulse before. Who was he? To *test* Big Drum?

'I doubt,' he said, 'that Kremnitz was arguing George Channing's case. He may have been arguing the case of some other members of the Joint Chiefs. But you might remember, General, George Channing told me about the Presidential visit to Hawaii, and the opportunity it gave us . . . '

'It's nice of you to think well of your fellow humans, Galt. But Channing was pursuing another line altogether. He wasn't doing us a favour. He was softening us up. He was trying to make me relax in front of Kremnitz's onslaught. Believe me.'

But Galt didn't. To him Big Drum looked like any old man likely to die shadow-boxing with ghosts.

'General, it's my impression George Channing's been very fair in all this. Maybe he doesn't like us. But he's treated us with some justice.'

'Galt, for God's sake,' said Big Drum. 'You don't know him.'

Galt did not bother saying, *But I know what I know*.

He left Big Drum's bedroom a little confused, a little empty, but also excitedly aware of new opportunities. I am a fallen member of the Big Drum fan club, he thought. In other words, I am liberated.

There was a cocktail party the following evening to welcome Big Drum to Hollandia. Nursing officers from the great Hollandia hospital where Dim lay were brought in to leaven the company of males. Some of these women were Australians. Galt wished he could have had Dim there, to serve in a way as his declaration of independence, as a frankly cherished companion.

It was Saturday evening and Galt knew that if Ernie and Harry hadn't suppressed those stories, the tale of Galt Sandforth and his Aussie girlfriend, and of their Hollandia cavortings, would now be in the process of being typeset in newspapers from Hobart, Tasmania, to Nome, Alaska. He was confident, however, that nothing would hit the headlines.

In the middle of the party, Buck Clancy arrived back from inspecting a new airstrip on Wakde Island. He took Galt aside and asked him in the most touching and – Galt was sure – unfeigned way about Dim. 'I don't know if this means anything to a Protestant, Galt, but I said the Rosary for her two nights back.'

'It must have done some good, Buck, that popish nonsense of yours. Because that's the night she came out of her coma.'

The gardens were full of young officers and women. Buck and Galt looked out on them. Buck said, 'It's great to be young, but I wouldn't swap what we're doing now for a chance to be young again. My Fortresses and Liberators are already clobbering Subiac Bay. The Japanese phenomenon is finished, Galt. It's a matter of time. Even Hal Metzger can't slow us down.'

Moving back inside to find another drink, Galt was detained by Big Drum, who sat in the big front window, looking out at the younger officers in the garden.

'Galt,' said Big Drum, 'while I remember. See those Australian girls out there. I've given a solemn promise to the Australian Prime Minister that I won't take any of his Australian women's forces or his militia north of the equator.'

Galt paused, he wondered what this meant. Was he being told as an administrative matter, or was he being warned? He looked at Big Drum's penetrating eyes and noticed that they seemed more like ciphers than he'd ever thought before. Is there a man behind them? Galt wondered.

To hell with you, he thought. You'll have to be smarter than that if you want to separate me from Dim.

What he said was, 'Would you like me to issue an order to that effect?'

Big Drum looked at him and the tension went out of his voice. 'Yes, just bear it in mind, Galt, and issue a general order to that effect some time next week.'

'I won't forget, General.'

'You're a good man, Galt. My right hand.'

If I weren't, Galt thought, I'd be General of the Sixth Army.

When Dim left hospital a week later, Big Drum had already

flown home to Brisbane to see Mrs Wraith. Galt let Dim rest a few days and then arranged for one of the army launches to take them both up Lake Sentani for a picnic. The water near the cascades was pure and cool from its long descent from the mountains. Dim and Galt sat on a rock overhung by foliage, and Dim even discussed the idea of going swimming herself. Galt did young men's dives into the deep, cool water while she applauded.

But he was uneasy because *they* had introduced an uneasiness. 'What did you do to Harry Strudwick?' she had asked him. And he had answered, 'What he would have done unto me.'

But he noticed she took the excuse of her recent illness as a reason rarely to emerge from her room when the conspirators were about.

'Dim?' he asked. 'How important is your Australian identity to you?'

'What do you mean?'

'Look, I've issued an order that no Australian women, officers or members of the militia, are to accompany us north of the equator. I think it's time you donned the uniform of a US captain.'

'But that wouldn't be legal, would it?' she asked.

'No. We've made an exception in your case. I'm not leaving you here.'

Dim thought about this. 'It doesn't seem right, Galt.'

'Well, maybe you have a boyfriend here then.'

'Of course I have. The hospital stint was a mere cover for that.'

'I'll fix you up with a US captain's uniform. And you can be sure that soon after we hit the Philippines, I'll send for you. I thought I'd lost you ten days ago. That's never going to happen again.'

'What does Big Drum say?'

He thought about this. She saw him cock his head. 'Big Drum is willing to make an exception in your case,' he said.

'But why, Galt? Harry Strudwick wouldn't.'

'Big Drum is a bigger man than Harry.' But having said that, he began to doubt it.

'I would be in hiding again though, wouldn't I?' she said.

'No.'

'I'd be in hiding in a foreign uniform.'

'Foreign?'

'In a foreign uniform,' she repeated. 'Under a rock.'

She looked at him with a sudden confusion. Her mind was not yet clear of the delirium which had so recently swamped it.

'Never, Dim. Never under a rock.' He found a shirt and put it on, because on this particular rock, the one they were sitting on above the water, the sun was beginning to bite at him.

'Would I live with the staff? In the Philippines? Would I live with Harry Strudwick and Ernie Sasser?'

He shook his head. 'No, Dim. There's no future in sharing quarters with those guys. I'll find you a place of your own. Call it *under a rock*, if you have to. But we may be in Manila by Christmas, and that will be the end of the Army for me, Dim. We can really emerge into the open then.'

'Big Drum will beg you to stay on.'

'Let him. It's time he came to depend on himself.'

Dim looked at him with great solemnity, very soberly. It was the first time she'd ever heard him use a phrase like that about Big Drum: 'depend on himself'.

'And your daughter Sandy – she'll create a stir and that worries you.'

Dim was suddenly so fretful.

'We'll have one awkward meeting, Dim. Sometime in the future. And after that Sandy and you will be the closest friends. I know it, Dim.'

The solemnity stayed there on her face.

'Dim,' he insisted, 'I'm fed up with being what I am! I'm sick of having to find levers to use against people, and buttons to push. I'm sick of being Big Drum's messenger boy to the Joint Chiefs. I want a human life, not an inhuman one.'

She nodded. The nod said, *OK, if that's what you want, we'll get it for you.* Then she became pensive.

'Galt, I had a lot of bad dreams about Allan. A python had hold of him.'

Galt could not stop himself shuddering for an instant. I know the name of that python, he could have said. That python is Death.

'Is there any news?'

'None,' he said. He could feel the inherent danger in that awful, potent lie.

'You wouldn't hide things from me?'

'No.'

Even if what Runcie had told intelligence *was* the truth, this wasn't the time to tell her. He took a second to wonder where Runcie was now. Still in the enclosed ward in Darwin? And Runcie's wife – she still knew nothing either. Galt would have to take a hand in this. The situation was inhuman. The Runcie woman deserved to know. At least that her husband was alive, even if she also had to be told that he was locked away, unvisitable, under treatment.

'You will tell me when you find out, won't you?' she asked in that debilitated, insistent way.

'Of course, Dim.' Inwardly this lie put him in panic. Could he claim it was kindly deceit. In any case, he knew that devising the manner of his breaking the news to her was the most crucial task ahead of him.

'Everything has to be settled,' she said, looking up the long silver thread of the waterfall. He could see it was time he took her home. The heat and glare of the picnic had been a bit too much.

All the way back to the White House, he held her against him, his arm around her frankly. He noticed the young Army helmsman glancing in his direction. In the old days, he would have said, 'Eyes front, soldier!'

In the old days, he wouldn't have been caught in this situation.

Chapter 16

The Leyte Broadcast

INTO GALT'S OFFICE, as into Big Drum's office back in Brisbane, came thousands of transmissions from the Filipino underground, who knew the time of their deliverance was near now. The Kempei Tai, the Japanese security police, were hunting down rebel leaders and beheading them at Fort Santiago, an old Spanish fort and prison. Every execution was graphically detailed in radio transmissions from the Filipino rebels, who bore the name Huks, or Hukbalahaps. Some of the transmissions mentioned the Minister of the Interior in the Filipino puppet government – Xavier Rivez. They dreamed of his execution. It was interesting for Galt to ask himself whether when Manila fell Big Drum *would* order the treason trial of an old friend who had delivered to him, without any strings, a gift of $400,000.

Pete Andrews's transports and escort carriers – old merchant ships transformed by the addition of guns and a landing deck – began to gather in Hollandia. Tanahmerah and Humboldt Bays slowly filled with ships. It was hard to look out there and believe that Big Drum was being starved by the Joint Chiefs. One of Kremnitz's carrier groups had also been assigned to the operation. It was to be under Kremnitz's command still, said the Joint Chiefs, but under Big Drum's direction – a curious exercise in semantics was involved here, in an effort to salve the egos of both Big Drum and Kremnitz. Galt just hoped it all wouldn't create problems when the landings in the Philippines began.

The sky seemed full, too, of enormous B-29 Super Fortresses, flying north to Morotai or west to Wakde, ultimately intended for bombing raids against the Japanese forces behind the beachheads where the troops of Bryant Gibbs's army (now grown to 150,000 men) and of Hal Metzger's (now grown to 200,000) would go ashore.

Under the drone of those huge and deadly planes, Dim slowly got her colour back, staying in the White House, sometimes even attending communal meals. Bravely waiting, as Galt had asked her to.

Big Drum and Galt had at the start planned the great Philippines return as beginning at the southern island of Mindanao and then moving north to Leyte and Luzon, embowered in whose western coast was the prize: Manila. But then they got a report from a young pilot from one of Kremnitz's carriers. Patrolling off Leyte, the young man had been shot down, had parachuted to the ground, been greeted by members of the Filipino Resistance, who, before long, had arranged by radio a rendezvous for him on a beach in Leyte Gulf, at which a US submarine arrived to take him aboard. In debriefing, he said that Leyte had been lightly defended – according to the guerrillas maybe no more than ten thousand troops. Kremnitz's admirals had also reported very little opposition from land-based enemy aircraft operating out of Luzon or Leyte. And so Big Drum had changed the proposed thrust from Mindanao to Leyte, to the beaches near the island capital of Tacloban.

'Tacloban is where I started in 1903,' Big Drum told Galt. 'The Visayan tribesmen didn't like us, and two of them ambushed me, and I shot both. And do you know what my Irish sergeant said to me? He looked at the corpses and said, *Beggin' your pardon, lieutenant, but in me sincere opinion, the rest of your life is goin' to run like silk*.

Or else Big Drum would sometimes say, 'Had my first bout of malaria in Tacloban.'

Or then again, 'I went to Tacloban as a one-bar lieutenant in 1903, and I'm going back as a five-star General forty-one years later.'

A logistic and personnel problem Galt had not solved was the question of what Dim would do once she got to Leyte. He had already raised it with her. 'You'll be wearing US uniform, with US captain's bars. But there'll be no specific task. Will you mind waiting round for a while?'

Dim smiled though she was not happy with the idea of idleness. 'You find me quarters, Galt, and I'll work with the nurses.

Unofficially. I'll empty buckets and write letters for the wounded.'

'It can't be for long,' he said, uttering it as an absolute guarantee. But he wondered if he should tempt destiny that way. In the past eighteen months, Big Drum had become accustomed to storming ashore with the troops of Metzger and Gibbs, to finding airstrips for Buck Clancy's planes; to the whole clockwork of planned operations. That was the way Leyte was intended to go too, and if it did, if the Japanese were as thin on the ground as Kremnitz's young pilot had said, the results would be equally superb, the Philippines would be cut in two, Big Drum would be in the Hotel Manila for Christmas.

Yet in any military event there were untold possibilities for chaos. He wondered if he should be talking about outcomes as if they were as regular as dividend payments.

Buck Clancy had made the point to Big Drum that Leyte was some hundreds of miles beyond the range of his land-based fighters operating from Moratai. It was unlike Buck to be hesitant like that. Big Drum was blithe enough. 'Until your fighters get up there, Buck, we'll depend on your bombers and Kremnitz's carrier-based fighters.'

'The carrier-based fighters aren't under my control, though, General. Or yours. We'll have to go cap in hand to Kremnitz.'

'I'm not above that,' said Big Drum, as if replying to an accusation.

There was another strangely disturbing piece of news. General Timoyuki Yamashita, the man who had made fools of the British in Malaya and who was called the 'Tiger of Malaya', had been kept by the Japanese equivalent of the Chaumont gang in the administrative shallows of the Japanese Army. Now he was appointed to command the defence of the Philippines.

Galt knew that the USS *Chattanooga* was the cruiser which would take Big Drum and his staff to Leyte. They were to go aboard on the afternoon of October 16th. On Monday, the morning of the 20th they would be anchored at Tacloban, blasting Japanese shore positions and then watching Bryant Gibbs's men go ashore on the beaches south of the town, and, a few miles further south but probably detectable from the bridge by binoculars, Hal Metzger's 1st Cavalry Division going in against Dulag.

Saying goodbye to Dim and leaving her US captain's uniform with her, Galt boarded *Chattanooga* and found his cabin more or less as cramped as the little cabin he had occupied on the USS *Tucson* at the time Big Drum invaded Los Negros. He felt anxious, and wondered whether it was merely shipboard claustrophobia. There had been some radio messages coming in about the reinforcement of General Suzuki's Thirty-Fifth Army on Leyte.

One of the reactions these radio signals produced in Galt was an even sharper awareness that if Big Drum had not so cherished him as right hand, he would be in Hal's place, taking on Suzuki. He would not be the participant in the struggle for Suzuki's mind and will. He would be the protagonist.

Various surviving politicians from the Philippines government-in-exile had been flown from the US and were now recuperating aboard a nearby transport called the *Bunyan*. They also would go ashore with Galt and Big Drum. The liberation government of the Philippines would be established on the beach near Tacloban on the first morning of the landings.

But though the Filipinos were all old pre-war friends of Big Drum's, Big Drum did not want them sharing the *Chattanooga* wardroom. 'It's all going to be very emotional, Galt,' said Big Drum. It was as if he believed, in part, that he himself bore enough emotion for the occasion; that he did not want to risk an overload.

On the first night out of Hollandia in the *Chattanooga*'s wardroom, while an ill-defined dread still hung over Galt, Big Drum set to work on his speech. That was another thing. The US Signal Corps was going to set up a broadcast unit on Red Beach south of Tacloban so that Big Drum could exhort the Filipino masses. He was still, two nights before the landing, working on the text. 'It's deliberately florid, boys,' he told his staff, as if he did not want them to believe he was *really* like his speech. But, as everyone knew, that really was his style. Melodramatic, baroque, overdone, and convinced of an identity of interest between himself and the Deity.

He circulated the text for members of the staff to make notes on. As it stood, it read thus:

> *People of the Philippines: I have returned to you as I said I would. By the grace of an all-powerful God, the forces of right have established themselves again upon Philippine soil, on earth consecrated by the blood of both the Philippine and the American people, upon soil holy for its evocations of the heroism of Bataan and Corregidor. I bring to you your own leaders, your former government-in-exile which is now your government in place. For your government is now robustly established here on the beaches of Leyte, and soon its beneficence will reach all of you. As we do reach you, as the troops of our army of liberation will see all your faces! For the supreme moment of your redemption has arrived. In the darkness you must often have repined for it, but now it is here. I call on you to rise now and support me. Let the memory of Bataan and Corregidor lead you on. As we bring the lines of battle forward to meet you, as our operations penetrate into your hinterland, rise and attack. Attack at every favourable and reasonable opportunity. For your memories and your God, attack! For the future generations of Filipinos, attack! In the name of your holy dead on Bataan and Corregidor, attack! Show them your steel, show them the light and strength of your hearts! It is divine God himself who will show you the way. Follow his strength to the tabernacle of indomitable victory!*

'What do you think?' asked Big Drum when everyone had had a chance to read it.

Harry Strudwick said, 'With respect, sir, it might have too many references to God to be a powerful instrument in activating the Marxists amongst the rebels, whom we need.'

Ernie Sasser said he thought that was a fair comment.

The new Surgeon-General, Meacham, ventured that it was just a touch flowery, but Galt said nothing, because he knew it was pure Big Drum, and Big Drum wasn't really going to change it, although the point about the Deity would probably be taken on board, and God would get one or two mentions fewer than He already did.

Buck Clancy said, 'The thing to remember is, this is written for the Filipinos, not for the American press. The Filipinos will love this. I promise you.'

'Galt?' insisted Big Drum.

'Perhaps you could mention the forces of progress, General. Instead of God himself. Isn't *Divine God* a tautology in any case? But basically, I'm with Buck. I know they'll recognize your style, and they'll like it.'

'I shall take everything you say on board, gentlemen,' said Big Drum.

They watched him begin working on his speech with a blue pencil. He cut a word here and a word there. The major sentiments remained. Buck winked at Galt, and Galt winked back. Soon, Galt thought, I'll be quit of the lot of you.

The eve of the landing, Galt did not sleep well. Like many others in the landing force, he wanted the next day to be over and the inshore airfields captured. It seemed to him grotesque now that the whole inverted pyramid of this enormous effort should be based on the word of one of Kremnitz's flyers who had parachuted down into Leyte, led a confused life there for some days, and whose impressions must have been – of their nature – patchy. A steward woke him with coffee about 5 a.m., and he shaved and showered and dressed, moving purely by habit. He felt like a man shaving before an operation, pretending that the doctors and nurses would give a damn how he looked as they gouged away at his disordered gizzards.

There were scrambled eggs in the wardroom but he barely touched them. Big Drum was already on the bridge. He specialized in being a jump ahead of the staff. Galt climbed up there and exchanged a salute with Big Drum, but conversation immediately became impossible, since *Chattanooga*'s guns began to sound. *Sound* was a pale description of the reality. The *Chattanooga* all at once felt like a fragile vehicle for such enormous thunders. Galt tried to look at the flashes of the barrage landing behind Red and White Beaches. The beaches near Dulag had been designated Violet and Yellow, the latter – Galt thought – an unfortunate adjective, though he had not intruded in the colour selection. Once he might have. It was an awful thing to consider that there might next week be young widows back home who would be able to say that their husbands had perished on Yellow Beach.

There was nothing subtle about any of the dawns Big Drum and Galt had shared together north and south of the equator, in the Philippines or New Guinea. They came up unambiguously or – as Kipling would have it – 'like thunder'. Such a full-throated dawn revealed that the tropical green waters all around were filled with Higgins boats, but almost at once as well the silver-azure sky was full of aircraft. Galt at first thought they were Kremnitz's planes, but then he picked up on the tension in the way Buck Clancy, who had also arrived on the bridge, was clutching his binoculars. They were Japanese fighters from Luzon, maybe from Leyte itself. Great ninety-millimetre anti-aircraft shells filled the sky with smudges of flame and black smoke. But it seemed that many of the aircraft were breaking through, and even some of those which fell from the sky seemed aimed unerringly at the decks of Andrews's cruisers and escort carriers.

It was not until after 9 a.m. that there was a lull. Galt could hear the sounds of battle ashore, but the Japanese aircraft had gone off to refuel. Buck Clancy spoke to Galt and Big Drum in a tight whisper. 'Some of those sons of bitches deliberately crashed on our ships. We know that from Japanese radio intercepts. It looks like it's a new movement amongst the Japanese.'

On top of the knowledge that he must go ashore later in the morning with Big Drum and stride around amidst the enemy's fire, Galt found Buck's news unnerving. It was a further sign from a dangerous world which he did not want to belong to except as a traveller and a lover.

Buck said, 'I hate these goddamn ships. Give me an aircraft any day, or even a tent on the edge of an airstrip crawling with mud. They don't build these damn things strong enough.'

Galt said, 'I thought all you good Catholics had faith, Buck.'

'I know it. But sometimes when I'm on these steel buckets, I get the sense that God mightn't know it. Let's get ashore, Galt, and find those airstrips we need.'

Galt felt that he was caught in an endless day, one in which the frenetic energy would never cease. He watched another wave of soldiers go ashore, another wave of enemy fighters come in from Luzon. But the messages from shore were reassuring. Near Tacloban, three miles from the *Chattanooga*, Bryant Gibbs's men had broken through the screen of Japanese defenders. At Violet and Yellow Beaches further south, the main problems were the crowds of grateful Filipinos who came down to the shore to greet the 1st Cavalry Division with gifts of food and liquor and garlands.

Towards mid-morning, Galt took some coffee and a tuna salad sandwich in the wardroom. Big Drum intended that they should be ashore by noon. Again, Galt had the sense that he should postpone the gestures of a live man – including the tuna salad – until he knew the outcome of the day. He was finishing his coffee when someone from Big Drum's press office came up. 'General, we have a ciné and news photography team ashore to record the General's landing. We'd be obliged if you would stick close to him on the way up the beach.'

Galt was tempted to ask, 'Do you want me for my own sake or for the reflected glamour of my daughter the actress and Democrat?' But he did not bother. He could hear and feel the anti-aircraft guns firing. More Japanese fighters and bombers from Luzon were overhead, and more Japanese youths were hurling themselves like arrows at Pete Andrews's fleet.

With a feeling therefore of unreal and quiescent terror, Galt climbed down the accommodation ladder of USS *Chattanooga* behind Big Drum and into the Higgins boat for the journey ashore. They took off in a wallowing manner for a nearby transport, where some young and aged Filipino politicians appeared in a loading gate in the ship's side and were lowered into the Higgins boat. Galt recognized some of them. He had never respected them much – all Filipino politicians had seemed to him to be privileged and opportunistic in a way which American politicians, even taking account of all their special backgrounds and prejudices, were not. He found himself shaking hands with them. They all looked drained of blood. There was harsh reality above them in the sky. Perhaps they had expected a more tranquil return to their homeland than this.

The engines of the Higgins boat cut in and drowned all conversation. Galt himself spread a map for Big Drum to consult.

Big Drum pointed over the high coping of the boat to a headland. 'Tanauan,' declared Big Drum. 'I used to take girls there for picnics when I was a boy.'

The landing barge jolted against shingle, and its steel ramp descended to show surf. They were not on the beach. Galt became aware that the commander of the Higgins boat was calling ashore to the beachmaster, and not getting much answer. This barge skipper was a young man, and now he came striding forward amongst the Filipino politicians and the staff.

'Gentlemen, you will have to wade ashore,' he cried.

Big Drum said, 'Did he say *wade*?'

He stepped off the end of the landing barge, tottered on the sandy bottom. Galt also stepped forward and landed in the warm waters of the Philippines. They strode ashore. Photographers shot them. Great plumes of scarlet and black smoke rose behind the beach. *This is history*, Galt thought.

Big Drum roared out of the corner of his mouth, 'Find the beachmaster, Galt, and pay him my most devout disrespects.'

This leonine scowl would also be photographed, would appear in newspapers throughout the world and on ciné film and, becoming one of the most famous photographs of the Pacific campaign, would add to Big Drum's imperial reputation.

Big Drum and the staff and three returning Filipino politicians went striding along the beach, pausing when Big Drum did to inspect landing barges which had run aground crippled. 'This is great, gentlemen,' called Big Drum, but Galt and Buck merely exchanged glances. They could hear combatants yelling to each other in the undergrowth a little way inland. In a gap in the noise, some Japanese soldier very close, was yelling in English, 'The President eat shit.'

This caused Big Drum to emit his customary chortle. 'You see?' he asked. 'You see? Even Yamashita's soldiers are Republicans!'

They reached a squad of eight men with a Browning who

were sheltered behind a log rampart, catching their breath. 'You gentlemen are 24th Division, are you?'

The section, who had thought the day unreal enough without the admixture of Big Drum and his staff, frowned, trying to absorb an extra confusing element in a berserk universe.

A young officer carrying a pistol emerged from the palms and told Galt that there was considerable resistance a little way inland. Big Drum asked him, 'How are you finding the enemy, lieutenant?'

Galt heard Buck interrupt, 'Perhaps we should not imperil the Filipino liberation government, General.' Buck meant the Filipino politicians who had come ashore with them. Buck was one of the few members of staff, perhaps the only one, who could get away with appealing to the presence of special guests as a means of avoiding getting shot at. In any case, Big Drum wasn't having any of that.

'Our Filipino friends are better soldiers than we are. They've always considered themselves in the front line. Isn't that so, gentlemen?'

And all the rest was an enlarged repetition of Los Negros. Along the trail Big Drum nudged the corpses of Japanese soldiers and announced, 'These guys are from the 16th Division. They were the ones who did all the dirty work on Bataan. Now the dirty work has been returned to them a thousandfold.'

Someone murmured, 'At least he hasn't mentioned Divine God.'

'Sir, there's the broadcast,' Harry Strudwick reminded Big Drum.

And so now everyone returned gratefully to the beach, although it was no safer. Shells were bursting above it, fighters would appear overhead and be gone. A mile offshore there was a loud discourse between the ships and enemy aircraft.

A colonel of signals was waiting for him. Galt could hear him shouting to Big Drum that the communications truck had broken down, that they were supplying power from a mobile generator. A mike had been set up on the beach – a classic radio broadcast mike on a tripod, aimed inland. Big Drum stepped up to it. All the noises of fire between aircraft and ships, all the sound of small-arms and mortars and tracked vehicles would go into this broadcast, which was bound to be so florid that cynics back home would believe the sound effects were dubbed in.

Big Drum began his great speech. The signals officer had said he could not be sure that the thing was transmitting, but he was hopeful. Big Drum transmitted by force of will. 'Citizens of the Philippines,' he began.

As Big Drum continued, Galt was horrified to see a flash of fire come down from the sky and pluck three men out of an entrenched position fifty yards up the beach. Does this man consider such phenomena mere background to his performance? Galt wondered.

When Big Drum had finished his resounding broadcast, he asked the Filipino politicians to say a few words. Then, after consultations by radio with a brigade commander, he decided that they should go and see the nearest airstrip. 'Gentlemen, we'll just have to be careful to keep away from the western end. It isn't *secured* yet.'

They were off down that jungle track again, where the Japanese dead had accumulated. Some of them showed by the headbands they wore that they had consecrated themselves to death this day and had now achieved what they were looking for.

US infantry fire teams laden with flame-throwers, mortars and Brownings overtook them, rushing forward, their faces taut. They looked very confident in a grim sort of way, Galt thought. How far we've come in how short a time! It gave you a certain pride in these citizen soldiers, these old-young men. His pride would be more unqualified if he knew that he was going to live through the day. But as the track opened up to an airstrip runway, Galt saw the fire teams peel off into the undergrowth to the west. They did not intend to expose themselves on the open reaches of the airfield. They left that to God's anointed, Big Drum.

It was a mean airstrip to die for anyhow. That much was apparent. Around its edges were thatch shelters and brush hangars, but they looked as though they were long abandoned. The surface was not of crumbled coral but of a grey, muddy sand in which recent rain had cut ridges. Big Drum plugged the corner of his mouth with his amber cigarette-holder – and strode about kicking the stuff with his shoe.

'Tell me what you think, Buck. Good or bad?'

Buck got down on his hands and knees, an enviable situation in this case, and dug at the surface with a scout knife. A large explosion of flame occurred at the other end of the airstrip, and there was an exchange of rapid fire. Buck said, 'I can see why the Japanese have abandoned this. The ground's too low. The soil won't hold. Even if we put in steel reinforcing, it would wash away in the wet season.'

'This *is* the wet season,' said Galt.

'Exactly,' said Buck. 'We're going to have to really build this up, put in drainage and aqueducts to get rid of the water. Sorry, General, but it's going to be a long time before we can land a B-17 here.'

'Ernie!' called the General. 'Get your engineers in here as soon as you can!'

Big Drum was frowning. He was going to be dependent for air cover on his old enemy Kremnitz. Galt realized too, that this meant it would be a long time before such rear echelon personnel as Dim Lewis could be flown in.

There were three further ear-splitting explosions at the western end of the airstrip. Is this hanging around real heroism on Big Drum's part? Galt asked himself. Or is it comic opera?

At last they were able to turn back to the beach yet again. Big Drum did not seem particularly flustered by the problems Buck had raised in connection with the airstrip. But if all the airstrips round Tacloban and Dulag were like this, the battle for Leyte might last months longer than planned. Back in the cool wardroom of *Chattanooga*, they ate tuna salad sandwiches and Big Drum cleared messages for transmission to rebels throughout the Philippines. *Chattanooga* had become a communications centre for all the guerrillas. From its radio shack they were informed on where to expect air drops. During lunch *Chattanooga*'s anti-aircraft guns kept firing, and its eight-inch guns continued to bombard the enemy positions, though not in Tacloban itself, which Big Drum wanted captured intact.

Even after dusk, the guns went on reverberating. Japanese fighters from Luzon were still active, though the *kamikaze* attacks had ceased for the moment. It seemed that the young pilots who were willing to crash their planes into US ships needed the full light of day so that the theatre of their sacrifice could be visible to everyone, could intimidate and awe the world.

In the morning, Big Drum insisted on going down to Dulag in a Higgins boat. There the 1st Cavalry Division had established a wide perimeter, and there were no signs of battle. Instead, just as they'd been warned, they encountered a chaos of grateful Filipino visitors. The Filipinos brought plantains, sugar cane, bananas and pineapples to the troops and garlanded them with flowers. Big Drum was mobbed. They knew who he was from his time in the Philippines before the war. Old men and women raised adoring faces to him, and children unabashedly sought his hand. Harry Strudwick asked, 'How many of these people are Japanese agents?' And despite Harry's normal negativism, it was a fair question.

Buck confided in Galt. 'I'm going into Tacloban this afternoon. The 29th Division have cleared the streets. I want to find a house we can take over. I'm fed up with that goddamn *Chattanooga*.'

That evening, while everyone was sipping Coca-Cola in the wardroom, Buck arrived back at the ship. He had found a fine Spanish-style villa in Santa Maria Street in Tacloban. It had formerly been the Japanese Officers' Club, and before that the property of Mr Edgar Scotland, the pineapple and sugar-cane magnate who was presently under detention by the Japanese somewhere else in the world, perhaps in Indo-China or Formosa or Japan itself. Some of Ernie Sasser's engineers were already repainting the place and preparing it for the arrival of Big Drum and his staff.

On the fourth day they all went ashore and drove into Tacloban. I am a man in my mid-fifties, Galt told himself, and still all I have to carry with me in the world are two suitcases.

Galt was allocated a fairly small room on the first floor of Scotland's house. Even Big Drum had no more than a spacious bedroom, at one end of which he placed his desk. But there was a verandah and an enclosed garden with a fountain which no longer worked. There were air raids every day, but it seemed to be against the rules to take advantage of the ornate shelter the Japanese had themselves provided in the garden.

On their second afternoon in Scotland's house, Galt heard a pounding on his door. Buck Clancy was there. 'You ought to come and listen to this, Galt.'

Galt followed him down into the room where the radio was kept. A pale sergeant was adjusting the dial to improve reception. He had Radio Tokyo.

'It seems that our friend Big Drum,' said a voice in accented English, 'has been foolish enough to make his headquarters in the Edgar Scotland house on Calle Santa Maria in the middle of Tacloban. Don't worry, General, our bombers and fighters are making their way to you.'

Big Drum had earlier ordered the 1st Cavalry Division unit who provided his headquarters guard to fill in the excellent air raid shelter in the garden. It spoiled the look, he'd said.

At dinner that night, Buck Clancy therefore earned everyone's gratitude by reminding Big Drum of the *kamikaze* pilots. 'General, you have to face it,' said Buck frankly. 'A whole squadron might dedicate themselves to wiping you out.'

Big Drum considered this. Galt could see the old-man obduracy in the muscles of his face, and so felt cold. At last Big Drum said, 'Then we'll see if God wants me round more than those blackguards want to bump me off!'

But Galt recognized that if God was involved, he himself might be punished for what had befallen Allan Lewis. He began to despair of a sane time on Leyte, and even late at night, no longer believing in Big Drum's immutable destiny, fearing the coming of dawn and the intentions of the enemy, doubted the survival of any of Big Drum's people.

The air attacks became more intense as Kremnitz's carriers were drawn away north by the arrival of an enemy task force in the San Bernardino Strait area. In the absence of the US Navy carriers, Pete Andrews found out by reconnaissance that a Japanese fleet from Singapore, which included the *Musima*, whose eighteen-inch guns could flatten Tacloban, was loose in Leyte Gulf to the south. Pete's old cruisers, such as *Chattanooga*, and his makeshift aircraft-carriers fabricated out of old transport ships, could not match this Japanese armada. And while Kremnitz's fighters were away hammering Japanese carriers to the north, the enemy's fighter bombers from Luzon had the sky over Tacloban, and over the Scotland house in Calle Santa Maria for that matter, very nearly to themselves.

After breakfast on their third morning ashore, Big Drum and the staff were just about to move out to a conference on the verandah when Galt felt himself pushed sideways and upwards in a curious way, flying across the breakfast room like a leaf in a vacuum. He bruised his right shoulder against the corner of an old Spanish *credenza* which stood against the far wall. He could not remember afterwards however having heard the noise of a detonation, but he had ringing of the ears for the next two days. For a bomb had landed next door at Calle Santa Maria number 49 and killed a Filipino family and their servants. The plane which had dropped it had no doubt been flying a precision mission, had been able to dodge its way amidst the fire from the many anti-aircraft crews stationed in the city square and around the cathedral. Some brave young enemy flyer had missed Big Drum by one household.

Apart from Galt a few other members of the staff suffered grazes, and Meacham had bitten his tongue to an extent which required stitching. So far as anyone remembered, Big Drum had simply kept on walking towards the verandah. The physics of the explosion had left him unswerving and untouched.

Two years ago Galt would have thought this wondrous, this detachment of Big Drum's, and would have wanted to remain associated with it. Now, however, he wanted to get out. He even began to think that if ever this man became President, he would expect all of America when faced with *kamikazes* to look with a primitive faith to the Deity to decide the issue.

The next morning three fighters strafed the street, laying down tracks of cannon fire from the cathedral square southwards and past the front gate of the Scotland house. Galt, in the living room downstairs, heard that weird metallic, penetrative sound of glass fragmenting, of cannon shells hitting the inside walls and zinging off them, and then re-zinging. He dragged himself up off the floor and found himself rushing up the stairwell. Big Drum, he knew, was at that moment in his bedroom office.

Arriving on the landing, Galt did not bother knocking but rushed inside. Big Drum was standing by the end of his bed, waving his hand in the air as if it had been burned. Blood dripped from the ends of three of the fingers. 'Look, Galt, I was hit by a splinter of wood from my bedhead.' He flicked more blood on to the polished wooden floor. 'I've had worse problems running up bookshelves for Mrs Wraith.'

A strange and fortuitous – or as Big Drum would have it – *Godsent* – thing happened then. The Japanese admiral who was bearing down on Pete Andrews's makeshift fleet with *Musima* and all the other heavy battleships, pulled away. The experts said afterwards that it was because he believed that Kremnitz would come back and block his passage out of Leyte Gulf. Others said it was because the Japanese admiral aboard *Musima* misread an order Pete Andrews gave to his inferior force of carrier-borne fighters. He ordered them to land on Leyte so that they wouldn't be destroyed on the decks of the escort carriers, to go to the bottom of the Gulf with the rest of Pete's force. The enemy may have misinterpreted the landing of these aircraft on Leyte's airstrips as a build-up. Whatever the cause, not only did the threat of the *Musima* recede, but Kremnitz came south again, and his fighters were available to further Big Drum's – and God's – intentions in Leyte. Above all, they were able to chase the enemy's raiders away from Tacloban.

You had to admire Ernie Sasser. His engineers had an airstrip near Tacloban fit to receive the big bombers within five days.

A day later Buck Clancy brought in his first Liberators and Super Fortresses. They landed on raised, drained and reinforced sand. Galt did not go out to see them touch down, but the report of their arrival cheered him. It meant that Dim could not be far behind.

Then, as a result of the capture of more airstrips in the Moluccas north of New Guinea and the enlargement of fuel tanks, Buck's fighters appeared. Hal Metzger had been panicking on the west coast of Leyte by the arrival of the Japanese 13th Division, shipped from Luzon overnight, but now their positions were hammered by Buck's fighters and Hal was more composed.

Galt, in his office-bedroom, had access through Captain Duncan to the lists of priority by which personnel should arrive in Leyte from Hollandia. When it was considered safe for senior administrative nursing and hospital staff to turn up, he advanced Dim's name to join them. There was a villa by the loamy road south to Dulag where the officer-nurses and Dim could be billeted. He made arrangements that they should be.

Wearing the uniform of a US Women's Army Corps captain, feeling that it was still alien to her and that she was acting a part, Dim touched down in Tacloban at dusk aboard a B-29 which carried five other female officers. They all felt tired and disgruntled – it had been nearly a twenty-four-hour flight across a monsoonal sky. Three of them had been airsick, and the irony was that Dim, who was the only one amongst them not a nurse, had spent a great part of the night and day on board tending one or other of her comrades.

Now they were led through the hordes of cheering Filipinos who met every plane and conducted the newly arrived heroes and heroines to their vehicles. Fortunately, it was only a ten-minute drive down a muddy road to the bungalow where she and the nurses were quartered. They approached its front steps across a steamy tropical garden of the kind they were all used to by now. The house looked large, but it lacked glass in its windows. For ventilation, the shutters were propped open. The young male driver who dropped them there told them there wasn't any electricity yet, but they'd find storm lanterns inside. The wash-houses – by which like all Americans he meant the lavatories as well – were at the back of the house.

He excused himself and drove away.

Inside, they found the promised lanterns, but there was no furniture at all. There were no chairs nor beds. But this after all was wartime, and they were all practical women, so everyone bravely spread her clothing and her musette bag, and lay on those.

Chatting before sleep in the faint light of a lantern, they all discussed Dim's accent and asked her where she'd nursed before. She told them she'd been Entertainment Officer in Moresby and then Hollandia. 'Maybe they shipped me up here a bit prematurely,' she said. 'Maybe I could come and help out at the hospital. I mean, write letters for the boys and so on.'

'Sure,' they said.

Their leader was a small, chunky lieutenant called Merle who said, 'Here we are, nervous of you and wondering if we ought to call you *Ma'am*. Because you outranked us.'

'I've been called *Ma'am* by the best,' said Dim, smiling. She told them to call her Dim, and then gave the inevitable explanation of her name, and then they all fell asleep.

In the morning, jeeps arrived to take the nurses to the base hospital, and Dim travelled with them. She was tormented by excitement. At some stage, she knew, Galt would turn up.

As she suggested she might, she went around the wards writing letters for soldiers. She had brought an extra supply of stationery. The hospital staff were politely mystified to see a captain engaged in such work, but on the scale of the other mysteries of war, it scarcely mattered and they did not spend time worrying about it.

When that afternoon she came back with the others, Galt's jeep was waiting. She could tell, because it had three stars on the bonnet, which confused the nurses. She knew she would have to bear them putting two and two together. As she and the others went up the stairs, he came out. As the others passed inside, he clung to her with a sort of gratitude. She felt that he was no longer in command, her Chief of Staff.

'There's no furniture,' he told her, almost at once. Obviously, he had been doing his own recce of the house.

'My friends and I are fully aware of that, Galt,' she told him. 'Doesn't matter to me, but they deserve a bed.'

'For Christ's sake, I'll talk to that little prick Sasser. You'll have beds by tomorrow night.'

'In the meantime, Galt,' she said, 'we have to do what can be done.' She drew him into the room where she had spread all the clothing from her musette bag to make a soft surface. There she astounded him, if he were not astounded already, with her tenderness and her hunger.

'This place will look like the Taj Mahal by the time I've finished with that little prick Sasser,' Galt promised her.

After he went that night, only Merle was still up. She said, 'The girls and I don't think you came up here too early. You came just in time for some people.'

'I suppose you all despise me,' Dim suggested.

'We don't despise anyone, honey. We've seen everything.'

'That's good. Because I love that man.'

'Oh dearie. He won't marry you. Generals never do.'

'At some stage, when we know each other better,' said Dim, 'I'll tell you all about it.'

The next morning Ernie Sasser, in the midst of arranging for the reinforcing and paving of a second field on Leyte, would receive a demand from Galt Sandforth that a certain villa down the coast, towards Dulag and quite near the major base hospital, should be furnished by his team as a matter of priority.

Galt would learn of subsequent events only afterwards, partly through reliable repute, and partly through overhearing the boasts of his enemies.

Ernie Sasser, it appears, went and complained to Harry Strudwick about Galt's demand for the immediate furnishing of a nurses' quarters near Dulag. Wondering what to do about Galt Sandforth's hubris, Harry fell back on suggesting that Ernie's powers of telepathy might be a possible strategy.

That afternoon there was yet another air raid on a nearby quarter of Tacloban. During it, Ernie sought his chief, Big Drum, who, he knew, would be pacing on the verandah. They exchanged a few items of rudimentary conversation, and then Ernie, at his invitation, sat down with him and – while Big Drum fell into a brown study – began to concentrate. What Ernie concentrated on was the image of Captain Dim Lewis, the triumphant and queenly Dim Lewis – so Ernie saw it – of Hollandia. A number of Zero Mitsubishis wheeled overhead, but everyone was used to them, and fortunately they gave up in the face of solid anti-aircraft fire from the town square and headed away. Big Drum, in particular, had assimilated them into his scheme of things long ago and was able to go on meditating throughout.

Ernie thought this reflective mood was exactly right for his own purposes.

'Thanksgiving coming up, Ernie,' murmured Big Drum dreamily. 'Impossible to dash down to Brisbane from here. There's the distance first. Then there's the situation. I don't like Mrs Wraith and the boy spending it on their own.'

Ernie did not bother offering any conventional regrets about this. He went on concentrating.

The trouble with the situation had been partly that Hal Metzger was moving his troops forward too slowly, and with unnecessary caution, southwards from Dulag, whereas Bryant Gibbs's men were already flying the Stars and Stripes and the Filipino national flag from the steeple of the church of Ormoc on the west coast of Leyte. Hal could, unless taken by the scruff, waste months achieving his objectives.

Then there were the unexpected quantities of Japanese aircraft still flying over from Luzon, Manila's island, every day. Kremnitz was due to pull his carriers out by early December, so Ernie's engineers were rushing to produce airstrips amidst the continual rain.

Not only did Ernie make little response to Big Drum's wistful reflection about Thanksgiving, he made himself feel calm about the fact that at a point when his engineers were needed for construction work, he was being harried by a confident Galt Sandforth into assigning some of them to move furniture down the road for Galt's paramour. More exactly, what Ernie did was feed out that anger carefully, thin as a spider web, sharp also and focused, in Big Drum's direction.

A middle-aged Filipino housekeeper who had attached herself to Big Drum and the staff, brought the two gentlemen a jug of lemonade. She had been Mr Scotland's maid, she had announced. She knew where Mrs Scotland was. Mrs Scotland was a Filipina herself and was with the Huks, the rebels. So were her two adolescent children. The General and his gentlemen, said the housekeeper, shouldn't be surprised if Mrs Scotland turned up some day to greet them. She would not want to intrude upon them though. She would be honoured that the General was using her house.

Setting down the lemonade for Big Drum and Ernie that morning the housekeeper said nothing. She could tell neither of the gentlemen wanted chatter.

Ernie was concentrating all the while on the image of Dim at her healthiest and – since he *did* find her desirable – most luscious. Delectable in her ill-fitting khakis and Aussie bush hat and gaiters. Big Drum said nothing more throughout this phase of Ernie's meditation. Perhaps he was even affected by it.

Then, after a time Ernie conjured up an image of the Australian Prime Minister, Big Drum's socialist friend, before returning again to – as it were – transmitting Captain Dim Lewis.

It seemed after perhaps ten minutes of this that the results were not going to be worth while.

Big Drum coughed and came out of his reverie. He sipped his lemonade and said, 'Do you know, Ernie, I wrote the President from Red Beach, on Signal Corps notepaper. A sincere letter. But I'm sure when he gets it, he'll tell himself that I wasn't really there, that I was probably writing it from somewhere safe offshore. Very hard to document these things, Ernie. If you want to be brave to impress others, you have to take account of the fact that people don't want to believe you're brave. That goes for a lot of people. Especially Democrats.'

Ernie made a few token noises of assent and kept projecting the appropriate images.

Suddenly, Big Drum said, very affirmatively, 'I should have taken the time to write to the Australian Prime Minister. Now he might be of the same political ilk as the Democrats, but he would have believed me.'

Ernie agreed and concentrated all the harder on memories of Dim, the jewel incongruously set in an ill-fitting Australian army uniform. This seemed to produce another long silence, during which Big Drum sipped more lemonade. Then he took out the amber cigarette-holder again from his breast pocket and began sucking on it, his normal instrument of reflection.

His mouth bunched up, he said, 'That Australian girl. You

know, the one who was at Lennon's and looked after our movies. What happened with her after we moved on up here to Leyte?'

'General,' said Ernie, 'I really hesitate to answer that.'

'Hesitate?'

'I don't want to earn Galt's enmity.'

Big Drum took the cigarette-holder clear of his mouth. It was buried in his fist.

'And you don't want to earn mine either. Anyhow, what's this stuff about Galt's enmity? She'd be back in Queensland or Moresby somewhere, wouldn't she? Or is she still in Hollandia?'

'Since the General asks, I can tell you that she is ten miles down the coast wearing a US captain's uniform and insisting that her house be furnished.'

That caused Big Drum to stand up abstractedly. He walked to the railing of the verandah.

'Ernie, you are certain about this?'

'If I weren't, General, I wouldn't have said it.'

'You saw her with your own eyes?'

'Not me personally. Some of my officers have.'

Big Drum thought about this. 'Son of a bitch,' he murmured. Then louder, '*Son of a bitch*! Ernie, be so kind as to fetch Captain Duncan and tell him I want to see Sandforth upstairs *quam primum*! You understand? Instantly.'

His voice had risen and grown in passion so that any bystander would have thought he was angry with Ernie. He stamped upstairs. Two soldiers of the 1st Cavalry Division stood at the base of the stairs, holding semi-automatics. They were there to protect Big Drum from assassination, since it would be quite feasible for the Japanese to send in a suicide hit squad, ideally consisting of a few Filipinos, who would have protective colouring amongst the population of Tacloban. Big Drum actually jostled these two young men as they stood to attention. They, too, wondered if he were angry with them.

The last thing Big Drum said before he went into his office was a loud, '*Now*!' It sounded as if he were making some cosmic demand.

Galt had already heard that one word. He wondered what it meant. Within seconds Duncan was at his office door telling him that the General wanted to see him. 'I was told, General Sandforth, it has to be immediate,' said Duncan apologetically.

Galt approached Big Drum's bedroom/office door with a strange mixture of taut apprehension and joy. Was this, he wondered, to be the settling of affairs with Big Drum, the letting loose of all the opinions both of them had kept secret since the Philippine days?

He had barely knocked before he was told to come in.

'Close the door, General Sandforth,' Big Drum roared from the place where he sat, by the window, presenting his back to any strafing aircraft. His face had gone dangerously puce.

Galt obeyed him and closed the door. 'You son of a bitch, Sandforth,' said Big Drum in a tight, low voice. He hadn't called Galt 'Sandforth' since the very earliest days of their association in Manila.

His voice rose. 'Didn't I tell you in Hollandia to issue an order about all Australian auxiliaries? Did you do that?'

'Yes, General.'

'And what in the fuck is your girlfriend doing down the coast? I believe she's wearing a US Army captain's uniform. What's she doing down there? Making demands of the engineers?'

'So Ernie Sasser's been whispering to you, General?' said Galt.

'Listen, Galt, Ernie answered a direct order for information. He did not volunteer this. Ernie has no malice. He's not the one wandering round the Pacific with his prick hanging out his flies.'

This is a different man, Galt thought. For Big Drum rarely descended to these barrack-room insults, and they had all the more impact for that now. He felt the blood leaving his face, rushing for shelter around his heart.

'And now the bitch,' raged Big Drum, 'is demanding furniture!'

'General, please moderate what you're saying. I am the one who demanded furniture. The nursing officers have none.'

'General Sandforth, you have been completely unhinged by this Australian woman . . . '

'No. I intend to marry her.'

'Well, that's just great!' Big Drum roared. Galt was sure that throughout the house, throughout the centre of town, officers were listening in to this exchange which, in military terms, Galt knew he couldn't win. 'That's just great,' Big Drum repeated. 'That will make great copy if I should choose to allow myself to be drafted for a political career! The Democrat press will love that. You're a fool, Galt. You're a damn fool. And you're a liar. You told me that you would not only issue that order but obey it.'

'Like all soldiers of good sense, I try to obey the letter of the law.'

'Letter of the law! For God's sake, Galt. I don't have Mrs Wraith here with me, and she's my lawful wife. You chose to introduce this damned whore into my headquarters and into my battlefront . . . '

'Again, General, I have to ask you to respect my feelings.'

'Feelings? You're driven by so-called feelings, Galt, especially those below the waist. You have lost moral bearings.' It wasn't any cigarette holder but the quite terrible instrument of his index finger which Big Drum now directed at Galt. 'You betrayed me. It's incredible.'

'I was encouraged to,' said Galt. He knew he was destroying his career, yet he felt liberated to be at such work. 'You betrayed me twice, General. The first time you betrayed me by betraying yourself – over that stupid matter of the Wisconsin primary.'

'Don't be absurd, General Sandforth. I wasn't meant to be in Washington this year. I was meant to be here. That is obvious. Everything that happens here, every thwarting of the enemy demonstrates that fact. I am not some priapic fool whose head is ruled by his testicles. This is an outrage, what you have done! It will stand as an historic outrage and betrayal.'

Galt waved that aside with his right hand. *Where does this daring come from?* he wondered. *They may very well court-martial you.* Yet reprimand, dismissal, reduction in rank, all meant so little to him he wondered why they had meant so much for thirty-five years of army life. As long as they let him explain it all first to Sandy, his daughter.

He insisted, 'I haven't finished talking about betrayal, General. I find that the Joint Chiefs were willing to give me command of Sixth Army, because no one's really happy with Metzger. Look what's happening down the coast with him now. Your army limps, General. Bryant Gibbs runs, Hal Metzger crawls. Anyhow, you didn't even ask me about it. About whether I'd make a good commander, or would like to be one? You didn't ask me what I thought. You told them no for me, and you told me nothing!'

'Who tells you this horseshit?' Big Drum roared. They would certainly be able to hear such a roar on the steps of the Tacloban cathedral. 'That's rubbish. I'm happy with Hal. He's a cool head. I was happy with you in your position too. But what sort of army commander would *you* make?'

'A damn good one, General!'

'You would? With your tart in tow? Well if you would have, you've blown it all out your ass now, General Sandforth. You are under house arrest. You'll eat your meals in your quarters and a corporal's guard will escort you to the bathroom. I forbid you under pain of court martial to communicate with Captain Lewis. Don't think of sliding down the ivy to visit her. You won't find her on Leyte. I am giving orders for her expulsion, and I assure you they will be very quickly effected.'

Galt felt genuinely frightened for the first time. 'Where are you sending her?'

'Hollandia, of course. I don't necessarily wish to punish her. You are the culprit, General Sandforth, God help you!'

For Dim's sake he was willing to plead. 'If she is not culpable then, let me talk to her. Just once.'

'She's heard from you too often,' said Big Drum. 'Staff-sergeant,' he bellowed then, and the door opened and there were the young men who were to keep this middle-aged lover under house arrest.

It was raining at the base hospital, that place of increasing size, which grew prefabricated wards every day it existed. There Surgeon-General Meacham had his headquarters, and Dim would sometimes see him in the wards and look up to him without being abashed, the way Galt had advised her to be in her demeanour towards the conspirators. He did not seem to notice her.

She had spent dispiriting days. Certainly she wrote letters for the wounded and the sufferers from malaria and gonorrhoea – Hal Metzger's boys had made eager contact already with the liberated Filipina women – but she knew she was supernumerary. At any stage, generally just after she had established contact, found out where the sick or wounded man was from, begun to write to his dictation, the real workers, the true professionals, would intrude and bear the patient off to surgery or therapy or for tests.

Galt had assured her that this situation would last only a matter of weeks or at most for a few months. But even a morning at the base hospital passed for Dim as slowly as a term at boarding school.

She was writing a letter for a boy from Georgia who had been struck in the hip by a Nambu machine gun round and who, it was expected, would have to spend the rest of his life with a stick, when an officer wearing the flashes of the US Military Police appeared. It was Karpinsky, who so long ago, in the garden of the Administration villa in Moresby, had nearly convinced Ray Harris that he was a saboteur.

'Captain Karpinsky, ma'am,' he told Dim, 'I wonder if I could see you for a second.'

Dim excused herself with the patient from Georgia and walked down the ward with Karpinsky.

'Ma'am,' he said, 'I have assigned a guard to take you to your quarters, where you are to collect your belongings. They are to stay with you until you are placed aboard a transport or a bomber returning to Hollandia, probably this evening.'

'You must be mistaken,' she told him. It was a sentence she would use a lot that day.

Karpinsky said, 'Ma'am, there's no room for argument. These orders come from the highest source.'

'Telephone General Sandforth. He'll clarify the whole thing. Obviously you have me mixed up with someone else.'

'General Sandforth is under house arrest, ma'am. Don't make things difficult. If you were a male, I'd cuff you, ma'am. But you're a lady, and I respect you, and I know you'll do the right thing.'

'I'll just call General Sandforth, nonetheless.'

'Ma'am, General Sandforth is incommunicado. And you're refused all calls. Don't make it hard.'

Dim began to weep and felt stupid for doing so. It was what Karpinsky would have expected. 'But I still have to write a letter for that boy.'

'That boy will find someone else to write his letter.'

He saw her into a jeep in which three armed MPs wearing the shiniest of helmets sat. The men who did the fighting never looked as martial as these fellows. As they drove her away, Karpinsky waved.

They went to the bungalow, where the nurses had been sleeping on rattan mats, their possessions bundled around them, and Dim uncomprehendingly packed her duffel bag and her suitcase, protesting all the time but being told she would not be permitted use of a phone, that that was specifically excluded in their orders.

She wanted to know one crucial thing: had Galt fallen from grace? She wanted to be there to comfort him if he had.

But there was an alternative scenario as well. Had Galt himself for some reason, under some pressure – blackmail, a sense of the danger of his situation – decided to ship her out? The sergeant of Military Police said in passing, to hurry her along, 'General Sandforth is under house arrest.' She felt cold as she had under the impact of the malaria. She impotently wanted to liberate him, to plead with Big Drum.

But as the afternoon wore on, as they waited at the airstrip for an evening transport to land, she began to get an irrational suspicion that it all might be different from what she was imagining, and that even if he was a prisoner he might not be a victim of the situation but a maker of it.

Not that she had the luxury of quiet thought. By four o'clock she was in the belly of a C-54, grinding its way down one of Ernie Sasser's new runways, finding height, leaving Leyte, wheeling north along the liberated coast before doing another turn and heading south down the gulf for Hollandia. The aircraft was empty, except for three wounded on stretchers and a medical orderly. Against the noise of the engines, she talked aloud, expressing her utter belief in Galt, because she knew that that would dispel her misery.

Night overtook the C-54 from the west and the medical orderly shared some K-rations with Dim.

She slept miserably for two hours, and then drowsed for the rest of the night. She was looking out on the port when the sun came up. The wounded were asleep – the orderly believed in sedation, and sedation was probably a good option to make the long flight tolerable.

Below her now she could see islands, but she was tired of the sight of islands and no longer speculated what they were – Moluccas? Marianas? The geography of the Pacific not only defeated her, she felt she was out of it now. Just as these three boys were out of it.

They landed at Hollandia at mid-morning. Dim left the plane not knowing whether she would be met by a guard of MPs or not. But there was no one waiting for her. There was no room for her in the ambulance which met the plane. She got a lift into town in the cabin of a truck which had met another plane, one flying in a new Army postal section from Hawaii.

'I'll tell you where my office is,' she said to the driver. She was so weary, so sapped of will. She knew that not only would she not be welcome at the White House, with whoever occupied it at the moment, but that she did not want to go there anyhow.

The first point of reference in nearly twenty-four dismal hours presented itself when she walked into her old office in a complex of prefabricated huts down the hill from the White House, and found her former assistant, Hutchinson, now a staff sergeant, sitting at the desk.

'Captain,' he said, 'Gee, you don't look so healthy. Allow me, ma'am, to find you some coffee. And I've got all your Aussie Army pay packets here. I really admire a lady who can afford to leave her pay behind.'

She reported to the US Personnel office and found that she was still seconded to Big Drum's army. Someone had sent a signal saying she was coming. So whoever had exiled her from Leyte had not been utterly lacking in humanity. For sleeping quarters she was given a room in a prefabricated hut occupied by American WAC officers. Hutchinson insisted that she sleep for the afternoon, which she did reluctantly. For though she was exhausted, she feared that she would awake to questions. If Big Drum had ordered her eviction, had Galt consented to it? Had old affections and old political ambitions in the end won out?

Lying on her bunk all afternoon, she found that her mind was drawn to the question of a child. She wished she had one. She wished she had Galt's child. Despite her fears about him, she wanted the growing comfort of his child within her. On top of the normal sweats of a monsoonal afternoon, she began to sweat with anxiety that she might be barren. The contraceptive device the gynaecologist had given her was not supposed to be one hundred per cent certain. Yet in all the time she had been with Galt, she had never felt the alarm or excitement of a potential pregnancy.

Chapter 17

Peanut Brittle

EVERYWHERE THAT EARLY December of 1944 there was victory. The Germans had been driven back to the Vistula by the Soviets, the British and Americans were on the western German border. The war would end soon. Half asleep, for the first time she imagined her post-war self. Lacking Galt, she had nowhere to go. She could not imagine herself living with Allan in Maneering while he law-clerked for his father. She could not imagine herself running the office and keeping the stud books for her father. The life with Galt made her a stranger to her parents. She wrote to them weekly, and received letters in reply. Her mother wanted to know why it was two and a half years since she had had a home leave. She said she knew combatants – Blue Riley's son, for example – who'd had a home leave from New Guinea in that time. Dim couldn't explain that her leave had been spent with Galt.

As the awesomely familiar afternoon rain pounded down on the roof of her quarters, she would have been nearly happy to have had her life end there.

Except she wanted to know what the hell had happened to Galt.

A corporal of the 1st Cavalry Division was under orders to lock Galt in when he went to wash or shave or perform bodily functions. Galt had to knock on the inside of the door when he was finished. Galt chose to be amused by all that rigmarole. He would do a jolly, jazzy rat-tat-tat on the door, and the young man with the semi-automatic would open it, looking far more uncomfortable than Galt himself intended ever to look.

'Soldier,' Galt said to him one morning in a lowered voice,

'this experience must answer one of the quandaries of life in the ranks. Namely, whether the shit of generals smells like roses.'

If they wanted to discuss anything with him, the others had to come to his room. He was still compiling plans for an amphibious landing in Lingayen Gulf on Luzon, north of Manila. Everyone in Tacloban knew that this would be the climax of their association with Big Drum. Harry and Ernie and Buck Clancy would come in singly or together for conferences and take pains to pretend they didn't know what had happened to Galt, or that they didn't know why he was under house arrest.

Ernie and Harry were studiously polite. They seemed to feel pretty secure anyhow. They knew that without direct access to telephone or radio contact with the United States – an absurd situation for a Chief of Staff, but one which did not impair his efficiency – he lacked means to punish them. In any case, if he tried to produce his evidence of graft against them now, Big Drum would certainly pull out all the stops against Galt. On massive evidence, Galt would be court-martialled, disgraced. What the army left of him, the press would devour.

And what Ernie and Harry could tell by instinct was that now he lacked the malice to take revenge against them. They could sense that the one thing he feared had happened – he had lost Dim through Big Drum's finding out about her and taking irreversible action. Dim was the one element of his life which mattered any more in a fundamental way.

Even Hal Metzger and Bryant Gibbs came sometimes to see him. Bryant made one frank reference to Galt's position. 'Sorry to see you in this fix, Galt. You're still our Chief of Staff, though.'

And Galt was confident that he would be able to talk things out with Buck, as soon as Buck had reason to visit Galt's bedroom/office on his own.

During his house-arrest, Galt had a little time to consider Big Drum's reasons for treating him in a way that some people would think was lenient. Was it sentiment, or the acute necessity not to disrupt staff work, or the fear that Galt knew about Rivez and the $400,000? Galt did not even know whether Big Drum knew about Galt's hold over him in the Rivez matter. It didn't matter anyhow. In a way, Galt didn't respect Big Drum enough anymore to blackmail him. He knew he couldn't win that particular game with Big Drum anyhow.

What preoccupied him were plans to contact and reassure Dim.

At last, on the third evening of Galt's house arrest, Buck Clancy appeared at the door on his own. He had brought some Scotch whisky with him, correctly surmising that such rare comforts of the household were forbidden to Galt. By bringing the bottle he indicated that he was willing for friendship's sake to violate the strict letter of Big Drum's law in Tacloban.

The corporal keeping guard closed the door on the two generals. Buck sat to one side of Galt's desk, which was covered with reports and maps and the massive operational plans, the final editing and collating of whose elements it was Galt's job to supervise.

Buck Clancy poured two tumblers of neat whisky. 'This is the way my Irish daddy drank it,' he told Galt.

They sipped together. After the turmoils and hostilities of the past days, it *was* like something Celtic, a kind of honest sacrament. The taste of reconciliation. Very bitter though.

'I'm not complaining, Buck. But I like it better with ice.'

'Most goddamn Protestants do,' said Buck, smiling and relishing a second mouthful. Then Buck looked him in the eye. 'We all need you, Galt. We need you to stay as good as you've been.'

'I'll work on as long as Big Drum wants me. Like clockwork, Buck.'

'I've already told him I can't do anything without you there, handling the negativism of Harry Strudwick and pushing Ernie along. You're a great co-ordinator, Galt.'

Galt laughed. 'It's not what I set out in life to be called, but it'll do.'

'You sound bitter,' said Buck. 'OK, I'll be frank with you, Galt. You can't expect people who don't know you to be sympathetic. There are young men dying. No one else has his girl with him. But here's this middle-aged general who does . . . '

'I've heard that argument. It's cogent as hell. It's particularly cogent if you're not in my skin.'

'OK, OK. I'm not judging. My background is that divorce is

contrary to God's will, but if it's so, maybe you're invincibly ignorant of that.'

'Come on, Buck. With the greatest respect, I don't want you trying to shoehorn me into Paddy heaven. As you rightly say, there are young men throughout Leyte having their blood and grey matter strewn around the jungle. There are Japanese nineteen-year-olds being frittered with napalm flamethrowers. What I'm saying is, beside all that, a little divorce barely breaks the contour of God's landscape.'

'I know,' said Buck. 'I know. There are two ways of looking at these things. But you can't expect outsiders to be sympathetic, that's all I'm saying, even though I may be. After all, I know you, I know the woman.'

'Buck, I have an enormous favour to ask. Big Drum had the Military Police ship her out instantaneously and without explanation. She won't know what's happened here – she may even think that I ordered her expulsion. I know you're a compassionate fellow, Buck. For sweet Christ's sake, could you send a signal to her. Give her some indication what's happened. Tell her everything stands between us.'

'Oh geez, I can't do that, Galt. Big Drum said there can't be any radio traffic involving you unless it's authorized by him.'

'No one's going to supervise a little routine radio transmission like this. Please.'

Buck shook his head – it was not a refusal to do what Galt asked but rather a sign that he felt beset. 'Look, Galt, you must have been on the lookout for a girl, for God's sake. When it all started. Sorry to sound like a father confessor, but you can't tell me you didn't court this.'

'I saw her at a silly cocktail party in Government House in Melbourne, long before you even arrived in Australia, Buck. And yes, I was looking for a convenient lover. But I wasn't asking for what's happened with Dim. I didn't expect to learn certain virtues – devotion and loyalty and a little humility. Look, Buck, this thing is decent, what I'm asking you to do. I would be enormously grateful. It would put me out of torment, and Dim too. I hope you're not quite ready yet to consign Dim to the flames.'

'I suppose you want her to be told you still intend to marry her?'

'I want you to tell her that in words suitable to radio transmissions.'

'Damn you, Galt. You ask for a lot.'

They composed a signal that read:

To Captain D. Lewis Australian Women's Army Corps on secondment US Army Headquarters Hollandia Dutch New Guinea stop

A senior officer of my acquaintance presently prevented by order of his superiors from communicating junior Australian staff wishes it placed on record that your recent transfer Hollandia not result of any order of his stop

Wishes me to communicate intention to make contact at earliest opportunity stop Orders are for you to remain at post pending further contact stop Indicates conditions of earlier arrangements yourself and Chief of Staff Southwest Pacific area remain as before stop

Signed: Lieutenant General Clancy Fifth US AAF

In Hollandia one steamy morning, the horror of a solitary Christmas ahead of her, Dim received and signed for Clancy's signal. Urgent radio communications were a rare event for her, and she opened the unsealed envelope in which the radio flimsy was delivered in some confusion. It might be news of Allan. But she soon found it was the sort of message she wanted.

It elated her and made the world habitable again for her. There was the miracle of Galt's having made contact, and the miraculous compassion of Buck Clancy who, though straitlaced about adultery, had enough soul to take pity on her desperate bewilderment. 'Presently prevented by order of his superiors . . .' There was only one superior to Galt in Leyte. Big Drum was punishing him. And it was her fault. The transfer to Leyte in the wrong uniform had never seemed a credible move to her, and she should have resisted it. But there was a reason to wait now: she needed to ask him to forgive her. She needed to soothe him for the humiliation she'd brought him. For some reason she couldn't understand, she was confident of her role.

Within two weeks a short note from Galt was delivered to her, not through the regular mail channels but by a young officer from Bryant Gibbs's staff on his way through to Brisbane. Galt was calling in all his old favours.

He was not, he said in the letter, Big Drum's number one boy. He said he was surprised how pleased he felt about that. Though under house arrest, he continued to operate as Chief of Staff, and would continue to do so until Manila fell. After that, he would arrange everything along the lines they had discussed earlier.

The letter was signed, 'Yours in the open and till the end, Galt'. That was the most expressive thing he said in the whole letter. The rest was written in a kind of code – phrases such as 'plans as earlier discussed'. Dim presumed that that was in case the letter fell into the hands of others.

There was other brief advice in the letter. One sentence: 'Be proud.'

And indeed, like Galt, she did not feel that she had fallen from grace, but that she had ascended to it.

She began to work with gusto again. She enjoyed Hollandia now that it was an exquisite backwater from which the Harry Strudwicks and Ernie Sassers of the world had passed on. It was good to examine herself apart from all that, to re-encounter herself, to look out over a Lake Sentani which was not connected anymore to the Big Plan or even to Galt, over a wildly blue surface with which she could now make contact in her own right.

Bombers kept taking off and landing around Humboldt and Tanahmerah Bays. There were hospitals where men who suffered malaria or had been hit by diehard snipers in the Vogelkop Peninsula were treated.

Since the Australian Army was still operating in New Guinea engaged in the long slow business of finishing things off in the hinterland between Aitape and Hollandia and in the island of Bougainville, she would occasionally see Australians – medical teams, journalists – running around Hollandia in jeeps. She sometimes looked to see if her friend Stacey was amongst them. She watched out for him because she would have liked to have a drink with him.

In fact, as if summoned by the thought, Stacey presented himself with a lean diffidence, appearing in her office as he had once before in Port Moresby. He seemed much more subdued than when she had first met him and was wary, too; she could see all the old insouciance was gone. He did not smile as easily, and she was aware – with relief but also a strange regret – that he was no longer burdened with painful and unreal respect for her.

'I've got plenty to tell you, Dim,' he said. 'But this isn't the right place for it. I don't suppose you've got time for a drink?' He suggested the new American Officers' Club up on the ridge by the White House.

The place – when they got there – was overdone with Christmas decorations. No wall was free of clammy lumps of cotton wool doing their best to imitate snow. Dim and Stacey signed themselves in and then sat at a table on the verandah. The monsoon which was causing Buck Clancy so much trouble on Leyte was in full swing above the waterfall where earlier Galt and Dim had enjoyed their picnic. Again, she felt gratitude that the view was untainted by the presence of the staff, by all the skilful deceptions and strategies of leverage by which she and Galt had felt bound to live.

She ordered a gin and tonic. There was no doubt that it was the drink for this climate, though tea was still her favourite. Stacey ordered a bottle of iced Carlton beer. The drink of his home city, Melbourne. Stacey was a local patriot!

He drank the first half glass at a gulp. Then, after two seconds of savouring, he announced, 'I know about you and Big Drum's Chief of Staff, Dim.'

She was not prepared for this. She had expected him to talk about his own problems as a correspondent under the regimen of Big Drum's press office. Taken by surprise, she blushed primitively. But she felt angry at him, too, for springing this on her.

'Obviously, he didn't tell you that I knew. Well, no reason he should have. But anyhow, I know.'

'Have you come to stone the woman taken in adultery?' Dim asked, just firmly enough to let him know that he wasn't to take liberties, that she'd had enough of people doing that.

'Don't be silly. He loves you, Dim. I think he's an absolute bastard, if you want to know. But the fact that he loves you so well speaks in his favour.'

'Did he tell you he was going to marry me?'

'Yes. He's definite about that. You've opened doors for him, Dim. You've made him a different sort of man. As I say, you're the redeeming feature. He'd be mad not to marry you, and he understands it. Again, top marks to him . . . '

'Bastard that he is,' said Dim, half smiling – but again with an edge of protest at Stacey's attitude.

'Exactly,' said Stacey.

'How did you and he have a conversation?' Dim wanted to know.

'I'm a newsman. Strudwick tried to involve me in the big Chief-of-Staff-has-a-girlfriend scandal.'

'My God. And you mean you wouldn't do it?'

'Of course not. My God, you know I wouldn't, Dim. I warned Sandforth.' He showed a trace of a smile, but there was bitterness on his side too.

Dim thought about that. She felt tears burning one eye, the left. How ridiculous. She felt a little sweat too break out on her brow and her upper lip. That had happened regularly since her fever. She must have had some tear duct problem with the right eye. She could weep lopsidedly, as was appropriate for a person in a bit of a moral fix.

'I'm very honoured, Paul,' she said. 'I'm a very ordinary woman. I don't have high intelligence or even astounding good looks. But I'm honoured by friends like you.'

'Enough of the plaudits then,' said Stacey shaking his head. 'Dim, I wanted to get that out of the way. I didn't want you to think that what I'm going to tell you has anything to do with hurt pride for having suffered a rebuff. But you obviously haven't heard anything about what I now have to say. When I heard that you were in Hollandia, I thought you might know. But it's obvious that you don't.'

She was frowning, but he put a hand up to prevent questions and kept on. 'And I think you should know. I think you ought to talk to Honor Runcie too. Or I will.' He shook his head. 'Jesus, Dim, this is the worst story I've had to tell anyone. It looks as though Allan is dead.'

Her head began to ring as if she had been struck a blow. She wondered would she simply fall forward on the table. Stacey held up her gin and tonic to her mouth and made her take a sip.

'Sorry, Dim,' he said with a compassion she couldn't doubt.

It was frightful and yet she had always known it. Why had there been no news all this time? No letters? Do people stay on Special Operations, living underground on some island, for as long as that? She had convinced herself they did, and yet now that conviction looked shabby and insupportable.

'He can't be,' she pleaded.

'I'm sorry, Dim. There are eye-witnesses.'

'Gordon Runcie too?' she asked.

'No. But there are a few people who think he might be better off that way.'

The idea first occurred to her right then: Galt must have known. Though someone might have kept the knowledge from him. Clearly lots of people felt malice towards Galt, something she couldn't understand. So he didn't know. She was sure, she told herself, that he didn't know. He'd said so a number of times.

'Look, Dim,' said Stacey, 'I was in Darwin two months ago. Now I went to school with a fellow who is in intelligence there. His name doesn't matter. But one night when we were drinking, he told me about something that had been worrying him for some months. It seemed that there was a Royal Navy fellow in the closed psychiatric ward at Darwin Base Hospital. He had, my friend said, escaped from Timor on a native boat, and one of our vessels on patrol had picked him up. He had been physically ill treated – he was in a mess from beatings and disease. But it was considered he needed mental care. Hence the psychiatric ward.'

'Are you saying that was Runcie,' said Dim with dawning horror. 'But what happened to Allan? What happened? Oh God, if you're saying Runcie's barmy . . . He could be wrong about Allan . . . '

She began to weep uncontrollably now. Earlier, when she'd felt gratified by Stacey's friendship, the tears had come unevenly, the left eye but not to both. There was no question now: they both flowed wildly. Poor, stupid Allan. She felt two convictions – that her infidelity had somehow generated the force which pushed him into his mad endeavours with Runcie. And the second thing she thought was: if Runcie's been in hospital for months, Galt would have been told.

Stacey continued his story. 'My friend thought that Runcie wasn't mad, just angry. It was presumed he was mad though because, even after intelligence explained things to him, he was still furious. So they decided to commit him, more or less until he became calmer about things.'

A wild hope occurred to her. 'But you haven't seen him. You don't know it is Runcie.'

Stacey shook his head to disabuse her. 'I decided I *did* want to see this commander. By this stage Runcie's been there for three months, and people have forgotten him, and security isn't very intense. It took me half a dozen bottles of beer to buy off a ward orderly and get in to see Runcie. I found he's very thin. But he seemed very sharp, very intelligent. His eyes stared a little, and he obviously wasn't getting much sleep. But he certainly told me things, Dim.'

'Things? What damn things, Paul?'

'He claimed that Allan and he had been set up – landed on Timor with instructions to look for landing beaches for amphibious operations and to radio back information of enemy strength, and all that stuff. They were captured within two days. Allan and he were both forced to transmit against their will – apparently they were savagely tortured. I'm sorry Dim. They were forced to transmit Japanese misinformation to Australia. And we transmitted them misinformation in return. Although at the time, Runcie didn't know it was misinformation, and so he and Allan were half-demented from the torture itself and from having given in to it.

'I'm sorry to put things so brutally, Dim. But basically, Allan went mad, so they beheaded him. Apparently his end was quite tranquil, and the beheading sounds barbaric, but they put him out of his misery that way in recognition of his bravery.'

Dim wept more copiously. How was such cruelty possible? Not the brutality of the enemy, but the inhumanity of keeping such essential tidings from her. Evil was supposed to be on the other side.

Stacey now concluded his tale quickly. 'Runcie escaped from his cage, was rescued by the Timorese Resistance and put on the prau on which he was found by our navy. He was already raving at that stage about how he was convinced it was a set-up. If it hadn't been, he said, the Allied troops would have landed on Timor by now. Intelligence tried to explain to him that Timor had been just one option which they wanted explored.'

'But he could have been mistaken,' Dim kept insisting. 'Allan might still be alive. I mean, you say Gordon's a little bit deranged . . . '

'I don't say he's deranged. Army Intelligence does. Those well-known assessors of mental stability. I'm afraid, though, the news of Allan's death doesn't come just from Runcie. Timorese rebels who were taken off the island by a submarine last month confirmed that Allan had been beheaded.'

'Oh God! Oh Jesus!'

He helped her drink some more gin and tonic. 'I'm sorry, Dim. But no one was doing the right thing for you. No one was going to tell you what had happened. Those bastards might well have kept it a secret for years. Might well have told you he was missing in action. So, given that that would have been a crucifixion for you, and no help at all, I've taken it on myself.'

'I've had letters from Honor Runcie, you know.' She'd passed on the inquiries to Galt.

'Well, I'm going to let her know her husband is ultimately coming home. It'll be easier to tell her the news than it was to tell you.'

Now she was able to help herself to her gin and tonic, and took a big draught of it, enough to sting her eyes and cause her to gag a little. 'They could all be wrong. Even those Timorese Resistance people. They could be wrong.'

Stacey merely looked at her and said nothing.
'Why didn't Galt tell me?' she wanted to know, plaintively.
'I don't know. Maybe they weren't telling him either.'
He could see though the tortured scepticism in her.
'Perhaps,' he pursued, 'he didn't want to distress you. And then perhaps his silence went on too long for him to break it without waiting for the right moment. I don't know. Again, I'm sorry to have to raise all these questions.'
She could tell he was: that he was not enjoying this. She felt angry at him for taking away her innocence, and yet contradictorily thankful. She felt a surge of compassion for Allan who would now never be a solicitor in Maneering's main street, would never draft the wills and mortgages of Maneeringites, would never occupy those dull offices within sight of the railway station.
And then there was the question of his parents. They deserved to know. About that there was no doubt between Stacey and Dim. No doubt either about Stacey's neutral morality in all this. Stacey had done the right thing. Knowledge in these matters was essential, a profoundly valued right of the bereaved, if bereaved was what Dim was. 'Let me get you another drink,' suggested Stacey.
'No,' said Dim. 'I wonder could you take me for a drive.'
'Of course.'
She tried not to cry as they left. She knew that the stewards and other guests would make the wrong assumption. This was a lovers' tiff. The tall young Australian had just told his girlfriend that he had a fiancée or wife somewhere at home; had just broken the news. She knew that such assumptions embarrassed a man like Stacey, but she couldn't help him out by refusing to shed tears. No such refusal was possible for the moment.
She felt immediately better once she entered the jeep. It gave her a sort of immunity and privacy she had not had in the club.
'Is there anywhere you'd like me to drive?'
'Let's go and watch the bombers,' said Dim.
They drove to the bomber field near the beach at Humboldt Bay. Here the giant B-29s were lined up on the perimeter, very safe from marauders these days and in this place. She watched

some of them returning from amongst the monsoonal thunderheads. With their huge tanks, they would have been as far away as Luzon or maybe as far as the Japanese bases on Formosa from which reinforcements for the Philippines were sent. God knew what havoc they had wrought where they had been, but it was extraordinarily soothing to watch them come in one by one. She could not believe Allan was gone from this world of graceful American bombers and of monsoons and sheeptowns in Victoria.

'Oh Jesus, I have to talk to Galt,' said Dim.

'I'm not unsympathetic, Dim,' said Stacey. 'But why the rush?'

She looked at an immense bomber banking against the backdrop of coastal mountains. She felt sick and hollowed. If Galt had known, she should have been told. *She* should have been told as soon as *he* knew. There was no other way of looking at it. The two of them were the one mind. That was – as Galt would have said – the deal.

But the hope remained that someone had kept it from him for their own reasons.

'This operation – the one Runcie and Allan were on?' she asked, not quite knowing where the question came from, the tears suddenly stopping. 'Would Galt have known about it? I mean beforehand? I mean, he wouldn't have had to authorize it . . .?'

Before Stacey gave his uncertain and confused answer, she was ashamed of herself for thinking this of Galt.

After two weeks, the young captain of the headquarters company, 1st Cavalry, commanding the troops whose job it had been to guard Galt and accompany him to the bathroom and back, knocked on Galt's door and entered. Galt was at his desk writing a memo to Hal Metzger on logistical support for the proposed Lingayen Gulf landings. One of the purposes of the memo was to reassure Hal on logistical grounds so that he could move ahead with greater confidence. For Hal had expressed his temperamental fear of advancing vigorously and then finding himself at a loss for fuel and ammunition.

The young man was carrying Galt's pistol and gun belt, and laid them on the desk in a cleared space.

'Sir, General Wraith instructed me to inform you that you are now free to go out and about at your will. He also instructed me to return to you your sidearms.'

'Will you please thank the General for me. And captain, I would like to thank you and your men also for the consideration shown to me during my internment.'

Saying this, Galt smiled broadly and ironically at the young man, who allowed himself to join in the smile. Rising, Galt strapped on the gun belt with as un-contrite an air as he could manage. Then he sat down again and went on with his memo.

'Is there anything I can get the General?' the young man asked.

Obviously, Galt thought, they expect me to get up straight away and run out the door whooping.

'No. You could tell the kitchen staff that I'll be down for lunch.'

The young man saluted and left.

At lunchtime he went downstairs. As well as the regulars, Bryant Gibbs was at the table, looking a little less starched than the snappily dressed staff. His men had done wonderfully in Leyte, and would do wonderfully in Luzon. But they weren't getting any press, Galt knew, because the press office thought that it was bad business to let the US public know Big Drum now had two full-strength armies at his disposal. It might discourage Washington from sending the *more* which Big Drum had always said he had been deprived of. Bryant was philosophic about all this. He didn't seem to grieve about the colouring and forcing of the news the way he once had on the verandah of the Administration villa in Moresby. Although for a time after Buna he had been one of America's military stars, he had never demonstrated any lasting ambition for personal press coverage. Yet, undoubtedly, he deserved to be as famous as General Patton was in the European theatre.

All this cunning of the press office, of the Big Drum circus, would have once seemed valid, significant and urgent business to Galt. Now, after the sea change of discovery and arrest, after all the other sea changes he'd undergone, it seemed to be no more than a morbid preoccupation.

Everyone at table, including Big Drum, behaved as if Galt had not been locked away upstairs for two weeks. That too made Galt feel that there was unreality in this household.

The table conversation was largely about how poorly Wendell Fryer had done for the Republicans in the Presidential elections. Meacham, a latecomer but by now a staunch supporter of Big Drum, said, 'Wagner's at least crept away to his law office in the Dakotas. But Fryer's still talking as if he's the only hope of Republicanism. I mean, he's telling all the journalists what he'll do in '48. Though he doesn't say it aloud, he thinks our Democrat friend will have died by '48, and he'll walk into the White House just about unopposed.'

Galt noticed the phrase: 'our Democrat friend.' Pure Big Drum.

Big Drum produced a *Life* magazine which was by his side. Galt wondered whether it was strategically placed to allow Big Drum to make some remark about the Chaumont gang or to back Meacham up on the poor health of the Democrat President, or the poor calibre and intelligence of the Democrat Vice-President.

Big Drum waved the magazine.

'Galt, look at this. Not even a pony edition.' He spread it open and passed it across the table. There was a double-page spread of stills from Alexandra Sandforth's new film, a tale about an *ingénue* on Broadway and a jealous older actress who comes close to destroying her.

'They talk about motion pictures now,' Big Drum remarked, 'as if they're the new art form. I always thought they were just somewhere you took your girl.'

There was laughter. It was not loaded. No one seemed to take any malicious joy in the fact that Galt's girl was in Hollandia. They had all too thoroughly won their argument with him to get any ungentlemanly pleasure from that fact.

Galt for some reason decided not to read the piece there at the table. His upbringing said that you weren't supposed to show too much eagerness to read about yourself in the press anyhow. 'May I keep this, General?' he asked Big Drum.

'Of course. Naturally you'll have to read all about Bradley and Patton.'

'I'll be interested in that too, General. My son used to work with General Bradley.'

'Of course, Galt,' said Big Drum reprovingly. 'I hadn't forgotten that fact.'

After lunch everyone went to the verandah for coffee. Ernie Sasser had produced some peanut brittle from home. He offered it around, including to Galt. 'This isn't poisoned, is it, Ernie?' asked Galt, holding up the piece he had chosen.

'I think you can trust me, Galt,' said Ernie, warily grinning.

Putting the candy in his mouth, Galt began to read the article on Sandy's new film. The writer said that *Pandora* was to be the film of the year, and would establish Alexandra Sandforth – if there was ever any doubt about the matter – as the supreme actress of the American cinema.

The screenplay for *Pandora* had been written by Anthony Wellman, the playwright whom Sandy had mentioned to Galt during the photo session in California earlier in the year. The article referred to the likelihood of a marriage between Wellman and the great lady.

This possibility filled Galt with an obscure joy. He bit into Ernie Sasser's peanut brittle. A section of a molar of the upper left hand side of his jaw came away from the rest of the tooth, but without dropping out by its roots. The sugars of the peanut brittle hit the nerve and made him open his mouth in a soundless scream. Then, by pushing with his tongue the parted section together with the mass of the tooth, he was able temporarily to put a stop to the pain. Whenever he released the pressure however, the tooth began to scream again. He knew he would have to go to an army dentist before dark. His first act of freedom beyond the walls of the Scotland house.

It came to him that his pain was an opportunity. He finished the article, folded the copy of *Life* in his hand, and strolled off upstairs to his office. The pistol and gun belt were on the back of his office chair – he had not worn them since he strapped them on as a gesture in front of the young captain.

He took out his Smith and Wesson, opened the chamber and shook out the bullets. Choosing one of the bullets, he put it in between his teeth, below the fragmented molar. Then, with deliberation, he bit down on it. He felt something radical befall his tooth – not only did the separated section come completely away, but the main part of the tooth simply broke away also, exposing the nerve end to the air. Whimpering, he spat the bullet out, wiped the spittle off on his shirt sleeve, reloaded the pistol and placed it back in the gun belt behind the chair.

He left the office and went looking for Meacham. Along with other staff members, Meacham was still on the verandah, waiting for the afternoon conference to begin.

'Look at this,' Galt begged him. 'Ernie's goddamned peanut brittle has done for me.'

He opened his mouth and Meacham looked in. 'Jesus Christ, Galt. I'm no dentist, but it looks bad.'

Galt had himself driven to the Tacloban Base Hospital, where a young dental surgeon whistled as he looked at the damage. 'That's root canal work, sir. I can do it. But if I were you, I'd take it back to Hollandia, where they've got better facilities.'

He provided Galt with codeine. Throughout the afternoon, the pills took the edge off the pain, but did not touch the central jet of fire which seemed to occupy his upper jaw.

Galt presumed that Big Drum would become suspicious when he knew his chief of staff had to return to Hollandia. Surprisingly though, Galt encountered no resistance. 'Give yourself a few days to get over it, Galt,' Big Drum suggested. 'If you can be back by Saturday, I think we'll all be happy.'

Galt thought, he must know I'll visit Dim. Perhaps he doesn't care as long as I keep it secret and away from the press. Perhaps he's willing to give me what he thinks of as one last fling.

He had one of those new and well-fitted out transports for his journey to Hollandia. He could not sleep in his bunk, however, and neither could he read. Pain and the anticipation of seeing Dim kept him wide-eyed. Occasionally he would rouse the steward's bell and get them to bring him a little Scotch, which he'd roll around his mouth and swill through the broken tooth. This was excruciating, too, but in a different way, one that was a relief from the monotone agony which filled the night.

They came in to land at Hollandia at first light. A driver in a jeep with three stars on the bonnet was waiting for Galt. The driver said, 'Straight to the hospital, General?' expecting Galt to say, 'Of course.'

All communication caused the pain to rise from his jaw and occupy his entire skull. Galt spoke at length, just the same. 'I want to go to the headquarters offices first. You know, on the slope below the White House. I'll show you the building.'

When they reached the place, he told the driver to wait.

The offices Galt went to were miserable little prefabs which had been humanized now by what seemed like a long occupation, beginning earlier that year. There was a large central area of the kind which had been used to make the officers' mess at the White House but which was used here as a press office for the Southwest Pacific edition of the Army paper *Stars and Stripes*. On the walls above each desk were pinned postcards and *Saturday Evening Post* cartoons, photographs from *Life* magazine, columns from *Time*. Already there were a few young army journalists at work, and the teleprinter machines were chattering with news of other places where it was not dawn, where a day's fighting had already taken place.

He knew where Dim's office used to be. He intended to wait there for whoever turned up. They could tell him if there was a change of address for Dim or not.

He found the door and went in, switching on an overhead fan, since it was already so hot in here.

There were two desks, and it was easy to tell which was Dim's and which was her assistant's. What was his name? Hutchinson. The wall space behind Hutchinson's desk was covered with picture posters and the front covers of film magazines. Hutchinson was a film exhibitor at heart. Dim was not. Though there was one film photograph on a bulletin board by her desk. Alexandra Sandforth's. Sandy half smiling and half threatening above the desk of a woman she would have to get to know as stepmother.

He did not sit at either desk. He was too tormented with pain and with the unreality yet certainty of seeing Dim again. He walked. He read all Hutchinson's posters so frequently he became familiar with the names of costume designers and executive producers. He even found one with Anthony Wellman's name on it as co-writer. Sandy's beloved playwright. Screen play-writer-by-convenience. His name calling to Sandy's picture across the human spaces of an office in Hollandia.

He wondered with an indifference he would not once have felt whether the name Wellman was Jewish?

He began to hear more staff arriving in the office outside. So that the meeting wouldn't be spoiled by outrageous pain, he took another two codeine pills, swallowing them without water. He was crazed with the drug and the pain and the frequent overnight infusions of whisky.

At last, sometime after 8.30, Hutchinson opened the door. He didn't know Galt. He saw the three stars and the ribbons, and like any sensible citizen became alarmed. God knew what minor irregularities and guilts made Hutchinson's jaw hang. For he must have had, up to now, a cosy, uninhibited war, Dim being his main contact with authority.

'Sir,' he said, finding somewhere from memory his rarely used salute.

Galt went in for none of the normal jovialities the big brass exercised in benign moments with ordinary soldiers. No 'At ease, soldier.' No tolerant smile. He simply said, holding the tips of his finger under the left side of his jaw and speaking over the agony. 'Does Captain Lewis still use this office?'

'Yes sir. She should be in any time.'

'Good. Do you think, sergeant, you could make yourself scarce?'

'Yes sir. If you say so.'

'I mean, clear off to the sergeants' mess or something like that?'

Hutchinson smiled. 'If the General would like to make that an order . . . '

'Certainly, sergeant. As long as you stay at least an hour.'

Hutchinson saluted again, a gesture of wild enthusiasm, a

movement like a wave of the hand at a baseball game, and turned to leave. 'Is there anything I can get the General?'

'No. Clear out.'

And so Galt kept waiting in solitude and read all the movie posters again, and dared to wink at that photograph of the first lady of the cinema. He wondered if he himself might possibly, at this late stage of life, make a plausible screen writer?

In any case it was a daydream compounded of codeine and ache of all kinds.

The door opened and Galt stationed himself out of sight, steering the point of his tongue at a place on the roof of his mouth which when pressed seemed to offer temporary relief. He knew he must have looked ashen with exhaustion, and his shave aboard the transport that morning had been perfunctory and influenced by his tender jaw. But he hoped she would see him as a man who'd been through something for her.

She came in looking wan herself, and Stacey was with her, and his arm was around her shoulder.

Now Galt could only say, feeling stupid, the words breaking from his mouth like hot stones, 'I thought I'd surprise you, Dim.'

'As always, Galt,' she said, not – he noticed – sounding in any way ironic. 'As always you have.'

He believed he could see what had happened. He wished he could be philosophic and forgiving, but he was in too much pain. He wished he had the virtue to acknowledge that she might have blamed him for her sudden expulsion from Leyte, blamed him because his power had failed her. And so, in return, it was understandable she would fail him.

But he also knew there wasn't a chance of his taking that attitude. He looked at tall Stacey and felt a sort of acid running to the corners of his mouth.

'Did you spend the night with him?'

Stacey said, 'We shared the same room, that's all.'

'I see. You shared the same room? Is that the latest euphemism for it?'

'For Christ's sake, I didn't want to be alone, Galt.'

'Yes. I've managed to get that message.'

He picked up his cap from Hutchinson's chair, where he had

hidden it so she wouldn't see it from the door. 'Well, I know you'll excuse me. I've got a dental appointment. These damn molars, Dim. Old men's teeth are a hell of a problem.'

Dim had come well inside the office, but Stacey was still in front of the door. *I wish he'd move out of the way*, Galt thought. Otherwise he himself might throw a punch.

The pain was of course all at once twice as dementing as it had been half an hour before.

'Please, Galt,' said Dim. Her eyes were quiescent, he saw. They weren't like the eyes of a woman embroiled in a fight over sexual fidelity. This fact scared him.

She said, 'I know about Commander Runcie. I know about Allan. Please . . . please, tell me *you* know nothing about all this.'

This was the second which, much later, he would curse. If the matter had been less important he could have easily lied, but he was confused by drugs, the fire in his mouth, despair and fury. He knew that he was lost if he did not deny all knowledge instantly. Yet he could not manage it. And he couldn't believe anyhow that it would all come down to this. A two or three second delay. How could it all depend on timing? After all the kindnesses and shared eons and intimacies, what could timing count for? He shook his head. He knew he must look like a man who was temporizing. But it was too massive a lie to utter. Above all, it could not get out over the fire in his jaw.

'Oh, Jesus!' he heard Dim cry. 'No!'

Even then he was thinking, I can explain it all. His first, superficial and yet most obvious urge was one of anger at Stacey. That was item one on the agenda. Dim could then be won around as a separate issue. 'You're dealing in classified information,' he told Stacey. 'I'll have you destroyed for this.'

'Whatever you wish, General,' said Stacey, calmly. 'The war will be over soon, and I'll tell my own story in my own way. One of the saddest you could come across, I think.'

Now Dim came up to Galt and looked him in the eyes. She had no interest, he could see at once, in the threats of vengeance he and Stacey were uttering. He was somehow terrified of her.

She looked as ageless now as she had when she had seemed under the power of that fever, months ago.

'I could never forget this, Galt,' she told him, pleading and accusing at the same time. 'It would never go away. For Christ's sake, why didn't you just tell me?'

Galt covered all the pain of his jaw by putting his hands in front of his face and talking through them. 'I didn't choose him by name, for God's sake, Dim. Our headquarters approved the general strategy. But others chose him. For Christ's sake, do you think I chose him by name? It didn't happen that way. It would have happened even if I'd never met you . . . '

She shook her head. 'But you did meet me, and you've known. You've known for a long time. You were able to keep that from me? How was that? How were you able to do that?'

'You know now, Dim. I wasn't able to stop the thing on my own. And so then I kept it from you. Okay. I'll admit something. I kept you in the dark for love, for Christ's sake.'

But he was really alarmed at how stricken she looked. He hoped she was using all these terms – 'Could never forget' in particular – in an attempt to do just that: to forget, to let him off the hook.

She said it all again. 'Oh, Jesus, I can't forget it, Galt. You always knew that. You and I were together, and you were smiling and not telling me. That can't ever be forgotten, Galt. I'd forget it if I could. But how can I, Galt?'

He shook his head. His agony surged point-first into his brain. 'I have a dental appointment, Dim. I'm in great pain.'

'Goddamn you, Galt,' she said, shaking her head distractedly. 'Oh, dear God, I can't believe it . . . !'

'I can talk to you clearly after they've fixed my mouth,' said Galt, hopeful of buying time.

'If only talk was possible, Galt,' she said. He could see in her a genuine desolation, one he couldn't deal with at the moment.

So he decided to be firm then and to go. He was working by instinct, and yet he had a fearful suspicion that the intuitive offers and gestures which had brought them together were failing him now.

Stacey could see his intention and moved out of the doorway.

Galt was tempted to turn back and say to Dim, 'I got this pain for you.' But he did not want to sound stupid in front of Stacey. Above all, he did not want to waste such a powerful token at such an unsteady moment. He paused to stare at Stacey, feeling for this abominable Australian hack a hatred as vast as the fire beneath his skull. It defeated, however, any attempt at expression. He cried out over his shoulder to Dim. 'We'll talk it all out later,' he promised.

'Oh Galt,' she pleaded. 'If we could. If we could do that . . . '

She seemed to be saying that she wanted him to attempt it: a mending of what she knew. She knew that by mistake she was giving him hope. She opened her mouth to take it away, and couldn't find the breath for it. Something in her chest was crushing out her breathing. Galt went. It was inhuman how he moved in the instant before he disappeared into the corridor – what they called *military bearing*.

The lack of breath was serious now. She knew she was dying, that there wasn't any mercy for her and Galt, and that that was a just arrangement. She took two steps forward towards Stacey, as if he could do something about it all. She lost her feet and fell against Hutchinson's desk. Stacey came forward and pulled her upright. She could feel a sharp, irrelevant pain where her upper arm had hit the desk. And she found words. 'For God's sake,' she pleaded. 'Get me out.'

He seemed to know exactly what she meant. 'Where are your papers? With the Americans or with us?'

'US personnel,' she muttered.

'First, I'll get you some tea.'

She heard herself wail. 'They don't drink tea. They're not like us.'

He sat her down and then went out to the *Stars and Stripes* office and found her both coffee and lemonade. Then he led her out and to his Jeep. He drove her through the neatly signposted streets of the American cantonment. They *were* astounding, Dim saw. Their temporary camps had better roads and a look of greater permanence than many Australian remote towns.

At Personnel, Stacey helped her fill out an urgent application for compassionate leave. 'What will I put as the reason?' she asked. She did not want to put down that her husband had died. There was in any case no evidence of it. The Australians would deny it.

'Say your father is dying,' said Stacey.

'No,' she pleaded.

'Say your father is dying,' Stacey insisted. Then he smiled, broadly and grimly at once. 'He can make a miraculous recovery once you're airborne.'

When the time came for her interview, the personnel officer was suspicious of Stacey's presence. 'She's very upset,' said Stacey. 'I'm her cousin. She wants me to be with her.'

It was apparent to the personnel officer how distressed she was. Her grief was so obviously unfeigned and had great authority. So Stacey was allowed to help her into the office and to sit beside her.

'Holy Gee,' said the officer, opening her file. 'You haven't been home in two years, Captain Lewis. Do you have the radio signal about your father there?'

He obviously wanted a copy for his records.

'Damn,' said Stacey. 'We were so confused we left it back at your quarters.'

'OK,' said the officer. 'You qualify anyhow. Look, there's a troop plane leaving direct for Darwin at 1400. You'll have to line up further flights from Darwin on, but I'll stamp your papers *Compassionate* and you shouldn't have any problem. I'm giving you a month, captain. You're entitled. I hope your father is better by then.'

While she packed, she wondered how she would be able to function in Darwin, talking herself onto further planes, without Stacey to talk for her and hold her upright. Stacey reassured you. 'I know enough people in the Australian side of things. And you needn't work for the Americans again unless you want to.'

He agreed that after her plane took off he would deliver an order from her to the relaxed Sergeant Hutchinson, instructing him to deliver personally the canisters of a feature film named *Indiscreet* to an artillery unit fifteen miles west at a place called Haarstkopf. He was to wait and return with them after they were screened that night.

Galt spent five hours sucking on laughing gas and enduring pain. They dug the tooth out by its root, and he sat for an hour or so, drinking water with his pain-and-anaesthetic unbalanced face and getting better from the shock of it all. As soon as he could stand steadily, though, he went looking for her. He was astounded to discover from his watch it was already mid-afternoon. Her office was locked. He went looking then for Hutchinson, in the sergeants' mess, but Hutchinson wasn't there.

Next, he found out from the personnel office where she was billeted. It was a women officers' quarters well down the hill from the White House. He got his driver to take him down there and checked in with the WAC corporal who ran the front desk.

The corporal was just a kid. 'Oh,' she said, 'Captain Lewis flew back to Brisbane this afternoon. She was due for leave. You know, she hasn't had leave for two years.'

Postscript

Galt Sandforth continued as Big Drum's Chief of Staff for the length of the war and then for three years afterwards, during Big Drum's regency of Japan. His attempts to make contact with Captain Dim Lewis were consistently rebuffed. He divorced his wife Sandy and in early 1946 married a freelance journalist he had met during the surrender signing ceremony aboard USS *Mississippi* in Tokyo Harbour the year before. After leaving the Army, he became a director for a number of companies and a strong post war campaigner on the question of the impact of communism on Asia. In 1953, he was made US Ambassador to Spain, a post he held for three years.

His failure to be given further Government posts was believed to have arisen not from a poor performance in Spain but from his atypical championing of a number of Hollywood people targeted by the House Un-American Activities Committee. Amongst them was his son-in-law, Anthony Wellman, who went with his wife, the great Alexandra Sandforth to London, where Alexandra found a continuity of trans-Atlantic and European vehicles for her extraordinary talent and where her husband ultimately directed a number of large budget films and wrote for the West End stage.

Galt Sandforth would live on through the Vietnam years and, in his late eighties and while still an active lecturer and occasional contributor to the journalism of the Vietnam conflict, die of a stroke in 1973.

Dim Lewis married Paul Stacey in 1948, at a time when she was working as an administrative officer for the Melbourne *Age*, the rival paper to that of the Stacey family. She and Stacey moved to London that year, where Stacey worked in Fleet Street, building up a certain renown and ultimately subsuming a

London evening newspaper and adding it to his family's assets. Dimity Stacey became active in the administration of television. They had no family of their own but adopted two Asian children.

They lived between Melbourne, London and New York, where Paul Stacey eventually acquired television and further press interests. Now in their early seventies, they are both still in good health. An occasional biography of Big Drum makes guarded and generally snide reference to her but she shrugs that off.

Because she knows: they weren't there.

Author's Note

In the making of this fiction, the author drew with gratitude upon a range of works on the era in which the love affair of Galt Sandforth and Dim Lewis is set.

He acknowledges the following works with particular gratitude:

American Caesar and *The Glory and the Dream* by William Manchester;

The Years of MacArthur, Vols I & II by Dorris Clayton James;

MacArthur as Military Commander by Gavin M. Long;

South-West Pacific Area First Year; Kokoda to Wau by Dudley McCarthy.